Patriot of Last Resort

CHRISTOPHER WILDE

Published by The Bend Publishing Co.

Cover Design and Illustration by Nick James (www.nickjam.es)
Cover Photograph (Author) By Kristy Merrill Photography (www.kristymerrill.com)

ISBN: 0-9965307-0-3
ISBN-13: 978-0-9965307-0-5

DEDICATION

For Theodora, and for Pat & Bob.
Thank you for believing in and inspiring me.

ACKNOWLEDGMENTS

Special thanks to Bryce Anderson and William Hampton, for educating me and editing this work, Kristy Merrill Photography for shooting my cover photograph, to Nick James for his phenomenal cover art, and to Jeanette and Melinda for your support and encouragement. To Emily Marie, my unintentional muse, your strength and charm inspires.

CHAPTER ONE

Kyle,

Do you remember the first time we made love? Afterwards you started that little game, "How far would you go to change the world? Would you steal food to feed the homeless? Would you kill the bad to save the good? Would you avenge my death?" You asked the easy questions and ignored the hard ones. I don't want one act of brutality to be my only impact. It's the little contributions we make every day that make a lasting difference.

It seems like all we've done for the last six months is fight. I don't want to fight about goodbye. I love you, but I can't stay holed up anymore.

Laura

I don't stop to think. I follow the hidden signs: colored chalk marks, tape, or the occasional dab of spray paint that tells me where to go and what to do. A green dot—I'm running along the top of this wall and it's a fifty-foot drop to hard pavement below. A blue circle—at the end of the wall I do a running flip onto the roof. A red arrow followed by a red dash—I sprint full bore and jump across a fifteen-foot gap to the roof of another building.

Parkour is sometimes called free-running. It's often seen in movies and documentaries. Practitioners run up walls on all fours, climb, flip, and vault. It is a form of holistic movement, derived from a military obstacle-course form of training. It's beautiful, utilitarian gymnastics are most often practiced in urban environments. The motto of its founder: Be strong, be useful.

You might think this was a kind of greatness. After all, only a few people in any given city can do parkour at a professional level, but that's not why I did it. It was therapy to deal with stress, trauma, and the general purposelessness of life. I could slip through the railings of a fire escape, jump from one small spot to another, fall a significant distance, rolling away safely, and complete a course in record time. I felt that as long as I could do those things there was hope for my life. I could believe that greatness was on the horizon.

I had no real plan to achieve greatness, and no idea what I would do or what I had to offer the world. Instead, I had the quickening beat of my own pulse and the knowledge that no matter how much I wanted to, I could not afford to think about Laura. Not then. Not while every step I took required complete focus.

For the last couple of weeks I'd been agitated. It started from the moment she crept into my thoughts. Wrecking my body by working out excessively was not chasing her out of my mind.

I had not seen her in five years—not since she'd taken up with Ray. It did not escape me that I was still in love with her, or traumatized by her; I don't really know if there is a difference. So when I *did* bump into her, it felt like my mind had magically reached out and called her back to me.

Of course, if such a thing were possible I would have done it years ago. There was no logical reason to still be in love with her. I figured that by now the only thing that we had left in common was that we had each killed a man.

In front of me was the side of a concrete apartment complex. Every five feet, rectangular alcoves protruded from the wall, with windows set at the back. They created solid vertical stacks that climbed the length of the building. The indention between alcoves could only be climbed by "chimneying," but the distance between the stacks was too great to use my back and feet. I had to place my feet on one side, my hands on the other, climbing while facing the ground.

The last time I ran this route I slipped at the second story. There was no way to stop my fall. This time I was determined to make it to the top. I placed my hands on the south wall, kicked up, and locked my feet to the north side. I began to climb.

I'd been told not to try this alone because at the back of the building no one might find me. Pain from the injuries of the previous fall radiated through my body. That fall had left my head spinning for a week—a memory that now returned. I kept climbing.

The flat roof was surrounded by a small wall covered in slippery brown metal; my fingers only had a grasp on the lip. Kicking with my legs, I pushed off and lifted my hands from the wall. I reached over the wall and grabbed the edge. Now, hanging on one side of the alcove, I kicked out and swung my legs upward until I was doing a handstand, then flipped onto the roof.

I ran across the roof and caught the smell of fresh coffee from the café on the street below. I jumped the breach to the next building and hung from a balcony. I pushed off, turned in midair, and descended by catching a second-floor balcony on the first building. Two more zigzag descents and I was on the ground.

The narrow alley between the two buildings deposited me in front of the café. It was the first time I had completed this route without incident. The best parkour athletes in the world were in their early twenties, some still in their teens; few if any were in their early thirties. Out of breath, I put my hands to my knees.

When I looked up, Laura was sitting outside the café watching me as she sipped her coffee. She looked different. She was a little fuller in the cheek and projected a more regal sense of strength and confidence. When we were together she still had the slender, sinewy look of a girl. Now, in her thirties, she was an exquisite woman. Even her smile was different: it was warm and inviting. Before, it had been a mischievous grin that implied she might eat you.

There was nothing about her that looked humbled, or regretful, or suggested she was in any way interested in looking backward. There wasn't a ring on her finger, but my gut told me she was still with Ray.

Ray had been my friend since junior high school. He probably still believed I owed him because he went to prison. If that debt ever existed, it was wiped clean when I killed the man who snitched on him. After he got out, he demanded interest on his half of the take. I'd risked my half day-trading and several times nearly lost it all, something I wasn't willing to do with his money. I stuck to trading, and by the time he got out, I was earning a steady income. All Ray saw was that I had a comfortable living. We argued, and then parted ways.

"Hello, Laura," I said, as if seeing her around town was a normal occurrence. We'd broken up two-and-a-half years before Ray was released from prison. It didn't help that Ray took up with her as soon as he was released.

"It's good to see you, Kyle," she said, then came to greet me.

She filled my nose. I could smell her in layers. There was the fresh warm scent of her shampoo, the faint undertone from the powder in her makeup, but underneath it all there was her: the scent that I remembered strongest in the early morning hours when my nose had been against her neck and her natural aroma had filled our bed and settled like fog among the sheets.

It's not a smell I can describe, but it triggers the same emotions I feel when smelling slow-stewed home cooking, baked chocolate, or fresh bread. My mouth watered.

I straightened my back and stared at her for a moment. Her hair, the vibrant amber color of whisky, exhilarated my eyes; they traced the lobe of her ear to the curve of her neck, and settled on the begging pout of her lips.

I've been thinking about you, I thought, but didn't say, because it made this feel like it wasn't a coincidence. My mind hadn't called her to me—though I'd often wished it could.

"You've been running," she said, tilting her head and showing some pleasure and surprise. Then in a hushed tone she asked, "Does it help with the PTSD?"

I winced a little. I've never been officially diagnosed, and using that term feels like stealing from veterans. My self-inflicted hand-to-hand combat experience seems tame by comparison. She saw my expression and tenderly touched my arm.

"Kyle, it's so good to see you out in public." Her touch lingered and she added a squeeze. There was a shocked look that quickly vanished. She let go of my arm and examined me more closely. "You look...like you're doing well."

"How's Ray?" I asked, but I didn't really want to know.

"Ray is great. He misses you."

Their relationship had outlived my predictions and hopes. Ray, generally a blithe individual, was also a lifelong incessant conspiracy theorist. Ray and I used to argue about his conspiracies constantly. Laura had a keen analytical mind, a healthy skepticism, and an inflated sense of justice that I've always believed would serve her well as a lawyer, but undermine her tolerance of Ray.

"We've been meaning to look you up," she said, and then in a beseeching feminine tone. "We have a problem and could use your help."

Help?

I'd helped her when she dropped out of law school and turned up at my door. It's what I did when she acted out in anger—I saw past the facade and soothed her underlying pain. When her consistently positive attitude dissolved and she succumbed to a fear of family depression, I helped quiet her panic. Equity demanded I turn and walk away, but I could not fault her expert knowledge of me or for knowing and exploiting my weakness.

"Why don't you come have dinner with us? Let's all catch up together."

We exchanged phone numbers. She hailed a cab and left; I stayed and imagined she hadn't.

CHAPTER TWO

The Cherry Bloom Tavern is a local favorite. It's the kind of place where people rave about the food, but their enthusiasm is misplaced. They have childhood memories of cherry blossoms on the trees that line the tavern's walkways. They forget that, in winter, cherry trees are scraggly and haunting, or that decades of old dried cherries litter the ground and stab your feet through the bottom of your shoes.

As teenagers, they remember the feeling of maturity they had drinking their first beers and forget that it was because the Cherry Bloom dangerously shirked liquor laws. Right up until the turn of the century, if you asked at the bar and paid extra you could buy a pack of cigarettes at sixteen.

The most impressive memories of the tavern are kept under glass: its giant models of our nation's capital, a place most locals have never been. Patrons stand over and then kneel down beside the Washington Monument, the Capitol Building, and the White House. Walking behind the display, they marvel at the fact that they can look inside, find every stick of furniture hand-carved and to scale.

If the food had as much effort and detail put into it as the models did, it would be a five-star restaurant. Instead, you got fare a grade below what you'd find at a national chain, and it might have been edible were it consistently prepared. Should you ever have the audacity to point this fact out to a local, they would shrug you off, tell you not to worry, and rightly add, "But the beer is fantastic." The Cherry Bloom Tavern had been brewing its own beer since it opened in 1977—one year late for massive nationwide bicentennial celebrations.

The place was frequently written up in guidebooks for its "historic charm." Ray and I had been here a few times as kids. From the display in the glass counter, under the register, you could still purchase a miniature copy of the Declaration of Independence, a feather quill, or a felt tri-corner hat.

Inside, I followed Ray's voice to a table in the back.

"The water glasses used to have the pictures of our first five presidents on them, but no one liked drinking from John Adams' face and so the tavern gave them up," he said to Laura, eliciting a chuckle.

He looked slightly older. The only difference was that now he'd gone hipster, complete with a thin-sculpted Old Dutch-style beard, a pinstriped hat with a baby-blue ribbon around it, and the requisite wallet chain.

I don't know what Ray was expecting or what he saw, but as I came toward their table he looked me over with a nervous flit of his eyes. He'd been casually leaning back, but now sat up straight and pushed back with his shoulders. Laura read his expression, reached out and tucked her arm under his and scooted a little closer to him. He broke into a self-satisfied smile and relaxed back into his chair.

"Kyle, sit down. Let's get you a beer."

"I'm fine," I said, taking the seat opposite them.

Laura's words outside the café came back to me clearer now. *We*—not—*she*, needed my help. Each day, before I ever place a stock trade, I ask myself, *What do I expect from this transaction?* The question helps me clear away the emotion and focus on the numbers. Realizing I'd failed to do that here, I began to catch up quickly.

Ray said to Laura, "Did I ever tell you the story of how Kyle dragged my butt to college?" Laura leaned in expectantly.

"We dragged each other," I corrected.

"No, Kyle here had it all planned before we were even in high school. You had those spreadsheets you made on the school computer. You made us save every dime from every job we ever worked, just so we could go to fucking college." Ray rapped his fingers on the table so hard it rattled the silverware and my butter knife fell underneath. I couldn't tell if he was mad or had already had too much to drink.

"You managed to get an associate's degree. Are you upset about it?" I asked, perplexed.

"Correction: a bachelor's degree I finished in prison. And, hell no, I'm not upset, but there were times I hated you." He went back to telling his story to Laura. "I'd just turned sixteen and we had, what was it, fifteen hundred in the bank from working farms two summers straight. I was going to buy a car and work an after-school job. Kyle wouldn't let me."

"How'd he stop you?"

"First he showed me how I couldn't afford a car plus the cost of insurance, gas, and repairs. He drove every ounce of excitement out of the very idea of owning a car. So, you know we both come from dirt-poor families. There's nothing harder than watching every other kid in town get their first car.

"When Kyle wasn't around, I took all my money out of the bank. My plan was to buy this six hundred dollar car and have the rest for gas and insurance. I'm not two steps outside of the bank and here comes Kyle running up to me all panting and out of breath."

Laura pretended not to pick up on the underlying current of bitterness in the way Ray told his version of events. It made me uncomfortable. I leaned down under the tablecloth and looked for the knife. I grabbed it near Ray's shoe and then caught sight of a 9mm in the holster strapped to his leg. I came back up with my knife and said nothing about the gun. Ray was taking a terrible risk; as a felon, possessing a gun could land him another ten years in the penitentiary.

"Kyle, you never told me how you knew I was at the bank." Ray said.

"I'd begged Mr. Bernstein to let me know if you ever tried to take out any money," I said unapologetically. Laura gasped.

"Bernie Bernstein? Holy shit, I haven't heard that name in a long time. That guy did not like me." Ray cracked his knuckles. Laura turned to me.

"I can't believe at sixteen, you had the presence of mind to not only save money, but make him do it too."

"We fought that day right in front of the bank," Ray told her.

"With punches?"

I shook my head and Ray picked up the story. "My mind was made up—I was buying that car. Kyle was practically in tears, and then he said that, if I did, he'd never speak to me again. I knew he meant it."

"I seem to remember you saying a couple of hurtful things," I added.

Ray turned to me with a cold look and said, "It takes a special kind of resourcefulness to bring our absentee fathers into the fight."

"I was young; it was the only frame of reference I had."

"You capped it off by telling me I was going to end up like my mom's loser boyfriend. You know how I felt about him."

Laura looked jolted.

"Wasn't that the first year you got A's in school?" I said.

The waitress came and took our orders. She was very young and very pretty, trying hard to mask her boredom. She wrinkled her nose when all I asked for was a side of steamed vegetables.

Ray was leaning over and pointing at Laura's menu. The waitress stood by.

"I'm having that," he said in a hushed voice, then acknowledging Laura's choice, "I don't know—I've never had it. You should risk it."

"Are you sure you want to get that? Remember last time you had some?"

"I think that was the flu that got me," Ray reassured. "I'm having the roast beef and she'll have the...um...sal-ma-gondi." The waitress smiled then opened her mouth.

"I think it's pronounced sal-muh-guhn-dee," Laura corrected, her cheerfulness buoying the moment as she gave Ray's arm a comforting hug. Ray patted her hand tenderly and gave her an affectionate wink. The waitress stuck the order in her apron and disappeared.

Laura and Ray's habitual affection might have been disarming were it not for the deadly imprudence under the table. Laura rushed to protect Ray from an embarrassing mispronunciation, but ignored that he carried a weapon that could get him incarcerated. It was not like her to have her priorities backwards. Doting was only one of Laura's attributes. She was a very shrewd individual and—though never in disservice to me during our relationship—she could be exceptionally cunning. I would be wise to keep on guard.

"That car you wanted to buy—didn't Pete Drummond end up with two broken legs before he even got home with it?" I asked, intent upon rehabilitating my reputation.

Ray shot back, "That's because he didn't know how to drive."

"Without brakes," I tacked on.

Ray's tone was confrontational, "Next you're going to blame me for keeping you out of the military."

With that statement, his lack of appreciation for what we'd accomplished together got the better of me. He was putting me on trial in front of Laura. Publicly, she would never be less than a partisan judge and so I wondered if he was testing her loyalty or mine.

If Ray were going to play the part of prosecutor then I reasoned the battle could be won with humility.

"Ray, maybe I never said this directly, but I would not have made it to college without you. When we first met I didn't have a single friend, my parents taught me so little I wouldn't have known how to make one." Turning to Laura I said, "The first summer I got a job, the manager at the feed store took me aside gave me a stick of deodorant and told me how to properly bathe. I listened and learned, but I was mortified," and then back to Ray, "I was so embarrassed that I didn't know basic hygiene I quit that job."

Laura knew this stuff, but from the expression on her face, had never heard it put this way.

"I remember," Ray cut in with some remorse, "He was talking to both of us, not just you."

"That's right, and you were my friend. You talked me into coming back and convinced him to re-hire me."

"We debated for a month whether we could even get jobs; I wasn't going to let you bail."

"I don't understand," Laura asked me. "Why wouldn't you be able to get jobs?"

Talking about this was more painful than I'd expected.

"We didn't believe we could," I said taking a deep breath. "Between us we had three decent pairs of jeans. In school, I'm sure there were other poor kids. Maybe they hid it better, but it felt like Ray and I were the only ones. At the start of school, the other kids would talk about these vacations they'd take with their parents. They'd go see all these movies and go to each other's birthday parties. We didn't have any of that. When you grow up poor, you feel undeserving and powerless. Who would give someone like us jobs?"

Laura reached over and gave Ray's hand a compassionate squeeze and me a sympathetic frown.

"I don't know where the idea came from to go to college or why it resonated with me as our only hope, but without Ray I would never have been able to do it." The first part of that was a lie; I did remember, but it was too painful to discuss. The second part was true.

"We both could have gone into the military," I continued, "and they would have paid for our college. Ray talked me out of it. I listened because when we were fifteen we promised to stick together."

"You can't trust the government," Ray interjected, "especially the military."

The conversation was interrupted by the food. Ray's roast beef was a working cut; it looked really chewy. My vegetables had been overcooked, but with a little salt they were palatable. Laura's salmagundi looked more like a chef salad, but instead of grapes, they'd thrown in dried cranberries. She poured her dressing on the side. She seemed to enjoy digging out the parts she liked, dipping them, and then pushing away the rest.

Laura glanced over at Ray, saw that he was absorbed in cutting his beef, and then looked over to me. She held her focus on my eyes. Her expression grew more serene with each second, a familiar look, meaning her mind was caught in review of some complex emotion. Her top teeth pressed gently on her bottom lip and pushed it to one side. I smiled at this. Her blush revealed it had been involuntary. She stopped and returned to her food. Then, as if to assuage her own guilt, she reached out and stroked Ray's hair.

My twinge of jealousy confirmed that I still loved her. I decided that what I wanted from this transaction was Laura. I gave a moment of consideration to the moral implications of trying to interfere in their relationship. I decided that if I could entice Laura to leave Ray for me then my actions only served to validate her choice. Laura and I had been together first, and that made Ray the interloper.

"Where do you guys live now?"

A childlike smile spread across his face.

"I inherited my grandmother's house," he said. Ray and I grew up two counties away from the city. Occasionally we spent weekends with his grandmother who lived on the west side of the city. "We've really fixed it up," Ray said with pride.

"Laura mentioned you guys needed some help with something?"

Ray put down his fork and took a drink.

"Kyle," Laura said, "You're still trading, right?"

I nodded.

"We have some money saved up," she continued. "Not much, but enough to invest, and we'd like your help growing it."

"How much?"

"Forty thousand," Ray said with a slight smile. It was the amount I'd given him when he got out of prison.

Laura said, dropping her voice and leaning in, "We're hoping you could help us find a way to keep it off-book."

"We want to leave the country and go off the grid. We don't want money that can be tracked back to us." Ray added.

"Why?" I asked and—realizing I sounded suspicious—turned it into a joke. "Have you two done something you're running from?" They laughed, but it had occurred to me that Ray could be involved in some criminal enterprise.

"No," said Ray as if he weren't at this moment breaking the law, "This country is headed in the wrong direction. We don't believe it's safe to live in any urban area. We want our money in an offshore account."

I wanted to laugh. Forty thousand in an offshore account is preposterous. The kind of anonymous banking they were talking about wasn't meant for play money. It was for people with hundreds of millions of dollars. You could spend forty thousand just trying to make the right connections.

"I've never opened an offshore account, but I'm happy to look into it," I said.

"That's fantastic," Ray replied.

"Yes. That's all we ask," Laura added.

"But we really would like to do this right away," Ray said with a hopeful curl of his lips.

They seemed extremely satisfied when I told them I'd do it this week.

CHAPTER THREE

A twenty-yard thicket of woods separated Ray's childhood home from a drainage culvert that ran under his street. The concrete pipe was a great place to lie down and escape the heat of summer. It was also a great place to escape the man inside Ray's house. His mother's boyfriend, who'd looked down at me with a disgusted snarl, misted me with alcohol as he said, "He took off."

I looked down into the dry ravine and into the tunnel. The sun was high over the road, casting shadows. I couldn't see Ray, but I felt certain he could see me. I skidded down the side, getting pebbles and dirt into a hole in the side of my shoe. As I walked toward the edge of the pipe Ray's voice, laced with tears and still cracking with puberty, came from inside.

"Go away."

I stopped short at the edge, leaned my back over the exposed pipe and closed my eyes in the sun.

"Fuck'em Ray, we don't need them."

Ray groaned and then sighed. "Go away Kyle."

"I'm not going away. I've got your back. I'm your friend."

Ray barked through his tears, "Why?"

"Because I said so and friends stick together. We have to, Ray. We have no one else."

"You can't help me. You can't stop him."

"I can call the cops."

"No, they won't do anything. It will just get worse and he'll kill me."

"Yeah, and I'll fucking kill him."

Ray kicked his foot against the side of the concrete, and then threw a stone down the pipe. I listened as it cracked on the sides and rolled somewhere near the other opening.

"I'd do it too, man, swear to God. Even, if I have to wait until I'm older, I'll fucking kill him."

"Sure you will."

"You don't believe me? Go ahead; tell me I'm a fucking liar. Have I ever broken my word?"

"No."

"Then I give you my word. I'll kill him."

"I know you will."

It was a promise I never had to keep. One night two months later, the boyfriend got blind drunk, fell into the river, and drowned. At the funeral,

Ray and I stood beside the grave and listened to the priest's hollow words. At the conclusion, the adults bowed their heads. Ray rolled his eyes, looked at me, and smiled. We bumped fists.

As outcasts, Ray and I first came together because of our *us against the rest of the world* outlook. Were it not for our mutual investment in escaping miserable circumstances, I don't believe the friendship would have lasted. Academically, Ray tended toward the artistic while I preferred the scientific. By college, small differences in our personalities as children had become grating. That, as adults, our friendship had now deteriorated—to the point where I'd actively plot against him—was a long time coming.

Ray was carrying a gun and he and Laura had said they wanted to "go off-grid." That's the sort of sentiment I knew to be the product of Ray's fearful conspiracy theories. Through high school our arguments about conspiracies were the mainstay of our friendship. Were it not for misguided loyalty, we would have unraveled then.

I remember it started at about fourteen with a shared enjoyment of science fiction. That branched into an obsessive speculation about aliens at Area 51. It seemed only natural to fantasize about the 'what if' of escaping our lives in a stolen alien spaceship. At fifteen, it was fun to engage in these daydreams, but I knew them for what they were.

At first, I was not bothered by his talk of an order from the Crusades known as the Knights Templar. They were history, a favorite subject of mine. I considered his suggestion that they were still around and hiding in the Masonic order to be an example of Ray's abundant creativity.

I became concerned when he started watching videos about shadowy organizations that "control everything." We started arguing when he brought to me names like the Illuminati, the Bilderberg group, and the Trilateral Commission.

"They all want to push us into a one-world government," Ray once said, while hanging from the rope swing we'd installed in his grandmother's barn. He said it as if an invasion force were imminent.

By this time in our lives, I'd taken to playing devil's advocate.

"What would be so wrong with a one-world government?" I replied.

"Man, do you want to be communist or like one of those socialist countries?"

"Is that a bad thing?" I asked.

We'd taken a round wooden disk, drilled a hole in the center, and threaded the rope through it. By tying a knot at the bottom we'd created a seat. I snuffed out the joint we'd been smoking, grabbed the knot, and dragged him to the edge of the barn.

"Yes, it's a bad thing. Do you want someone telling you what you have to do all the time, your job chosen for you, and no right to speak out?"

I released the rope and watched him go flying. He reached the other side of the barn but did not jump off into the pile of hay below.

"Well, if it's going to happen, what do you think you can do about it?" I asked as he came spinning back. I climbed up the ladder nailed in the corner of the barn, held to the rung, and put my feet on his rear. With one swift kick I sent him flying hard to the other side. Once there, if he didn't jump off he would collide painfully with the floor of the hayloft.

"Bastard!" Ray shouted and jumped from the rope.

I turned and looked though the gaps in the barn walls. Ray's grandmother, who didn't mind an occasional 'shit' or even a 'god damn,' had an unusual sensitivity to aspersions cast on someone's lineage. With the coast clear, I caught the rope and carried it higher up the ladder. She was not opposed to taking a belt to him for such an utterance and had once done so in my presence. It mystified me that he worried about a New World Order when the real threat was the authority figure in the house.

"We need to wake people up. If everyone knew about this stuff we could put an end to it," Ray said, after rolling out of the pile and shaking the straw from his hair.

I held high to the rope and swung off twice as hard and fast as Ray had. Lifting my legs and holding my weight by my arms, I avoided smacking into the floor of the loft. Instead, I flew above the loft, turned, and landed on the edge. Ray did not have the upper body strength to pull off this maneuver.

Knowing what was coming next, he tried to grab the bottom of the rope and tug it from me. With a quick jerk I dangled it from his reach. If he wanted it now, he would have to wait. His other option was to go outside the barn, around to the back and up another ladder to the loft. By the time he did that, I would have swung back across the barn. If I wanted to, I could keep the rope from him all day.

"Well then," I said with intentional smugness, "If you don't want us to end up under the thumb of a world government, we had better go to college and become part of the educated elite."

All of Ray's conspiracy theories centered around one idea: that our destiny was not our own, that we lived our lives as pawns of more powerful forces. Though I tried, no amount of facts or data ever seemed to change Ray's mind.

It wasn't that I didn't believe in conspiracies. They occur—otherwise we would never know about mass graves where despots murdered and buried thousands of their own people or that radiation from American atomic bomb tests poisoned our own citizens. I could never get Ray to see that there were just too many factors at play for anyone to keep really big secrets over time, especially not the elaborate conspiracies he believed.

The strain that most threatened to destroy the relationship between Ray and me were our debates about the World Trade Towers. Conspiracies gained a new strength after the tragedy that killed nearly 3000 people. What had been a trickle of books, websites, and seminar speakers circulating on late-night talk radio quickly became an industry churning out a relentless deluge of deliberate misinformation.

Ray believed it all. He believed that a black-ops military team working from within the U.S. government planted explosives and blew up the towers and he believed that a missile, not a plane, was shot into the Pentagon. He believed that the motive for this was to hide billions of dollars in banking losses, and simultaneously believed that it was done to justify spending billions of dollars on wars in Iraq and Afghanistan.

Our first two years of higher education were spent at the local community college. It was during this time that Ray's obsession with 9/11 got out of hand. Arguing with him became a full-time job.

His opinions were drawn largely from documentary-style videos he found on the Internet. The videos used scary music, ominous-sounding narrators, and out-of-context images to create the illusion of treachery.

My response was to sit him down and dissect each video. I would play, side by side, the clips he watched against the primary source video to demonstrate the deliberate misrepresentations. Ray fought back by drawing on the "professional opinions" of a listing of "architectural experts." Their names had been used to bolster the very video I'd already completely rebutted. With a few clicks I was able to show most of these experts were not working professionals and that they had little to no credibility when it came to the causes and analysis of this horrendous terrorist act.

Our debates were acrimonious, and what I couldn't admit then was that they hurt. Ray was capable, highly intelligent, and very loyal. He was sweet-natured, generous, and—when paying attention—very empathetic. Were it not for those qualities, I never would have tried so hard to get through to him, but my efforts always ended in complete frustration. We never got past this aberration in his personality. What hurt was that I felt his beliefs reflected negatively on me. I've always tried to keep his good qualities in mind, but the end result of our debates was that I thought less of him. All of these memories came back to me as I drove home from the tavern. I was furious to think that after all these years, Ray not only still counted himself among the lunatic fringe but that he had dragged my beautiful Laura into that dark corner as well.

"After we transfer we're going to make bank," Ray said, referring to the pot I'd been dealing since high school. We were in community college at the time.

"I was thinking about getting out of it," I said. The source of marijuana and the customers were mine. I only used Ray for deliveries and then only so I had an excuse to give him some money without damaging his pride. "We've got the grants and with the loans I don't need to deal at all."

"Come on man. We will be surrounded by a built-in market. How could you pass that up?" Ray paused, and then with a wave of his hand added, "Never mind, if you don't want to I can do it on my own."

While I didn't doubt that Ray could get himself started, he had a fondness toward get-rich-quick ideas that I believed would ultimately lead him into trouble as a dealer.

"Are you still planning on majoring in art?" I asked, to change the subject.

"I'm not going to change my mind," Ray said, and then in a snarky voice, "Are you still planning on majoring in history?"

It had been my suggestion that Ray take something offering greater career potential. It was a suggestion he was all too happy to throw back.

"We need the pot money," Ray said. "We can't afford to throw it away."

When we got to college, it turned out Ray was right: our living expenses proved to be higher than anticipated. Selling marijuana around campus wasn't really an option. The college market was already filled with a glut of high-quality kush.

It was dealt by rich kids. Ray liked to call them hipster douchebags. They also controlled the bigger market in amphetamines. I just couldn't compete. Instead, I drove our shared car two and a half hours home, twice a week, to maintain existing customers.

Though it had not yet opened, there was a freshly constructed Owens Co. Jewelry Store just a few blocks from the freeway. A mainstay of the county where Ray and I grew up, they had been very slow in making their way into the big city. It was during one of my trips back home that the plan to rob the Owens family was born.

Running back and forth from college to home was a grueling enterprise, especially since I was often expected to get high, shoot the breeze, and feign interest in the lives of small-town people with whom I was, day by day, losing touch. So much so that in a few months I would never see these people again.

My customers constantly reminded me of the dead-end jobs that waited if I didn't finish college. There was John, the high-pitched, squirrel-faced auto mechanic who kowtowed to his boss, then behind his back, bitched about him constantly. Sue, the hairdresser, had been a beautiful and popular girl in high school. Though she was bright and clever, she'd put on a few pounds and now spent most of her time sitting home, getting high, and lamenting her fading looks. Skip, the electrician, had just knocked up his girlfriend and was pretending to be excited about a new baby.

Not all were so miserable. Fred owned a small cottage on the south side of town. He was a satellite installer and generally very affable. He loved to talk about work, particularly the luxury homes where he'd installed television. When he did, it was with all the enthusiasm of a fanboy meeting his favorite celebrities.

I endured their stories because they paid me a premium for weed, smoked a lot of it, and, had they bothered to step out of their comfort zones even a little, would have discovered I was overcharging.

Fred's warm, clean place was always my last stop. Though he was a pudgy bachelor with pug features, he decorated his house like a wife was going to step through the door at any moment. I always gave him points for optimism, and I appreciated that he was a bit of a high-strung neat freak.

He had a sort of innate loneliness about him, counting among his close friends the people he only knew as acquaintances. It was really apparent in his tendency to look up to anyone who showed him a kind word. He'd give me a beer when I came in, often had food, and if the hour got late he'd let me crash in his spare bedroom. I could trust him and always left a backup ounce in case any of my customers ran out between trips.

"Hey check it out, have you ever seen the Owenses' hot daughter?" he said as if about to confide a dirty story.

"Shaun Owens' daughter?" I asked.

Shaun Owens inherited the family jewelry business. They had five stores around the county. Fred brought up a picture from his phone. Janice Owens was eighteen, and as Fred had promised, she was hot. She was wearing a red bikini covered in small blue flowers. Having just pulled herself out of a recessed hot tub, she was leaning back on the deck with only her calves still submerged. She did not appear to know she was being photographed.

"How did you come by that vantage point? Were you on a balcony?"

"Ladder. They'd just changed services and I was slinging cable around their house. Man I would love a piece of that," he said, with a reluctant smile.

"Go ask her out."

"Me, no way, a rich girl like that—oh shit, that reminds me. So, I'm there and her folks leave while I'm tacking cable to the wall outside the master bedroom. I'm right by the window and I see Janice come in. She moves a painting and there's a safe."

"Oh?" I said somewhat disinterested. "Did you get the combination?"

"No, only part of it, like an 86 and a 54, but it's what was inside that was so cool."

"Cash?" I inquired.

"Well yeah, she stole about five hundred dollars from her father. The big thing was that there were diamonds, lots of raw uncut diamonds." Fred spread out his hands like he was rolling diamonds off and on to a table. "He's got five stores. There was more than enough diamonds for all of them."

As if you would know how many diamonds a typical jewelry store goes through, I thought to myself.

"I still think you should ask her out. The worst that can happen is she can say no," I said, changing the subject. Fred shook his head *no* so violently his jowls flopped back and forth. "Don't be so hard on yourself. You've got your charms; look what you've done with this place. Any girl who isn't impressed by your decorating skill alone isn't worth having."

Fred took that in, leaned back, and began to ponder. I began thinking about the two times in my life that I'd met Shaun Owens. The first time, I was a freshman in high school and he tried to sell me an overpriced, gaudy class ring. Because I wasn't interested (and couldn't afford it had I wanted one), he came off as smarmy and condescending.

The second time I'd met him, I was standing on the street corner next to his store. He pulled out of the parking lot in a hurry and crashed headlong into a black Mercedes trying to pull in. The man in the Mercedes broke his wrist, and so I helped him from the car to the curb.

Owens mumbled a brief, "I'm sorry, Arnaud." He then looked at his watch and said, "I'll call an ambulance but I've got to go, I'm late for an appointment. " Owens paused for a second, but not long enough to see if anyone would object.

After Owens drove off, I introduced myself; then I stayed with Arnaud until the ambulance came. Arnaud was a thin man, dressed in a slightly wrinkled silk-blend brown suit. His hair was straight and came to his shoulder. He had sparse facial hair, shaved into a Van Dyke.

"Thank you Kyle," Arnaud said to me. His accent was thick but pleasant.

"Where are you from?" I inquired politely.

"Israel. I do business with this piece of shit," he said, nodding at the Owens name on the store front. "Can you do me a favor? Grab my keys from the car and my case from behind the front seat."

I opened the driver's side door and yanked the keys out. Over on the curb, Arnaud pulled out a brightly colored pack of cigarettes covered in foreign writing. Using a single hand, he shook one into his mouth. I lifted the tab and pushed the seat back.

There was a hard-sided metal briefcase. Around the handle was a pair of handcuffs; the other cuff was run through a ring bolt in the floor of the Mercedes. I hesitated and heard Arnaud calling from the curb.

"The key is on the ring."

I pulled up the handcuff key, released it off the floor, and brought the case to Arnaud. Sitting down next to him, I got a heavy whiff of the tobacco in his cigarette. It had a strong musky smell that made me think of old men smoking pipes.

Arnaud quickly clamped the cuff around his good wrist, watching me suspiciously as he did. I stared at him but gave no expression of curiosity. He looked around cautiously, but at this time of afternoon there were few people on the street. He unlocked the case, sat it on its side, and lifted the lid. The case was lined with black velvet. There were little indentations where it looked as though you could set something, but there was nothing inside.

"Go ahead," Arnaud said, "grab the little loop at the front and lift it up."

Following his instructions, I pulled on the loop that raised a lid, revealing a case full of cut and uncut diamonds. I found this interesting and hoped that was all my face showed. There was a very large diamond tucked in a pocket at the back.

"May I touch?" I asked.

Arnaud shook his head and then said gently, "No, go ahead and close it now."

I lowered the lid and applied enough pressure to seal it back in place. Because of Arnaud's wrist, I helped secure the handcuffs.

"You know," he said, "I used to come to this town with my father. Even on my first plane ride, I came to sell diamonds when I was a young boy. Shaun Owens' father was a good man. He would have us over to dinner. He knew a good diamond from bad, and he knew a good price. We haggled, but that's just business.

"When I took over I dealt with the father. He was much older but always nice to me, and then he died. And this piece of shit, he thinks everyone is trying to take advantage of him. He only buys the cheapest diamonds and then marks them up like as if they were cut from the most precious Star Diamond."

"You should sue the fucker for what he did to your wrist," I said, showing my righteous indignation. Arnaud smiled brightly.

"No. Owens' insurance will pay, but for the next twenty years I'm going to come in here clutching my wrist and moaning about the pain. He will feel so guilty. I'll stick him on price for years to come." Arnaud looked up and I could see he was gleefully imagining it.

The ambulance pulled up, and a second behind it came a tow truck for Arnaud's car.

"Is it a good business?" I asked, before the paramedics could get out. "Selling diamonds?"

Arnaud got to his feet and looked me over.

"Are you going to college?" he asked.

I nodded that I was. Arnaud reached into his pocket and handed me his card. "You finish college and give me a call." Then the paramedics walked him around and put him in the back of the ambulance.

I still have that card.

Listening to Fred's story about the safe made me think it might be worth giving Arnaud a call early. Though Fred did not realize it, the two numbers he'd given me were very significant.

The Owenses' had been in the jewelry business for three generations. They advertised their stores constantly on the radio. Their radio ads were memorable because of the way Shaun Owens tagged their stores at the end of the commercials.

"Come to our central store—at the corner of 1700 and Vine in Mapleton, our 2900 store—at Price Street in Monroe, our 5400 store... our 8600 store... and our 2200 store in downtown Chesterfield." This was always followed by a bright little jingle I'd once been told was recorded thirty years ago.

The radio commercials were a tradition started by Shaun's grandfather in the late '30s after they added their second store. It continued as a matter of pride even though it became very cumbersome to say by the addition of their fourth and fifth stores.

22-86-54-29-17. I knew he was that arrogant, but was it possible Owens was that dumb? Had he not been such a dick or had I not the misfortune to witness it for myself, I probably would have just forgotten about the whole thing. Instead I was plagued by two mysteries: Could I unravel the correct order of the numbers, and (not that I would) was it possible to actually break in and steal them?

On subsequent trips into town, I always made a point of casing the Owens estate. Their property sat alone on the rolling hills at the outskirts of town, surrounded by a six-foot brick wall. At first, I dragged a cut log from the nearby woods and stood on it to peer over the wall. Then I discovered that by lying atop a nearby hill, flat on my belly, I could hide in the tall grass and observe much of the house with a pair of high-powered binoculars. I had a clear view into the master bedroom and of the painting covering the safe. Watching their house and recording the family's movements became a favorite pastime. I brought my textbooks and when nothing was going on, I'd study.

Shaun Owens had grown rather large over the years, and his fat hands made it very difficult to see the numbers as he spun the dial. I had much better luck with his long-fingered trophy wife, who had clearly bestowed Janice with her good looks. In either case, it was much more fruitful ascertaining the numbers by looking at the bottom or sides of the dial than the number stopped at the top. It took me four weeks to confirm the combination.

For a long time, I thought the alarm system would be a problem. Shaun and his wife always parked in the garage and used the interior door. I had no clear vantage point to view the code panel. Janice, on the other hand, parked in the driveway and frequently went through the front door. Many times she came into the house and ran to the top of the stairs where I could see her turn on the landing. If she pushed a code into a panel, she did it with blazing speed. Eventually, my suspicions were confirmed when she started sneaking boys into the house by throwing them the key from her bedroom window. If they had an alarm, they never used it.

My curiosity satisfied, I stopped watching their house and went back to school. Afraid that Ray would insist on doing the job (and if I refused, attempt it on his own); I told him nothing. It was my work, my side project, my little secret. I enjoyed keeping it to myself.

CHAPTER FOUR

"We really enjoyed your company at dinner. I look forward to finding out what you uncover. Thank you," read the text message from Laura. It came across my phone as I was walking to the elevator from my car. I could hear her voice in my mind as I read it. I stared at the phone and contemplated any hidden meanings while listened to the echo of my footfalls in the parking garage of my building.

In college, while helping Laura study for an exam, I came across the Latin word *gratia*. It's my word to describe her. The full meaning, not just the surface definition; with Laura you always need to go to the root. *Gratia*: full of favor, popular, acceptable, beloved, agreeable, and belonging to the people.

During our final year of community college, Ray and I made several trips to four-year schools around the state. We took tours, went to parties, and slowly acclimated ourselves to what life would be like on a real campus. The state university was our last trip, and while we were there we agreed that this was the school we would attend.

That night, invitation in hand, we took the drive that wound around the hills west of the college. The houses to the right and left of us enjoyed gorgeous views of the city. At a break in the houses to the north, we turned up a private drive but were stopped at the gate. A burly student, no doubt a football player, barely looked at our invitation. He seemed content that we looked like college students.

"No more cars," he said, and indicated we should drive around the corner to park.

As we walked back we found ourselves in a throng that converged at the gate and then spread out as we passed through. Slowly we trudged up the brick-lined concrete drive, following the glow of lamp posts that provided only the bare minimum of luminance. Around us were the sounds of excited chatter and the click of heels. Ahead, through a grove of spruce, was the distant sound of house music with its thudding base and distinctive hydraulic hiss. Beyond the trees, we found a modern mansion buzzing with the activities of hundreds of students.

Most surprising was that these students were nowhere near as loud, raucous, or out of control as one might expect at a party of this size. All booze—a bottle was the fee for admission—was brought to one of three bars, where it was redistributed equally. Inside, the crowd was so tightly packed that all movement was made along snakelike paths that wound between clusters of people. The sheer size of it was overwhelming.

In recent years, Ray had learned to enjoy winning the acceptance of small crowds. He was particularly fond of winning the approval of gregarious women with limited conversational depth. I felt a friendly tap on my shoulder and turned to see his red shirt enveloped in the crowd, like a sliver of apple being pulled into an anthill.

Still blind to the market forces at work, I sought to uncover my potential to sell marijuana. I smiled a lot, stood on the edge of conversations, and joined them when introductions seemed appropriate. Not wanting to step on anyone's toes, I did not mention that I was a dealer. I made two passes through the house and did not once smell pot or see a person who looked as if they were high. The crowed was energetic, pumped on designer drugs, and from what I could surmise, uninterested in old-school pot. I resigned myself to the reality that increasing distribution was unlikely and put an end to my machinations. It was time to enjoy the party.

My first sight of her was from the side. I was looking through the channel of people and contemplating the wait at the bar in the next room over. She stepped backward onto the path and turned. Seeing some friends, she gave a sincere laugh, crossed over, and joined them in conversation. I had a quick view of her hair, her smile, her tight torso, and perky breasts. In the moment, she was just a pretty girl among dozens of pretty girls, except for that twirl and laugh which imprinted her on my mind.

The second time I saw her, my impression was that she was a player. She garnered the kind of attention I would get when people were desperate for my product. In retrospect, it is clear the label "player" revealed a deficit in my vocabulary. It would be more accurate to say that I observed her "belonging to the people."

She wasn't a dealer, not of drugs anyway; she was a distributor of social glue. I stood on a step just off the bar in the largest room. Here, I had a view clear through the doors into the room beyond. At the far end I saw her stand on toe looking for the bar. She looked at me, presumably as a reference point, and began to make her way.

Had I not already met him, I would have mistaken her to be the host of this party. Every few steps she was drawn into a conversation with a different group. She was tugged at to receive hugs from people who sought her at their arrival and others before leaving. Twice she got lured into telling and reenacting past stories that erupted in a cascade of laughter from its new audience. And then, there was the varied, persistent flirting she received from both men and women. I did not want to take my eyes off her, but for the sake of appearances I engaged in conversation with those next to me and kept her in my peripheral vision.

It took her nearly thirty-five minutes to make her way. The entire time she smiled and was smiled back at, like she was the emissary of joy. Ten minutes before her arrival, the bar was down to beer and vodka. I had a drink mixed and took a beer.

By the time Laura had arrived the drinks were gone. Even her false disappointment became a game. She stood on the bar and shouted, "Oh no!" The phrase was then repeated by the crowd in unison, moved from the bar, and spread outward like an echo.

After someone helped her down, she looked my way and I motioned for her to come over.

"You have your choice of beer or vodka and cranberry juice," I said, holding them out to her.

On the spot she managed to coax forth yet another look: surprise and happiness, one I had not already witnessed. It was hard not to immediately fall in love with that expressive face. With a curtsy she took the vodka. I came off my step to stand beside her.

"Hi, I'm Kyle."

"I'm Laura," she said.

With the bar now closed, a silent space had opened around us that made conversation easier. We turned outward watching the crowd and she said, "You've been standing on that perch for a long time, birdy. What did you see?"

I turned my head toward her. With a sly, pointed smile and in my most melodious voice replied, "I—see you."

With that statement, I'd hope to convey something deep in my observations: that what I saw in Laura conversing so fluidly with so many disparate people wasn't social climbing, neediness or calculated self-promotion. It was social athleticism. Even at a distance, I could tell it was sincere and intuitive beyond anything I have ever in my life witnessed.

"Oh do you?" she asked rhetorically and then she fixed her eyes on me in speculative contemplation. "And now I see you," she said and grabbed my arm in hers. "Let's go see what we see together." She towed me into motion and for the rest of the night I was hers.

On the steps behind me, one of the bartenders directed the others: boxes were carried down, the bar was restocked, and the crowd surged again.

She never let me venture away by more than a foot. Not that I would have. Throughout the evening she whispered in my ear and peppered me with questions. Between answers, she moved me around the party, making more introductions than I could possibly digest. More than once, I caught faint scowls from those who saw her arm around mine and viewed me as an interloper, a competitor for her affections.

Following her lead, I ignored them, and for the first time in my life I glimpsed what it was like to be popular. With each greeting, I noted her observing me carefully. It dawned on me that how I dealt with this social acceptance was a test of my character. Hoping to pass the test and win Laura's favor, I willingly endured her exam.

We enjoyed the night and slept in the next day. We then stayed in touch while I finished at the community college. Laura seemed to find great comfort in the distance. We communicated by phone, spent the occasional weekend together, and after my matriculation in the fall we became an item.

Laura later told me that what she found attractive in me, that first night, was the combination of boldness and courtesy I'd displayed at the bar. What I learned from a close friend of hers, months later, was that I'm generally oblivious to the attention of others. It seems there were a great many girls at the party who'd found me very attractive and that I'd come to Laura's notice far earlier than she let on.

Our time together was marked by honest and sincere communication that made us both great lovers and friends. This was something neither of us had gotten from our previous relationships. We discovered we each shared a secret personality trait. Growing up, we had developed edges as sharp as knives and, early on, had both learned to sheath them.

I carried a chip on my shoulder that was the result of poor parenting and childhood poverty. Laura had grown up with very wealthy parents. She hinted that their money had not been legitimately earned. Laura felt as if she'd been treated coldly as a child, expected to maintain false appearances, and sent away when she grew troublesome. She despised the class distinctions inherent in her status and felt a strong desire to avenge social transgressions quickly. That she sometimes reacted to injustice with violence was likely representative of an unbridled privilege she'd enjoyed in her childhood.

"There are some things that I don't want to talk about even with you, dear," Laura said as we were walking hand-in-hand in the park. "Please don't take it personally. If I wanted to share, it would only be with you."

I'd been pressing her again for details of her childhood. Perhaps to offset the many tear-jerking childhood stories she'd elicited from me. In telling her my past I'd felt we'd grown closer. Her way of shutting down a conversation, while leaving open the door and building me up, was very effective.

As we followed the path that led past the baseball diamond, we heard the cracking of a bat. When the balls flew to the outfielder he shouted, "Nice one," and when they didn't, he cussed.

Each time he cussed, the pitcher dressed him down, "Liam, shut your filth hole! I don't want to hear that kind of talk." The three of them were college age and very athletic, but we did not recognize them from school.

In the bleachers were two young teenagers. One had on a furry hat and gloves. He wore black leggings under white shorts, at the back of which he'd pinned a bushy tail. The other boy wore lipstick and eyeliner. He had on a leather jacket over a white T-shirt, wore his pant legs cuffed, and had his hair slicked back. The jacketed boy had his left hand rested on the inner thigh of his furry friend. With his other he stroked the tail.

Seeing their affection inspired me—I kissed Laura. I thought to take her to the other side of the bleachers and perhaps stroke her a little. She returned my kiss and pulled at me eagerly. Behind us on the field, we heard the discordant whine of intolerance.

"Ooh, those faggots are kissing!"

I winced and felt the sting of shame from the memory of mean things said to me when I was a teenage outcast.

I let go of Laura as we turned to look. They had not been speaking of me.

The voice had come from the batter. He extended his bat with a slow sweep and pointed to the two teens. The kid in the leather jacket flashed his middle finger.

The pitcher wound up and sent a speed ball hurtling into the stands. The ball hit the furry boy with such force it knocked him over like a milk jug at a carnival booth.

I could hardly believe what my eyes were seeing. The one in the leather jacket clutched at his friend, who could no longer move his arm. Their faces were now showing the horror and fear of victimization I knew too well. My mind struggled to process the shock. I reacted slowly.

"We need to call someone...the police," I said to Laura.

She did not respond. I turned my head to her; she was gone. I looked down at the field, just as she disappeared behind the dugout. She came back into view as she crossed the baseline. In her hand she dragged a metal bat. Her head was hung down so that her hair fell around her face.

Motion in the corner of my eye caused me to turn my head. I caught the teenagers fleeing the stands and not looking back. Unsure of what was happening, I started moving toward the field.

"What the fuck do you think you're doing?" the pitcher said derisively as she came near.

Laura did not reply. Now in reach, she slowly raised her head.

I'm not sure what expression was on her face. He was six foot three, Laura five-eight, but whatever he saw in her eyes it caused him to jerk his head back as if he'd smelled something foul.

The first hit struck his shoulder and elicited a scream. The next, and the next, smashed into his humerus, three inches above his elbow. Her speed was blindingly fast and very accurate even as he fell to his knees. With the next hit I heard a crack and a new agonizing scream from the pitcher.

I was down on the field and turning the corner through the fence. The batter was running up behind her, bat in hand. She took another swing, hitting the pitcher in the shoulder. Instead of pulling up she shoved the tip of the bat into the crook of his neck and sent him to the ground.

"Behind you!" I warned. The batter was readying a swing.

Without looking Laura swung around, arms fully extended. This caused her attacker to comically step back and nearly fall off his toes. The outfielder had made his way in, his hands raised in submission as he tried to aid the pitcher.

"We're sorry, it was just a joke. Sorry," the outfielder pleaded.

Laura waved the bat, threatening them to keep their distance. They did not pursue her as she slowly backed away.

She dropped the bat as she left the field and did not once look back. We walked away at a quick pace, my eyes constantly over my shoulder until we got to her car. She hit the button to unlock the doors and then tossed me the keys. I sat behind the wheel and started the car as she got in and closed the door.

"Are you okay?" I asked. "Can we talk about what just happened?"

She smiled at me affectionately, as if nothing had happened.

"You understand. Some things just have to be done," she said.

"I understand," I said coolly, as I pulled away from the curb. Then gently, "but I'm here for you if you want to." Again she smiled and patted me on the leg.

"Thank you, you're wonderful," she said, turning and giving me a wink. "Thanks for having my back."

The following day, Laura sat for the LSAT, the test given for law school admissions. She scored in the ninety-eighth percentile, three points higher than expected for admission to programs at Harvard and Yale.

Laura and I spent eight months together. I have always thought of it as our honeymoon period. By the end of it I loved her. Yet, when the time came for her to leave for grad school, we agreed to break up. It didn't seem prudent at our age to risk being long-distance lovers. Without that pressure, we were able to wait a few months, then pick up the phone and stay long-distance friends.

CHAPTER FIVE

My major in college was history, with a long-term plan to go to graduate school and study international relations. Ray was working on a bachelor's degree in art. He dreamed of working in an L.A. gallery and of discovering several of the next great artists. Laura planned to finish law school and work as social justice advocate.

The year after Laura had gone was Ray's and my senior year. That summer we'd gotten jobs near the university. We had been sharing an apartment together that was largely paid for by the pot I was selling back home.

The previous year had gone very well for both of us. I'd had Laura, and Ray, for the first time ever, had classes in a subject he loved. He'd found a peer group among the art students, dancers, and the theatre crowd. Some of his friends took very fondly to his passion for conspiracies. A few of them would even sleep with him. More than once I'd woken to find a beautiful, half-naked girl making us morning coffee.

While I was not without the occasional affection of others, Laura had set an impossibly high standard for other women to live up to. Besides, my job that summer was a commission sales job that consumed a lot of my time.

One afternoon, Ray came around the office and called me out for a break.

"They fucked us. We're screwed," he said, so furious that spittle flew from his mouth.

"What are you talking about?" I asked, wiping saliva from my cheek.

Seeing that he had spit on me, Ray calmed considerably, "Fuck, I'm sorry man. It's the fucking government. They just cut our grants."

That fall, conservatives had swept the government, promising to balance the budget. They slipped education cuts into a military spending bill, and last night it had been signed into law.

"You're the mastermind, Kyle. What are we going to do?" Ray implored.

"Calm down. Give me some time to crunch the numbers and see what we can do," I said, but Ray was not placated.

"Maybe we should look into selling something more than insurance," he said, mocking my current job. Ray wanted us to give up marijuana for amphetamines and even believed he had a great source. I was opposed to the idea. Amphetamines sometimes made addicts out of people. I didn't want that on my conscience.

"Give me some time," I asked, and then sent him away.

Back at my desk, between sales calls, I began to run the numbers. Slowly I came to the conclusion that we could make it, but only if we took the coming school year off and both picked up second jobs.

The thought of getting set back a whole year was agony. Together we had come so far from such humble beginnings. By contrast, most other students on campus relied on mommy and daddy for cars, clothes, and spending money. They didn't have to purchase their own health insurance or pay the other numerous bills that arise while going to school, whereas we had endured—without a safety net and without a single material possession we didn't buy on our own.

We'd come far, and gotten so close to the end, only to have the assistance we'd been promised snatched away from us. As I considered our predicament and weighed our options in the back of my mind, there was the constant lure of Owens' safe.

If it were just me, I'd do the job and be done. If Owens didn't have insurance, then the asshole would get what he had coming. My moral quandary was with Ray. I could do the job alone and then give Ray enough money to make up what he'd lost in government assistance. If I did that, I'd be taking all the risk and giving Ray a free ride. My other option was to make Ray a partner, have him help with the job, and split it all fifty-fifty. My final option was to do the job alone—cut ties with Ray, and let him fend for himself.

The last option was tempting. Ray had been getting on my nerves: just three days before, we'd been arguing again about one of his conspiracy theories. If I let Ray participate, I'd get to enjoy the delicious irony of making him a co-conspirator. Unfortunately, I had no real idea of the value of the safe's contents, and thus, no idea of how much delicious irony would cost me.

When we argued, I invested my time and energy trying to get him to separate fact from fiction. I always failed and so I questioned his judgment. In order to pull off the heist, we had to be a team. I had to be able to trust him with my life. I feared that something would go wrong and I wouldn't be able to count on him.

"So, what did you figure out?" Ray asked me as I walked in the door from work.

I sighed and then answered him, "If we make a serious sacrifice we can do it."

"No," Ray said, his voice flat and his face expressionless. "I'm not going to take a year off from school and work two jobs."

That he knew what I was about to say shocked me.

"What?" Ray inquired, "Did you think you were the only one who could do math and put together a spreadsheet?"

"I didn't think you were inclined to," I said, feeling a little defensive. I went into the kitchen to grab some dinner.

"There's a better way," Ray said. "You don't have to do it."

Ray followed and came to the living room side of the kitchen counter. I could see a giant bulge in his front pocket.

"You cleaned out your savings for this?" I asked, knowing that was the only way he'd have been able to raise the money. Ray nodded.

"Kyle, you have helped me a lot. If we tallied up a balance sheet I'd be deep in the red to you. I'm going to do this on my own, and then for once I'm going to take care of you."

"And what happens when you go to make this purchase and they take all your money and fuck you? What happens if you get busted holding ounces, or pills, or tablets or whatever you're holding? What happens if, like those kids in New York, someone dies because of what you've given them? That's never been a problem with pot," I said, my voice rising to a near panic. I don't know why I took Ray's risks so personally. I did and it showed. I feared for him and I could not hide it.

"Hey man, it's my life. You don't have a better solution. This is my decision," Ray said, his voice cracking.

"You're willing to risk jail for that?" I asked, letting it hang in the air. I looked down and put the finishing touches on my sandwich.

"I'm not going to get busted, but if that happens—I'll do my time," Ray had on that annoyed expression he gave me whenever I challenged one of his ideas.

"Alright, so if you could pull off a heist instead of selling speed you'd be down for that?" I asked as if raising a hypothetical question.

"Hell yes. There would be less people involved and if it was planned right, there would be less chance of getting caught," Ray said.

"You think you could keep your mouth shut and be patient enough to pull off a major theft?" I asked, goading him a little.

"Fuck you. Why do you always have to act like you're better than me? Anything you can do, I can do. I'm not a fucking blab or some snot-nose kid. I don't need you to wipe my ass."

Knowing that I'd gotten Ray hot under the collar had made me feel as if I had regained control over the situation.

"Put your money back in the bank," I said, smiling.

I started going back to the Owens' house to observe their current movements. In addition, I began drilling Ray on every possible eventuality. We had a backup plan if we tripped a silent alarm, if we got separated, or if we discovered someone at the house who wasn't supposed to be there. There was a plan in case one of us was arrested, and we both had detailed alibis.

After four weeks of following the Owenses, and after some legwork on the side, we were ready. We approached the house dressed in black, brought backpacks and the proper tools. The three Owenses had taken the family boat four hours away to Mountain Reservoir, where they had a cabin.

The first step was to cut the phone line at the back of the house. Looking in a window, I verified my suspicion: they had an alarm but it wasn't in use. We pried a window open, I slipped through and then let Ray in the front door. Our only light was from headlamps and flashlights.

"Man this place is garish," Ray said as we slowly climbed the stairs. The house was decorated in elaborate furniture pieces topped with marble, the floor was covered in white carpet, and the scroll work on the crown molding was painted gold. Upstairs the walls had silver and red wallpaper imprinted with fleurs-de-lis.

"Try not to look," I said, responding to Ray's exasperation over the décor. We entered the master bedroom. I took down the painting, spun the dial to clear the safe and began entering the combination.

Ray moved from window to window checking to see if there were any cars moving in the vicinity. The safe opened right up. I quickly slipped the diamonds into a felt bag I'd brought, and then stuffed it in my backpack along with a wad of cash from the safe.

"Oh my God," Ray shouted. "Quick, come here!"

With the safe closed and the painting back in place, I followed Ray's voice and the glow of his flashlight to a sitting room off the master bedroom. There, on a pedestal near the far wall was a small bronze statuette. It was fifteen inches in height, about four inches in diameter, and weighed nearly forty pounds.

"Isn't she beautiful?" Ray said in awe as I drew near.

The statue was of a very lovely woman who had been augmented with cybernetics. Her left eye was a protruding cylinder that partially obscured her face. She had a robotic arm and opposing robotic leg. Aside from her machine parts, she was naked. There was an empty cavity in her chest and her heart was in her hand. On her robot leg she wore a high heel and on her human leg she wore a Greek sandal. She had beautifully flowing hair but when you walked behind her you could see that, except a tiny part at center, her brain was mostly computer.

"Sure," I said, more concerned about focusing on the job at hand.

"You don't understand," Ray said, his wonderment taking on new depth; "It's a Nick Planne."

"You're right, I don't understand. Let's go before this whole thing falls apart."

"Oh, Jesus, Nick Planne, he's one of the hottest living sculptors in the country and he graduated from our university just three years ago."

"That's great, good for him," I said, becoming annoyed. Ray began lifting the statue. "What the fuck are you doing?" I asked.

"I'm taking this with me."

"No, are you insane? What's it even worth? You'll never fence that," I said.

"He's still living. This piece sold for five; it's probably worth ten, maybe twenty, but— I would never sell this statue," Ray said as he placed it in his backpack and zipped it up.

"You can never even show it to anyone," I added.

"Don't worry, I won't keep it in the house or car or anything. No one will ever see it," Ray assured.

The forty thousand in cash was enough to get us through the school year. The diamonds would take a long time to fence. I hid them and reached out to Arnaud. Arnaud was happy to hear from me and we struck up a friendship. It would be another year before I felt that I trusted him and knew his character well enough to even broach the subject of the diamonds. I was offering a 40/60 split and taking the smaller share. Eventually, Arnaud took great pleasure in selling many of the diamonds right back to Owens. In the interim, Ray and I returned to school, feeling less stressed than we'd ever felt in our lives.

CHAPTER SIX

The lecture hall for my "Economic History of the World" class was still decorated in the seventies style from when it was built. Against the painted white cinderblocks of the wall hung large, dark pieces of wood cut at an angle and spaced an inch apart, so that they resembled a pan flute. All of the chairs were orange plastic with a folding, side-style desktop. On the opposite side of the wall, large squares floated over the cinderblock in blue and yellow.

Tasteless and distracting. I tried not to look at the decor and instead focused on the screen behind the professor. We had advanced through the economic systems of the Paleolithic, Neolithic, and Bronze Ages and were now at the Classical Era, when Alexander the Great established world trade routes and a stable currency.

As I put this in my notes I saw a campus police officer enter the hall. He came to the front of the room and handed the professor a small piece of paper. Every student in the room raised their heads and looked forward.

"Kyle Everett, this officer would like to speak with you. Something about your car?" The professor looked around the room. The class was large enough he did not know me from the other students.

The officer had his hand casually resting on his gun. He began scanning the room.

The car was in Ray's name, and so I wondered why the ruse? My guess was the officer wanted to get me out of the lecture hall without incident. Whether he kept his hand on his gun out of habit or caution I didn't know.

This almost certainly had to do with the robbery. *How much could they know?* I wondered. I considered making a break for it. There were several exits in the hall. I looked around the room, but no deputies were posted.

They didn't yet know enough to make an arrest. I weighed whether or not I should run. Unfortunately, there were enough people in the room who knew me by name. Those that did locked their eyes on me, and this led others to do the same until I was clearly marked. The officer started toward the stairs. I quickly gathered my things, pretending as if nothing was wrong. It would be better to play along with the ruse than create a scene. Besides, Ray and I had planned for this; I'd covered every contingency.

I grabbed my books and noticed my hand was shaking. I couldn't afford to look nervous or guilty. I dropped my book, then leaned down to pick it up. While I was hidden behind the seats I took two very deep breaths, closed my eyes, and forced myself to relax. I've done nothing wrong, I told myself;

therefore I must act as if I've done nothing wrong. I stood up smiling, and made a point of adding a spring to my step as I came down the stairs. This seemed to work on the class and the professor, who resumed his lecture. The officer seemed to relax as well; he took his hand off his gun and did not move to touch me as I exited the class.

There were two men in the hall. One was a uniformed state trooper. The other was mild-mannered and a little paunchy. He wore a tan suit with brown-laced dress shoes. His face was lined and he had large bushy eyebrows that drooped overtop clear blue eyes. The gray around the temples gave him a fatherly appearance that I'm sure caused many people to drop their guard.

The campus officer pointed in the direction of the man, and as I approached, his eyes gave him away. He examined me carefully and when he spoke he looked right into my eyes with a very intense, penetrating stare. I had the sense that if this man came after me, he wasn't going to stop until he made an arrest.

"Hi Kyle, I'm detective Kirkwall. We would like you to come down to the station and answer a few questions," he said, as if extending a cordial invitation.

"I'm right in the middle of class. How long will it take? My last class lets out at four," I said, wondering if I sounded authentic.

In a firm tone Kirkwall said, "I'm afraid it can't wait."

"Am I in trouble for something?" I asked, trying to sound perplexed while pushing down my fear and panic.

I searched the detective's face intently and then looked at the trooper and the campus officer who had been standing behind me. The state trooper kept checking his phone; the campus officer leaned forward on his toes, as if he was witnessing a great drama unfolding.

"No, not at all," Kirkwall said sounding very warm and inviting. "We need to ask you about a case, and unfortunately, time is of the essence."

The detective was a good liar. I continued with my perplexed expression and looked down at my shoes. I needed time to think, to work out what was happening. If I go voluntarily they'll say I wasn't arrested. If I refuse to go and they have a hair of evidence on me they will arrest me. Depending on how sophisticated they presume me to be they might arrest me without evidence. If I refuse I'm going to look guilty. I had to assume they didn't have any evidence on me directly. So what did they want? They wanted me to incriminate myself or someone else. *Ray, where's Ray?* I began to wonder.

It felt like I was losing the battle to hide my anxiety. For a moment I lost my sense of time and did not know how long I'd been looking at my shoes. I could see the detective was leaning forward, his eyes on me as he searched me for a sign of guilt. I needed information. The only way I was going to get it was by going with them. They suspected me; that was certain.

I needed time to think and the longer I stood there looking down, the more suspicious they were going to become. I summoned the emotions of the innocent.

"Oh my," I exclaimed, allowing a panicked concern to spread across my face, "Please tell me no one is hurt? Is my mother okay?" Kirkwall turned his head and looked at me with one eye.

"No one is hurt," he said, without compassion. He then extended his arm, pointing the way. I followed him out to a plain car, where I was asked to sit in the back. From the driver's seat, he passed through the Plexiglas several pieces of paper, folded over and stapled in the corner.

"What's this?" I asked as the car began to move.

"It's a warrant to search the apartment and car you share with Ray Barr," Kirkwall said smugly and then added, "We are searching now. Will we find anything?"

Had he come yesterday, he would have found four ounces of marijuana. When they looked in the plastic box under the coffee table they would find less than a dime bag, a pipe, and some rolling papers.

"Is Ray in some kind of trouble?" I asked, sounding sincere.

Kirkwall just let out a "hrmph" and gave me a quick glance in the rearview.

Quietly I texted Laura, told her that I was being taken for questioning, and asked that she try to contract Ray.

Even then Laura was sharp as a tack, never more so than in a crisis. We exchanged a flurry of texts between us before Kirkwall pulled into the station.

Inside, Kirkwall dropped me off in an interrogation room. Two cameras hung from the ceiling, a two-way mirrored window on the wall, and a microphone on the table. The room was painted off-white and overly bright.

Fifteen minutes later, Kirkwall returned.

"Do you know Shaun Owens?" he asked in a calm, even tone as he sat down across from me.

I paused and waited. Then just as he was about to speak again I opened my mouth.

"At this time I'm going to invoke my Fifth Amendment right against self-incrimination," I said matching his tone.

Kirkwall's head jerked ever so slightly. Then he looked up at me and gave a great big outbreath.

"You're not under arrest. I just want to ask you some questions. If you are not guilty of anything, why wouldn't you just answer them?" he inquired with muted curiosity.

"Because of *Salinas v. Texas*, in which a defendant who had not been charged had his silence used against him in a court of law to imply he was guilty." I turned to look right up at the camera. "I am not guilty of anything. You have served a warrant on the home and the car I share with my roommate. I have no idea if he is guilty of anything. If he put something illegal in our apartment I don't know about it," I said, hoping that Ray had stuck to the plan.

Kirkwall's face tightened; he dropped his pen on top of his legal pad and pushed himself back from the table.

"I don't like your attitude, Mr. Everett. People with nothing to hide don't try and obstruct justice."

"Good officers don't threaten people with obstruction of justice for exercising their lawful rights," I said and then added, "If we are done here I'd like to go."

Kirkwall grimaced. "You're not going anywhere. Your friend Ray—has already been arrested. We caught him in possession of a statue worth about $850,000. We've charged him with the burglary at the Owens estate."

I let a look of surprise and absolute disbelief wash across my face.

"Never, not Ray," I responded.

"We are going to recover the diamonds, and when we do I'm going to find some evidence tying you to this crime. You two didn't hurt anyone. There's no reason for this to be hard on either of you. Ray has confessed. He's going to serve the maximum sentence. We could split that sentence and make both your burdens a little easier. We just need to get the diamonds back. Come clean and I can help you out."

"Again I'm going to assert my Fifth Amendment right," I said, in the same plain tone as before.

Kirkwall narrowed his eyes.

"You had better get used to saying that. I can hold you for questioning and that's what I'm going to do."

Before I could say another word, there was a knock on the door. A uniformed officer stuck his head in the room. Behind the officer stood a man in a suit who began to push his way into the room.

"Kyle Everett?" he asked me. I nodded. "I'm your lawyer. Don't say another word."

"I've only asserted my Fifth Amendment rights," I replied.

The lawyer shot me a pleased little nod, before turning back to Kirkwall. "Do you have a cause to charge my client?" he asked the detective.

"I will," said Kirkwall with absolute confidence.

"Then until that time we are leaving—let's go."

I stood and followed him out of the police station. Outside, he advised me to go home, talk to no one, and be in his office the next morning. He then went back inside to act as Ray's attorney. Laura had come through and quickly.

Eventually, I learned that Nick Planne had died a few months ago. Subsequently, the stolen sculpture had soared in value. Ray turned to Mike Cox, a friend from art class and the nephew of a well-known art dealer in the city. Ray felt him out a little and then told Cox he knew of a hot piece. Slowly Mike lured Ray in with promises of a huge payday. Ultimately, he turned Ray in for a $10,000 reward and his picture in the newspaper.

Having been busted holding the statue, Ray (despite all we'd rehearsed) broke down and confessed. Fortunately, he didn't admit to more than the statue.

The lawyer turned out to be a good one. He discovered that Owens had reported to the police one missing amount from his safe and filed a higher amount with his insurance company. The mistake may or may not have been intentional. The attorney successfully argued that Ray had stolen the statue and when Owens saw it gone, he stole from his own safe. He got Ray's sentence knocked down from twenty years to four.

Ray could have confessed and implicated me in the crime for his own personal gain. He didn't sell me out. I owed him for that. Even though Ray got on my nerves, he was still my friend. He stayed loyal.

"Some things just have to be done," Laura had said. Her words kept coming to my mind when I thought about Mike Cox's betrayal. Cox needed to pay and I intended to make him pay with his life. It may be hard to understand my reason for going after Cox. There are certain things you don't do, snitching is one of them. Mike could have not gotten involved and walked away. He didn't; he used Ray to enrich himself. He had committed an unpardonable offense.

I used cash to purchase two stainless steel fighting knives with five-and-a-half-inch blades.

Cox worked at a night club in the city. Eventually, I caught him in the early morning hours in a back alley as he walked to his car. Even with his crime it was not right just to kill him. Just like a duel among gentleman or an old-fashioned gunfight, every man deserves a right to fight for his life.

As he approached I sidled out from around a corner and threw down the knife. It hit the ground with a clink and then skidded to Mike's feet. I stood in front of him, my knife in hand. He took a hard, long look at me and then squinted.

"Because of Ray Barr?" he asked.

I nodded yes, but didn't say anything.

Mike was about five-eleven and about three hundred pounds. He leaned over and picked up the knife. He held the knife with confidence. A pale, sickly fear washed over me as I began to realize I was in over my head.

I lunged at him like an awkward fencer. Because he walked slowly and was fat, I'd made the foolish assumption that he was dumb and weak. He moved with unpredictable speed. He knocked my arm away with his empty hand. Striking, he plunged his knife into my thigh up to the hilt. As he pulled it back out he elbowed me in the chin. I screamed in pain. I readied my knife should he come at me again. He backed up a little.

I'd come here with resolve, a plan, and very primitive notion of honor. Now my mind flashed with doubts. My righteousness was about to get me killed.

He came at me again and I drove him back with a couple of wild slashes. He could see I was bleeding badly and he was smart enough to know he could wait me out.

This had been my choice. No matter how great the pain, if I was going to die every ounce of my strength would be used fighting.

I charged him screaming. Not a rebel yell—I screamed in pain because when I put pressure on my injured leg it hurt so badly I thought I was going to pass out. To get to him I put weight on it twice. On the second step I jumped in the air. The look on his face told me it was unexpected.

I flew towards him. He swung but was blocked by my arm. With the damaged leg I kicked him as hard as I could in the chest. Blood from my thigh spurted all over him. It was in his hair, on his face, and covering his arms. It rained on the ground and on the wall behind him.

Coming down, I shoved my knife into his chest as deeply as I could. Landing on my good leg, I came back up and pulled the knife out. He took another swing. It was wide, closed around me, and caught me in a bear hug. His wound gushed all over me.

My knife was pointed up and so I drove it into the V of his neck, imagining I could slice him. Instead it went into his throat. I pulled it back and forth, side to side, and up and down. His heavy breaths wheezed in and out the hole, over and over again. Eventually he released his hold on me, stumbled back, and fell to his knees.

I tore a piece of my shirt and tied it around my leg, keeping a watchful eye on my dying foe. I was shaking. My heart was pounding with adrenaline. It felt like I was going to throw up or pass out, but I could not afford to do either.

Mike's DNA and my DNA were all that was needed to send me away. It was everywhere. It was especially all over Mike. I picked up his knife.

"Come on," I said, "let's get you to the hospital." Mike used his last ounce of strength helping me drag him into the passenger seat of his car. Then from my trunk I grabbed an old sheet and two five-gallon cans of gasoline, put them into Mike's car and drove far away. We weren't going to the hospital.

Mike Cox died in the car. I poured five gallons of gas on Mike, making sure I let it pour down his back and pool up in the seat as well as cover the front of him. I saved the other five for the car and stuck the old sheet in the gas pipe before setting the whole thing on fire. Later, I would go back to the scene of the fight and wash the area with bleach.

One week later, sometime in the middle of the night, someone tried to smother me in my sleep. My fingers reached across the night table sending the lamp to the floor; they closed around a knife. I stabbed at my attacker, again and again with no effect. A huge weight rested on my chest, the pressure increasing the harder I fought. I couldn't breathe. In a last ditch effort to save myself I pushed back with every ounce of strength and fell to the floor. I woke up in a cold sweat and realized it was just a dream. I'd been stabbing at the mattress.

The dreams continued for months. At their worst I'd have them four or five times a week. In order to sleep better, I ran until I exhausted myself. Around this time I finished college, stopped selling pot, and got a job in the financial industry. I still had the dreams two or three times a week, but having whittled it down I felt I had control over the problem. It was around this time there was a knock on my door.

"Hi, I need a place to stay," she said. She looked tired as if she'd driven nonstop.

I looked past her, saw behind her that her car was packed full and knew she'd dropped out of law school. I opened my arms, felt her press against my chest and selfishly buried my nose in her hair and sucked up her scent. She wouldn't say why she'd left school and got angry when I pressed her to tell me.

Sleeping next to Laura brought me a week's reprieve from the dreams. Then they returned in full force. I made excuses to explain my behavior. After the fourth time I woke up next to her shaking with fear and waving an imaginary knife, she demanded I see someone.

When I told her I couldn't see anyone, she forced the truth out of me. I told her how I'd killed Mike Cox. She looked solemn as I told her, as if the information had resolved a great dilemma. Telling her sent the dreams away for a while.

The typewritten note taped to the lamp shade said: *Please go to the store right now and get night and day cold medicine, mentholatum, and milk.*

Laura was not home. I followed her instructions. When I returned she was still gone. I opened the fridge and placed the milk inside. Inside was another note. It said: *Be back in two days. Tell no one I'm gone, let no one in the house.*

Around midnight of the second day Laura quietly slipped in the back door. She found me in the kitchen. She smiled and came over and stood.

"I was miserably sick for the last couple of days but now I'm feeling much better," she said, locking eyes with me for emphasis. She leaned her head and paused until I nodded in acknowledgment. "Where did you put the notes I left you?"

I pointed to a magnet on the fridge. She took the notes down and burned them on the gas stove. She dumped two bottles of cold medicine out in the sink and threw the bottles in the trash.

I shrugged in confusion. She frowned in sympathy.

"Since I'm feeling so much better, let's take a walk. She stroked my hair and then pulled me up into a hug.

A few minutes later we walked arm-in-arm on the lighted path by the river.

"Thank you for being so patient," she said, then stopped and kissed me. "I love you. I've never met anyone who has shown me so much faith and patience." We walked again until we came to a bench. She sat me down and stood in front of me.

"I left school—because I was raped." She allowed this disturbing news to sit on me, but did not seem bothered herself. Behind her the river churned.

I felt helpless and it stirred my anger. I imagined things but had no idea what had happened or anything about her attacker. I tied up my fear and sorrow and drowned it in rage.

"It's okay," she said, kneeling beside me, "I took care of it—he's dead." Seeing that I was still burdened she whispered, "I killed him."

The profundity of her actions soaked into me. I was cleansed of any doubt: never would I find a woman more amazing than this.

"I love you," I said, standing and pulling her to me. She nodded knowingly and put her head on my chest and held me.

After a few minutes she coaxed me to walk, steering us toward the water's edge.

From inside her jacket she produced a cloth that unwrapped to reveal a knife.

"Can you toss this right about there for me?" she asked, pointing to a spot toward the center of the river.

I threw it hard, watched it spin, and then splash close to the center. As it sunk I began to worry that this act of violence would change Laura for the worse. I ruminated over her choice of weapons. Did she sneak up behind her attacker or did she face him head on, I thought to myself.

"The deepest part of the river is called the thalweg," Laura informed me.

As we turned and walked back toward the house she continued talking about thalwegs: their geographic significance, that the word was derived from old German, and so on. I took comfort in her telling me. It was typical Laura to over-research everything. Once her head was stuffed full of knowledge she would blow a little steam valve and it would all come whistling out.

I nodded along but I'd stopped listening, wondering instead if she'd leave me and return to school.

CHAPTER SEVEN

Three Hispanic men looked up from the car they were working on as I walked by; I gave them a reassuring head nod and continued on my way. Four houses down, two young black kids were shooting hoops off a detached garage. They didn't notice me as I walked past their driveway. Across the street an old man, sitting on his AstroTurf-covered porch, lit a cigarette. At his feet was an old coffee can overflowing with butts—it was still smoking from his last. Over his shoulder, through the plate glass, an older woman in a green housecoat was clearing the dining room table and tidying the kitchen.

The man was looking down the street where a Honda had just pulled into a driveway; the car had a wrap of neon underneath and in the dark it looked like it floated. Techno music blared from the open window along with the annoying *thump, thump* of a disproportionate subwoofer. The driver, a young Asian kid dressed in a suit, left the car running, got out, and came around to the passenger side, where he leaned back on the car's hood. A wispy, six-foot-tall girl with long blond hair, pale skin, and a short skirt came out of the house to greet him. Dressed in high heels, she traversed the stairs like a pro—though judging by her skinny frame she was barely sixteen. She pressed her pelvis against the kid. Towering over him she leaned down, her upper body resembling the long neck of a giraffe, and gave him a passionate kiss.

This seemed to disturb the man with the cigarette; he growled with disgust until it turned into a hacking coughing fit. He snuffed out his cigarette and went into the house, slamming the door. Through the window I saw him approach the plump woman. He came at her with a ferocity that caused her to freeze, the dishtowel she was using to wipe the dining room table still in hand. He snapped out his arm, pointing. She turned and bent over, jutted, and putting her hands on the table. He lifted the house coat, revealing naked, plump, but firm marbled buttocks that showed signs of light bruising. With one hand he dropped his trousers and started in on her unconcerned—or perhaps excited by the prospect—that someone might observe from outside. I turned away.

As I neared my target, the cars parked along the street stopped blending into the neighborhood. The tight cluster in question contained brand new SUVs and older foreign cars, rugged cars: a couple of Jeeps, a Subaru or two, and a mix of faded pickups. I would have assumed someone was having a house party, but there were none of the tell-tale signs. The Asian kid and the girl had pulled away, clearing the street of noise. There was no muffled music, no laughter, and none of the occasional break-away voices from people who'd stepped out for a breath of fresh air. The newer cars had few if any extra emblems, but the older cars had plenty. The stickers were contradictory, with individual cars bearing both hard-right and hard-left political positions. Every car featured at least one pro-gun message.

Far down the sidewalk, a small group of men in brightly colored high-top sneakers were walking in my direction. They had yet to see me. The driveway on my right was shielded with a six-foot hedge. I stepped onto the driveway and walked down it until I was standing between two cars. I placed my back against the hedge. I kept an ear tuned to their voices and waited, hoping the men would quickly pass.

It had been two weeks since I'd met Laura and Ray for dinner. In that time, I had been on this street once before—sitting in the back of a taxi cab. Not much had changed since the old days. The house had a fresh coat of paint and the front yard had been landscaped to make better use of the two large, overhanging trees. Tasteful ground cover bordered the front yard while tall, willowy shrubs in the four corners drew the eye and all but made the metal fence disappear. The house, though only a small, two-bedroom clapboard, now looked homey and slightly out of place among the chain-linked, sun-dried yards of its neighbors.

Another advantage of the house was its age. It pre-dated the neighborhood and had a backyard that could easily have held three or four houses its size. The reason it hadn't been carved up was that, back in '76, they ran the loop for the Interstate down in the ravine just beyond the property line. Now the backyard was bordered by an effective, 20-foot tall sound barrier.

The wall, though slightly shorter, appeared to loom over the large barn that in its day held farm equipment. The fields were long gone, replaced by the houses that lined the street. When Ray and I were twelve, the barn was used as a garage to hold his alcoholic grandmother's red Eldorado Cadillac and the rusting hull of his deceased grandfather's 1954 Chevy truck. Sometime in the last ten years someone built a two-car garage onto the house. Despite a fresh coat of red paint on the barn, the garage all but obscured it from the street.

I had ridden by a few days ago and was now standing in the dark with my back to the bushes, because I was consumed with Laura. I wanted to get closer. I needed information, specifically, to size up her relationship with Ray. Most importantly, I hoped to impress her—to get and keep her attention.

To that end, I spent a lot of time researching offshore accounts so I could show off my expertise at our next meeting. It turns out they are easy to set up. It only costs a few thousand dollars. The hard part is managing the accounts. It requires watching the countries in question with diligence, always ready to move your money at the first sign of political unrest.

It didn't seem enough to know where and how to set up accounts. I dug deeper, more exhaustively, and didn't stop until I felt like I was an expert. Over the years I have lived frugally and banked a tidy sum of cash. Having recognized some of the benefits of offshore banking, I'd already moved my own savings.

I could certainly help them if they wanted to proceed. Armed with my knowledge on the subject, I decided that tonight would be a good time to drop by on a surprise visit. "You know," as I'd planned to say, "since I was in the neighborhood."

The men in the sneakers didn't pass. I walked to the edge of the driveway and peered around the corner. They had barely moved. They stood on the sidewalk and alternated leaning on the fence while they drank and shared a spliff.

Ray's house, on this side of the street, was just one door down. What I didn't want was to knock on their door and wake them if they'd crashed or approach their house if they weren't home. It had been my hope to walk past and observe without being observed. I didn't want to turn back and forth in front of their house and I didn't want to walk directly through the men smoking and drinking just a few doors down.

Ray's porch light was off, but a light on the garage brightened the path leading to the barn. The barn was illuminated by two more lights. The numerous cars and the darkened house drew my attention to the barn. The only approach was on the path past the garage. If anyone was watching they would see me coming first.

The house of the driveway where I was standing had its porch light on but was otherwise dark, suggesting the occupants had gone to bed. At the end of the driveway, a low fence separated the front and backyard. Beyond that was a tall tree, next to the sound barrier that ran behind all the houses on this side of the street.

Neatly folded into my jacket pocket were my two-finger parkour gloves. I put them on and began considering my options. The trunk of the tree was too far from the wall for a chimney climb and, due to some unusual trimming over the years, had a strange gap between its upper and lower branches. Parts of it looked dead. I worried that if I climbed it directly, branches would crack and make a racket. As I peered through the dark, I noticed a single, thick branch about ten feet high, jutting out four feet toward the wall and terminating where it had been sawed off.

I turned, walked to the edge of the driveway and took another look at the men down the sidewalk. Now, out of alcohol, they appeared to be playfully sparring. I turned back toward the driveway and began moving closer to the backyard fence, looking carefully for obstructions in the yard beyond. My biggest concern wasn't the climb; it was the fear that once I'd cleared the fence somewhere, just beyond in the dark, there might be a loud, vicious dog.

I took off running, easily side-vaulting over the fence. Then I increased my speed, determined to surprise and outrun a dog should one appear. Looking right, I found myself clearly in the window of the homeowner. His only light was the flickering T.V. over his shoulder. He was at the window, looking toward the night sky. My heart was thumping. I fell into the closest shadow, and waited until he drew the blinds. Then I was back up and running at the wall. Good foot placement propelled me and let me run fourteen feet up the barrier. Just as I started to fall I turned sidewise and gripped the protruding tree limb.

The limb, at its longest part, proved strong and supple. I put my back to the tree then ran along the sawed branch, springboarding at the end, and used that momentum to run up the remaining distance of the wall until my fingers could clutch the top edge. I pulled myself up. Balancing on the six-inch cap, I quietly ran the distance between the properties until I was alongside Ray's barn.

It was a quick hop to the crest of the barn's roof; I paused before making it. The house was completely dark, the barn was not. There was a light on over the paddock door and another over the large alley doors. I listened closely; the barn seemed alive with the chatter of many voices.

I aimed for the widow's peak, fearful of the noise a direct landing on the roof might make. Hopefully, the ancient center beam would hold my weight. I landed with barely a sound and silently thanked the long-dead craftsmen who'd roughhewed such a thick beam. I turned and hung from it, then dropped carefully onto the hay hood, rocking its pulley slightly. Now I was just above the hay door, a double door that had broken away from its interior latch so that it bowed in the center. I had a clear view into the loft, whose floor slats were widely spaced. With little side-to-side head movements, I was able to glean a clear view of the entire meeting below.

When Ray and I were kids, this was just a barn with side walls made of three-quarter-inch wood that had weathered and shrunk enough to produce gaps on nearly every side. Rather than replace the wood and shore up the gaps, Ray had constructed a room inside the barn. Where once there was a dirt floor littered with decades of mashed up straw, he'd built a wood floor, constructed ten-foot-high walls all around and lit the room with track lighting. At the back he'd built a little one-foot dais where I found him sitting alongside Laura. Off to their left, pushed back and out of the way, was a simple podium.

Ray and Laura had turned the barn into a meeting space. In the common area sat a surprising number of people on cushioned folded chairs. I did a quick count: twenty-four. As I looked them over I felt keenly aware of my precarious position: standing high without cover on a four-inch beam. Below me was a roomful of armed men and women participating in a secret meeting. I only knew two of them and at best we were on shaky ground.

Laura was dressed in a black skirt and soft-looking khaki top with a high collar, unbuttoned to show the V of her chest and throat, but not so low as to show cleavage. She wore a shoulder holster, but I could only see enough to tell that her pistol was a semi-automatic. Around her waist was a blue and red silk sash. It set apart and brought together her top and bottom to create a business-casual, paramilitary outfit. Laura was dressed sharper and with greater class than any of the other three women in the room. It seemed appropriate that, sitting there on the dais, she should look the part of the strong, capable leader. To me, in that outfit, she looked like a sexy guerilla CEO.

I felt jealous that she played this part, standing next to Ray when she should be standing next to me. A wave of jealousy washed over me, made me forget that I was peering down on an armed group that would shoot first and ask questions later. All I could think was how much I wanted to stand there next to Laura, and what pleasure I'd take in shoving Ray aside.

This reconnaissance was proving fruitful. It was unlikely I could gain better insight into their lives than right now. The collection of cars outside, Ray's long-standing affinity for conspiracies, and the guns all added up: Ray and Laura had formed some kind of patriot group.

If this was all the members, it was a small group. There was no telling if they were a committee, the main body of membership, or just the police force. These people didn't look shuffled in off the streets. They had good jobs; they did not fit the stereotype of the average slack-jawed weekend warrior.

Were it not for my training I probably would have been more

frightened. Not long after Laura left me, I hired my first fitness expert. Six months later I hired a professional to teach me how to fight with a knife and properly disarm an attacker. I've never felt a need or desire to have a gun, but it seemed foolish to know how to take a gun out of someone's hands and not be able use it. I trained intensively until I reached the level of marksman with both pistol and rifle. Now, I took inventory of their possessions and tried to determine their socio-economic status as well as to specifically draw on my knowledge of firearms to assess the danger below.

Each week when I went to the range, I walked past these guns in display cases. I spotted a $2,500 .45 caliber in the shoulder holster of a sleek-headed man—well-built, strong, but doughy around the middle. It was an expensive sidearm, but a bigger giveaway was the handcrafted, monogrammed, leather shoulder holster. He'd spent a lot of money on a specially made vanity holster meant to be hidden under a jacket. He was also wearing a $900 Equip watch; it was the same watch advertised on a glossy flyer mailed to me in with my credit card statement. My guess was that he was self-employed, perhaps a contractor or other small business owner.

Not too far away from him was an even larger man, about six-six with a linebacker's girth. He carried a Glock 9mm alongside a double magazine holster that carried only one clip. His clothes were not shabby, but faded. In the calloused fingers of his enormous hand, he flipped a Zippo lighter over his knuckles the same way a normal hand might walk a quarter.

These were the enforcers, standing at the back close to the doors. That made sense, since the first man had the look of someone who was used to giving orders.

A man and a woman, settled in the middle, had matching wedding rings and matching Smith and Wessons. They leaned forward together, as if leaning would help them catch every word. Seated one chair to the right was an older fellow, mid-fifties, long hair, and very skinny. He carried a snub-nosed revolver. He wore a comfortable-looking flannel shirt and was leaning back with his legs crossed, head nodding in agreement.

On the opposite side, one row forward, sat a scruffy-looking twenty-something with a great many tattoos. He wore no gun, but just two feet away leaning against the wall was a shoulder strap attached to an AR-15. Next to him was a mousey-looking girl, about the same age and of Indian descent. She had round silver glasses that stood out from her creamed-coffee complexion and thick black hair. She dressed in a velvety silk blouse and a tight pair of skinny jeans. If she carried a weapon it was likely concealed in the large handbag seated next to her. I guessed the grip on her gun would be pink to match her nails and lipstick.

Toward the front a small crowd sat together. Their familiarity with one another suggested their friendships pre-dated the group. They wore various firearms of intermediate value and I could see nothing particularly noteworthy about them: mid-thirties, probably here escaping families, strictly followers. They were largely paying attention when they weren't gawking at Laura. When Ray spoke, it was from this group that I occasionally heard audible signs of agreement.

Most interesting was a blond-headed young man sitting in the front row. He wore a pale suit with a salmon dress shirt. His weapon was a small, inexpensive 9mm Beretta in a belt clip holster. His jacket sat neatly folded on the chair next to him and his gun lay on the seat. His expensive phone was tucked into a leather carrier clipped to his belt. He sat with his legs crossed, elbows out, arms coming to a point under his chin. Occasionally, in response to the vocalizations from the group, he turned his head slowly and I caught a glimpse of the ivory face and the twinkle of a green eye. His expression was serene and unreadable; he looked like a handsome mantis. Were it not for his front-row seat I would have pegged him for a right-out-of-college spook— but no undercover Fed would leave his gun casually on the next chair.

A light rain began to fall, giving me a shiver. I ignored the chill and focused on Ray as he stood before the assemblage. As I looked closer I realized small cameras surrounded him. Ray wasn't just speaking to the room. He was broadcasting over the web.

"Free speech isn't just the power to speak but the right to be heard," Ray said, his voice carrying all the passion of a Baptist minister. "You cannot have a free press if they refuse to broadcast the truth!" he said, pointing into the audience for emphasis. "There is no savior; there is only you, and you, and you. Together we must grow our numbers so that we have the power to report the truth."

Ray's voice captivated as it vibrated around the room.

"Our First Amendment guarantees us the right to petition our government." As he spoke he pounded his fist into his palm, hammering out his words, "We are guaranteed a right to be heard!" He thrust both his hands into the air and shouted, "We will be heard!"

Ray displayed more confidence than I'd ever known him to show. As he spoke I studied the walls. They were lined with charts. I could see organized mapping of some common conspiratorial themes. Names like the Illuminati, the Trilateral Commission, and the Bilderberg Group headed lists printed with the names of people allegedly connected. In several locations there were photos with blue yarn attached and stretched to make lines that ran to the names of people.

"We have seen the ravages of living in a police state. No one person can defend our freedoms. We must do it together. We need your support. We need your action!"

If Ray and Laura had any big plans for this group, it was not immediately evident. There was nothing listed on the walls that could spark a revolution. There wasn't even enough tinder to wick a candle.

"We need you to wake up your neighbor, wake up your friends. Bring them forth and get involved. Hold a bake sale. Clean out your garage and sell what you don't need. Knock on doors and share this message of freedom.

"Tell them what you know. You are the free press. When the words come out of your mouth they will carry the powerful truth. Do not be dismayed by naysayers."

Ray paused and dropped his head. His hair fell in front of his eyes. He pushed it back up as he rose and began to speak again. This time more softly.

"There is just a little further to go now. Soon we will have the information I promised and we will prove them all wrong. The eyes of every American will be opened."

I wondered who was watching this fiery broadcast and whether it was motivating them. There could have been ten, a hundred, or a thousand. As powerful a speaker as Ray was, all I could see here were the same old arguments he and I had been having for years.

My heart sank. I realized that even though I didn't agree with Ray, part of me was secretly hoping he had something to back up this rhetoric. I was impressed that he'd built this room and gathered these followers. He was using them to raise money. It was my guess he would waste it publishing the nutty ideas plastered to the walls.

I didn't take his followers seriously. I couldn't see them making terrorist actions against a real target. As far as I could tell they were just a bunch of hobbyists crying that someone had changed their favorite role-playing game.

Throughout Ray's speech I'd been keeping an eye on Laura. Laura, who so lovingly gazed at Ray as if he were the messiah, come to lead them all to the promised land. It wasn't just her admiration for Ray that stuck in my craw; it was the fear that she bought into all of Ray's nonsense. I had always believed that Laura was smarter and wiser than Ray and I put together. How could she have been so brainwashed as to sit upon the stage and have a hand in leading this group?

I began to think that maybe I'd been mistaken. Maybe the image of her

I'd held in my mind all this time had been just a fantasy. I've always known that I am chemically addicted to her. Had her pheromonal sway left me blind?

Perhaps she was a better match for Ray, in part because he wasn't standing twenty-five feet off the ground, on a night that grew colder and damper by the second, ruminating about the hows and whys of whether or not two people are a good match. Like the statue that sent Ray to prison, he saw what he wanted and when the opportunity presented itself he took it.

A small thud at the back of the room drew my attention and erased these thoughts from my mind. The big guy with the lighter had dropped it. He bent over and picked it up. Ray had concluded speaking and the members of the group now stood, vying for his attention. The big guy at the back took out a cigarette. *Oh shit,* I thought, *if he comes out, he will see me.*

I jumped up, grabbed the edge, and slipped onto the roof just as the door below me opened. I lay flat, positioned my head above the light, and looked down. Sure enough, the man with the lighter was puffing away on a cigarette, staring aimlessly at the barn.

If I jumped back to the wall I'd be stuck, a large shadow framed against a full and bright, low-hanging moon. It would be better to come down the side of the barn and drop next to the wall. From there I could exit behind, in the shadow of the barn. After the big guy went back in I could come around and surprise Ray and Laura.

I pulled back from the edge of the roof and stood on the crest, then slowly started to walk down as silently as possible. I reached the top of the side shed and began to relax; under my feet were the wooden shingles of what was technically a second building attached to the barn. If a shingle had cracked or split it would have been unlikely anyone in the meeting could have heard it.

What I did not account for was the fresh mist of rain that had turned the wood into a frictionless slope. My feet slid out from under me and with surprising speed I was hurtling down the roof. My stealth forgotten I hastily rolled, turning face down as my legs careened over the side; my fingers frantically clutching at the edges of old shingles that crumbled and came free in my hands.

Finally my right hand caught the top of an exposed end-jack. I hung for a few seconds. It bought me enough time to safely position for the eight foot drop. My hand tore from its feeble grasp. I shifted my momentum into a roll and got in three good turns, and then came to an abrupt rest. I was in the shadows, surrounded by creeping ivy.

That's when I heard him racking the slide on his Glock, loading one into the chamber. Knowing a gun is being drawn on you is unnerving. Knowing that the person was a novice who didn't keep a bullet in the chamber was terrifying.

The voice was rasping and panicked "Get up, come out of there."

I stood slowly, putting my hands out in front of me rather than over my head. I could feel pain in the muscles of my right shoulder and left leg. They were mild injuries, but I pretended they were severe. I feared that this yahoo would shoot me, but he was less likely to see me as a threat if I looked like a wounded puppy. I kept my back to the building, moved sideways and then backward toward the door—drawing us both into the light.

"I'm a good friend of Ray and Laura's; please put the gun down."

Perhaps I said it too fast or too close together. He raised the gun and then used it to gesture at me as he talked.

"Then why were you hiding?" he barked.

"Put the gun down," I said, starting to get angry at the way he handled it.

"Everyone, hurry, come out here!" he shouted at the top of his lungs. Then to me, "Stand up straight! Put your hands over your head."

This time, with both hands on his gun he jerked it at me. He extended his arms from his body then pulled the gun back in, jerked it out, and finally directed it upward. Had he fired at that moment the bullet would have gone right through my face.

Behind me, I could hear bodies piling out of the barn. How many of them would join him in drawing on me? Which one of them would "accidently" shoot me? Here, I was trespassing: the law was on their side. If they wanted, any one of them could shoot me for fun.

"I said, put your hands up!" Again with his finger on the trigger, he jerked his arms out.

"Okay, okay," I said, allowing my voice to waver, doing my best to project submissiveness. His eyes watched my hands as they seemed to rise when actually I was lowering my body, simultaneously stepping closer to him. In that second, I sidestepped his barrel and in one quick motion slammed my right hand into his wrist. My left hand grabbed the barrel and jerked it up and back. The gun came free, easily turning in my hand. From behind me I heard a gasp, but I did not stop my sideways travel. My opponent was too shocked to move. In another second I was behind him. I gave a quick hard kick to the back of his legs, dropping him, then put the gun to the back of his head and knelt behind him. He was now my human shield.

I heard guns being drawn and looked up in the crowd. My eyes traveled down the line until they fell upon the mantis man who stood next to Ray and Laura. He was unarmed. Ray and Laura were not among those who had drawn on me. Ray and I locked eyes and then Ray was throwing out his arms and shouting.

"Wait, wait! Lower your weapons, lower your weapons. I know this man."

As guns began to fall I relaxed my stance and stepped back from the man on the ground. I looked up. The mantis man was staring at me. His handsome face was an expressionless mask but his eyes seemed to sparkle with glee. I turned my gaze to Laura, who stood there saying nothing while looking at me with the faintest of smiles. She realized I was looking back, raised an eyebrow, and then turned and disappeared back into the barn, taking that lovely smile with her.

If I had been entertaining any doubts that I wanted her, they evaporated on the slightest beam from that gorgeous face.

I could tell Ray was mulling over how he wanted to explain a group of armed men and women gathered in his barn.

"I'm here with the information you requested," I said, looking around and acknowledging all the faces. "I'm impressed, Ray. This is fortuitous. I've showed up at the right time," I added with a smile. Ray cocked his head. Hopping to ease the tension I came around and offered my hand to the big guy, "I'm very sorry. Please accept my apologies. I was terrified you were going to shoot me."

He hesitated but ultimately took my hand. Once he was on his feet I held his gun up for him, palm first. I put my other arm on his shoulder and pulled him down to me. I whispered, "You're a worthy opponent. If you don't know how to take a gun away like that already, I'd be happy to teach you."

"Yeah, that would be nice," he mumbled back.

It couldn't hurt to ingratiate myself with the group. I walked over to Ray and extended my hand. He took it and I pulled him in and patted him firmly on the back.

"It's good to see you. Maybe we should all go in so we don't attract attention," I said, in my most charming voice.

That resonated with Ray; he led us all back into the barn. As I walked in I removed my gloves and doubled them back into my pocket. Laura was folding and stacking chairs; several of the men rushed to help her. I stopped to more closely examine the conspiracy collage that adorned the walls. I nodded approvingly at the lists of people.

"Ah, these here," I said, pointing to specific names, "are actually connected to these banks. But, I didn't learn that until just recently."

The mantis man took his gun and jacket from the chair just as it was about to be stacked, then came back to stand next to Ray and me.

"Hi, I'm Charles Reid." His voice was warm and soothing. He reached past Ray to shake my hand. His face was still expressionless but as we shook he smiled and broke into a boyish grin. He had a good, firm handshake. He leaned in and said, "That was impressive. I'd like to learn how you did that."

I nodded without affirming that I'd teach him. Ray was looking perplexed. My fear was that he was feeling threatened. Laura came up behind Ray and wrapped her arms around him. She stood on her toes and kissed him on the ear.

"Introduce him around," she said.

Ray's demeanor changed as if he'd suddenly recognized an opportunity. The group had gathered behind him, talking softly as they waited to discover this interloper's status.

Ray turned to them with a big smile. "I'd like to introduce you to my oldest friend, Kyle Everett." Then to me he preached, "We are the First and Second. We are the defenders of free speech. From the First Amendment comes our natural right to express ourselves freely, and from the Second Amendment we draw our inalienable right to arm ourselves against oppression. These are the rights from which all others flow."

It seemed best not to challenge Ray's use of the word inalienable. I tried to keep from wincing, but must have failed. Charles turned and eyed me carefully. I redoubled my efforts to mask my true feelings.

Around the room heads nodded and voices chimed in unison, "Aye." I opened my mouth and joined them. We then went around, learning everyone's names and making general small talk. I shook hands, touched arms like a first-rate politician, and literally bit my tongue as every third person rambled on about their favorite conspiracy.

I learned that the big guy with the Equip watch was in fact a contractor named Rich Buntem, head of security for the First and Second, and a major contributor. The only other person in security was the big guy, Scott Randal, the man I'd disarmed. Scott worked construction for Rich's firm.

The scruffy kid with the tattoos and the AR-15 was named Paul Bradford. Paul was an electrician who believed that we are regularly visited by extraterrestrials and that if Tesla's work had not been lost to history we would be driving flying cars and enjoying interstellar travel.

Standing next to Paul was the Indian girl whom I'd initially thought was his girlfriend. Reading her body language, I began to think not. Several times I caught her looking at me and when I was done with Paul she spoke.

"Hi, I'm Katrina Varma." She smiled and extended her right hand. In her left hand she was twisting a strand of her hair. "I do the accounting for the group," she said as we shook.

We made small talk. I learned that she was a CPA and a serious contributor. I couldn't quite ascertain exactly why she belonged to the group. A young professional, very educated, and highly organized—she seemed out of place. She said nothing of conspiracies.

"You have some impressive moves. Were you wearing parkour gloves?" she asked with great interest.

"Yes," I said, looking her over more carefully now.

The muscles in her calf and forearms suggested she was in great shape. She was thin, but healthy. I began to see past the pink lip gloss and nails. My mind wondered how her naked midriff looked, followed by a deep curiosity about the shape of her pubic hair. She noticed that others were waiting to talk to me and graciously stepped aside.

I continued introductions for about an hour until most everyone had left.

"The information you have for us," Ray spoke quietly, out of earshot from the remaining members of the group, "as soon as everyone has left I'd like you to share it with Charles, Laura, and me."

"Do you want to include Katrina? She might find it interesting?" I asked, wondering if Katrina's obvious interest in me might make Laura feel jealous.

Ray looked over at Katrina and waved at her as she, and the remainder of the group disappeared, shutting the barn door behind them.

"No, not just yet," Ray said, leading me to the platform where Laura and Charles had set up chairs for us.

"Ray, there's something I need to explain to you," I laced my words with the utmost sincerity. "I know we used to go the rounds about a lot of stuff, but I've had experiences that have changed me."

We took our seats. Laura and Ray urged me to continue.

"After college..." I paused, looking at Laura and Ray; I was unsure if this was the right time to inform Charles that Laura and I had a history. "...after the three of us stopped hanging out, I got a job with a brokerage firm and started studying for my Series 7 exam. To be more accurate, the brokerage was a boiler room: mostly we cold called potential clients and pushed shady stock. The main guy there, Colin, took a shine to me. I was under his tutelage until I got my license. When the feds came he protected me and kept me out of jail. Most of the guys I worked with went to prison. I got lucky, and not for the first time," I said, pausing and looking Ray in the eye.

He reached over and patted me on the shoulder.

"While Colin was out on bail, he confided in me that the whole operation was funded by some very big names on Wall Street. They used firms like his to manipulate the market and to act on inside information. When boiler rooms get raided, they just start up another one.

"It was a shock to me. I knew what we were doing wasn't right, but I didn't realize we were pawns in a much bigger conspiracy. We were playing with millions, but the Wall Street banks that were using us played with billions. After the banking crash I began to see how conspiracies go on all the time. It bothers me, but I've never known what to do about it. These people are incredibly powerful.

"Since then, I've just kept my head way down and stuck to day trading for myself."

The three of them nodded as if nothing I said was surprising. For the most part, everything I told them was true except the part about not knowing what to do. Corporate malfeasance is the kind of problem that gets solved with heavy-duty regulation and a judicial system willing to prosecute. It wasn't the kind of problem that was going to be solved by a day trader or a handful of guys with guns.

Charles leaned in, fascinated by my story. He was a bit of a mystery to me: a computer programmer who left a high paying job to start his own company making phone apps. He'd had some mild success with a couple of popular, short-lived games and had developed an app for teams to use while playing paintball. In order to improve his app he took a tactical firearms course, where he met Ray.

Charles generally took time to consider his words carefully, though if you got him speaking about one of his apps his enthusiasm spilled out like a toddler with a shiny new toy.

"Is it possible to set up the accounts we asked for?" Laura asked.

A little contemplative crease appeared on her forehead. I couldn't help but smile. I remembered that crease from all those times in college I use to stare at her while she studied. So many of those study sessions started with me staring, then kissing the back of her neck while she read, eventually leading to...

"Yes, it costs $5,000 to set up the paperwork and another thousand to cover the licensing fees." Ray and Laura looked at one another. I could see a mixture of relief and concern. They were happy it could be done, but not thrilled at the cost.

"Is there any way to make it less expensive?" Ray asked.

"Do you plan to use this money for a specific project? It's not worth setting up the accounts if the money is going in and then coming right back out. It's an ideal place to squirrel money or if you want a tax-free haven to invest and avoid capital gains."

Ray gave Laura a pained expression. Something wasn't right. Whatever they wanted to do with it wasn't as obvious as printing leaflets or creating a website to "open everyone's eyes" to their version of the truth.

"Go on Ray. Tell him," Laura urged. "You know that there is no one more loyal than Kyle. He'd kill for you."

Ray took a deep breath and started to speak. "The money is for a contact, an informant. He's an ex-black ops guy that is willing to go on the record. He was part of a crew responsible for blowing up the Trade Towers." Ray let those words hang in the air for a minute.

Over the years Ray and I had engaged in a lot of debates. None were more fierce or heated than our debate over his unwavering belief that the Trade Towers were exploded from the inside under orders from our own government.

I felt my eyes starting to roll and instead closed them and shook my head as if I'd been rattled by an earth-shaking revelation. I opened my eyes wide.

"That's incredible, I said, "but why does he need forty grand in an offshore account?"

"He's dying of cancer and he knows that when he goes on record they are going to kill him and confiscate his assets under the National Security Act. The money is for his daughter."

"How do you know he's telling the truth?"

"He's got video, names, a journal—everything," Ray said with excitement, "I've seen a video."

There was a pause. Ray looked at me, anticipating all the old arguments to surface again. I remained silent.

"I've met him; I believe him," Laura added, breaking the tension.

Now it all made sense. They were being conned, and not by an amateur.

"It's more than forty-thousand," she continued, "We just didn't want to tell you how much we really had."

"How much?" I gently inquired.

"A hundred and fifty," Laura said.

Ray shot her a look. She put her hand on Ray's arm and pressed on.

"Kyle, his orders didn't just come from the government. They received the money to pull off the operation from a major bank and the largest military contractor in the world."

A knot formed in the pit of my stomach. It was like I was hearing Ray's voice coming out of her mouth.

It wasn't that Ray and I loved to argue. We fought because there are real-world consequences to fallacious thinking. Ray suffers from the kind of faulty logic that leads parents to keep their children from getting vaccinated. Diseases once thought eradicated were now on the rise again because children were not getting immunized. It's hard not to have disdain for people who think vaccinations are part of an alien tag-and-release program or some form of government mind control. We argued because I cared about Ray and didn't want him to spend his life stewing in a cesspool of fear and paranoia. I knew he could be so much more.

I used to painfully joke that one day I'd tear through a wall of newspaper clippings and find him naked on the floor, rocking back and forth, and mumbling about little gray men. Hearing that Laura was enchanted by his delusions reignited all my fears.

My terror about real-world consequences was the driving force that got Ray and me to college. I could feel my protective instinct coming back. It was a desperate urge to save them both. Arguing never worked before. It wasn't going to work now. If I wanted to change them I needed to take a different tack.

"Listen," I said, "if you guys will pay the thousand for the filing fees, I'll contribute the five thousand for the legal work to set up the shell corporations and bank accounts."

Ray's mouth fell open. Laura joyfully slapped him on the knee. She smiled at me with a sort of "I knew it all along" expression.

Charles nodded, and with a grin said, "It's official Kyle; you're now part of the group."

He shook my hand as we both stood up. Ray kept my hand and pulled me in for a hug. He let go and Laura lunged for me. She wrapped her arms around me and kissed me on the cheek.

CHAPTER EIGHT

Train tracks used to cut along the edge of the city. For two decades, the area just west of them was littered with old warehouses and the run-down industrial buildings of a bygone era. I used all of my savings and took my first big risk day-trading about six months after Ray got out of prison. It paid off. I took another by being one of the first to buy a condo in a warehouse about to be renovated. This was before the redevelopment agency came in and declared the area ripe for urban renewal.

Eventually, the neighborhood was completely transformed. With ready access to fiber optics, it has become the favorite home of startup tech companies. There was a high-end, open-air mall, lots of luxury apartments, and several buildings dedicated to artist space. The city built a theatre and concert hall just four blocks away from my condo. It seemed like every week there was a new restaurant opening down the street. I'd bought my condo there not because I was hoping it would rise dramatically in value, but because I was hoping it wouldn't.

When I first moved in, it wasn't safe to go out at night. At that time, this area was frequented by the drug-addled, the criminal contingent that supplied them, and the homeless. There were frequent carjackings and murders. After my apartment was completed, it was six months before I saw another tenant. By then, the building had been broken into three times. They never got as far as my apartment. Twice I got into fights, and once I stopped a gang rape in the lobby.

When you love someone with your whole heart and they leave you, risking your life on a daily basis seems like a good idea. Instead of fighting for Laura, I'd fought defending this apartment. It was my fortress and sanctuary. I'd lived here alone and avoided people, even as a vibrant population had grown around me.

The condo was two-story with an open floor plan. At the back there were bedrooms, I used mostly for storage. On top of them was a loft, I used as my master bedroom. It overlooked the rest of the apartment. There was a bathroom above and one below. The kitchen was to the far right opposite the door as you come in; it had a wraparound counter where I sat on one of the barstools and ate my meals. Out front a large balcony overlooked the street, and in an area close to the door sat my desk. It was at the desk, with its four large computer monitors, that I did my day-trading.

At the center of the condo was my living room. There was no furniture.

Instead, I used it as a gym. It was where I practiced with my trainers. One was the krav maga teacher who convinced me to try parkour. It had taken him some coaxing to lure me outdoors, but that was the start of my getting better.

I'd told Ray and Laura it would take three days to prepare the paperwork, but really I wanted the three days to figure things out. My workout was sour the morning after I left them at the barn. I was filled with angst, which I'd tried to excise with brute force and agility. Having failed, I'd taken to pacing and arguing with myself.

I felt a personal responsibility to step in and protect Laura (and Ray by proxy). They were about to give all their money to a con man to purchase a large quantity of humiliation. I knew there was no way to get through to Ray, but if I could get Laura alone, then perhaps I could talk some sense into her. However, if I tried and failed, she might be offended. I could easily lose my opportunity to steal her back. When she hugged and kissed me on the cheek, she pressed herself against me. I'd left the barn covered in her delicious scent. That night, I tossed and turned, remembering how wonderful it was to make love to her. I woke up hating myself for being so weak. When I got tired of hating myself, I got angry at her.

After the markets had closed, I took off for the shooting range. Wreaking destruction upon paper targets didn't help. I went back to blaming myself. *If I had been a better boyfriend, she never would have left. She wouldn't have gotten mixed up with Ray.* I then stopped and beat myself up for thinking that way.

On the third day, I decided to walk away from Laura and Ray. I'd promised to contribute money to draw up the paperwork. I'd left out that I'd already spent the money on my own accounts. I was just going to copy the paperwork and let them pay the filing fees. My only cost would be a little more time.

After their accounts were set up and the money transferred, I'd back out. I'd say to Ray and Laura, "It's too dangerous. If '*they*' find out that you have this information '*they*' are going to kill you."

Then I'd pack up and move. There was no reason for me to stay in this city. I can trade stocks from anywhere in the world. I could travel down to that lovely little island where I'd stashed some of my money and when I got tired of all that sun, I'd take a break and travel around Europe. Maybe I'd meet a girl who didn't speak a lot of English. I'd fool myself into believing she was exotic, put her on a pedestal, and pretend to fall in love.

I ran to my desk and dug into the back of the top drawer. Somewhere was a card from the flirty Realtor I'd run into while getting coffee one day.

She had vacillated between trying to seduce me and telling me that my loft had quadrupled in value. She had said, while touching my knee under the table, she would do just about anything for the chance to sell it. Ah, there was the card. Her name was Valarie Astley. It was 4:30 in the afternoon. I picked up the phone and began to dial Valarie, when there was a knock on the door.

I spied out the peephole and saw a nervous-looking Ray.

"Hey, did you come to get a final look at the paperwork?" I pointed to the fourth screen at my desk. Ray wasn't as dressed up as he'd been at dinner or at the meeting. He was wearing a leather jacket over a black t-shirt, jeans, and a pair of boots. He hadn't shaved, making his stylized beard look like a half-mowed lawn. A pair of leather gloves was tucked into his jacket pocket, suggesting he may have come here on a motorcycle.

"Kyle, listen. I've got a lot to say and it's hard for me." He stood close enough to make me uncomfortable. He put his arm on my shoulder and said, "Thank you." My ears drew back and my eyebrows came down, silently questioning. "Thank you for being the bigger man. I know when I got out of prison I was being a dick." He let go of me and took a deep breath. "You did the right thing by holding my money and not risking it. I was just—I don't know—bitter. I came out of prison in the same clothes I went in with and when I saw all you'd accumulated in that time, I was jealous. I didn't know what I was going to do with my life. I'd learned a few trades in the pen and you made it so I could start my own business."

"We were both in the wrong," I said, in a tone I hoped indicated it was all in the past. "It hurt to see you'd taken up with my old girlfriend."

"I know man, but it wasn't like that. She started writing to me in prison about a year before I got out. I think...I was kind of a project for her. We didn't even kiss until after you and I stopped speaking. Eventually, she told me what happened to her at law school and it wasn't," Ray stopped, took a deep breath and swallowed hard, "I saw a lot of shit in prison, so I understood. We bonded."

"Man, I did everything I could to get you out. All your college money went to the lawyers. Then all I had was the diamonds. I sat on them for a long time until the heat was off. They were watching me hard. When I visited you in prison they listened to everything we said. I was afraid one of us was going to slip up accidently."

"You were right to stop coming. I know you did everything you could. All these years we haven't been talking. I really missed you. You were my best friend. Outside of Laura, I've never had a friend like you. It means so much that you trust me enough to contribute to our group."

That was all well and good, but he still had Laura. That he was finally apologetic just made it that much easier for me to wash my hands of them. Maybe I'd let the Realtor seduce me and see if I couldn't just fuck the memory of Laura right out of my system.

"About that," I said, walking over to my desk and preparing to print out his paperwork.

"Wait, there's more I need to say," Ray interrupted. I stopped and tried to mask my mild annoyance. "Okay," I said, as I turned and gave him my full attention.

"This money, the hundred and fifty-thousand, it's...it's just a lot of fucking money and when we told you about it, I...I was expecting an argument from you. It's been three days since I've told you and you haven't raised a single doubt. You seem so happy to go along with it," Ray said, showing his disappointment.

"Wait a minute, you *want* me to fucking argue with you?" I threw up my arms in familiar exasperation.

"It's a lot of fucking money," And now Ray's voice was sharp, "What if he's not legit?"

"You have doubts? Laura was going to be a lawyer. She's wicked bright. If that guy wasn't legit, she'd be the first to tell you."

"Kyle, I don't know. I don't think she's willing to look at it that critically. She's so loyal and supportive of me. I think in order for her to really be objective she would feel like she was attacking me, and you know her. That's just not who she is, she's doesn't want to be the sour grape in the wine of our relationship."

"No? You and I have different experiences of Laura. Did she ever tell you why we broke up?"

"Not really, something about you guys wanting different things."

"Well, sure. She wanted to be more politically active. She wanted us to go to protest rallies, chain ourselves to buildings, and fight the good fight. And even though I agreed with a lot of her politics, I just didn't think that a couple of murderers should be getting hauled off to jail on a regular basis. I didn't think it was right to invite that kind of scrutiny.

"And do you know what she said to that? She said that, precisely because we were murderers, we needed to participate. She said we needed to be fearless and to fight for change as a way of paying back our debt to society: 'to set right the balance of karma.' I said no. Now she's with you and you two have this group." I caught my breath and realized that I'd tapped into a well of emotion I wasn't sure I really wanted to share.

"She didn't leave me without picking a few fights. We fought all the time," I continued. "Trust me, she has no problem being a sour grape if she really believes in something," I regretted the bitterness in my voice. It's true that we fought all the time, but we also made up all the time and somehow the fighting just made the sex better. That is—until she left.

"Then you understand why I need your help," Ray said. "I need you to argue with me. I need your objectivity. I need to know if I'm making a mistake by giving this guy the money. Kyle, when we pulled off the job you covered all the angles, except me. It was flawless, but I got greedy and tried to sell the statue. Please, I need your help."

I stood there in stunned silence. I kept wondering, where was all of Laura's loyalty when we were together? Was she so anxious to feel like she was making a difference in the world that it didn't matter if her efforts were smoke and mirrors?

And then there was Ray. Three days ago I played contrite in an effort to curry favor. Now he was practically on bended knee asking for my help. In that moment, I realized I'd been successful at infiltrating the group. I felt an exhilarating rush of power. My mind began to foment ways to use this influence to get Laura back.

I went to the back of a closet and found a folding chair, brought it around for Ray, and took a seat at my desk.

"Alright, I'll help. Tell me everything you know about this guy. How you found him, where he lives, everything."

CHAPTER NINE

Ray's enforcer, Rich Buntem, had a home just outside of the city in a newly created subdivision. His four-acre lot was surrounded by an impressive stone wall that hid the fact that his property lacked sod or finished landscaping. The houses in this neighborhood started at a half-million and were intended to be equestrian properties, though I saw no horses.

We drove past the house and around the outer wall. At the back of the lot we pulled up to a large building that was about half the size of the house.

"He runs his contracting business from here," Ray said as we pulled in. "His security company is on the second floor."

We exited the car in front of two twenty-foot garage doors that faced the street. Rich met us outside and walked us into the building. The main area was crowded with three trailers. We walked around two open trailers and alongside the third. It was enclosed by white metal. The words "Wells Cargo" were stamped on the outside in black. In back, the door was open and so I peeked inside. It was loaded with well-worn tools, strapped down to shelves.

"I started as a framer," Rich said. "After I got my license, I took every job I could get. Nowadays, I use subcontractors for everything. I hardly take the trailers out anymore."

Halfway through this cavernous shop, Rich stopped and opened a door to a stairwell. He was still wearing his monogrammed shoulder holster. It read: *R.P.B.* I stared at it, wondering what his middle name was.

"Do you have your concealed-carry?" he asked me. I shook my head, wondering what part of "concealed" he didn't understand. "I wear this all the time," he said, as we climbed the stairs.

"That's got to be awkward in the shower," I quipped.

Ray chuckled. I got the feeling that were it not for Ray's laughter, Rich would have told me to go fuck myself.

"I know you've got fancy moves and all," Rich said, "but they aren't going to help you at a distance." Then he said to Ray, "You should take him out and get him outfitted right away."

I bit my tongue and swallowed my snarky response. I wasn't planning on getting into any firefights. If I did, the last thing I'd want on this operation was a registered weapon and a permit.

At the top of the stairs Rich opened the door and led us into a spacious, three-bedroom apartment. The living room, dining room, and family room had been subverted into store rooms. They were filled with row after row of metal shelves.

The first we came to was loaded with maneuverable, dome-style, 180-degree security cameras. Ray picked one up off the shelf.

"I see the power hookup, but where does the coax go?" Ray asked, perplexed. Rich pointed to another shelf on the other side of the room.

"The traditional tail-fed cameras are over there; the one you're holding transmits the video wirelessly. I don't normally keep this much stock, but a guy in Tucson was going out of business and I won the bid on his entire inventory. This stuff is pretty common; wait till you see the *really* cool devices."

Rich led us back farther, stopping along the way to proudly show us cameras that had been hidden in stuffed animals, sprinkler heads, electric outlets, clocks, and a host of other surprisingly mundane objects.

"I used to buy a lot of these," Rich said, holding up a clock radio, "but then people started catching on to the fact that they weren't brand names."

We continued on. Behind a door that led into the master bedroom, we saw several work tables, soldering equipment, and piles of tiny circuit boards wrapped in anti-static packaging. Rich opened one up and slid out a tiny circuit board, smaller than a dime, with a small lens attached.

"These days I use cameras like this and install them myself. That way you can swap their existing device for one that looks just like it, but with a camera inside." Rich looked around the room and then took us over to a shelf at the far corner.

"Alright, you guys are going to need some GPS trackers. Now, the average trackers on the market are like this," Rich held up a small device a little smaller and thicker than a thumb drive. "These things have a battery life of about thirty days. However, I've been taking these apart and changing out the batteries. I produced this." He held up a silver pen. "Smaller, it lasts eight to sixteen hours, but it really writes too. The problem with the other tracker is that it's too obvious. It's hard to slip onto a target, whereas no one thinks twice about taking your pen. It's best if you take two pens; that way if they try and give it back to you just say, 'No thanks—I've got an extra.'"

"Brilliant!" I exclaimed, and—given the smile Rich flashed me—I could tell I'd just earned some points.

"I'm going to send you with a couple of trackers that have strong magnets. You can attach them to a car or really anything metal. You're going to need a variety of bugs, and I'm going to send you with some of the cameras you've already seen, but"—Rich held up a handful of USB drives separated between his fingers on two hands—"these here are way more valuable. On my left, plug these into any computer, start the program, and they'll quickly mine the machine for data. On my right, jailbreak the phone and install the software. You'll have real-time tracking and a visual on everything he does with his phone. The ability to hear his calls, read his text messages and web history. You can even get a copy of every keystroke he makes. The downside is—it can take you about ten minutes to jailbreak the phone and another five to ten to install the tracking software. Now, that doesn't seem like a lot of time. But ask yourself, when was the last time you went thirty minutes without your phone?"

"When I was asleep," Ray and I answered in unison.

"Exactly," said Rich.

Ray and I spent a week there. We practiced picking locks, installing cameras and bugs, and then testing all of these tools until we could do it in our sleep.

There had been a gestation period in Ray and Laura's relationship. With her help, he got his business together. She helped him fix up the house. He built the room in the barn and—again with Laura's help—started the group. Together they traveled to gun shows around the country. There, they met with other patriot groups before returning home and feeding stories of their travels to the members of First and Second.

Ray's natural passion for conspiracy theories, coupled with Laura's encouragement, led to several speaking invitations. It was after a speaking engagement in Salt Lake City that Ray met the man who called himself "The Ranger."

On first meeting, he introduced himself as a veteran and a medal winner who ended his career as an interrogator and intelligence specialist. He praised Ray for his speech on chemtrails. Over the following year, they met up anytime Ray and Laura happened to travel to the western states.

As we sat on the floor in my living room, Ray was reluctant to answer some of my more specific questions.

"That first conversation you had with him, close your eyes. Try and remember exactly what was said."

"I already told you!" He raised his voice. Ray was unaccustomed to being called into question. I wondered exactly how long he'd surrounded himself with adoring followers.

"No, you paraphrased," I replied.

"Um, okay. I'd come off stage, I was shaking hands and he was standing off to the side. He's pretty tall. The next speaker was starting and so I went out into the hall to get a drink of water. He followed me and told me I'd given a great speech. I thanked him. He shook my hand." Ray paused and looked up, trying to remember. "Then he started our conversation saying, 'When I was in the military...'"

"He didn't say what branch?"

"No, he called himself 'The Ranger' and that's the Army, so I assumed he was in the Army. He said, 'I was in intelligence. You have the voice this community needs.' He asked if I was going to speak at the Idaho rally. I told him I was. We agreed to meet up for a drink that night, and then we went back to the conference. We stayed for two other presenters."

"So what happened after you got drinks?"

"I brought Laura. We had dinner. He told me that he was bringing some friends to the Idaho rally. 'Doubters,' he called them. He said he needed my help to convince them and asked if I would focus on a few key points in my speech."

"He changed your speech?"

"No, not at all!" Ray was indignant at the suggestion. "He asked me to emphasize a few key points. Then he told me a couple of things about the kind of charges that were used to bring down the Twin Towers."

"He told you he was in on it that night?"

"No, he told me a year later. At that time, he said that he and a buddy had built their own thermite charge. They'd shot a video, proving it could be used to cut steel. That's common knowledge now, but back then it was just speculation. He gave me a printout of his notes and I used a lot of it in my speech."

I resisted the urge to roll my eyes. "How did you get in contact with him over that year?"

"Cell phone, text messages and occasionally email. He's really smart."

"What makes you say that?"

"They don't let idiots into intelligence. Kyle, I've thought about this a lot. He took a long time before telling me what he'd done. Right from the beginning, he was taking precautions. He changed his phone number all the time. Whenever we talked over the computer, he insisted we use encryption."

"So, how did the speech in Idaho go? Did you convince his friends?"

"Yes," Ray brightened with pride.

"What did The Ranger's friends say to you?"

"I never met them. After my speech, they left. He and I caught up the next day; we've been tight ever since."

CHAPTER TEN

The temperature grew hotter and hotter as we rode southward. It had been years since I'd ridden a motorcycle, but my reflexes hadn't abandoned me. The hardest part was keeping our speed down so as to not attract attention. Ray and I had liberated the bikes from an auto storage facility and attached a set of stolen license plates. So long as we didn't get pulled over and kept our helmets on when gassing up, everything would be fine. We carried fully loaded saddlebags and our bedrolls were strapped to our seats—up against the small of our backs to provide more support.

Planning is my specialty. I enjoy it and I'm good at it. We left our cell phones at home and carried burner phones in their place. When we got to Vegas, we'd ditch those and pick up new phones. Ray moaned every time I set up a new hoop for us to jump through, but relaxed once they were implemented. In addition to protecting us, these safeguards gave Ray the impression that I was keeping an open mind about The Ranger.

We knew next to nothing about The Ranger. I presumed he was very dangerous and if for some reason the job went south, I wanted us to be able to prove we were never there.

"Hey, Ranger," Ray said, when he'd called him two weeks ago. I listened in and pointed to lines on a prepared script. "Are you sure this line is secure?" Ray asked, sounding concerned.

"What's up?" asked The Ranger. He sounded oddly amused.

"I'm worried I'm being bugged," At my prompting, Ray dropped into a whisper, "I've got to come see you."

"What's wrong, what's the matter?" I noted that the Ranger did not seem all that conspiratorial. He didn't match Ray's tone of voice. He sounded rather jovial.

"I was paid a visit by Homeland Security."

"What? What for? Did they say what they wanted?"

"I was moving the money, slowly, in small increments. $500 every couple of days, but they said it triggered an audit."

"Wait, so you have all the money?" The Ranger asked, sounding surprised.

"Yeah. I was wiring it into the offshore account. That's why they paid me a visit. I'm worried; they're watching me now."

"Hold on, hold on." The Ranger sounded excited.

I started pointing to the script frantically, indicating to Ray that he should start speaking with the urgency we'd practiced.

"They aren't supposed to flag small increments," The Ranger continued, sounding perplexed.

"Yeah, they said that the government didn't flag strictly on increment but that they used an algorithm to catch anything suspicious. They acted like it was no big deal, claimed they were just checking it out to be sure. They seemed satisfied that I was an American, but as they were leaving my accountant showed up. She is an American, but of Indian decent. They've been watching my house ever since."

"Alright, calm down. The best thing to do is to transfer that money to me."

"I know, I know. Where can you meet me?" Ray asked.

"I'm going to be in Las Vegas in three days. Can you get there?

"Yeah, I can be there. It's best if you don't call me," Ray added.

"Be ready to transfer the money."

"I've got to go," Ray said. I hung up the phone.

"That was excellent, Ray. Now he's on the hook," I said, patting him on the back.

That's how we found ourselves off Vegas Drive, at a greasy-spoon called the Sunshine Café. The restaurant sat second from the end in a strip four stores long. Ray was already seated inside. The motorcycles were parked down the block and out of sight. Street entry to the parking lot is from behind, and so I stood casually against a wall toward the back corner of the building with a good view of the cars coming and going.

Ray and I shared two-way communication via tiny earpieces and microphones. The Ranger was thirty minutes late. Ray sat inside, sipping coffee, unable to say too much for fear it would look like he was talking to himself. I stood outside, unwilling to say too much for fear I would start trying to convince Ray that The Ranger was a total fraud. I was already deeply annoyed at how many times I'd had to say, "The Ranger," and I was looking forward to uncovering his real name.

"I think we've got something," I said to Ray as I spotted a brand new Ford Taurus pull into the lot. The driver seemed to match Ray's description. He was six-two, reddish-blond hair, and balding at the front making his thick, bushy eye brows stand out against the pale, freckled face. He wore jeans and a bright blue shirt. He looked like a man who had once carried a bit of muscle but was no longer working out. He walked with a spring in his step. He entered through the back door of the restaurant and disappeared.

"I think he's on his way to you," I whispered into the mic. "He doesn't look like he's suffering cancer to me; certainly not someone who's undergoing chemo."

I walked around his car. Like most of the cars in Nevada, the windows bore a dark tint. On the back bumper there was a small rental sticker next to the Nevada plate. I quickly placed the tracker on the underside and went around to the front windshield where the tinting was the lightest. Looking in, I could see no hotel key, rental agreement, or other clue that would suggest the man's identity. I walked to the end of the building and around the corner, hoping to minimize traffic noise so that I could better hear them over my earpiece. Accounting for the fact that he entered through the back door, it still seemed like it was taking The Ranger an abnormally long time to get to Ray's table.

"Ranger," Ray said, the legs of his wooden chair squeaking on the tile. "Jesus man, you look terrible. If I'd seen you come in, I would have helped you to the table. Here take my chair; I can move to the other side."

"Thanks, my friend," the Ranger said weakly, followed by a cough, "I just started chemo this week. You know, they tell you it's going to be bad, but nothing can prepare you."

"Is that why you're in Vegas?"

"They have some amazing doctors here."

"Hi, can I get you anything?" a female voice asked.

"Just water for me," The Ranger replied.

"Nothing for me," Ray added. And then, after she walked away, "I'm so sorry you are going through this. Does that mean you have a chance of recovery?"

"I don't know, Ray. It's the choice between doing something and nothing. I'll try anything if it buys me a little more time to spend with my daughter. All those years in the military, I wasn't around for her. It strained our relationship, and this is the only time I have to show her another side of me. Once it comes out what I've done, she's never going to forgive me. I need her to have a few decent memories of me." Then his voice became urgent, "Ray, you must promise me. I hope I didn't make the wrong decision. I have no choice but to take you as a man of your word. Please reassure me again that you won't release any of this information until after I'm gone."

"I promise, I promise. You can trust me," Ray urged.

If Ray was lying, he had me fooled.

"Stick to the plan," I said into the mic, not hiding my annoyance with him.

"I'm sorry Ray. I know I can trust you. This medicine has me feeling so desperate." The Ranger coughed. There was a long pause of silence. Then, I heard his breathing so loud I could only imagine he'd leaned his body over the table until he was close to Ray. I heard a deep, wheezing breath, followed by a long, audible sigh. His voice was dripping with regret. "Ray, it's only right that I should be in this much pain. This sickness started when I followed that order and has grown every year I've kept it a secret. Thank you for giving me this chance. You are going to free my soul."

I could not picture this big man weeping, but I heard it. It was believable, though I did not believe it. Ray did, because he only managed two more of the lines I'd scripted for him.

"The paperwork should be here in a few days. It was posted before I left." This prompted an audible change in the Ranger.

"You mean, you didn't bring it? Post—why didn't you send it electronically?"

"I did everything not to lead Homeland Security to you. I was afraid they would intercept it."

"Oh, Ray. I'd hoped that by tomorrow I would have started to unload this burden. I know this is the cancer talking, but I'm just not that strong anymore."

"I'm so sorry. It's for your protection."

Ray's empathy for The Ranger was really starting to grate on me.

The Ranger began to cough, rather loud, and a bit overly dramatic.

"I need to go lie down. Please, don't call me until you're ready to do this."

Their chairs slid back, the sound reverberating off the floor. Ray chimed in, high-voiced and childlike.

"Okay, I understand. I'm so sorry. Please call me if you need anything—anything!"

Ambient noise from forks scraping plates and low chatter filled Ray's mic, suggesting he was standing witless in the middle of the restaurant.

"What the *fuck*, Ray? What the fuck was that?" I shouted, and then crept to the corner in time to see The Ranger come out of the building and rush to his car. He opened his car door and before his face disappeared behind the glass I caught his smug, self-congratulatory smile. He started the car, revved the engine, and backed out with such swiftness his tires screeched when he switched into forward gear. He pulled out onto Vegas Drive without stopping for oncoming traffic and sped away.

I pulled out my shiny new phone and loaded the tracking app. Ray walked out of the restaurant, looking sad and dismayed.

"What the fuck was that?" I shouted again, this time throwing up my arms. "Come on, let's get to the bikes."

"Jesus fucking Christ, can't you see the man is dying?" Ray screamed back.

We were walking fast down the sidewalk. The map on my phone came up quickly, populated with the names of nearby businesses.

"Ray, he's faking. He was laughing at you as he came out."

"That's bullshit. You don't know him like I do. He's not faking."

"Oh shit! Come on, we have to move." I started running and did not look back at Ray. The motorcycles were still a quarter-mile away.

"Why are we running?" I heard Ray say. His voice came mostly through my earpiece and I knew he wasn't keeping up.

"He's going to the rental car agency. If he transfers cars, we lose him. Did you get a tracker on him?" I could hear Ray's footfalls coming up fast. His staggered breath in my ear let me know he wouldn't be able to keep up the pace for long.

"No," he whined.

I stepped onto the bike, not bothering with my helmet. I took off at top speed toward the rental agency. A few minutes later I slowed as I approached. It was a small lot, with the typical glass building in the center. I could see The Ranger inside at the desk. I quickly pulled over, put on my helmet, and then cruised into the lot. The Ranger was gesticulating wildly at the clerk inside, then turned, and made an angry exit—walking right by me and heading toward a dirty and dust-covered Lincoln. He opened the dented door and took out a laptop case from the back seat. He then walked over to the rental car and drove off. I snapped a couple of pictures of the Lincoln, discreetly attached a tracker, and then walked into the rental office.

"What the hell was his problem?" I asked the desk agent, after I'd removed my helmet.

"He wanted to return the car for a full refund because he hadn't used it for more than an hour. The minimum is for a day. It's his until this time tomorrow." The clerk then stared at me, wanting to know what he could do for me.

"Do you have one of those brochure racks, you know, with all the little maps and sights to see?" The clerk pointed me to the corner and I went over, pretending to read while I tracked The Ranger on my phone until Ray arrived.

CHAPTER ELEVEN

The Ranger lived an hour out of Las Vegas. Neither Ray nor I had spent much time in the desert. The suburban houses of Ailanto Avenue in Pahrump, Nevada, stood out for their complete lack of grass. The streets were lined with rows of identical ramblers topped with terracotta, barrel roof tiles. The yards consisted of crushed red rock, pocked with short, plastic-looking Palo Verde trees and small, green bushes that reminded us of sea urchins. The whole place had the feel of a bromidic fish tank, drained of water.

The Ranger's house was the last on the street. Beyond his place the road turned and became Toscana Way: a street that had been cut into parcels but never developed. There were four houses for sale on his street and at least two or three more on every street in the development. We chose the closest house to his, close enough to pick up a strong Wi-Fi signal from his router.

That night, we quietly broke in and parked our motorcycles in the garage. Inside, we set up and began our surveillance. After five minutes, we'd uncovered that The Ranger's real name was Tabor Irvin. In ten minutes, we'd confirmed that he'd served in the Army, that he grew up in Idaho, and that he'd lived in Pahrump for the last four years. Within an hour, we knew that he had self-published (under the name Tom T. Irvin) three small conspiracy books that had decent ratings on Amazon, but which did not appear to have many sales. From the foreword we ascertained that Tabor liked to go by the name Tom.

Tom was married to a plain-looking, pear-shaped woman, who stood about five-four with walnut, shoulder-length hair. Her name was Beth and they'd been married for thirteen years. They had no children between them.

Like many suburbs, every morning Pahrump spewed the majority of its residents, to choke and clog the highways on their way to work. We saw Beth and Tom among them, leaving in the rental car. We presumed that they were going in to Las Vegas to return it.

We tracked the rental car in case Tom should turn back. Then we broke into their home, planted audio and video equipment, and installed software to hack their computers. We replaced their chargers with duplicate devices that would load software onto their cell phones, giving us complete access.

There were two ATVs in the garage, but unfortunately we'd run out of GPS devices. Behind the ATVs, covering the back wall from floor to ceiling, sat small boxes about a foot-and-a-half square. Inside the boxes we found thousands of copies of his little books.

During the operation to plant the bugs, Ray functioned perfectly. Once we were back across the street he became surly and morose.

"We should call this off and go home," Ray said, not looking to see if I agreed. He then began pacing furiously back and forth in the master bedroom where we'd set up our operation. Watching him, I had an image of what he must have looked like trapped in his cell all those years ago. "This is wrong. We shouldn't be invading his privacy like this," Ray said, and rapped his knuckles on the wall.

"I don't understand why you have so much sympathy for this man," I responded. "If he's honest he's a mass murder and if not, he's a liar trying to con you out of your money." As the words left my lips I could see a new level of animation come over Ray.

"Because he has a secret so big, it's going to change the world. I will finally be able to prove to the sheeple and doubters that it was our government all along. Doubters like you!" He said, raising his voice unconscionably loud for such a bare room. I maintained my composure. "Don't you get it man?" he asked, relenting a little. "Everyone in this country is finally going to see what this movement has been trying to expose for years."

When we were in college, I might have tried to contrast Ray's fantasy with the thousands of real criminal conspiracies on the law books. I would have argued that mass murders like Jonestown, were in fact, criminal conspiracies that become footnotes of history.

I did not say these things, because it dawned on me that Ray's anger was not about rational arguments. His anger was out of fear that he was about to lose the elusive "Truth" he so desperately wanted to believe. Moreover, when we proved Tom was a fraud, he would lose a friend. He looked up to Tom on some level, and felt rewarded that his friend trusted him with this great "secret." Again, never mind that it was a lie.

In many ways Ray still seemed an innocent child. His time in prison might have stunted his emotional growth. I wondered if Laura mothered him on a regular basis and if that was why she found him appealing. Ray continued to drone on for some time. I stayed silent, waiting for him to wind himself down. He kept looking to me for an argument.

Three times he muttered, "Are you going to say anything?"

Eventually, he grew silent. I stood and approached him with the thought that if Laura was going to mother him, then perhaps, I should play the tough-love father. Hopefully, I could guide him to a more productive place.

"Do you really want to make a positive change in the world or is it all about your ego?" I asked. "Is it about you being right or believing you are smarter than everyone else? You have all this investment in exposing this "great lie." We are here for one reason and one reason only: the truth. Not your truth, not what you want to believe, the actual truth. We are going to learn that man's secrets," I pointed across the street, "even if they do not conform to your expectations."

Rays looked small and retreating. He seemed cowed by my onslaught, but I wanted more.

"I came down here because you asked for my help, and I'm in. I'm going to learn the truth, because that is what I'm committed to. When you say you want to get out of here, what you are saying is that you are sheeple. You want to live in a lie. You don't want to risk finding out if he's telling the truth, because that would hurt your feelings. It would be too hard for you to deal with."

Ray's mouth opened to protest, but I cut him off.

"This is it Ray, today is the day. Are you committed to your fantasies, or are you committed to actual truth? Are you ready to hear the truth about this man?"

Ray did not answer me.

"It was not a rhetorical question. If you are not one hundred percent committed, then get the fuck out of here. I'll do it on my own."

"I am committed."

"Good," I said, and was thinking of Laura when I added, "because there is a lot of uncomfortable news in the world and you need to be ready."

Ray was now looking under my arm at the laptop screen on the floor. "He's pulling in."

We went to the front window and watched as the Lincoln entered the garage. Tom popped the trunk and got out of the car. His wife was not with him. He pulled two red, five-gallon cans of gasoline from the trunk. Their weight pulled down his arms as he carried them over and sat them next to the ATVs. He hit the button to close the garage door and went inside.

For the next four-and-a-half hours Tom played first-person shooter games, messed around on Facebook while listening to conservative talk radio, and occasionally took breaks to stuff his face. I did not point out to Ray that people undergoing chemo generally lack appetite and the ability to concentrate for long periods of time.

In the evening, a white rideshare van pulled up and dropped Beth off. She found Tom playing video games, made a face, but said nothing to him. After changing clothes, she quietly started making dinner. Tom's phone rang.

Because he had not yet connected it to the charger, we could only capture one side of the conversation.

"Hello? Yes, this is he. Ah, fantastic. Thank you for returning my call. I got your name from my friend...You spoke with him? Great. I would like your help promoting my books. A big push...I do but I was thinking more." And then he whispered, presumably so his wife would not hear. "Seventy-five...yes...no, not a tour. I want radio ads, direct email, interviews—anything that will drive traffic. Yes, of course. I'm in the process of liquidating some assets. It should only be a few days.

I turned and looked at Ray, but he did not meet my eyes.

"It's my understanding that you put together a marketing plan. How long will that take? A retainer, how much? Five...thousand," he hesitated. "You can take a card?" Tom took out his wallet, looked back at the kitchen, and then put his wallet back in his pocket. "You'll need copies of the book, won't you? Will digital be okay? Let me email you a copy and I'll call to issue the retainer in the morning. Alright, thank you. Goodbye."

Tom sat down to dinner with his wife. He indulged her in some small talk then they watched TV for a few hours. When they went to bed, Tom plugged his phone into the charger by his nightstand. After what sounded like four minutes of rough throttling and eerie squeals from his wife they drifted off to sleep. Twenty minutes later, his phone was hacked and we began siphoning off his data. It would be early morning before we had a complete copy of all his messages, files, and logs.

I woke up before dawn. Ray was sleeping in the corner with his head resting on his rolled-up jacket. I sat quietly, listening to Ray's breathing, while I analyzed the data from Tom's phone. The data from his phone and personal computer provided a much clearer picture of our target.

Mr. Irvin was living off of a disability payment that was less than his wife made each year working as a housekeeping manager at one of the larger hotels in Vegas. Twice a month since moving here, he withdrew several hundred dollars in cash from his bank. Based on his browser history, I suspected he spent it at Pahrump's legal brothels. Digging a little deeper into his computer, I found multiple anonymous email accounts. There were exchanges between Tom and two other people looking to buy his 9/11 "confession." That was enough for me, but would it be enough for Ray?

I longed for a cup of coffee. My head was groggy and I'd tired of digging through Tom's life. I decided to spend a few minutes digging into my own.

Before we'd left, I'd suspended all of my active trading. However, there were several companies on which I'd purchased stock options. If the price went high enough, it would trigger an automatic order to sell them.

The top headline of the financial news was yet another report highlighting income equality. It reminded me of how poor Ray and I were growing up. Back then, there were still plenty of industrial jobs. The world has changed. I wouldn't want to grow up poor in today's climate.

Navigating over to the journal, I discovered that yesterday, Massive Energy & Mining's stock had shot up on the news that its former CEO would not be indicted for the coal mine disaster that killed twenty-six workers in West Virginia.

Two years ago, an independent, government safety investigation blamed the accident on gross negligence. Its report highlighted over $4 million in bribes paid to government inspectors over the last ten years. Those inspectors underreported the mine's safety violations. Ultimately, this led to the fire and collapse that killed the workers.

The panel concluded that Blake Donaldson—husband of Sue Massive-Donaldson, heir of the Massive mining fortune—had authorized the creation of the fund that provided the bribes. Because the panel had no legal authority of their own, they recommended a special prosecutor to investigate. The final reported stated: "We conclude that there is more than sufficient evidence to warrant an indictment against Blake Donaldson."

Immediately, Donaldson made more than $7 million in donations to congressional political action groups. The federal government authorizing $5 million to compensate the families of the mine workers killed in the accident, provided those families signed away their right to sue the government or Massive Energy & Mining. No special prosecutor was ever appointed and no direct evidence was ever found linking Donaldson to the bribes. Three years after the accident a local reporter, Diana Holston, printed a substantial newspaper exposé suggesting that mine safety was still far under par and that another disaster was imminent.

These types of stories boil my blood. Growing up, Ray and I knew plenty of kids whose parents worked low-paying jobs in factories and who from time to time suffered indignity at the hands of their employers. When a single industry is the largest employer in a region, no one wants to rock the boat. No one wants to risk losing their job. When you're making just above minimum wage and have been wronged by your employer, you can't afford to sue, unless the payout is certain and substantial.

Massive Energy & Mining could get away with killing workers because they held hostage the rural towns where they operate their mines. They make hundreds of millions, sometimes billions, every year. Millions in bribes over ten years is nothing to them, just a cost of doing business.

Investors had been waiting for a ruling on the case by the Department of Labor. I predicted the company would get off with a wrist slap. A month ago, I spent a couple of thousand dollars to purchase an option on Massive Energy & Mining. This morning, I was fifteen thousand dollars richer. Two days ago, the Department of Labor released an administrative order. The case was closed, and Massive Energy & Mining was fined a half-million dollars. No further action could be taken against the company or its former CEO.

Were I home in my loft, sitting in my big comfortable desk chair, I would have simply cursed Massive, cashed out my stock, and patted myself on the back for being so shrewd. Then, to assuage my guilt I'd have made a small charitable donation before skipping down to the corner shop for a celebratory latte.

Instead, I was in Pahrump, Nevada, sore and tired from sleeping on the floor, in an attempt to prove that Tom Irvin (who was now up drinking his coffee) wasn't part of a criminal conspiracy, an inside job that blew up the Twin Towers in New York City on September 11, 2001. I was doing this to prove to Ray what I already knew—that Tom was a con artist. He was pulling a scam so despicable that when I thought about the victims of the tragedy, it made me sick with fury. I wanted nothing more than to walk across the street, kick in his door, and shove my knife into his sternum so that I could twist it back and forth, interrupting the arterial spray with a flick of my wrist.

If I did that, I would never prove Tom's guilt to Ray. More importantly, I would lose any shot at Laura. Ray mumbled something and rolled over in his sleep.

I was seized by the urge to close the laptop, carry it over to Ray, and begin beating him over the head while screaming, "Massive Energy & Mining is a fucking conspiracy, a *real* fucking conspiracy, you goddamned, self-serving idiot!"

I did not close the laptop. I set it down and walked into the living room where I did physical exercises to calm myself down. I was glad for the high ceilings, as I ran in place and did backflips. While working out, I began to feel that I'd missed something in Tom Irvin's data, but I was still frustrated about Donaldson's criminal evasion and couldn't keep my mind on task. I stopped running in place and started walking on my hands. *Someone should do something about Massive Energy & Mining*, I thought. *Someone should do something about Blake Donaldson.*

I put that thought into the back of my mind and forced myself to think about Irvin. What was I missing? We had used this surveillance equipment to great effect, hacking into every corner of his computer and phone with relative ease. Two powerful thoughts came to me at once. I lost my balance and fell over hard onto my back, knocking the wind out of me.

Why couldn't I track down and set up surveillance on Blake Donaldson and Massive Energy & Mining? Given that coal mining did not require cutting-edge R&D, their security would likely be low. I could publish any evidence I found and embarrass the company. I could use any information I found to make pre-emptive trades against the company stock, potentially making millions of dollars.

My second thought was about Irvin. I had been spending all my brain power on the enormous amount of data I'd collected from him and none thinking about what was not there. I ran back into the bedroom and to the computer just as Ray was waking up.

"Good morning. I've been combing through Tom's computers. Do you know what he doesn't have?"

"Huh? What doesn't he have?" Ray asked with a yawn.

"Neither he nor his wife has a single credit card: debit cards, sure, but no credit. What's more, they don't have five thousand between them." While I was in the other room, Tom had been busy. He had logged into an offshore account and transferred $5,000 into his local bank account. "You said he wanted the money for his child, but there is no evidence he *has* a daughter. No records of any kind. When we were over there, did you find any photos, documents or anything that would prove he has a kid?"

"No, but that doesn't mean anything. He served overseas. She could have been fathered over there."

"Would it surprise you to know that Tom was offering to sell his story to several other people at the same time he's selling it exclusively to you?"

"What?" Ray asked, and then stopped and stood silent.

"I've got to go to the bathroom." He turned and walked out of the room.

Every morning, Tom drove his wife to work and then she took the carpool home. Ray came back into the room just as they were pulling out of the garage.

"I can't really blame him if he put out feelers to other people. I didn't know if I'd be able to raise the money. That's why he was so surprised when I called him and told him I had it."

I turned around and looked Ray in the eye. "Are you prepared for this?"

"Did you find something?" Ray sounded perturbed.

"Yes. He has an offshore account with $8,000 left from multiple deposits going back the last five years. The first deposit was for $20,000, then $40,000, and the last was $75,000."

"That doesn't prove anything."

"Then I went and recovered deleted files and old email accounts from the same period. I found emails from three different people screaming at him because he'd taken their money and not delivered the goods."

At this point, I stood with the open laptop in my hand and turned to face Ray. "Here," I said, handing it to him to read. "You had better be ready to accept the truth." Then I stood silently as Ray read the emails. As he read each one and then clicked to the next I could see him growing visibly angrier and angrier. Finally he handed the computer back to me.

"Okay, where is he now?" Ray's tone was icy.

I looked up the tracker on my phone. "He's on his way back from Vegas."

"Let's get the bugs and get out of here," Ray said, and began packing the equipment in the room. Ten minutes later we were across the street at Tom's. We quickly retrieved the equipment, took it back across the street, and stowed it in our saddle bags.

"Shit, I forgot the camera in the garage," I said to Ray, hoping he'd run over and save me the trip. Ray nodded.

No longer concerned with stealth, I opened the garage door of the house we'd been holed up in and watched as Ray ran over to Tom's. When he got there, Ray opened the garage door. He stood on the ATV and quickly retrieved the camera we'd hidden in the rafters. He tucked it into his pocket and opened the door to the house.

I sat on the motorcycle and watched as Ray started carrying boxes of books from garage into the house. He quickly cleared half a wall and then came back out to the ATVs. There he picked up the two red plastic containers of gasoline and disappeared into the house. Five minutes later, he emerged with a gleaming smile. At the front window, flames licked the curtains.

Ray took his seat, put on his helmet and started his engine. Flames were now emerging from the house. He turned his head to me and raised his visor. I had not yet put on my helmet; Ray flashed me an inquisitive look. I took a look at my phone and estimated two, maybe three minutes. I leaned over and shouted at Ray.

"Close your visor, wait for my signal and we leave together." Ray nodded in acknowledgment. I put on my helmet and waited.

It was only a few minutes, but it seemed like an hour before the black Lincoln arrived. The house was now fully engulfed in flames. Tom rushed from his car to the house but was pushed back by the heat. He began running back and forth, as if he thought there might still be a way to salvage something.

I started my bike and revved the engine. Ray did the same. Eventually the noise drew Tom's attention. I gave the signal and we pulled out. The heat of the fire had now driven Tom into the center of the street. We drove right at him. I passed him on his right, Ray on his left, sending him an unmistakable message. I hoped the look of fear on Tom's face brought Ray immense satisfaction.

We made a few stops on the way home. During our first, Ray took off his helmet. He stared at me, searching for a reaction. He wanted to know if he'd messed up the plan. Burning down the house was a brash act. If he got caught, he'd go back to jail.

I didn't say a word, just stared back with a look of indifference. While Ray was off in the restroom, I smirked. Tom got what he deserved, but that's not what made me giddy. I now had something on Ray, and if I needed to I could use it as leverage.

Back in the city, we dumped the bikes. I took the train downtown. Ray grabbed a cab out to the burbs. Back at my loft, I crawled into my comfortable bed and slept for the next fifteen hours.

CHAPTER TWELVE

I awoke excited. I had a renewed sense of purpose. I spent my morning researching Massive Energy & Mining. Its corporate offices were located in Charleston, West Virginia, and its mines were in West Virginia, Virginia, and Kentucky. I familiarized myself with its executives and officers. Then I printed their pictures and hung them on my wall next to the satellite imagery I'd used to construct a map. I discovered all of their personal property holdings and attached them to the map. I wrote a list of questions, and those which I could not answer by searching online, I put into a list to be investigated when I got to Charleston. After a few hours I was ready for a break, so I left for a run.

I would have preferred to run a course. My muscles begged to be climbing and jumping, but I had spent the better part of a week riding a motorcycle and sitting in an empty house. I needed a few days of straight running to restore my cardio. I would follow this with a few days of muscle work and then slowly work my way back into parkour.

Before leaving, I'd gotten a call from Charles, asking me to teach him the defensive techniques I'd used to disarm Scott Randall. There was something to Charles. He didn't fit among Ray's group of misfits. He seemed too polished and educated. He was a curiosity I wanted to explore. I found myself wondering why I cared; it was not my way to make new friends. Perhaps I was interested because I saw him and myself as more grounded than Ray and Laura. Charles was part of their inner circle. I took him to have a sharp intellect.

My exercise had been a way to focus my brain, to be in the moment and not think about anything else. Parkour does that for you. Let your mind slip one time and you'll fall and break your neck. It's not often that I run. It doesn't require much attention and so my mind is open to a massive flood of thoughts.

In Pahrump, when the idea had come to me to infiltrate Massive Energy & Mining, I'd briefly considered letting Ray in on the job. I doubted he'd recognize the value of exposing a real conspiracy. On the ride home I concluded that it was my issue, my shot at making a difference in the world. The project could take weeks, likely a month, maybe longer. Charleston was a long way from Laura and Ray. It was a great opportunity to change direction and free myself from her spell. Perhaps, I could fill my nose with the state flower of West Virginia, the rhododendron, and drown out her scent for good.

The sun had been rising steadily, beating down on me. Its warmth felt great. I turned the corner and headed home, my blood pumping with endorphins. I felt exhilarated. My nose was opened to all the smells of the city. The grime of the street mixed with the sundry aroma of dozens of restaurants and was topped with a bouquet of spring flowers planted across numerous balconies. I didn't even mind the occasional whiff of tobacco from some wayward smoker.

For the first time I had a cause that was mine. If I could take down Massive Energy & Mining I could have a positive impact on the world. I licked the salty taste of sweat from my lips and realized that my mouth was frozen into a giant smile. The thought of my project, particularly, that I would risk something personal to accomplish—it made me happy, happier than I'd been in years.

I took the stairs to my apartment, walking—rather than running up by twos and threes as I typically do. I was sweat-drenched and could feel it between my toes and soaked through to my underwear. I would have to peel these clothes from my body. I could feel my runner's-high intensely; as I opened the stairwell door I began to laugh.

"What's so funny?" she asked, as I turned the corner to my apartment.

Standing in the frame of my door, her arms outstretched as if she were holding it up, was Laura. She looked despondent.

I smelled her, felt her attraction taking hold, and it angered me.

"Nothing," I said flatly. "Stand aside."

She moved out of the doorway, but not without a scornful stare. I opened the door and she followed me into the apartment. She wanted something, but I wanted her to leave. I would have admonished her for not calling first, but I broke that protocol when I showed up at her and Ray's place.

Instead I said, "Sorry, you caught me at a bad time." Then, without looking at her, I began stripping off my clothes. It wasn't as if she hadn't seen me naked before, but perhaps being this forward would scare her off.

"Wow, you've put on muscle since we were together," she said, followed by a wistful sigh.

Her comment left me feeling exposed. Instead of her getting embarrassed, I was the one turning flush.

"Is that why you're here? You have some unfinished business you'd like to consummate?"

"I'm here because of Ray," she said, turning away from me and fixing her focus on the collage of printouts lining my wall. I dried the sweat from my body, wrapped a fresh towel around my waist and walked over to where she was standing.

"Is he going to go back to prison?" she asked, her voice sharp and tight. Was she angry? No, I knew better; she was scared.

"We covered our trail."

"You don't think The Ranger—Tom, is going to put two and two together?"

"He doesn't know that Ray knows where he lives. He probably thinks one of the other people he ripped off burned down his house."

"And then you pulled that stunt, riding by him like that. The Ranger's not an idiot. He's going to suspect Ray."

She had a point. It was unlikely he'd go to the authorities and risk drawing out all the other people he'd defrauded. I could see him coming after Ray, looking for revenge. That would be just as bad. It doesn't matter how many guns you own if someone wants to take a shot at you with a high-powered rifle. I began thinking up a strategy.

"And when you discussed all this with Ray, what did he say?"

"He blew it off, but what other option does he have?"

"Why does this fall on me? I'm not the one who was about to give $150,000 to a con man. I didn't make him burn that house down. He did that on his own."

"It would be better to have lost the money if saving it means Ray is going to jail. It's not your responsibility, but you're the mastermind who came up with the plan. So, I'm asking if you have any ideas." She turned back to the wall. "What is this? " She asked pointing to the maps and building addresses. "This company's been in the news lately. You don't need all this to trade. "

It was refreshing to hear that she still stayed abreast of current events.

"What are you planning?" she asked, a shrewd expression on her face. "You're going here, but why?"

Now I really wanted her to leave.

"Alright, I think I have a way to throw suspicion off of Ray. I'm going to need a burner phone," I said, grabbing my wallet and pulling out some cash. She brightened immediately and then waved the money away.

"I've got it. There's a store a few blocks over. I'll run and grab it; you can take a shower while I'm gone." She walked off toward the door.

"Does Ray know you're here?"

"Yes," she said, shooting me a quizzical look before disappearing behind the door.

That left me with a smile. I could always tell when she was lying.

"Hello, am I speaking to the gentleman who goes by the name of The Ranger?" I kept my voice cool and staid. There was silence on the line. "My name is Mike Kenneth. I'm the attorney representing Ray Barrett. He asked me to give you a call at this number. This is—The Ranger?"

"Yes," he responded, taking the bait.

Laura smiled.

"Unfortunately Mr. Barrett couldn't call you himself. He's currently in custody. He was picked up by federal officers in Las Vegas and is under investigation for money laundering."

"That's got nothing to do with me," Tom said.

"As his attorney, it is my job to protect his interests. Mr. Barrett has given me the details of his pending transaction with you. It was my professional opinion that you two have no further contact. He believes that he can trust you, but having me make this call puts his defense at risk."

"Will he get out?" There was a smidgeon of sympathy in his voice.

"I believe I have struck a deal in which Mr. Barrett will forfeit certain offshore accounts in exchange for probation. Ranger, I'm very concerned that if I arrange for his freedom, Mr. Barrett will try to raise the money again in order to complete the transaction. I'm sure that will be very tempting for you. However, while Mr. Barrett believes in your story, I know a con when I see one.

"I have close ties with the Justice Department." I let the statement hang. "If you have any contact with Mr. Barrett or anyone associated with him, I guarantee there will be no rock under which you can hide. Are we understood?" There was another long pause. It was my calculation that Tom Irvin was fundamentally a coward.

The pause had now gone on too long.

"Mr. Barrett says he doesn't know your name, but I'm sure Homeland Security would have no trouble tracking you down. Should I call them or do we have an understanding?"

"We understand each other." Tom's voice was solemn, not fearful, but convincing.

"Very good," I waited a few beats and then hung up.

Laura took off her headset. She sat with her hands in her lap, looking flushed, and staring at me as if it was for the first time.

"Does that satisfy you?" I asked.

"I'm impressed," she replied in a soft tone.

I shrugged, stood up, and walked over to the wall. "I'm going to leave in a week. I don't know when I'll be back." Laura followed and stood beside me.

"What is this about?" she said, gesturing toward the wall. "I won't tell anyone."

"Blake Donaldson got away with murder. I'm going to break in, set up surveillance, and prove he's guilty."

"They won't be able to convict him over anything you find."

"I'll publish it on the web. There will be such an outcry; he will be forced to live in hiding from angry mobs."

"Will you be able to trade on any information you recover?"

"The company price is up, but only temporarily. Coal is in free fall. Natural gas is so much cheaper. There could be a rich opportunity to short the stock."

"Then, Ray and I are coming with you."

"What? No. I'm doing this on my own," I said firmly.

"I won't allow you. This guy deserves to go down, and you need the help. We need the money. We have one-hundred-and-fifty-thousand to trade with."

Laura slipped her arm in mine and rested her head on my shoulder. "This is a good plan. We can do this."

Was she trying to be solicitous? I wasn't sure. She was right. Everything would go smoother with two extra pairs of hands.

"Alright, but you two have to follow my every order." She let go and walked away from me.

"I wouldn't have it any other way. I'll go tell Ray we're doing this."

"Will he fight you?"

"Ray never fights me." Laura said, and then pulled out her phone in response to a chime. "Charles wants you to call him. He wants you to teach him how to disarm an attacker."

"I have his number. I'll give him a call. What can you tell me about that guy?"

Laura put her phone back away. "We trust him completely."

CHAPTER THIRTEEN

The addition of two more people postponed my trip to Charleston another month. I took the opportunity to spar with Charles, the pleasant mantis, and teach him the moves to disarm an opponent. Charles proved to be an excellent student. He listened carefully, tried hard, and didn't mind a bruise or two.

"Alright, we need to take a break—your form is off," I said. Charles looked disappointed. "It's just the way it is. If you want it to become a reflex action, you are going to need thousands of hours of practice." We walked into the kitchen where I poured us each some water. "Did Ray mention that he and I have been friends since junior high?"

"I put together that it has been a long time. Was the break in your relationship over the First and the Second?"

"No, we've been hashing conspiracies since we were kids. I got that you met Ray over something to do with playing paintball, but how long have you been following conspiracies?"

Charles did not answer immediately. He looked at me carefully, as if he were carrying the weight of a great secret he wasn't sure he could tell.

"Just between you and me, I bristle at the overuse of the word 'conspiracy.' I have a slightly different focus from the other members of the First and the Second. It's not that I don't appreciate their ideas, but we have different interests."

The prospect of hearing a new angle was intriguing. I pulled myself up onto the kitchen counter and gestured to one of the bar stools for Charles to have a seat.

"Back in college, I had a friend who defended himself on a traffic ticket. These things are usually decided by a judge, but since he wasn't a lawyer he didn't think he'd get a fair trial. He freaked out when he discovered the jury was going to be seven people instead of twelve. We started looking into it and discovered that it's been okay since the 70's to have a smaller jury for minor cases. That's when I first read about jury nullification.

"It's when a jury agrees that the person is guilty but acquits them anyway because they feel that the laws are wrong or unfair. Judges and prosecutors hate jury nullification. They restrict any attempt to argue that a jury has the right to nullify the law. That really sticks in my craw. Most people don't want to send a guy to prison for a year because he gets busted with an ounce of marijuana. Juries don't know they have the power to stop the conviction. It's a travesty.

"From then on I studied the law on my own. Thanks to DNA evidence we are constantly seeing people exonerated for crimes they didn't commit, and yet most of the time the prosecutors who put these people away just can't bear to admit they were wrong. It drives me crazy, especially because this mostly happens to poor people who can't afford a good legal defense. These prosecutors, judges, and dirty cops are all immune from prosecution.

"Anyway, I can go on about this a long time. It's a passion of mine."

"Sounds like you should go to law school," I said, jumping off the counter. "Come on, let's get back to sparring."

"It would be nice, but I have a decent thing going with the programming, and by and large hanging out with Ray, Laura, and the gang helps me exorcise my demons."

"Alright, back to first position." I was now holding a plastic gun for Charles to remove. You would think this was the easy part, but it's very hard to stand still, let someone come at you, and resist taking them down. Charles came at me with surprising force and executed each motion meticulously. He took the gun from my hands as if he'd been doing it his whole life.

"Wow, nice job. You're a fast study."

Charles, when enthusiastic, had a freakishly large smile.

"Do you share the same beliefs about 9/11 as Ray and the rest of them?" I asked while we went through the motions several more times.

"Well, I wouldn't say 'share.' I'm a skeptic by nature."

I was pleased to hear it. I found myself liking Charles more and more, but I was curious as to why he belonged to Ray's group.

"Look, you have to understand, I'm kind of a nerd. I met Ray and Laura and they just invited me right into their lives. They got me doing things that I'd never done before. The three of us have gone hiking, camping, boating, shooting, rock climbing. When Ray started the group, they let me in as a founding member and I donated a few thousand to help pull it all together."

"I was under the impression that you were a major contributor to the $150,000 they were using to pay The Ranger."

A bashful expression came over Charles.

"They're like family to me and I have the money to spare. Besides, you know how much passion Ray has; it's infectious. I'm very grateful you kept him from getting conned."

We practiced the methods to disarm a knife.

"Kyle, are you saying you don't believe 9/11 was an inside job?"

"It was absolutely not an inside job. It's one of the oldest arguments Ray and I have debated. I've read every report that's been written about it and watched countless hours of video over the years trying to prove the truth to Ray. It hasn't done any good."

Charles nodded in agreement, but then shrugged as if it didn't matter. He appreciated his friendship with Ray and Laura more than he cared about Ray's sanity. "I was kind of hoping that I could interest them in using the money to educate people about jury nullification. I found a trial room we can rent and I'd like to shoot a video we could circulate on the web."

The following day, in addition to practicing, I took Charles on a run and was pleased to see that he kept up very well. I found myself taking greater interest in him. A couple of nights we hung out at his place. I discovered he was more organized and fastidious than me. He was a voracious reader and we both shared a love of history. He was a bit of a geek, with a passion for micro-robots: his house was filled with prototypes of flying robots—some the size of insects.

He kept himself fit with daily exercise, but didn't see any need to take it to the extreme level I did. I pushed him anyway and we hung out nearly every day until it was time to go to Charleston. Over that time I brushed off his questions about where Ray, Laura and I were going.

Charles reminded me of myself, or maybe the self I could have been. He was younger and more accomplished than I was at his age, but he hadn't come out of bone-crushing poverty either. Perhaps because of this familiarity or because of Laura's recommendation, he won my trust.

We were having dinner with Ray and Laura when, at Laura's urging, I decided to tell him where we were going and why. His reaction was enthusiastic.

"I want in."

"It's too late to bring a fourth along," I said.

"No, no, that's not what I mean. You want to expose this guy in a big way. I want to help. Bring me every scrap of data you find on the guy. It will be my job to package and deliver it to the public."

Charles, who ran his own business, had far more marketing experience than any of us. Still I hesitated.

"Don't agree—just promise you won't do anything until you get back. By then I'll have a complete plan together. Listen to my presentation and then decide."

CHAPTER FOURTEEN

The city of Charleston, West Virginia, was nestled in the tops of the Appalachian Mountains, but at the bottom of a Gallup Poll for well-being. In measures of physical and emotional health, access to basic necessities and work environment, Charleston was indexed among the worst in the nation. The city's visitor's bureau dubbed it "Almost Heaven." I couldn't help wondering if that meant, "Last stop before heaven, you will die here."

The city's political offices were equally divided between the two major parties, but like nearly all small, Southern towns, the residents were largely conservative. The people of Charleston struggled to cope with a world that was changing around them. Clashes were common. The city had a yearly gay pride parade and festival that was always swarmed with evangelicals who did everything possible to disrupt it. Racism and sexism were not hard to find and showed up frequently in news reports.

Flying into the airport was harrowing. The meager runways had been formed by shearing off the tops of mountains. The cost of making the runways was so great the airport had to share them with the West Virginia Air National Guard base—a detail the pilot pointed out as we began our descent. Ray immediately perked up at the mention of a military installation and began looking for the base through the window. I crossed to the empty seats on the other side of the aisle, hoping to catch a glimpse of the Elk and Kanawha rivers, upon whose banks Charleston was built.

Our cover story was that we had come to Charleston to take photos, particularly of the birds that could be found at the Kanawha State Forest, just seven miles south of Charleston. That meant that on the plane we restricted our conversation to photography and current events. Neither subject much appealed to Ray, who sat silent, listening to music for nearly the entire trip. Laura and I had brought photography magazines and we talked about the articles we read. We'd brought a significant amount of freshly purchased camera equipment and high-end lenses to survey Blake Donaldson. Since none of us were professional photographers, the conversation was welcome and instructive. I noticed that Laura had stopped fawning over and petting Ray, though they held hands as they left the airport.

We rented a car and drove down into the city. It was a good time to arrive. The spring foliage was fresh and in full display, while the sky was overcast, giving the city a gritty feel that reminded us of the seriousness of our mission.

Ray had been bottled up on the long flight. He came to life in the car and began sharing his notions that the National Guard base was actually a satellite base for the Emergency Operation Center at Mount Weather. Mount Weather, a five-hour drive east across the border into Virginia, was run by FEMA and had long been speculated to be the President's bunker in case of nuclear war.

"You know, during 9/11 they sent most of the congressmen to Mount Weather," Ray said.

I mumbled, "Is that so?" and continued to focus on the drive into the city.

"What most people don't know," Ray continued, "is that there are a series of underground tunnels that connect Mount Weather with the air base here in Charleston. They get the politicians out to Mount Weather and then ferry them underground until they arrive here."

I wanted to ask why "they" would go to such lengths as to dig a 280-mile tunnel. What purpose could it serve when there were so many less-expensive means of protecting our nation's leaders during even the worst possible war? Ray started whistling the theme to "The X-Files." Sometimes it felt as if he was deliberately taunting me.

I was grateful when we entered the city limits and I could tell Ray that he would have to explain it all to me later tonight over dinner. We checked into our hotel; Ray and Laura had an adjoining room to mine. It was still early in the morning, so we took a three-hour break from each other to rest and refresh.

After a nap and a shower, I knocked on the door between our rooms. Laura welcomed me into their suite. Ray was on the couch, wearing a pair of headphones, crouched over his laptop. One of the ear buds fell out, and without looking at either of us he grabbed it and shoved it back into place.

"Are you ready to finally practice with these cameras?" I asked Laura.

She smiled at me. "Finally, what do you mean? I've been out and back already." She couldn't have been out taking pictures; I had all the cameras in my room. She ignored my puzzlement and added, "Come on, let's go get some snaps."

I pointed to Ray.

"He's been like that since I got back," she said. "He's keeping up on his radio shows and articles—he's still got the First and the Second to lead."

Ray had a voracious appetite for anything that fed his theories. He was probably looking to corroborate his ideas about Mount Weather and the underground tunnel to Charleston.

I felt a twinge of excitement that I would get to spend the day with Laura, but promptly shoved it back down, reminding myself that my desire for her was irrational. She would always have an intoxicating sway over me, but that didn't mean I couldn't mentally override it.

We stepped into the empty hotel elevator and Laura relieved my shoulder of a camera bag.

"You went out?" I said. "Where did you go?"

"Local research on Donaldson. It turns out he's opened up offices here in the city. He's going back into the coal business. "

After the mine accident, Donaldson sold his interests in several of the company's mines, collecting hundreds of millions of dollars. Then, to quell some of the investor's complaints about the scandal, he stepped down from Massive Energy & Mining. Now that the investigations were over, he had bought back some of the mines and with his partners was preparing to start a new mining business. Massive Energy & Mining was now an empty shell. Its mines—and most of its assets—had been sold back to Donaldson.

Laura and I walked silently to the Kanawha River. When we got there, she removed the camera from her bag and began taking photographs. A barge moved past us: two long troughs loaded with piles of black coal, pulled by a towboat. Looking at the coal reminded me of the miners who had died for Donaldson's greed; their bodies were never recovered. Mining is dangerous work. More than a hundred thousand miners were killed in the last century. I wondered how many more would die as a result of Donaldson's latest venture.

Laura continued snapping pictures, unaware that I had diverted my attention to her. I was deeply impressed with her enthusiasm for this project. While I'd been napping, she'd found Donaldson's office and home address, and discovered his latest business plans. I'd forgotten how studious and energetic she could be and wondered how much of her talent was wasted on managing Ray. Had I been more ambitious in our relationship, what might she and I have accomplished?

I wiped these thoughts from my mind, took out my own camera and began shooting pictures. Every now and then, I would sweep around and snap a picture of Laura. We began walking, Laura leading the way, down Kanawha Boulevard toward the steel truss, Dickson Street Bridge. A few blocks past the bridge we turned up Court Street and kept walking until we came to a large, glass tower.

"His new office is on the fourteenth floor," Laura said as we stood across the street.

"Unbelievable. You would think after what he's done he would be hiding under a rock. Yet here is he is, in plain daylight as if nothing had happened," I said.

Laura started, a memory coming to her that turned her ashen. She put her hand on my forearm and turned to me.

"I never told you this—when my attacker lay dying I wanted him to see my face, to know what he'd done to deserve it. I looked him straight in the eye as he bled to death. With no remorse at all he asked me, 'Why?' I said, 'Because you raped me.' His dying words were: 'You wanted me.'

"I had never looked twice at him before he raped me," she said. "Kyle, people like that, like Donaldson, they don't understand what they do is wrong. They justify their actions in their own heads. They're monsters."

Laura was shaking. I put my arms around her and held her tightly. She folded hers around me and we breathed together for a moment, remembering what we shared: that sense of righteous indignation and insatiable passion that, in both of us, came from the same place, deep down. I felt her body begin to relax, her hands flattened on my back pulling me into her tighter, like they used to when we made love. Standing on the street corner, next to the roar of midday traffic, it felt like there was nothing but her and me.

I buried my nose in her hair, suffused with that irresistible smell and felt her lips against my neck. They were not pressed into a kiss, just against, moistened by her hot breath, as if they were tired and needed a place to rest. I felt the urge to say something, to acknowledge the flood of emotion I was feeling—something to harken back to a time when there wasn't a third person between us.

"I remember—" I started to say and then paused as my brain frantically tried to gather the right words.

Laura spoke quietly, sweetly, in my ear.

"I remember too." She did not reclose her lips and I felt her teeth ever so gently on my neck, the slightest nibble that came and went. While I had been thinking of the great expanse of consuming love I had for her, now those teeth were reminding me of a small, vivid detail: that in the throes of passion, Laura bites.

She brought her lips to mine.

I had longed for it, a sign of recognition that she still had feelings for me. The kiss consumed me, brought me to the moment, and stayed my mind from all the other thoughts that would rush in the second she pulled away. I met the passion of her kiss and was stripped naked by it. She broke the kiss and looked into my eyes. I moved to kiss her again, but she shook her head.

"I'm sorry. I shouldn't have done that to you. I don't mean to give you false hope." Again she rested her head against my body and I put my face back into her hair. We ended our embrace without word and turned back toward the building.

The white walk symbol flashed. We crossed the intersection and approached the doors of the building. I noticed the security cameras and stopped us before we got too close. On a plaque outside, I could see the building housed two other major coal companies and several investment firms.

"The building gets a lot of protests and has its own security team," Laura said. "Right now, there are three empty floors. There are always two guards walking the property and a second in the security office, monitoring the cameras and fire systems."

Something caught Laura's eye and together we turned to the right. We were standing on the first of a series of low steps up to the corner entrance. Three-story-tall pillars lined the building on the right and left; below that, a little wall topped with bushes followed the length of the sidewalk.

At the turn of the wall stood a mother and her little girl. The girl couldn't have been more than eight. The mother was extremely skinny, painted with freckles, and had crinkled red hair that suggested she descended from the Scotch-Irish who settled in the Appalachian Mountains back in the eighteenth century. She held a large poster board that read, "Donaldson Murders Miners."

The little girl was not as skinny as her mother; she had a healthy glow to her full cheeks and hair that matched Laura's. Even from ten yards away, we could see the bright blue-green of her eyes. She too held a sign. It read: "Donaldson killed my Daddy."

"I thought you said he paid off all the miners' families."

"I thought he had," I replied, but Laura was already walking toward them. The woman must have mistaken us for journalists, because she held up her sign and nudged her daughter to do the same. Laura obliged them by snapping photos.

"Have you two had lunch?" Laura asked the mother while smiling down at the child. That's how the four of us ended up at the steak house, back across the street, next to the mall. The mother was named Lucy Clark, and her daughter was Cassandra, Cassie for short. Cassie was hungry; Lucy had to remind her several times to slow down.

Over lunch, we learned that they had been offered $400,000 in settlement money, but turned it down. "If we took the money, then we had to agree to be silent. I can't make that promise for Cassie. She has to be able to speak about how and why her father died."

They had a case in court suing Donaldson, but his legal team had been using every trick in the book to stall. The judge who had presided over the settlements believed they should have taken the money that was offered. He had not been favorable to them. Currently, they were living off her late husband's Social Security and a small death benefit, all of which barely met the monthly bills.

As Laura listened, the tips of her ears became a crimson red. I excused myself and got up from the table to call Ray. I told him to grab the equipment and meet us at the restaurant. While I was standing near the door, a gentleman in a suit came in and was seated. He took off his suit jacket and hung it on the hook to the outside of his booth. In the process his jacket flipped open. I glanced at his security badge, clipped to the inside of the jacket's breast pocket. I stayed at the front, pretending to talk on the phone. After placing his order, he walked off to the restroom. When no one was looking, I grabbed the badge and returned to my seat. Lucy had just finished copying down her contact information for Laura.

"Were not journalists we are here to photograph birds," Laura was saying as I sat down. Disappointment washed across Lucy's face. Quickly, Laura took out the camera and turned it around to show Lucy the pictures of the two of them. "They're really great pictures. I'll email them to you tonight. Maybe you can use them to make up a press release."

Lucy nodded and said, "We don't have email anymore. Thank you for the meal. We had better get back." She stood up, taking Cassie's hand. I stepped out of the booth and allowed Laura to stand. As soon as she did, Cassie wrapped her arms around Laura, putting her ear to Laura's belly and squeezing her tight. "Thank you so much for the meal," Cassie said, in a small squeaky voice. "The pictures are lovely."

"You're welcome." Laura choked back tears.

Lucy seemed touched by the display and reached out a long arm, resting it on Laura's shoulder.

"We will be alright. You don't need to worry about us," she said. The two women stared at one another for a moment and then mother and daughter quietly walked out of the restaurant.

We paid the check and by the time we made it outside, they had already taken up their previous spot at the corner of the building. While we looked on, Ray pulled up.

I had Ray drive around to the back of the building and enter the parking garage. Hanging from a hook in the back was the suit I'd asked Ray to bring. I tore off my clothes and quickly put on the suit.

"I've got a security badge into the building. I'm going to see if I can get into his offices and plant our taps. You two drive out to Donaldson's house and get some pictures, and then we can make a plan to go back and break in later."

The fourth floor of the parking garage was connected to the building by a glass walkway. I left my camera bag in the car and grabbed one of the two equipment cases in the trunk. I said my goodbyes and didn't look after them as they pulled away.

The badge turned out to be a boon. I kept my head down as I passed the security cameras, and pressing the badge to the terminal outside the glass doors, walked right into the building. There was no receptionist desk and no security guard present at this entrance. There were five elevators. I took one to the tenth floor and then slipped into a stairwell and walked the additional flights. At each floor, I cracked the door enough to get a glimpse of the corridors. When I got to the thirteenth, I was surprised to find that it was completely empty. Not just empty, but gutted of every wall, ceiling tile, and doorway. All that remained were the outer walls of the buildings, the elevator stacks, the bathrooms, utility closets, and carpet that surrounded the granite tile outside the elevators. There were no cameras, so I left my case in the stairwell and stepped out onto the floor.

Standing nearly anywhere, I could turn and have a 360-degree view of Charleston. The afternoon sun touched down on the golden tops of the Greek Orthodox Church across the street. The ripples of the river in the distance and the surrounding green mountains were breathtaking. I regretted leaving my camera in the car and so I reached for the camera on my phone.

As I clicked the camera, I heard an odd ding along with the traditional sound of the shutter. It was a new phone and this was the first picture I'd taken with it. I took another and this time I heard the unmistakable sound of elevator doors opening. Someone had just stepped out onto the floor.

In a panic, I ran as fast as I could and pressed my back against the elevator stack, listening intensely for the direction of the footfalls on the granite tile. They were heavy, but did not produce the clicking of a pair of dress shoes. Slowly, I moved around the stack, away from the sound toward the elevators. At the corner I knelt down and pushed just the camera portion of my phone around the corner, tilting the screen so I could use the phone like a periscope.

My chest pounded; just inches from my phone stood a pair of black boots draped in the hem of a pair of polyester pants. I held my breath and did not move. His footfalls had echoed around the empty room and misdirected me. He stood there, not moving, giving me time to plan. Should I incapacitate him, make up an excuse for my presence on the floor, or knock him over and make a break for the stairwell? None of these seemed like great options, they would certainly trigger additional security and make it that much harder to spy on Donaldson.

Quietly, I exhaled and then slowly drew in a fresh breath. When my lungs were full, I held my breath again. At that moment, inches from my face, the guard farted. He followed it with a deep groan of satisfaction.

He turned and started walking across the granite toward the bathrooms. I exhaled and immediately regretted it. I should have incapacitated him in retaliation for cloaking me in that rank bomb. Instead, I watched him, through my phone, approach the bathroom door. Under his arm were a couple of magazines. At the door he removed a giant ring of keys from his belt and fingered through until he found the one for the bathroom. He unlocked the door and went in, leaving the ring hanging from the lock outside. I quickly moved to the bathroom door. I heard another explosion, groan, and then the turn of pages.

I knelt and examined the keys, careful not to rattle them. They were labeled. I selected the key for the 14th floor utility closet and with my most delicate touch removed it from the ring. From inside the bathroom I heard the guard's radio. "Dan, come in Dan."

"I'm on a break," Dan belted into the radio.

"You know they lock those bathrooms so the janitors don't have to clean them."

"What do you want?"

"Keep an eye out for Mr. Manning's security badge; he thinks he dropped it somewhere between the eighteenth and lobby."

"That couldn't wait until I'm off break?"

"You're still in the building aren't you?"

"Yeah!"

"Then you can use your eyes wherever you go—sheesh."

"Fuck you," he said, but I don't think it was into the radio.

I looked at the badge in my pocket. Across the top was the name, "Manning, J." It would probably be deactivated by morning. I quickly headed up the stairwell to the fourteenth floor. There was no one in the corridor. It appeared the floor was divided up into two offices: to the left was a law firm, to the right was River Energy Group. I entered the hall and pushed the key into the lock of the server closet, walked inside, and closed the door behind me.

What I thought would be hard was suddenly easy. The servers for the entire floor sat here. In an hour I had hacked into the only two active computers at River Energy Group.

There was a computer at the front desk for the receptionist. She kept an appointment book, played games on Facebook, and looked at celebrity websites. The other belonged to Donaldson. As yet the company wasn't fully funded. No other employees had been hired. Reading his email, I learned that his partners had put their money in escrow for the purchase of new mines, but Donaldson had been waiting for his name to be cleared. Now he was waiting for the government to approve the transfer of the mines to his new company—at which point, he assured his partners, he would transfer his $200 million into the escrow account. I found a letter of credit from his bank in the Cayman Islands authenticating his funds, but I could not find any indication that he had accessed that account from this computer.

I'd been in the closet a couple of hours when I received a text from Laura: she and Ray were on their way back and would meet me at the hotel. Now that my taps were in place, I could access these computers from anywhere. I packed up my gear, took the stairwell to the fourth floor, and dropped Manning's security badge outside the elevator. Fifteen minutes later I met Laura and Ray back at the hotel.

Ray, his face expressionless, his eyes twinkling, let me into the suite.

"How did it go?" Laura asked. She had a beaming smile. She came up behind Ray, ran her hand lovingly across his back, and tucked herself under his arm.

"I had one close call, but it turned out to be amazingly easy." I said, and then quickly filled them in on the details. "How did it go for you two?"

"He has a nice estate, but very lax security." Ray spoke flatly. "There were no fences or cameras and the woods provided great cover."

"While we were there, a water delivery truck showed up and we were able to get access," Laura added.

"His wife wasn't home?"

"I don't think she lives there. She didn't have any clothes in the closet," Laura said.

"Wait, you went in?"

"Ray went in, I stayed outside and kept watch. You should have seen him, Kyle. He was very brave." A smug smile crossed Ray's face.

"If he'd had better security I might have waited, but I was able to penetrate his computer, change out his phone charger, and find his safe. I planted a camera over the safe and tied it into his Wi-Fi, so the next time he opens it we'll have his combination."

"Nice job," I said, hoping I came across genuinely enthusiastic. In the back of my mind, I had a nagging worry. What if there was a camera in the house that saw him? Did he wear a mask? I doubted it. If he had enough sense to check the closets and get a feel for who was living there, chances are he would have found interior cameras. Donaldson didn't have any children living at home, so it is unlikely he'd have a nanny camera. In any case, I would double-check Donaldson's computer for evidence that Ray had missed additional security.

Ray was soaking in the attention from Laura, and it was well deserved. He'd done a good job. I thought to consider that maybe my reservations about him going into Donaldson's had more to do with my jealously and a feeling that I needed to control everything.

It was another three days before Donaldson had cause to open his safe. The event was precipitated by a call from his wife.

"I need my jewelry sent to New York," she said following his hello.

"Of course, let me bring it to you." There was a pause on the line, followed by her sigh.

"That won't be necessary, Blake. Please just ship it and be sure to properly insure it."

"You're never going to forgive me, are you?"

"No," she said without hesitation.

"I did no less than your father would have done. Has—had done," Donaldson argued.

"I never wanted to marry my father," Sue Massive-Donaldson replied, then hung up.

Blake Donaldson put down the phone and opened the cabinet in his office that hid the safe. He typed in the code, pushed down the handle, and swung open the door. He reached in and lifted three soft, black boxes. He opened the top one, revealing a sparkling necklace comprised of fat diamonds and sapphires. He removed them from the safe, out of view of the camera. In the seconds before he closed the safe we could see several thumb drives, a mass of paperwork, and some cash at the back.

The next day, I slipped a stocking over my head, broke into Donaldson's home, and copied every scrap of data found in his safe. Robbing the house of a multi-millionaire proved to be a hundred times simpler than robbing the house of a man owning a small chain of jewelry stores.

A preliminary look at the data showed Donaldson used a separate email account to communicate with his mine supervisor. He'd kept these emails on a thumb drive, probably for easy disposal. They confirmed that Donaldson had directly ordered the deception and bribery of federal mine safety officials leading to the disaster.

Additionally we found that Donaldson actions had been spurred by a 50-page report.

The introduction to this report stated that it was written at Donaldson's request and contained "out-of-the-box thinking," and "fringe contingency analysis" regarding the mitigation of culpability in "the advent of a mine disaster resulting from the subversion of standard safety protocols." The report was penned by the same law firm whose offices shared a floor with Donaldson's new company.

We now had the proof on Donaldson. I felt good about this, Laura was ecstatic. Like a freshly-popped champagne bottle, she bubbled all over Ray, filling his glass the entire plane ride home. If I was restrained in my enthusiasm, it was only because I had in my possession a file from Donaldson that I had not shared with either of them.

Our flight had a one-hour layover in New York while we transferred planes. When Ray and Laura were off getting a bite to eat, I used security codes found in the safe to transfer Donaldson's $200 million into a newly created offshore account.

CHAPTER FIFTEEN

Charles had requested to meet with us the hour—if not the second—we returned. We put him off for a day so that the three of us could rest. I awoke the following morning and lay in bed thinking about the direction my life might take when my foot hit the floor. The day before, I'd arrived home and washed all my clothes, cleaned the house, and repacked my bags. I'd stayed up late cleaning. Not just cleaning; I was purifying: throwing out things I would not need, packing up mementos, wiping away the evidence of habitation. A couple of phone calls and then I could move a few boxes into storage, put the apartment on the market, and disappear forever.

Everything that had ever rooted me in one spot was gone. I no longer felt like a recluse. Money would never be an issue again. With that kiss from Laura, I'd gained an acknowledgment that she still had feelings for me. I had decided that I'd won enough; from here on I was resolved to accept her choice. If she still clung to Ray, with all his deficiencies and crazy conspiracies, it was because she had a hole of her own to fill. It was a mistake to believe her need for Ray reflected negatively on me.

Wherever I travel there will be other women. There will be women whose minds and temperament have been shaped by ideals and experiences that I cannot even begin to fathom. What would it be like to date a girl schooled all over Europe, multilingual, and largely untouched by America's disposable culture? I don't know. I've never met a woman like that, but they are out there. I now had the power to thrust myself into a lifestyle where I could encounter untold possibilities.

My plan was to spend three months in another country, learn its language, run its streets, and vault up and over its walls. I would formalize my education with the experience of doing, of being part of the planet in a way only a few people could afford.

I felt certain that I could turn the information over to Charles and that he would be able to publish it in a way that would bring the prick down. It may not send Donaldson to jail, but it would destroy his reputation. As Laura and I discussed privately, it might also give Lucy and Cassandra the edge they needed to win their suit against Donaldson. He still had plenty of money, but the millions of dollars he needed to get back into business were out of his grasp. He probably didn't yet know it was missing.

It was now 9 a.m. Still I had not moved. I should get up and make those calls, not say goodbye to Laura, and then disappear. There was a force that kept me in bed, the feeling of gravity, the weight of expectation for a life I never thought I would achieve.

I breathed in deeply and imagined the oxygen passing through my lungs and entering my bloodstream to awaken all my muscles. Eventually, all that potential energy seemed too much to sit still any longer. I'd run only once on our trip. I needed to exercise, to shake off the days of travel, and set my pulse to full speed.

Hopping out of bed, I noticed a text message on my phone: Charles asking if I wanted to join him on a run. Twenty minutes later we were jogging city streets, trying to outpace one another. After four miles, standing at the top of a hill, looking down into the park, we took a break. From this vantage point we could see every shrub, park bench, and low wall.

"You do all that crazy parkour stuff, don't you?" Charles asked. Our heavy breathing had subsided. I nodded. "Did I ever mention that I was track and field in high school and college?" I smiled wide. I could see it now. His long legs and slender frame were such a contrast to my more muscled, gymnast-like body. "Hurdles," Charles added and smiled deviously. He stretched out his arm and began pointing. "We start here, then to that bench, that shrub, the next bench, that wall." He outlined a perfect course.

My excitement was palpable. Parkour did not lend itself well to direct competition. Participants ran against the times of other runners, as most courses do not permit side-by-side negotiation. From the mark we were neck-and-neck, but at the first bench Charles pulled ahead. My method was to side vault over each obstacle while Charles, with his long legs and perfect form, sailed over each one.

I was inclined to mimic him, but the risk of blowing a form I had not practiced was too great. I decided to throw him off. I sprinted full speed between the next set of hurdles, getting just enough ahead of him that I crossed in front of him and side vaulted. Charles would have to hurdle over both the bench and my body. Instead, he stepped onto the bench just as I was putting my feet on the ground. His other foot hit the back of the bench and he leapt, landing beside me. My little gambit had only served to move me to his left and him to my right.

Ahead, I saw my chance: a high wall between us and the next hurdle. Charles would have to run around, but I could go over. I winked at Charles and headed up the wall, just as I reached the top I felt a hand push on my right foot. The sneaky bastard had jumped up and tapped me. I lost my balance, tumbling over the other side of the wall. To compensate, I tucked into a roll which gave Charles plenty of time to come around the wall and pull ahead. I hopped up, shook myself off, and then sprinted. He was good, an excellent sprinter and clever competitor. There was simply no outclassing him on basic hurdles. It took every last ounce of my energy to catch up, but in the end he beat me by about five seconds.

We crashed on the ground; our bodies were shot, but our spirits were high. We lay there for a while, recuperating and occasionally laughing.

"Kyle, I need your help." Charles' earnest expression was completely disarming. "If this goes well we could have a real impact on the world. We won't be just a bunch of urban kooks clinging to their guns in a barn." He conveyed the sense that something great was afoot. "I'm worried that Ray will feel threatened by me proposing changes to the group."

"What is it you'd like me to do?"

"A very small thing: if you like my presentation then vocally support it." I rolled onto my back and sat up on my elbows.

Off in the distance a young woman jogged along, pushing a stroller and walking a dog. The stroller was a long-handled running model and the woman wore tight-fitting running pants. She did not look as though she had just had a baby. The dog ran ahead, and then around the stroller, causing the leash to tangle, forcing the woman to stop. Her frustration was audible. It made me smile, reminding me that I would never have children or dogs.

Considering Charles, a quote I could only paraphrase came to mind: Great leaders ask small things of their people that are really big things in disguise. With this trick they shape a world of change. Was there to be a coup? Did Charles know I was leaving? He'd piqued my curiosity.

That afternoon, when I arrived at the barn, Ray and Laura were standing outside the door. I motioned to go inside.

"We'll camp at the flat and then it's only a three-mile hike to the hot springs," Ray said, discussing their next trip. Laura looked over at me and touched Ray lightly on the chest to stop him.

"Charles is still setting up. He's been in there an hour. He insists we all come in together," she said with a wink.

"There's some land up there we should look at, too," Ray continued.

I started to tune into their conversation, but then heard footsteps as Charles drew toward the door. He opened it with a smile, stood in the doorway, and looked to each of our faces. He was dressed in white slacks, a white jacket, and a pale blue shirt with no tie. With a brisk turn in place that caused his jacket to flutter, Charles spun and walked toward the stage.

We followed him in, stopping along the way to see the large posters he'd attached to the wall. The posters were the product of a wide-format printer; they were architectural drawings and several logo design proofs. The posters depicted strong lines surrounded by dark, stately colors. The ink was so vivid and fresh against the bright white, glossy paper that my hands unconsciously reached out. My fingers flicked the edges and then ran themselves over the corner marks, as if my digits thought they could add to or suck something from the artistry depicted.

Laura fixated on the first poster: a shiny courtroom, framed from a perspective just behind the bar, facing the judge's mahogany bench. A rough-hewn metal plaque, with traces of silver and copper in the lettering, was fixed at the front of the bench, presenting a raised capital J and S. The corner of Laura's mouth was elevated and curled. I suspected she was remembering her past legal ambitions.

On my way to the next poster, I walked around Ray and Laura, noticing that her hand gripped his in a tight squeeze. Ray was paying more attention to Laura than he was the poster and I could not tell if his muted expression was hiding fear, adulation, or a mixture of both.

Out of the corner of my eye, I caught another rendition of the logo on the next poster, this one curved in a half circle. It immediately drew my mind to where I'd seen this kind of raised metal lettering—on every manhole cover. The difference here is that manhole covers are cast iron while this metal lettering was silver and copper on a brushed pewter background. The artwork was phenomenal. The letters invoked the feeling that they were elevated by force, as if the words had erupted through the collision of tectonic plates. The logo read: The Justice Syndicate.

Further along, another poster depicted an overhead drawing of the courtroom that indicated camera placement. Down one side of the poster, little rectangles showed the area of coverage for each camera. The next two posters showed website design and sample press releases.

I turned to Charles, who was standing at the podium on the dais. Below him on the main floor was a long wooden table, the kind found in courtrooms for the use of attorneys. On the table was an architectural model of the courtroom shown in the posters. A few feet behind the table was an elegant wood bench, the style found in courtrooms for public seating, except that these were draped in padded leather. They were far more comfortable-looking and elegant than any I had ever seen, and as I remembered from a long ago trip to Washington D.C., outclassed even those found in the Supreme Court.

On the bench, carefully laid out, were three booklets, wrapped in thick blue paper covers. I took a seat on the far end, picked up a booklet, and began thumbing through it. I've had considerable experience reading annual and financial analyst reports. Charles' proposal was more clear, logically presented, and honestly stated then anything I'd ever read intended for investors. I got a quick look at the table of contents and a couple of pages on the inside before Ray and Laura joined me on the bench. Ray and Laura placed their booklets in their laps and with our attention facing forward—Charles began.

"As I've shared with you all before, in the past I've spent a great deal of time studying our jury system. During that time, I began going to court to observe the process. I was watching criminal cases, mostly minor stuff. One time I observed an older woman, in her forties, who looked like she'd had a rough road in life. She appeared to be in a panic, like she was waiting for someone. When the prosecutor came in she rushed up to him, and I overheard their conversation.

"Apparently she and her husband had gotten into a drunken brawl. The police came and she was arrested. In between the arrest and the case she and her husband reconciled. She said that he was supposed to show up to tell the judge that she was not guilty. The prosecutor was perturbed, because the husband was his only witness."

Laura's arm slid down the back of the bench behind me; her hand found my shoulder and gave it a reassuring and soothing squeeze. I looked down the bench. Her other arm was draped around Ray, pulling him tightly against her.

"This woman was clearly not well educated and like many poor people, she was unaware of her rights. She did not understand that without a witness or evidence, the prosecution had no case. She had no attorney, most likely because she couldn't afford one. She didn't know what to do and was badly in need of a helping hand. Unfortunately, the person she turned to was the prosecutor."

Charles' voice ached with regret.

"As I sat there listening," he said, "I was overcome with the desire to interject. Instead, I kept my mouth shut. The prosecutor told her that the best thing for her to do was to plead guilty. If I stood up and told this woman the truth about her constitutional rights, I was afraid this prosecutor would come after me," Charles said, dropping his fist on the podium. "She was tricked into pleading guilty.

"It was a small thing," he said, "to stand up for someone else and speak out. I wasn't in any real danger. Maybe I could have been arrested, but I certainly wasn't going to lose my life. I regret every day that I wasn't able to stand up and speak for that woman. To this day, I get so angry that we have a system that fails to protect the weakest and most vulnerable members of our society.

"Ray, you and Laura created a group with the intention of making a difference against injustice. With the help of friends, Kyle, motivated by injustices that led to the death of twenty-six miners, has brought back information that will prove they were murdered. You have all taken a far greater risk than I. This is my chance to take a stand.

"The person responsible for those crimes has already gotten away with it. Though the information proves Donaldson is guilty beyond a shadow of a doubt. "Inspired by you, I'm motivated to correct an injustice. That's why I want your help in establishing The Justice Syndicate: a courtroom where we can present online, concrete evidence of crimes against humanity perpetrated by people who would otherwise use their money and power to avoid prosecution. We have seen with experiments like Wiki Leaks that when nothing more than raw data is given to the public, the impact of those crimes is reduced to whatever sound bites fit into a 30-second news story.

"We will film a courtroom drama that will provide a vivid presentation of evidence to ensure we keep the public's attention. They don't have to read through countless documents; instead, they will be able to watch a riveting courtroom drama designed to expose them to the facts. Those found guilty in our court will forever be known for their crimes against the public."

Laura withdrew her arms from around each of us and instead took Ray's and my hand in each of her own and sat rapt, on the edge of her seat.

"We have seen CEO after CEO getting away with crimes that financially damage the country, cause the loss of life, and manipulate our democracy for their own benefit without so much as a single subpoena issued. If we do this right, that will change; people will start to demand that these companies be prosecuted and CEOs will be scared that we are going to tap their phones, break into their offices, and expose their guilt to the world.

"I have to do this and I need your support. I swore to myself a long time ago that I would make a difference. That's why I've donated so much. You three, by entrusting me with the information you got from Blake Donaldson, have made it possible for me to fulfill a promise I made to myself: to never walk away without standing up for what is right. Thank you for believing in me, for making me part of your group, and for hearing me out today."

Charles stopped speaking, took his arms off the podium, and let his hands fall to his sides. Laura immediately sprang from her seat and began to clap, and then was joined by Ray and me. Charles looked humbled. Laura was patting Ray on the back like it was his idea.

"Would you stream this live?" Ray asked.

"No, we would shoot it, edit, and the put everything online at once, leading with the verdict."

Immediately, I could see the implications of Charles' proposal. It would hit with the public like a bombshell, dramatically alter corporate behavior, and elevate the Justice Syndicate from obscurity to a national stage overnight. It had the potential to strike fear into CEOs. Charles' proposal was brilliant.

By taking this action, the Justice Syndicate would come under attack. It would suffer the full force of the U.S. government. The FBI would open an investigation and there would be wire taps, 24-hour surveillance, and background checks into the lives of everyone involved.

In the end though, so long as Charles was extremely careful, and kept his and the behavior of the organization above board, an investigation would only serve to increase the Syndicate's notoriety.

The publicity would bring in some money, but Charles would need more, a lot more, to get this thing off the ground and keep it in the air. The government cut off Wiki Leaks' donations; without a war chest they would do the same to the Justice Syndicate.

Ray looked a little pale, frozen in place, with a half-smile that showed his upper teeth, making him look slack-jawed. To the other side of him, Laura tilted back her head and gave me a stare. Silently, we acknowledged our agreement with Charles' proposal, and then, with a tiny head nod she communicated her concern about Ray.

Right now, Ray was most likely wondering where he fit into Charles' plan. What would become of his group and his leadership of it? It was obvious to Laura and me that the First and Second would be disbanded and that Ray's, Laura's, and my participation in the Justice Syndicate would be deep in the background.

Ray's mouth started to move but it was clear he had not yet figured out how to put the words together to vocalize his dissent. He was silently mouthing the word "wait," and waiting himself until he could figure out a way to tell Charles no.

Laura was whispering in his ear, "This is exciting; we need to be a part of this," she said, but clearly it was not having the intended effect.

"No. I will not participate in this scheme," I said, loud enough to drown out anything Ray could have hoped to have stated. My disapproval sounded angry. "You want the three of us to play the heroes in your little game, take all the risk, and face all the danger. While you get in front of the cameras and expose these bastards with the information we steal."

Charles' normally serene and composed face began to crack. His eyebrows began to waver, crawled together, and dropped expressing a deep betrayal. Ray was no longer trying to speak. He looked at Charles and then back at me. I could see he'd been filled with a fierce protective desire.

Laura was furtively staring at me, an eyebrow raised to mark her skepticism.

"Don't you get it, Ray? He wants us to go out there, break into companies and steal information to prove they're guilty of crimes. Have no doubt, I have a long list of great target companies, but I'm not doing it," I shot to Charles before turning back to Ray. "He wants us to be soldiers in a war. He wants us to be on the frontlines of the revolution. I see what you are doing, Charles. I want no part of it. If you participate in this, Ray, you're going to get caught and you're going to go back to prison. If you're smart, you'll stick with your little clubhouse and kick Charles the fuck out. I'm done." I started to walk out.

"Wait," Ray said to my back.

There it is, I thought, but I did not stop walking.

CHAPTER SIXTEEN

I returned to my apartment, turned off my ringer, and bolted my door. It wasn't that I didn't believe Charles' plan could succeed. I'd put on a show for Ray because I needed an excuse to break away and disappear. If I wasn't for it, then there was a good chance Ray would get behind it.

He must have accepted the plan because Ray, Charles, and Laura blew up my phone in the first hour. In the second, Charles came, stood at my door and rang the bell—two short rings at first, followed by a series of long rings that adequately expressed his frustration. I left him standing at the door.

Charles was asking me to exchange my life as a day trader for the life of a corporate spy, completely unaware that I had already retired. I saw it as the choice between watching the stars from a yacht in the Mediterranean or standing on the roof of a skyscraper with a cold wind whipping around me while I eavesdropped on Fortune 500 companies. It didn't take a lot of thought.

Except that it did. Every year corporate America used its vast wealth to evade taxes, commit fraud, poison the environment, and generally manipulate the free market in ways that were destroying or had already destroyed the planet. The greatness that I'd always wanted for myself was not the kind that came with fame and fortune. It was the kind of greatness that was bestowed upon the Founding Fathers when they gave up monarchy and sacrificed some of their own personal power and wealth to found a new democracy. This is what I had been telling myself for years: that when the opportunity presented itself I was going to get on board, sacrifice myself, and serve the greater good.

This inflated sense of justice was the kind of mentality I had when I picked a knife fight with Ray's snitch: a willingness to sacrifice everything for that which I believed was just. Charles' plan did encompass what I believed was right. His plan resonated with me so deeply he could have snatched the idea from the recesses of my mind. The real, fundamental difference between all those years ago, when I drove my knife deep into the chest of Ray's snitch, and now was that back then I had nothing. It's easy to sacrifice everything, even your life, when you have nothing to lose. At the moment, and for the first time in my life, I had the freedom that vast wealth could buy.

On the second day Ray came by, rang the bell. I didn't answer. He rapped on the door. I ignored him. "Come on, man," he shouted. "You don't have to do it, okay. But I am; Laura is. I want your advice. I need your advice." That was hard to hear, because I really wanted to give my advice. "Kyle, I'm the last one to come by. If you're waiting for Laura she won't be coming; she said she wouldn't, that she's been down that road before." He then stood there silently for a minute, gave the door one solid thump, and said, "You know where to find us."

CHAPTER SEVENTEEN

I hired Valerie to put my condo on the market, but did not sleep with her. I took down my computers, with their four shiny screens, and sold my desk. I closed all of my trading accounts, turning my back on the toil which had, for years, yielded my sustenance. Finally, I packed off the few remaining possessions worth keeping. With the help of the agent, I dressed my condo and we waited for a cavalcade of potential buyers to walk through my door.

I was not there when the first couple came through. I returned home and the perfume of a stranger lingered in the air. The solitude I had associated with my home was now gone. I could no longer sleep there. It was time for me to put the past behind me and start my life over.

I checked into the downtown Monaco and tipped heavily to ensure I was treated to every luxury available. It seemed fitting that I should start early and discover if I had a threshold for comfort. I took massages, met with travel agents, and leisured in high-priced shops, inspecting goods which I could now easily purchase, but had no real desire to own. I read books, got started on a new language, and at night kept up my workouts.

On the second Thursday of my stay in the hotel, in the evening after my run, I took a walk through the park. I crossed the places where Charles and I had competed. I walked around the pond twice and settled on a park bench thirty feet from a tall, ornate park lamp. I stretched out on the bench, looked up at the sky, and regretted that the city lights blocked out nearly all the stars. In the morning I was roused by a police officer, who cautioned me against passing out in the park. I had not been drinking, but I did not argue with him. I made my way back to the hotel, showered, and felt better than I had in weeks. From then on, for every night I spent in the hotel I forced myself to spend a night outdoors on various benches around the city.

On the third week, I accepted an offer on the condo and was positively giddy about it. Released from my self-imposed prison, I was no longer a recluse and in no danger of returning to that state.

Maybe sleeping outside had been a way to balance the feeling that I didn't deserve this wealth, and the residual guilt I felt about not helping with the Justice Syndicate. However, I grew so accustomed to sleeping outside that I wanted my first trip to be a backpacking excursion around Europe. My plan was to rough it: walk, sleep outside, and spend as little as possible. The first night after the condo sold, I took a cab far out of town and slept under the open stars, free of the light pollution that usually obscured my view.

Tomorrow, I would book my flight and never look back.

The next morning I walked into the hotel, grinning widely. Dirt and grass stains marred my face and clothes. I smiled at the desk clerks, waved at the concierge, and considered for a moment the amount of talk generated the nights that I came in from sleeping in the streets. As the doors closed and the elevator began to move, I looked long and hard at myself in the silver reflection of the metal walls. Yep, I looked a mess. The laugh that emanated from my mouth was large and throaty; it bounced around the elevator, reverberating into my ear. I was still laughing as the elevator doors opened, my appearance startling the old blue-bloods waiting to board. I ignored them, walked casually to my room, and continued laughing until I was inside.

After a hot shower, I draped myself in one of the hotel's super soft cotton towels and opened my laptop, intending to book my flight. While checking my email I discovered a news alert related to Blake Donaldson.

> by Diana Holston
>
> Charleston, WV-- Eight year old Cassandra Clark was struck by a car and died today. The girl was trying to evade police, who had come to stop her from protesting at the offices of the River Energy Group. For months now, Cassie and her mother, Lucy Clark, have been standing faithfully outside the building to protest Blake Donaldson, former CEO of Massive Energy & Mining. The high-rise is the headquarters of Donaldson's new coal company, River Energy Group. Quietly holding signs, they have been a silent reminder of the Massive Energy mine disaster that took the life of Cassie's father and twenty-five other miners over two years ago.
>
> Three weeks ago, Lucy Clark accosted Mr. Donaldson as he left the building for lunch. A confrontation ensued. Mrs. Clark spat on Mr. Donaldson, who had her arrested. Cassie was placed in foster care, but frequently ran away to continue the protest started by her mother. Each time the police were called and Cassie was returned to her foster family. This time however, Cassie tried to run from the police, entered the street, and was struck by a car. No charges have been filed against the driver. The medical examiner believes Cassie died on impact.

Cassie and Lucy's image sprang to my mind and my heart leapt into my throat. I pounded my fist on the table, slammed the laptop, and successfully choked back tears. I sat stunned for a minute, and then realized Laura would have read this too. Laura! As fast as I could, I toweled off, got dressed, and called down to have a cab hailed.

The cab couldn't move fast enough. My anxiety was so conspicuous that more than once I caught the wrinkle-encircled eyes of the cabbie as he nervously starred through the rear-view mirror. At Ray's house, I left him waiting with the meter running and banged on the front door. When no one answered, I went round to the barn and found Charles and Ray huddled over the table, reviewing a mass of corporate documents. Their surprise at seeing me was dichotomous: Charles looked hopeful, while Ray appeared faintly annoyed.

"Where's Laura?" I asked, as plainly as I could. Ray answered without the faintest sign of comprehension.

"Did you try calling her? She left an hour ago to go shooting."

"What range?"

"Not sure; she took her Glock. I'm guessing she went to Brad's. What's going on?"

His blind ignorance heightened my annoyance with the relationship they shared. He did not know his girlfriend's character like I did. If Laura had read about Cassie, then she would be hurting. She would channel her pain into righteous indignation and then begin fishing around for baseball bats.

"A mutual friend just passed away. She and Laura were close. I need to tell her."

"Man that sucks. Come back when you are done, I want to show you some of this," Ray said, pointing to the paperwork.

Without acknowledging him, I turned and ran back to the cab. Twenty minutes later I found Laura's blue-and-red Mini parked in the lot of Brad's Barrels and Bullets. I paid the cabbie and went in to look for her.

Brad's wasn't a small gun shop; it was a gleaming firearms supercenter with ten salespeople on the floor at all times. Unlike other stores that mounted their guns to the walls and stored them in racks behind counters, Brad's was marked by a showroom of plush carpet upon which sat gleaming aluminum and granite display cases. Inside, the top guns rotated slowly, bathed in crisp, warm light. In this presentation the sculpted metal appeared fluid and alive, begging to be touched. But the smooth glass prevents and frustrates, leaving you longing. The agony is short-lived; in moments, a flirtatious and buxom saleswoman is at your side to take your credit card and give you satisfaction.

I walked past all of this, deeper into the store, where I was forced to snake through row upon row of shelves carrying every imaginable accessory. I pushed toward the back. Faintly, in the distance, I could hear the *pop, pop* of expanding gas expelling lead at high velocity.

At a small desk in the back sat a bored-looking teenager wearing the crooked nose seen so prominently on Brad in all his television commercials.

He examined my ID, handed it back to me, and then returned his attention to his cell phone. I hesitated, waiting to see if he would utter a syllable of approval. Rather than speaking, with a ring master's jerk of his wrist, he spread his palm and swept his arm in a showy gracious curve that waved me to the door behind him.

I ran down a full story of the stairs. The gunfire grew louder. On the landing, at a counter, I was met by heavyset woman who issued me eye and sound protection. Behind her was a door marked *Employees Only*. This floor was Brad's storage and gunsmith workshop. I continued down the stairs to the sub-basement.

The bottom of the stairs terminated at a door which opened onto a pleasant hallway leading in three directions. To the right was a traditional range where paper targets zipped forward and back while the shooters propped in little windows. Straight ahead led to "Brad's Town," a firearm test range on a mock city street where metal targets sprang up at practice shooters. To the left was a third range, a modern version of the test range that used a screen and digital projections to simulate every imaginable shooting circumstance.

I turned to the right, entered, and proceeded walking behind each of the shooters until I came to the end, where I found Laura in the process of emptying her entire clip rapidly into a paper target. On the stand next to her were four loaded clips and three plastic boxes holding a hundred and fifty reloaded rounds. Down the range, Laura's paper target, a black silhouette on white paper, was decimated. As she emptied her clip, the bottom half of the target fell to the ground. She did not retrieve the target to attach a fresh one. Without moving her head she removed her clip, laid it on the stand, and reached for another. As her fingers curled around it, I placed my hand over hers. Startled, she swung around and in the last second thought to lower her weapon. Anger brought out the lines in her forehead. Her jaw was tight, her teeth slightly bared. Through our safety glasses she looked at my eyes, put the gun down, and welcomed me as I pulled her into an embrace. I held her until her body relaxed into mine and then led her out of the range, leaving the bullets behind.

Outside, I escorted her into the passenger seat of her car and then drove us away. Just as we pulled onto the street our phones beeped simultaneously. Laura pulled hers out and gasped at the message, then buried her face in her hands.

"What is it? Tell me!"

Laura struggled to form the words. "Lucy," she said, "Lucy... in jail, just hanged herself." Laura began to pound furiously on the dash. "I'm going to kill him; I'm going to fucking *kill* Donaldson." There was no doubt. Laura would kill him, and if I didn't intervene, she would walk right up to him on the street, put her Glock under his chin, and pull the trigger in broad daylight.

"Pull over, pull the fuck over now!" she thundered.

I pulled the car off to a side street beside an empty field. Laura jumped out of the car and stomped off into the field. I got out and followed her.

"Do you hear me Donaldson? I'm coming for you! I'm going to kill you, motherfucker!" She screamed so loud I feared someone would hear us, though the nearby traffic from the highway was more than enough to drown it out. I walked up to her.

"Laura, I'll help. We'll do it together, but we'll do it right." She stopped and looked at me as if seeing a different person.

She knew that if I say I'm going to do something, I do it. I would take this stand, commit this crime for her, because despite my best efforts I loved her.

She reached out, grasped my hand, and we kissed. She poured passion into that kiss that I hadn't felt since we were together. It made me feel weak. I felt vulnerable, because no matter what she may have been feeling for me in that moment, she was still with Ray. I pulled back from the kiss, ran my fingers along her bangs and down her cheek.

"If we want to really make this count, we need Charles and Ray," I said.

She nodded her understanding, gave me a hug, and we walked back to the car.

CHAPTER EIGHTEEN

"We have to go into hiding," I said to Charles. "I'm going separately from Ray and Laura."

Charles nodded in agreement as the four of us sat around the table in the barn. He was unaware that Laura and I planned to kill Donaldson. Sitting just to the left of him was Ray, who didn't know either. We'd agreed to keep this secret until the time was right, so that there would be no objections until it was too late.

It was two days ago that Laura and I had kissed. The emotion of that moment had begun to subside, replaced by a new, profound secret. Once Donaldson was dispatched, Laura and I would be bound together in a new kind of intimacy. Ever since that kiss, I desperately wanted to make love to her. I was frequently reaching into my pockets, shifting to hide my erection. It didn't help that I would catch her looking at me, or that she gave me little touches on the arm or shoulder when no one was paying attention. This secret had invisible tendrils that reached out, curled around us, and pulsated until we resonated in unison. My frustration was made worse by the fact that Laura didn't seem to pull away from Ray at all.

The plan was that I would fly to New York, hire an agent to begin the search for an apartment, and then leave for Europe. The First and Second was over; some of those members would be chosen to join the Justice Syndicate. Ray and Laura would travel the country, on the pretext of drumming up support for the new group. They would ultimately go to L.A. to establish a safe house and new identities, just as I would do in New York.

Charles would go Chicago and open the official office for the Justice Syndicate, build the court room, and establish the website. He would then choose and prep a jury.

"We're going to need to raise a lot of funds," Charles said. "Once my face and the faces of those in our courtroom appear on camera, our livelihoods will be in jeopardy."

"There will be plenty of money," I said. "I've created several accounts and dispersed funds into them. Some of these accounts will be for the surveillance operations, the rest are for the Justice Syndicate."

"How much money?" Charles asked, perplexed.

Everyone stopped to look at me.

"About fifty million," I said.

Mouths hung agape. Ray stood up, his chair falling backward. His voice rising in volume to display his anger, "Where the hell did you get that kind of money?"

Laura's ears jumped back behind the faintest smile.

"Blake Donaldson."

"I knew it. When? When did that happen?" Ray's face flushed crimson.

"It happened while we were in Charleston."

"And you've been sitting on this money the whole fucking time. You didn't tell us and you didn't give us a cut."

Laura said, "That's because the right thing to do was to give it to the group now. That's the way it should be used." She stood and picked up Ray's chair. "Honey, sit. We've talked about this, everything changes now."

Ray turned on her, "You knew about this?"

Laura raised her voice slightly, "No, I didn't, but since it's not about me and what I get or don't get, I'm not upset about it. This is our operation, yours and mine, an outgrowth of everything we've worked for all of these years. We are lucky to have Kyle. With this money the only excuse we have for failure is our egos. Please. Sit. Down."

Ray sat down. He glared at me with that look of betrayal he'd had when he'd gotten out of prison and discovered I'd not invested his share of the diamonds. Charles immediately adjusted to the situation.

"This will accelerate all our plans," he said, his steady hopeful voice bringing calm to the room.

"Once we split, there can be no unsecured communication between our cell and the group, "I said." Charles, it was my hope that you would set up multiple levels of secure communication. I will establish old-school drops around the city. If there is ever a failure of one communication system we can resort to the other."

"I can do that," Charles eagerly replied.

Laura had a hand on Ray, again trying to soothe him. Did she ever used to do that with me? No, I don't think so, and of course, that thought spurned a fresh batch of conflicted emotions. My desire for her left me feeling out of control, a feeling I once enjoyed when we were together as it meant my passion for her was so large it couldn't be contained. Now it left me feeling weak and shamefaced and had me making unfair comparisons between the ways she loved us.

Ray was bleeding animosity. He started terse, heard himself, and then softened his sentence at the end. "How are these communication systems going to work?"

Now, more than ever, I wanted him out of the picture and I had to stop my mind from drifting off to plan ways to do it. Instead, I rationalized. When I signed up to go underground, I made a firm commitment. I wanted Laura, but not at the price of jeopardizing our goal. Besides, was a relationship between us really worth having if she didn't eventually choose me over him?

"Once the Justice Department gets wind of us, they are going to try and invade every computer and phone system we have," Charles said, "We need to anticipate that intrusion right from the beginning. We'll need a cache of burner phones and separate computers in another building that are not part of the Justice Syndicate. If they don't know a network exists, then they can't hack it. Additionally, we can use steganography and hide messages on public web pages, like dating sites."

Ray seemed satisfied by Charles' answer, perhaps because he wasn't really invested in the question.

"We will have our own assets," I said to Laura and Ray. "Ten million each. If push comes to shove we can operate as independent cells and have enough funds to recruit new members. We will stay together as long as we can, but in the end our mission must come first."

I was looking at Charles and Laura, but watching Ray through my peripheral vision. His shoulders dropped and the tension left his body. It dawned on him that he was going to have complete control over more money than he'd ever expected to see in his life.

"We need to hit the rifle range as much as possible before we separate," Laura said. "Whenever we break in, one of us has to always remain at a distance and cover the other two."

"I'll buy the weapons," Ray added, "We'll need some expensive, high-end rifles."

Ray sounded as if he'd been coveting the opportunity to purchase expensive guns for a long time. No one complained at his suggestion and from then on Ray dropped his animosity and began to act as if he were an equal partner in our endeavors.

Two months had passed since the four of us met in the barn. Since then, I'd checked out of the Monaco and into a less-expensive hotel closer to the airport. It was neat and clean, but nowhere near as luxurious. I returned from lunch, entered my room, and found Laura lounging on the bed.

"How the hell did you get in here? You need a card just to get up the elevator."

Laura smiled deviously. "I've been practicing in secret. First on traditional locks and just recently I got this." She held up a small device about the size of a cell phone, with a key card attached to a ribbon cable.

She stood and danced in a little circle. "I can get in anywhere," she sung. She was in an unusually playful mood. I couldn't remember her ever being this giddy.

"You're not supposed to be here. We have a plan."

Laura sat the card machine on the table and sidled up to me. "That plan doesn't start until you get on that plane." She ran the flat of her hand on my shoulder and across my back. "Everything changes tomorrow." She came around the front of me, put her arm around, and kissed me. I did not resist.

Both her hands found me and pulled me close. Then they were under my shirt, her fingers finding and pushing down on the muscles in my back. I felt a familiar melting sensation and suddenly didn't know where her hands were. She still knew all the right places to touch me. Each kiss seemed more passionate then the last.

Every backward step was telling me that she wanted me. She pulled us toward the bed.

"You smell a little like gun powder. It's kind of hot," she said.

I'd met Ray at the range before we went to lunch. He'd insisted I fire a few rounds from his latest gun. We'd been going to lunch at my invitation because I wanted Ray to be ready. I needed to know where his mind was going to be when we finally told him about the plan to kill Donaldson.

Laura began unbuttoning her blouse. She smiled at me hungrily. I found myself wondering, when was the last time she smiled that way at Ray? When was the last time she made love to him? Her hands were on the second button and not on me. I pulled back.

"Stop. I'm not doing this."

She offered me a sad look. "What's wrong?"

"I'm still in love with you. I never stopped being in love with you."

She came close to me, gave me a hug, and put her hand behind my head with her thumb on my cheek.

"I love you, too," she said.

"No, no, don't say that. Not like this. If you did, you wouldn't still be with Ray. You'd be with me."

"Can't I love you both?"

"Don't! Don't start acting like you and Ray have been in some open *fucking* relationship all these years, because I know that's not true."

Laura reached down and put her hand on my crotch.

"Why can't you just enjoy the moment? Why can't you just do what we both want to do?"

"Because, you left me and then you chose my best friend over me..."

"No, it wasn't over you," she shouted, "It was never over you." She looked genuinely hurt. "It didn't start like that at all. We were friends; we wrote to each other. Ray needed me."

"I needed you!"

"No, you were trapped. You couldn't get past what you'd been through."

"Yes, trapped where you left me—in that cage."

"I tried, Kyle. You know I tried. You said so yourself: when you got the condo, you became a recluse. The only reason you left was because you started doing parkour. You had to find your own way out."

"I'm out now. So is that what this is? You're leaving Ray and coming back to me?"

"No, I don't know what I'm doing. I just want you. I need you."

"I want you too, but after—I'll need you more and you won't be there. Then I'll have to relive how lonely and abandoned I felt the first time you left me. And while I'm in pain, you'll be at home in bed with Ray."

"I'm sorry. I didn't come here to hurt you," she said.

"I know, but it still hurts."

Her eyes were moist. My anger was losing the battle to keep myself from crying. I grabbed her and pulled her into a kiss.

I hated myself for not making love to her. Isn't that what a normal man would do, take what was offered? I couldn't do that; she was right, I wasn't normal. I was the fatalistic recluse, who only left the comfort of his building for the chance to fall to his death jumping off buildings.

I walked her to the door, put her back to it, and kissed her again.

"I'm sorry, I love you and if you can ever love me back the way you used to I want us to be together. Otherwise, let's stick to the plan."

"Stick to the plan," she repeated distantly, and then with sweet insistence said, "Please, just for now. One more time, can we please pretend that it's like it was? I do love you." She looked into my eyes, washed away all her disappointment and said it again, "Kyle, I love you." It was very convincing. "I need you. Please, I need... only you can do this for me."

I don't know if she meant it, or if she was trying to be manipulative, but her words crushed me. They made me feel weak and needy and reminded me that when I feel vulnerable, I'm going to get hurt.

"I'm sorry," I said, then pushed her out the door.

CHAPTER NINETEEN

I was on the plane back to New York when the Justice Syndicate issued its sentence on Blake Donaldson. Justicesyndicate.org published all the evidence of Donaldson's crimes, touching video biographies of the victims of the mine disaster, and video of the mock court proceedings that played out like a thrilling courtroom drama. It garnered ten million views in the first twenty-four hours.

The judgment led the news on every network and in every paper. Charles had been opposed to my idea, but with this verdict he'd given me a clear answer.

Our last meeting occurred months ago, after another race through the park. We stood on the bridge and looked out over the river. Though the water was low, it moved rather forcefully over the large, round stones lining the bottom. They were too large and perfectly placed to be natural.

I had in mind to lead the conversation, but he beat me to the punch.

"I've been thinking about the separation. Ultimately, the three of you will have one another to confide in, but I will be left alone bearing this secret. I've decided that I need to have a confidant, someone I trust implicitly."

"Who do you have in mind?"

"Katrina Varma. She's already the CPA for the Justice Syndicate."

I looked Charles over carefully. Katrina was the attractive Indian woman who, like Charles, looked so out of place on the first day I encountered the First and the Second. He wanted to let her in on the fact that Ray, Laura, and I would be breaking into these companies and feeding Charles the data we stole.

"Do you have a romantic relationship with her?"

Charles laughed. "No, I don't think it would be a good idea to mix business. However, she seemed heartbroken that you disappeared so quickly. She has quite a crush on you."

I agreed that the burden was great. Charles might be able to trust Katrina initially, but would she stay loyal after we began executions? If I didn't give in to his request, he might tell her anyway. However, if I relented, I could give a little and perhaps get a little back in return.

"If you are wrong about her loyalty, she could implicate you."

"I know," Charles said, his tone unwavering.

"I agree, on one condition."

"Name it."

"Don't tell her that we have a two-way communication system. Let her think that all the information you have obtained came after we disappeared. Create some plausible deniability for yourself until she has proven her loyalty."

"Agreed."

His shoulders relaxed and he took several happy breaths, unaware I was about to burden him again.

"What happens after you find Donaldson guilty?" I asked.

"We'll put up the video of the trial, the evidence, and send out press releases."

"Are you willing to do everything possible to guarantee this story gains traction?" I challenged.

Charles had been looking over the side at the water. Now, he turned to me. "What are you getting at?"

"Just declaring them guilty isn't going to be enough."

"It's going to draw attention to the data you recovered," he insisted.

"It won't. You'll be just like Wiki Leaks. After a while interest will dissipate. We will create some shame for these CEOs, but then they'll band together and attack. You have to hit them harder."

Charles looked as if I'd stepped on his puppy.

"What's going on? I thought you were on board, are you backing out?" He kicked his heel against the railing of the bridge.

"You need something explosive."

"Like what?" he asked.

"You must always issue the same penalty," I said.

"I have no power to impose a penalty. What penalty would I impose?"

"You have no power to *carry out* a penalty," I clarified.

Exasperated, Charles raised both his hands.

"Death," I said as firmly as possible. "You have to issue a penalty of death."

"What?"

I stood there staring at him.

"What happens when someone, based on my verdict, kills one of these guys?"

"You won't be responsible," I soothed.

"I can't do that. Someone will murder one of them."

"And when they do, it will scare the shit out of every other CEO whose fingers are dripping with blood."

"Look, I see what you're saying. I understand we need the impact, but there has got to be another way."

"It doesn't matter if there is another way. This is what must happen. If you want this to work you have to issue a death sentence, every time."

"And the first time someone dies—"

"You will not be at fault. More importantly, you will be feared. The Justice Syndicate will be known internationally. When you go in front of the cameras to draw attention to corporate misdeeds, people will listen. If you use it sparingly, and with great discretion, you will have more power than you can imagine."

Charles rested his elbows on the wall and hung back his head. He was mulling over the potential. A thought came to him. He straightened up until we stood eye to eye.

"You seem pretty sure," he said.

I didn't reply.

"And if I don't issue a death sentence?"

"You have to," I commanded.

"But, if I don't?"

I paused, but did not break eye contact. Instead I leaned in, "If you don't—you will miss an opportunity."

Charles did not break away. Slowly, it dawned on him. "Are you saying...?"

"I'm saying that you will forever be on the defensive, so instead be proactive."

Those were the last words we had said to one another. We stood eye-to-eye for a few minutes and then nodded that we understood one another, even if we didn't agree. Then he turned and walked away.

I'd left it up to Charles to make the right decision, and he did. Phase one was complete, Donaldson's crimes were now public knowledge. The news organizations had a headline they could lead with, and now the threat of death hung over Donaldson. No one in the media wanted to talk about the potential for the sentence to be carried out. They didn't air an interview with Donaldson about it. Instead, they rushed to hear what Charles had to say.

Charles had chosen an old bank as the location of the Justice Syndicate. From the outside, large steps led up to doors between rough concrete pillars. Inside, the lobby floor was made up of green marbled tile and surrounded by granite walls. The lobby led to two ten-foot-high, wooden doors that opened onto the main floor of the bank. Charles had converted that main area into the courtroom.

He walked into the lobby, put his back to the wooden doors, and held a worldwide press conference. The podium in front of him was dripping with cables, filled with the microphones of all the major news organizations.

He wore a white suit which, against the dark wood and with his blond hair, made him look angelic. There was a commotion as the press surged forward, simultaneously shouting out questions. If Charles was unnerved by the thought that hundreds of millions of eyeballs were watching his every move, he didn't show it. He appeared serene, solemn, and nearly presidential as he looked around at the journalists. He smiled, nodding his head here and there, giving the impression that he knew these people and had been friendly with them before. The crowd calmed down and hands went up. Charles looked into the cameras and introduced himself.

"My name is Charles Reid. I am the Chief Executive Officer of the Justice Syndicate. The Justice Syndicate is a not-for-profit journalistic organization, dedicated to stopping the rise of corporate control; manipulation; the degradation of our government, laws, and individual freedoms. We do this by exposing corporate criminal activity. Our focus is on those businesses whose officers have used money and power to manipulate our government and avoid prosecution for their crimes.

"You are here today because the Justice Syndicate has found Blake Donaldson, formerly of Massive Energy & Mining, guilty of willfully directing the manipulation of safety protocols, ordering the payoff of government inspectors, and using his money and influence to avoid prosecution. These crimes led to the direct death of twenty-six individuals. We have demonstrated that Mr. Donaldson knew of the risk to human life and was willing to sacrifice those lives for his own personal gain. Having been found guilty, we issue a sentence of death and declare Blake Donaldson an outlaw. He should consider himself stripped of the protection of law: without rights, privileges, or recourse of any kind."

Charles paused and this caused another tremendous surge. So many questions were shouted out simultaneously the words were unintelligible as they came across the television. They must have been clear to Charles, because he pointed and selected a member of the press.

"Do you sincerely believe you have the power to issue judgment against anyone? Aren't you operating outside of the law as well?"

I could not see where the journalist was standing. Given the tilt of

Charles' head, I suspect he was close to the front.

"We are exercising a right of free speech, in a format that presents the facts to the world in a familiar setting. We are not breaking any laws by doing so and our decisions, like the government, have only the force the people give to them."

"You've ordered a death sentence against Blake Donaldson," said another unseen journalist. Her voice was firm and commanding. "Are you advocating murder?"

Charles was completely unruffled, firm in his response, and spoke without hesitation.

"We are saying that the crimes committed by Blake Donaldson warrant a death penalty. There will be additional trials and other companies found guilty. The sentence issued against Donaldson is a warning to executives of corporations everywhere: Stop your companies' unlawful activities immediately, divest yourselves of the individuals who have committed crimes and turn over to federal prosecutors all evidence of wrongdoing. If you do not do this, then count on that evidence finding its way here, where you will be exposed to the world and held liable by the public trust."

A deep raspy voice shouted out: "The FBI is reportedly investigating the theft of the information you've posted on the Justice Syndicate's website. How did you come by this information?"

"Last year, I began putting out requests for information on corporate crime, and eventually those seeds bore fruit. The information was provided anonymously, via a secure, encrypted data transfer."

"How can you establish a chain of custody for this evidence? Aren't your actions interfering with prosecuting him?"

"Blake Donaldson used his wealth to subvert the legal system; prior to our actions, he was walking around without shame. Anyone doing business with this man should be considered aiding and abetting a fugitive of justice."

Charles was a natural. This was working out better than I could have imagined. What had, just months ago, began with my attempts to reclaim Laura had turned into a thousand little actions that now formed a giant wave about to rain down on the world. I smiled and turned away from the screen.

I had not heard from Laura since our last meeting at the hotel. I'd had some brief communications from Ray. We would all be meeting up in New York in four weeks. I'd sent a message to Laura after I learned that Blake Donaldson had requested and been denied police protection. That was good news: it meant Donaldson was scared and undefended.

I'd hoped Laura would respond with some modicum of emotion, but she did not respond at all. She was sticking to the plan, and I couldn't fault her for that. Her silence probably meant that she had shaken off her foolish desire and fully recommitted to Ray.

I struggled with regret. I asked myself what would have happened if I'd made love to her. Would she have left Ray, or would she have gotten her itch scratched, and then decided she was over me? In my mind, I played out the fantasy that we did make love, that she was reminded of how well we work together, and that she left Ray to build a life with me.

Then, I remind myself that was a fantasy, reversed direction, and tried to accept reality. *We don't really work that well together, or if we do, it's impossible to tell because we just aren't the same kids we were all those years ago.*

I found solace in the fact that there was a greater cause afoot. What we were doing was going to change the world. Focusing my thoughts on the many missions ahead helped pull me away from my regrets.

Kyle had been lost backpacking in Europe. I was traveling under a new name. It was Jason Kohn who sat on the plane. When the seatbelt light came on, it was he and not I who, prepared for the descent into JFK. I took one last look out the window at the ocean below. The name was part of a bigger identity I'd been allowing to wash into and seep over everything.

I was now a revolutionary. I was highly organized and equipped to do the job that our government and legal system had failed to do. I was prepared to risk my own life for a cause greater than myself. I had no delusions: my actions would make me an outcast. If there were people who cheered what I would do, their voices would be small, drowned out by the public condemnation.

In the time I'd been out of county, I'd done parkour in London, Berlin, and Paris, and added rock climbing in the Alps to my repertoire of skills. I'd highlighted our next few targets and done as much background research as I could do at a distance. Once I'd settled into the new place in Brooklyn, I'd continue that research before meeting up with Laura and Ray.

CHAPTER TWENTY

Hochberg's CEO was Felix Chang. He came from a family of Englishmen who made their home in Hong Kong a hundred years ago. In the second generation the family picked up the Chang name. Future descendants kept the Chang name, but sent their children back to England for their education and to find their wives and husbands.

Chang, who grew up in Hong Kong, bore no resemblance to a man of Chinese descent. He was exceedingly tall, with pale freckled skin and alarmingly bright red hair. As a Young Turk with a degree in Chemistry, he began working in Hochberg's Hong Kong lab and just five years later was appointed head of the entire Asian division. Three years after that, he was appointed President of Hochberg Industries and moved to Ohio, home of their corporate offices.

Chang immediately sold off the company's chemical division, with the exception of its agri-chem business. Abandoning his own area of expertise he pushed the company, kicking and screaming, into biotech. Since then, Hochberg International had been on the forefront of genetically modified organisms. While the company liked to create the impression that its strains made for larger, better-tasting, and more durable fruits and vegetables, from a standpoint of edibility, Hochberg's products were identical to its unmodified counterparts. The only functional difference is that Hochberg's plants are engineered to resist the company's blend of chemical pesticides.

Chang drove Hochberg's profits into the billions while fighting back hard and smart against a rising tide of opposition to GMOs. He spent millions to turn back the effort to label genetically modified foods in half a dozen states, most notably California. He spent millions more on PR firms and government lobbyists.

When Hochberg's seeds blew (or were deliberately seeded) onto the farms of those who refused to buy it, Chang sued the small farmers out of business. Hochberg then swooped in and bought their land.

While Chang's fortunes were rising with Hochberg's, so were international complaints against the company. In Indonesia, Africa, and South America the company was fined between $1.5 million and $2 million for each of the eight different times it was caught paying bribes to government officials. The bribery scandal was most egregious in the Asian Pacific region, Chang's former domain. Four years after the bribery charges were settled, the company's CFO was implicated in a scheme to spend $150 million, much of it cash, as "trade incentives," the latest clever name for the company's continuing bribery efforts.

As pressure in the U.S. mounted, Hochberg poured money into its Washington lobbying efforts. When the farm subsidies bill rolled around for a renewal vote in Congress the company managed to get several profitable changes made to protect its products from disclosure to consumers. It was widely believed that Hochberg planned to use the provision to claim it was exempt from any GMO labeling laws.

When it was discovered that one of Hochberg's laboratories tossed discontinued strains of modified seeds into the wild, and that these strains had now become invasive, their efforts in Washington redoubled. In the dead of night the company managed to sneak a rider onto a Health and Human Services bill that made it immune from prosecution over the invasive seeds. The rider preserved the company's right to sue any farmer who knowingly chose to grow those seeds. It did nothing to protect farmers whose farms were accidently seeded by a neighbor's crops or by natural fertilization from wind, birds, or other animals carrying seeds.

Within legal circles, it was widely believed that there was a deeper purpose to both the rider and the agricultural bill: when taken together, they functioned like a two-part law. What Hochberg was really trying to avoid were lawsuits directly related to poisonings and deaths from Pestix, its signature pesticide. Due to better blood testing protocols, the number of deaths allegedly caused by Pestix jumped overnight from three to four thousand around the globe; more, in the range of tens of thousands, were expected to come forward.

Data about Hochberg lined my walls. Next to the CEO and executive's faces I placed maps, photos, and listings of personal property. Then, to get ahead of the curve, I started to work on our third target company.

CHAPTER TWENTY-ONE

"We've been broken up over six months now," Ray joked. Laura rolled her eyes. Part of their cover was convincing their friends at home that they'd split up. They told this story to create distance between Charles and the Justice Syndicate and to explain why Ray was never coming back to resume leadership of the First and the Second. The main theme of this lie was that, while on the road, Laura and Ray got into a fight in which Ray punched Laura. A few of their friends knew that Ray was a former con, so when that detail was thrown in with the aside that they'd, "been having problems for years," most found it believable, even if they didn't want to admit it.

Their friends were told the police had been called, but that Ray, not wanting to return to jail, had left before they arrived. Laura had gone off to live with a relative, and Ray had left the country and gone off-grid. This story was made even more believable when Ray, without returning home, liquidated his house and business.

"So Kyle—later, let's you and I hit the bars." Ray looked at Laura for a reaction. She gave him none. Ray laughed it off before turning back to me.

I had sympathy for Ray. After prison he'd spent many years rehabilitating his reputation, only to willingly trash it for our cause. Of the three of us, he had it hardest. I was already a recluse with few ties to cut, and, among their friends, Laura got to play the victim. It was understandable that he'd be bitter about it, and surprising that Laura made no attempts to comfort him.

We were all sitting in the kitchen–all dark wood, white tile floors, and light granite countertops. I had a big silver pot on the stove filled with hot soup and had loaded them both up with generous helpings. The two of them—with new identities in place—had flown to Washington, D.C., and then driven non-stop to New York City.

I'd been planning for their arrival: the house was furnished, the fridge stocked. While it had been tempting to cut corners and save money, I chose to go the other way. In case we ever had to go on the lam, I thought it best we enjoy comfort and style for as long as possible.

"This is a nice place," Ray said, trying to distract from Laura's apparent indifference. "I'm hoping you have some comfortable beds."

Laura, aside from casually greeting me when they arrived, had not said a word throughout the meal.

"Nothing but the best. You two are in the room at the top, to the right of the stairs." Ray shot Laura a concerned look which she saw, but did not acknowledge. "I'm sure you guys are beat. After you're done eating why don't you get some rest? We can go over my research in the morning. I've set up a planning room in the basement."

"That sounds great," Ray replied, and then added, "Have you done another board?"

I nodded, "Two."

"Well, if you don't mind I'd like to wander down and take a quick look; you can brief us in the morning."

"The basement door is under the stairs."

Ray quietly stood and walked off in the direction of the basement, leaving me alone with Laura in the kitchen. Laura returned to eating her soup. She did not make eye contact with me.

Ray and Laura looked very different from when last I saw them. Ray had shaved his sideburns, lost the hat and the wallet chain, and shortened his hair. Laura was leaner and had added some definition to her arms. They were dressed in plain, quality clothes of muted colors. Both had hats and sunglasses when they came in, though they seemed genuinely glad to get rid of them as soon as they came through the door.

"Where's the doorknob?" Ray shouted from the foyer.

"You see the outline? Push on the left side: it's a spring catch." I could hear the little latch click as Ray pushed open the flush panel door.

"Cool," Ray shouted back. "Did you have this put in?"

"No. It's a fun touch, but too visible to be a secret door." I could hear Ray enter, close the latch behind him, and start to descend the stairs.

I stared at Laura, but she kept her head down.

"Is there something you want to say?" I asked her. She looked up for a moment, wearing a bit of a scowl, and then put her head back down.

"No," she said in a disconsolate tone.

I pushed myself away from the sink and started walking to the door. As I went to pass her, she looked up again and spoke.

"I'm ready," she said.

My mind immediately jumped to, *Ready for us to be a couple*? I did my best to hide my thoughts.

"Donaldson," she clarified.

"I know," I replied, then left the room and went down to the basement to check in with Ray. Downstairs, I found Ray scouring over each of the printouts hanging from the wall. He glanced at me as I came down the stairs. I came and stood beside him.

135

"Is everything okay between you and Laura? She doesn't seem her usual self."

Ray straightened his back and looked at me closely. Then he went to sit on one of the overstuffed leather chairs in the center of the room.

"As soon as we got to L.A. she started working out every day, and after a week of that, she started harping on me to get in better shape. You know, I wasn't in bad shape. She demanded we hit the gym every day, but I drew the line at three to four times a week. That didn't make her happy, but it got her off my back."

His tone suggested that he wasn't bothered by this change in her demeanor, but I suspected it was far worse than he was letting on.

"I've never seen her so intense," Ray continued. "I think she's just been putting pressure on herself to be ready for anything. She does much better with clear, defined goals; once we start the mission she'll be fine."

I felt the momentary temptation to blame Ray. He and Laura had been together long enough that he should know her better. I knew Laura well, not so much for the time we spent together as for the time we spent apart. Having played our relationship together over and over in my head gave me a unique perspective on her that he couldn't hope to match. He shouldn't be expected to know that what was eating her up was being denied the justice she desired.

"Have you been doing any running?" I asked.

"I try to squeeze in a nine-mile run, three times a week."

"Great, you can come running with me in the morning."

"Oh, no, I'm not running with you, pal. You do all that crazy parkour shit."

"How about this: let's do a light three miles together. That will be enough of a warm-up for me and then I'll pull off and hit a course. You can finish your run and we'll meet back here."

Ray smiled. "Alright, I have to keep reminding myself it's not a contest," he said. "It's just being fit."

"Exactly!"

The following morning Ray and I left the house at a talking pace. We turned right at the river and kept Manhattan on our left as we jogged north.

"I stayed up last night researching Hochberg and Erhart," Ray said. "You know, for years I've known these were bad companies. Stuff used to fly by on Facebook and every now and again I would repost some of those articles. When you're living life, it's easy to focus on all the stuff in front of you that you think you have control over. These companies and their CEOs are horrible people.

"The whole time I was reading, I kept pinching myself. It's surreal. I stared out the window at the city and I thought—*this is it. We are going to change the world.*

"Kyle, I'm sorry for what I said. If I'd gotten my hands on the money I would have probably just built a castle, gone off-grid, and waited for Armageddon. I guess, what I'm really trying to say is, thank you for having the vision to make this a reality. I would rather spend my life making a real difference than hiding out."

"I can't take back the money. You still have more than enough to build a castle," I chided.

"Come on, you know I'm never going to pull out on you guys."

"As long as you keep your silence, no matter what, I would understand," I said, in a plain, even tone. "Any one of us must be free to walk way. How else are we going to maintain trust? There has to be an out if things get too intense."

"I'll bail when you bail." We jogged a little more in silence and then Ray flashed a big, toothy grin, and quipped, "Of course if Laura doesn't get her head together, I just might bolt and leave her with you."

For the next two miles we jogged at a steady pace and then stopped at the edge of my course. I pulled my gloves from my pocket and slipped them onto my hands.

"Do those gloves last long?" Ray asked.

"About as long as a good pair of shoes under hard use; maybe six months if I'm lucky." Ray nodded as if this were valuable information. "Are you headed back?" Ray had his phone out and was looking at a map.

"No, I'm just going to count that as a warm-up and still do nine. It will take me about an hour and a half, and then I'll catch you back at the house."

He looked up at me. I was standing by an old drain pipe. "Where is your course?" I pointed up and his eyes got wide. "You're going up *that*?"

I nodded, smiled deviously, and grabbed the pipe with both hands. I hopped up, placing my feet on the wall with the pipe between my legs, and scurried to the top of the building. From the roof, I looked down over the side at Ray.

"You're going to teach me that sometime, right?" Ray shouted, and then suddenly covered his mouth, afraid he would draw attention. I waved and disappeared from his view.

Before me were the tops of buildings as far as the eye could see. On the ground were the familiar spray-painted arrows pointing my direction. I didn't really need them. I'd run this course before; it was a favorite of mine. The creators of this course had gone to great lengths to span distances that were too far for any human to jump. Between buildings that crossed city streets they built narrow bridges and designed them to be obscured from people on the ground. At one junction they built a suspension bridge whose roadway was made of two-by-fours laid out end to end. They made sure to carefully place the bridge above clotheslines, power cables, and water pipes so that from the street you had to peer very carefully to even know it was there.

At another location, they welded a metal bottom to the legs of a mini-trampoline, and painted it with sky and shadows to camouflage it from the street. It sat suspended in the middle of an alleyway. The idea was to jump down onto it and bounce to the next building. The bottom provided a nice safety mechanism in case the trampoline ever broke.

I flipped, tightroped, and walked up walls. Each step filled me with joy. There were some in the parkour community who chided this route for its build-out. To them it wasn't authentic because it wasn't a truly natural, found route. They mockingly called it the Circus route because at one point it had a sort of hard trapeze: hard because instead of ropes it had pipes that attached to a gear at the top, so it automatically returned to its original position for the next runner.

I disagreed with the critics: since all urban environments are built and always changing, there are no truly "found" routes. Besides, this route was really fun! It made me feel like a kid. That it was abhorred by purists was a bonus: it usually meant fewer assholes crowding up the route. Today, I had it all to myself.

When I first got to New York my time on this course was twenty minutes; I'd shaved it down by five. I could complete it in fifteen minutes and be home two minutes after that. From the start, it had been my plan to get Ray out of the house so that I could get back to Laura. If in the process I could break my previous time all the better.

Another feature I loved about this route was that the final roofline passed by the house; it let me get a quick view of the front street. Then it took me directly behind the townhome, giving me a full view of the back of the house: if someone was watching the house or already inside, I could see everything. It made me feel safe and helped keep my stress levels down.

On this particular day, the "everything" that I saw was Laura. I slid to a stop, only momentarily lamenting blowing my record time. She exited the bathroom and threw off her towel, unknowingly showing off her naked body to me. Laura was far more toned and fit then I'd imagined. My attraction to her grew at the discovery of these new dimensions.

Having rebuilt my own body, I appreciated the dedication she had poured into hers. I found her self-discipline arousing. For all her muscle, she had not eradicated the beautiful curves of her body. Even at a distance I could see her strength. Laura checked herself in the mirror, turned toward the window, and then as if cued by my thoughts, performed a handstand and split her legs. My eye followed the line of her calves, up those beautiful hamstrings and onto her glutes.

I was entranced, and all the while I was watching, I was walking toward her. If she propositioned me again, it was unlikely I'd have the fortitude to resist.

That's when I started to fall.

I'd walked right to the edge of the building and tripped. Below was a six-story drop onto hard pavement or my choice of two cars, a painful-looking fence, and a couple of dumpsters. Surviving such a fall would mean a life of incapability.

It happened in hundredths of a second. The immediacy of fear was crushing. I felt a startling moment of imminent death. Then my reflexes took over. I'm glad no one observed what happened next. My arms flew out and my body wavered in what I'm sure was a half-second of pure physical comedy. There was no stopping myself. I was going over.

I regained my senses before the inevitable. Before my feet left the ground, I got just enough kick with my toes to roll me in toward the building. I extended my right arm and caught the top of the roof with my fingertips then held on for dear life. My feet flew off the roof and swung out. They circled out, down, and hard into the wall with a smack. My face hit the old brick building, scratching off skin and leaving a painful abrasion. The force of my body thudding into the side nearly tore my fingers from their thin hold and sent me into an absolute panic. In a desperate scramble I struggled to extend my other arm, but my body was not done. It bounced. I foolishly pushed with my toes, and my body swung like a chaotic pendulum.

On the second back swing I got my other arm on the ledge and refastened my grip with the first hand. I pulled myself onto the roof, where I lay face up and unmoving until my red-faced shame faded away and my breathing returned to normal. Less than a minute had passed. Eventually I stood.

"God damn that woman is dangerous," I muttered.

Inside, I checked my face in the hallway mirror. The wall had cut a scratch in a thatched pattern. It was not dripping blood, but there were painful specks of brick lodged in it, especially around the edges. I grabbed a paper towel from the kitchen and ran it under water that would not get warm fast enough. I wanted to talk to Laura before Ray returned. I put the cold towel up to my face and ran upstairs.

"Laura!" I shouted. It must have sounded more urgent then I intended because she came running out of her room with a look of panic on her face. She had on jeans and was buttoning up a gray silvery top over a smooth black bra. She saw blood on the towel.

"Jesus, what the fuck did you do?" she exclaimed.

"It's nothing, just an accident while I was doing parkour. Ray's still out running. I want to talk to you before he gets back."

"Alright, but let's get you cleaned up. Where do you keep the peroxide?" she clutched my chin and examined my face up close.

"My bathroom, "I said, then followed her into the master suite. I sat on the bed and waited as she went into the bathroom and returned with cotton balls, cleanser, and a pair of tweezers to pull out the brick.

"This place is amazingly clean. Did you hire a service?"

"Of course, it's huge as fuck. I'm not going to clean it all."

"Is that wise given the walls in the basement?"

"They don't come until tomorrow. I'll have it all down by then and we'll be out of the house."

"That's the best you're going to get. It stopped bleeding. I'll put some ointment on it, but if you want a bandage it's not going to look pretty."

"No, this will be fine."

Laura patted me on the shoulder and started to walk out of the room. "Hey, where are you going?" I asked, shooting up after her. She turned as I met her in the doorway.

"I don't want to have this talk. I want to fucking kill Donaldson. I'm goddamn tired of waiting."

"We have to wait. We have to get information on these other companies to Charles or the whole thing will get scrambled."

"You don't think I know all the arguments? Fuck the arguments! They don't get Cassandra and Lucy out of my mind." Laura was shaking with anger, practically snarling. I put my forearms on her shoulders.

"You're this angry because you're afraid to be vulnerable. It hurts, I know it hurts, but they aren't going to be able to get away with this shit any longer." I dropped my arms and pleaded, "I can't do this without you." Her eyes became a little wider, her body began to relax. I softened my tone, "We have a mission. I need you. Please, don't be afraid to let it hurt."

For a moment, Laura looked like a deer caught in headlights.

I pushed on, striving for a breakthrough, "There's no shame in crying about it. I promised you Donaldson will not get off the hook. I will not let it go. I give you my word, I will kill him."

"I've cried about it," she choked. "It doesn't help. She was right there in front of me. I could have done so much more than buy them a meal." Slowly, in the corner of her eye a tear began to form.

"We are doing more, what no amount of protests and boycotts have been able to do—we are going after those responsible. I need you to let this anger out and let it go." I grabbed her hand and put it to my chest. "Laura, I've never stopped being your friend. I know you. I'm here for you."

She looked into my face, her brow wavered, and she began to cry. I pulled her in and held her tightly as her tears grew into great sobs. The words formed in my mind, stuck on the end of my tongue, and begged to be spoken. Her arms were around me hugging me tightly. I imagined kissing her, picking her up in my arms, taking her to the bed. My nose found her hair, so close to her ear. Over and over again I could hear myself saying, "I love you." I did not say it. I could not say it now. It wasn't fair to any of us to complicate things. Nothing had changed since she had broken into my hotel room.

Eventually, Laura began calming down, her breathing returning to normal. When she pulled back, my shirt was wet with her tears. They felt pleasant, a substitute for all the exchanges we'd not shared.

"I'm sorry for letting loose like that," she said.

"Don't apologize. We needed this."

She looked into my face to see if I'd been crying. I had not, but what she glimpsed satisfied her.

"It's just that I've had no one to talk to, and I've been holding in this secret. You know...what we are going to do."

"It's been hard," I agreed.

"You don't seem to have as much trouble coping," she retorted.

"I express it differently. And, I distract myself with other obsessions." I don't know if she realized I was talking about her.

"I thought all the exercise would make a difference, that it would help me like it helped you."

"It's good that you and Ray have been keeping in shape. It will come in handy."

"I know. We won't stop," she said, and then leaned up and kissed me on the cheek. "Thank you. I needed that," she added.

"I'm always here for you."

"Good. I might need to do this again." We both smiled. Her hand lingered on my chest, her voice tender and relaxed. "Sometimes, I think no one else in the world knows me as well as you do."

That last one caused me a twinge. Laura seemed oblivious. I was gathering my words, but stopped. We could hear Ray coming in the front door. Laura disappeared to her room to freshen up. I went down to meet him, to show him my face and explain I'd had a tumble. I left out the part about eyeballing his naked girlfriend like a creeper.

That evening, we gathered in the basement and made plans. Everyone seemed more relaxed. I explained my stratagem, while Laura and Ray both questioned and offered suggestions. We felt like a team, we had begun to gel, and I looked forward to the coming days.

CHAPTER TWENTY-TWO

It was an eight-hour drive to Columbus. We got rooms in town, and in the morning we drove ten minutes south from the city to Hochberg Chemical's massive, sprawling campus. We were surprised to find that even on a Monday at nine AM, protesters quietly held picket signs on the sidewalk. Across the road from the protesters loomed the entrance to the company, a giant double arch sculpted from concrete and rising over two single lanes. There were two guards, one inspecting IDs as people drove in and another waving and checking people out as they left.

There was no fence bordering the property, nothing to prevent the protesters from storming the castle. Protests had become so commonplace as to be blasé. Public streets nearly encircled the campus and so we drove around it several times, casually examining the grounds from behind the tinted glass of the van. Guards frequented the grounds in electric carts, on Segways, and in at least two ATVs. All of them were armed, but they appeared to only be tasked with creating a visible presence. They merely waved and smiled as employees walked across the grounds, coming in to work.

That afternoon, we observed small groups of employees walking off campus for lunch and then returning an hour later. Every day there were thirty to forty of these clusters, mostly in groups of two to eight. Occasionally we spotted larger groups strolling along as if an auditorium-style meeting had just broke for lunch. The guards never stopped these groups to check badges or confirm identification.

There were perimeter cameras on poles, and in the distance on the buildings, we could see more cameras. Our assumption was that a single individual, crossing the street and entering the campus, could be tracked from the second they entered the property until they got inside. Laura followed some employees to a nearby restaurant and gleaned that their badges were simple scan passes, and not the more complicated RFID chips that could track step-by-step movements through a building.

Aside from the five-year-old computer center, all of the buildings on campus were constructed in the seventies. If Hochberg was like most companies, its security would only address existing danger levels. It is expensive to upgrade old construction in anticipation of unmade threats. It would be cheaper to demolish buildings and start from scratch. As expected, security was limited to what was justified by prior incidents.

We spent four weeks—sometimes sixteen hours a day—probing the security of Hochberg Chemical and Felix Chang. Mr. Chang traveled frequently and proved very difficult to track. Eventually we got word that he would be in Washington, D.C., to meet with the company's lobbyists and members of Congress. By pretending to be a congressional staffer we got hold of his itinerary. Ray and Laura flew off to D.C. and caught up with him as he was having lunch with his K Street cronies.

They followed his movements for a day and then, while he was at the hotel gym for his morning workout, broke into his room. Laura placed GPS trackers the size of a coin in his shoes and Ray cracked Chang's computer. He had his phone with him, so they replaced his charger with one that would hack the phone.

Meanwhile, I followed his wife.

Mrs. Margaret Chang was a prominent philanthropist who also frequently traveled to Washington. On the day Mr. Chang left, she returned by private jet. They kissed on the stairs of the plane and then went inside during refueling. Later she emerged, got into his car, and headed for home. He took off in the jet.

I was able to follow her to their house. I was driving around the neighborhood—looking for a place to park that would not draw attention—when she passed me going in the other direction. I could see she'd changed her clothes. I turned the van around and followed her to a downtown condominium. There was no way to follow as she disappeared into the building's underground parking garage.

I quickly parked on the street and ran to the front of the building. I strained to see the elevator through the glass but the glare made it too difficult. The call system was a receiver type. I picked up the phone and started to scroll through the numbers when an elderly lady walking two dogs left the building. I slipped in behind her and ran to the elevator just as it stopped on the ninth floor. I went back outside and copied every name out of the phone directory.

Using my phone, I searched the names until I came across René Olivier, an executive from the European branch of Hochberg, recently promoted to the home office. He'd been here less than a year, was a rising star with the company, and apparently didn't see any reason to scrub his address from the Internet. I identified his apartment as 6G, visible from the other side of the building.

I grabbed my camera bag and headed off on foot. On the opposite side of the street from his apartment, I found a narrow walkway between two buildings. I performed a chimney climb to make it onto the roof, ran up a seven-foot wall, and made it onto the next roof. Then with a full steam of speed I jumped an eight-foot gap to the apartment balcony of another building.

I dangled for a second over a six-story drop and then climbed from balcony to balcony until I was in view of Olivier's apartment.

The effort did not disappoint. The drapes on René's floor-length windows were wide open. I took out my long lens and began snapping pictures.

Mrs. Chang liked to live dangerously, very dangerously. A woman of her beauty and means could have had an affair with any other man, yet she recklessly chose to do so with a high-level employee, a man who worked in the corner office opposite her husband.

Motion complemented their conversation, a fluttering flirtation that appeared both deliberate and natural. She walked to him at the center of the room. He stayed a second, then rotated away and disappeared through a doorway. When he returned he was shirtless. With his hand on her side they spoke at a kissing distance, their foreheads nearly touching. She turned away, went into the kitchen, and grabbed a drink. Returning to center, she kicked off her shoes and now stood below his eye level. She pulled off her jewelry and laid it on the counter, took another drink, and with a laugh, put down her glass.

They moved to their own music. To hear them would have provided insight into the beat of their relationship. He pulled her by her hand; she extended it the length of her arm, then let her body follow, her other arm trailing behind. I thought for a moment they were going to dance; instead they stood close, touched lips along smiles, but did not kiss. She turned him around, ran her fingers through his hair. He reached back, and through her long dress, touched her thighs.

I was standing on someone's balcony. Behind the glass sliding door I could hear movement in the apartment, their steps causing vibrations under my feet. I pulled away from the camera and turned my head left and right, trying to peer between the vertical blinds. I could not really see inside and hoped they could not see me. I returned to my camera.

Margaret and René were in their late forties, both in great shape. The sandy-haired René was now on his knees in front of her, running his hands under her dress. She reached back and unclasped her bra. He withdrew his hands, stood, and in one motion dropped his pants and underwear: he'd need no more teasing. Again they brought their lips together but did not kiss, holding them there as if touching lips and sharing breath was its own kiss. She pulled up her dress and his hands reached under and slipped off her panties. Together they came down and lay on the wood floor—him on his back, she guiding him into her under the dress.

They were connected, but like the kiss not moving. She bent forward as they entwined their arms, and then they placed their lips in complete contact. A long, slow, passionate kiss while their bodies gently pressed to one another. They broke this kiss and she pulled her dress from her head, taking the bra with it. Completely naked, they gave way to one another. Their lovemaking was unrushed, fervent, and methodic.

To my right, I heard the clattering of cheap plastic blinds followed by the thud of angry hands on glass. I heard those hands fumble at the lock. I kept my face to the camera, my finger on the button snapping pictures, and waiting for the door to open.

"Why the fuck are you on my balcony?" screamed a coarse voice. The strong, putrid smell of sweat and mildew combined with stale cigarette smoke wafted from the apartment. Behind the voice I could hear the distinctive *puff, puff* of an oxygen machine. I did not pull my face from the camera. Instead I turned the camera on him, as if he had been my target all along, and shouted, "Gotcha!"

I continued to shoot pictures as I moved toward my startled victim. With the toe of my shoe, I caught the sliding glass door and slid it completely open. The man, heavy, thick, and tall, was mostly bald with heavy black eye brows. The crown of his head was unusually pointy and contained a single spurt of dark hair. He had a two day growth of white scruffy beard. I pushed through the narrow gap, past his body, and into the apartment. My lens was shoved less than an inch from his face.

He stepped back but then rightly gathered that I was not going to stop. He reached out with a surprisingly strong arm and grabbed the wrist of my camera hand. I could not afford for this to become a protracted engagement. With my free hand I punched him, not even a punch, more of a tap—right on the chest, just hard enough to remind him that he was on oxygen. He coughed, let my hand go, and then I was free, turning away from him and moving toward the door. I stepped over piles of magazines, food containers, and open UPS packages containing products labeled "As Seen On TV." At the door, I pulled back the chain. Behind me I heard the man recover; I should have hit him harder, but my guess was he was over sixty-five. As my fingers turned the deadbolt I heard a drawer open.

"Stop!" he shouted as I twisted the bottom lock.

My hand turned the door knob just as I heard the familiar click of a hammer being cocked. I had never been so glad as to not be in Florida—where "Stand Your Ground" laws had people shooting just because they could get away with it. I pulled open the door and lunged into the hallway, the door swung shut behind me. I ran. He did not fire. Down the hall I took the stairs and fled the building. Once outside I walked down the sidewalk, took the first alley I could find and then circled back to my car.

After Laura and Ray returned, we broke into Rene's place and the Chang home and set up our surveillance. Then we drove back to New York.

CHAPTER TWENTY-THREE

Data from Chang and his associates began to trickle in, especially after Mr. Chang and René connected their laptops at the office, giving us access to the corporate network. Analyzing the volume of information coming in from Hochberg was going to take a long time.

The three of us spent eight hours a day grinding through files, poking holes in their firewalls, and building backdoors into adjacent systems. I hired anonymous programmers, in China and the Ukraine, to write code that crept into the corporate network, self-replicated, and hid, ensuring we would always have access regardless of how many times passwords were changed. Our code jumped systems, rooted phones, and went home with staff. Eventually, we had the ability to track the location of practically every Hochberg employee, nearly 22,000 people.

We also took time to work on side projects. Ray, whose artistic ability had been dormant for years, became our hair and make-up specialist. He developed prosthetics, bought wigs, and collected a costume wardrobe. In addition, he added to our cache of false identities and passports. Laura took point on expanding our inventory of gadgets, including a very small surveillance drone, and various insect-like robots. I, in turn began training them both in combat and basic tumbling techniques.

Ray and Laura were already certified in scuba. I took classes alone, and then after my certification, we took a three-hour boat trip to "wreck valley"— a sixty mile zone of shipwrecks north to south from Long Island to New Jersey. None of us had ever jumped from a plane, so we added skydiving to our repertoire and that inspired us to learn to fly. In addition to the physical activities, we enjoyed much that New York had to offer. We saw plays, went to museums, and ate at some of the best restaurants.

We were surrounded by millions of people, but could not afford to make friends and so did our best to go unnoticed. This was hardest on Laura, who was prone to making conversation anywhere she went. A social person at heart, her *raison d'être* was to simultaneously elevate others with good cheer and kindness and then to bask in her ever-growing circle of friendships. In the past she had been the one to know everyone; now she knew only us. Without any effort on her part, people naturally flocked to her to make conversation, flirt, or offer help when she needed nothing.

Laura eventually recognized the inherent peril of her noticeability and altered her appearance and mannerisms to divert attention. Before going out she would joke that she was putting on her Norma Jeane–after the way that Marilyn Monroe dressed down and became invisible when she did not wish to be recognized. Laura did this to protect us and to protect the mission, but I could tell it took its toll on her.

Ever since my slip off the building, I'd had changed my demeanor toward Laura. I forced myself to put away any thought of intimacy and then surprised myself by how easy it was to do. No longer did I steal glances at her, give her long looks when we were alone, or fantasize about her in my private moments. Now, she was a member of the team and my dear friend.

Working so closely and enjoying so many activities brought the three of us together in a way we hadn't been before. My friendship with Ray rekindled. He no longer spoke of conspiracies outside of those we were investigating (and perpetuating). The three of us worked well as a team; we handled the little bumps with good communication and empathy. When we went out for a night on the town we left and returned in high spirits.

In early autumn we were celebrating having obtained our pilot's licenses. We dressed up and rewarded ourselves with a steak dinner and single malt scotch that had been aged twenty years. It had been our plan to make funny faces when posing for the photos on our pilot's licenses. During a cab ride to Keens Steakhouse, we lamented the fact that the licenses did not have photos.

"Let's do it anyway," Laura said.

"You mean make our own?" I asked.

"Yeah, take the photos and print them."

I nudged Ray, who was sitting in the middle, and looking very distant.

"I just can't believe we've come this far," Ray said. "I never would have believed I'd have the means to learn to fly a plane, live in New York, or be setting off to drink ridiculously expensive scotch."

Laura and I took in his comment. We were all beaming in agreement as the cab came to a stop. I pulled off a few bills and richly rewarded the cabbie. Laura put her back to the door and smiled sweetly.

In a very proper voice she proclaimed, "Well I never expected to be in company of such fine and accomplished gentlemen."

The thought that jumped into my mind was, *But I'm a killer*. It was the same thought that cost me Laura and drove me into seclusion. Ray was right, we'd come along way. I didn't want to spoil the night by allowing my mind to wander to a dark place. Instead, I jumped out of the cab into traffic, setting off a chorus of squealing tires and honking horns. I ran around, opened Laura's door, and bowed my nose to her knee. I held out my hand.

"My lady," I said guiding her from the car, then taking her hand and walking toward the restaurant.

Ray exited the vehicle and met us at the door.

"My lady," he said opening the door for her, taking her hand, and proceeding inside.

It went on like this all evening. I pulled out her chair and sat her. Ray pulled it out when she excused herself to the bathroom, and so on. Laura delighted in the attention. Adding her own touch, she adopted an awful cockney accent and behaved as unladylike as possible. She did not let up when the waiter arrived, purposely mispronouncing most of the menu. When it was time to go, I paid the bill in cash. Ray and I simultaneously rose and rushed to her chair. Rather than to fight over whose honor it would be, we each took a side and pulled her chair in unison. Laura rose.

"Thank yew fine gentleman," she said, still in her accent. She gave a little curtsey and then let loose a deafening fart that was heard throughout the restaurant. Though she claimed it was intentional, to this day I am unconvinced.

Our little game over, we stumbled out of Keens with our snoots full with scotch and decided to walk down Broadway until we'd sobered up a bit. Ray and I stood on either side of Laura; as we walked she slipped her arms in ours and then began to sing slowly.

I... no longer have to choose
To dance or sing the blues
To laugh or cry or muse
I've nothing left to lose

It had been so long since I'd heard Laura sing that I'd forgotten her melting voice. She dropped an octave and scaled into a playful, up-tempo melody.

Do I eat ice cream or chocolate bars
Choices that plagued me and broke my heart
Cease to detain and tear me apart
Cause I, no longer chase the stars

I... no longer have to choose
Between two and the truth
I give my heart to love
and so very proud of

I chose everything, all the things
All of the above

When I'm filled with lust
And ready to combust
There's always wood to burn
Everywhere I turn

She did not appear to be singing to either of us, nor did Ray or I care. She finished two more verses as we caught sight of the subway stairs. The song felt familiar, like an old musical number from the forties.

Do I drink brandy or smoke cigars?
Dance naked or drive fast cars?
I'll take what's before me into my heart
And cease to regret before I start

When there's nothing to hide
Pleasure's not denied
I want all of the above
of everything I love

We waited to cross the street and Laura hummed the melody, transitioning into the finale.

Hate me if you will
I'll gladly pay the bill
My Love is always free
Choosing one, two, or three

I... no longer have to choose
To dance or sing the blues
To laugh or cry or muse
I've nothing left to lose

A disheveled old lady, sitting on a piece of cardboard next to the stairs, clapped as we descended below ground. Laura smiled and tried to take a bow, but we urged her along.

"Oops, okay then," she said, her intoxication showing.

I sat across from Laura and Ray on the train. Ray took Laura's hand, leaned his head against the glass, and closed his eyes. She put her other hand on Ray's and stared at me stone faced, as if she were looking through me. We rode in silence.

I ran up to the door and opened it for them, then joined them in the living room.

"Yeah, we made it home again," Laura squealed, suddenly aroused. "One more, one more before bed."

Ray and I nodded. Our buzzes had worn off though neither of us was sure about Laura. He let go of Laura's hand and walked to the other room to retrieve our bottle of Macallan 30.

Laura, squinted, trotted two steps toward me, and touched the back of her hand to mine. As Ray entered the room she spun around. He poured our glasses and we raised them with a clink followed by a shout, "To us!"

"Time for me to turn in," I said, placing my glass on the table.

Ray collected Laura's glass and sat it alongside mine. Laura grabbed Ray and me around our waists. Thinking she was about to fall over, we both moved to steady her.

"My two big, strong men. I love you two."

Ray and I shrugged it off.

"Have you got her?" I asked.

Ray nodded yes and I left to go to bed.

CHAPTER TWENTY-FOUR

Erhart Pharmaceuticals and George Kennard were our third targets. Kennard joined the world's fifth largest drug company, Erhart Pharmaceuticals, as their general counsel just as the company was beset by a wave of lawsuits. These lawsuits stemmed from Erhart's mislabeling the side effects of its heart medications. At the heart of the case was whether the company knew that when taken in combination with other drugs almost always jointly prescribed for a heart condition, they had a very high incidence of causing nerve damage. Five people were dead and thirty-three others had such severe nerve damage they could not walk without canes or wheelchairs.

Kennard was rumored to have used a variety of questionable legal tactics to settle or quash the majority of the lawsuits. For the families who did not settle, Kennard launched a multimillion-dollar legal assault. He successfully prevented the plaintiffs' attorneys from obtaining the files from Erhart that would have proven their case. Monetarily, those families were asking for less money than the families that settled. To Kennard, the truth was far more valuable than money, and he saw to it that the families got neither money nor truth.

Five years later, Kennard was CEO and Chairman of the Board of Directors of Erhart Pharmaceutical. He inked a contract for a $2 million a year salary, a $3 million a year bonus and stock which paid him annually more than his salary and bonus combined.

The week he became CEO, the judge who had presided over all of the cases Kennard had originally been brought in to handle was indicted in a bribery scandal. Though the judge was proven to have accepted bribes in at least nineteen high-profile cases, no connection between Kennard, the judge, or Erhart was ever alleged. Nothing was made of the fact that when Kennard left Harvard Law school, his first job was clerking for the judge. The judge was stripped of his law license, served no jail time, and was quickly hired as a consultant at Erhart.

As CEO, Kennard began buying boutique pharmaceutical companies which made small-batch generics. According to analysts, these smaller companies seemingly had little to offer Erhart. Kennard did not strip these smaller companies of their assets. Instead, he gave them the patents of drugs that were within a few years of expiring. He bulked up the sales forces for these companies and they in turn systematically pushed those drugs for off-label uses. In just a few short years, Kennard's success with this formula made

Erhart the third-largest pharmaceutical company in the world.

Just five years later, hundreds were dead as a direct result of using these drugs for off-label purposes. Kennard had done a beautiful job of mitigating the company's risk. In order for the sales force to promote the off-label uses, they had to have the cooperation of thousands of doctors. The doctors—or rather their large insurance companies—pointed their fingers back at the smaller drug companies, whose legal teams pointed their fingers at what they called the "imprecise language in the FDA regulations of off-label uses." Erhart's corporate legal team, in turn, blamed the satellite companies for acting as lone wolves, independent from Erhart's management. These smaller companies went bankrupt under an onslaught of civil suits, just as the patent protection had run out on these drugs—their only real assets.

The federal government stepped up and—in cooperation with Erhart's legal team—arrived at a fine and settlement of $257.4 million; less than $100 million went to the states. This was roughly 0.02 percent of the profit Erhart made on the scheme resulting in the settlement. No one was criminally prosecuted, and the percentage of fines that trickled down to the injured families barely paid their continuing medical care. Part of the agreement with the federal government and states was that Erhart would be immune from future prosecution.

The same year Erhart settled with the federal government, Kennard and his wife donated $260 million to the Manhattan Research Hospital for the building of a new medical tower to replace its 89-year-old facility. While the deal sounded very generous, in reality Manhattan Research Hospital was a private organization specializing in R&D and clinical trials. Though it was not widely known to the public, the condition of the donation was that any pharmaceutical produced through the hospital was the property of Erhart.

Erhart's corporate offices were in New York. Kennard and his wife lived uptown, making the information we needed close by but difficult to get.

CHAPTER TWENTY-FIVE

"I just think we need some space," Ray said, coming in the front door with an armful of groceries.

"We had plenty of space in L.A.," Laura said behind him.

"That was different. We'd just left home and we were getting up to speed." Ray's voice grew a little louder. "It was a stressful time for both of us."

"Keep your voice down."

"He's not here; he said he was going uptown to shoot some more stills of the Erhart Pharmaceutical Building."

They were in the kitchen, unpacking and dancing a crisscross as they put the groceries away. Ray's voice grew sultry, "Remember Mexico?"

"I remember," she said with a hint of smile in her voice.

"We danced. We'd never danced before."

"I remember the coral reef," she said plainly.

"Oh, stop, you remember more than the coral reef. I know you didn't forget drinking tequila, clawing the sheets—screaming my name."

"I remember when we started drinking tequila. Everything after that is a blur," she teased.

"Liar! You remember. It's not like we didn't talk about it the next day or try and reenact it when we went to Vegas."

"I remember; it was nice."

"Just nice? Oh come on Laura. Is it your intention to wound me?"

"No," she replied in soft dry voice. "I love you Ray, I don't want to hurt you."

"But you don't want to make love to me? You're not attracted to me anymore? Tell me what I've done."

"Ray," Laura pled, "please, we've been through this before. It's not you. You haven't done anything."

"And I love you," Ray pined, "I always have. Even before…"

"Ray," her tone was sharp and biting.

"I'm sorry. I forgot you don't like to hear that."

"I didn't know about your feelings for me when I was with Kyle and I don't want to think about it. What you felt then has nothing to do with us today. "

"But Laura, I need you. I need to make love to you. I need to feel you next to me."

"And now you're hurting me."

"How—how am I hurting you?"

"Because I've told you I'm not having sex. I don't want to and you know I'm not doing it with anyone else." The groceries were all put away. They were standing across from one another.

"I don't know what to do." There was stress in Ray's voice, a choke like he was on the verge of tears.

"Ray, it's not fair to you, but it's something I need to do for myself. I need to be focused."

"And Kyle?"

"Don't you dare bring him into this or so help me I will sleep in another room and we are over!"

"That's not what I want. But what am I supposed to think? Our whole relationship, you have been the most passionate lover I have ever known. Your appetite has exceeded mine. I've done cartwheels to keep up and now you barely touch me, like I'm some fucking leper. "

"I'm sorry. I know you have needs. If you want to go elsewhere just tell me. It's okay. I understand."

"That's not what I want! I want you; I want things to be back to normal. Are you telling me your passion is gone—that you're not horny?"

"No, it's not gone at all. That's what you don't understand. It's very hard for me to do this, to turn you down, but it's something I need to do for me! And I don't need you making me feel like fucking crap about it!" The sound of her voice echoed around the kitchen. "Are we done here?"

Ray was contrite. "Yes."

"Good. I'm going to take a long hot bath; please give me some privacy."

Laura stomped over my head on her way upstairs. I could hear Ray slip into the living room, turn on the TV and raise the sound as if he could drown out her last shout.

My hand had been on the latch and with great effort I managed to engage the spring so that the panel door didn't fly open as I let go. I turned on the landing and tiptoed back into the basement.

I *had* intended to go uptown to Erhart, but I'd gotten distracted sifting through Hotchberg's data. I had stayed behind to tell them the good news, that I'd found the evidence on Felix Chang. Proof that he had directly ordered bribes in this country and fourteen others, proof that he knew his company products caused irreparable harm to the environment, and proof that he'd ordered modified seeds spread into farmers' fields so that they could turn around and sue those same farmers for violating their patents in order to take their land.

All of that would have to wait. Now was not the time to tell them I'd overheard their conversation. I was never so glad my camera bag was in the basement. I could hear water rushing from the hot water tanks, up three flights to fill the claw-footed tub in their bathroom. I looked at my watch: three o'clock. By the time I got uptown, took enough pictures to justify the trip, and came back, it would be dark. I'd miss dinner; I'd already skipped lunch. This was a fine mess.

I slipped out the basement door. If I cut through to the back gate, there was a chance they would look down and see me. I jumped up and grabbed the fence, lifted until I could glance into the neighbor's yard. This could be just as bad. I looked like a thief, fleeing my yard into another. It was worth the risk. No good could come of me getting in the middle of their fight.

My stomach was already churning over Ray and Laura. I jumped over the fence, landed on grass next door, and went straight to their gate. On the other side, I walked bent over so as to not be seen by either of them. A minute later, I was on the street headed to the Metro, cursing that taking a cab wouldn't save me any time.

So Laura and Ray weren't having sex anymore. Well that made three of us—two of us willingly. It made sense that I wasn't. Sure, I'd put my love for Laura on the back burner, but I didn't want anyone else either. Besides, it wasn't like I could have a girlfriend on the side while I was breaking into companies and planning murder. I'm sure I could find a hook-up, rent a room for the night, but it seemed wrong. Doing so would feel like I was cheating—cheating on my unrequited love.

"I'm officially crazy," I said out loud to myself. I looked around, embarrassed for having spoken, and then remembered I was in New York: it's officially okay to mutter to oneself.

I wondered if Laura felt the same way. Was she not sleeping with Ray because of a love for me? Whatever her reasons, they didn't matter if they broke up our little group and put all our hard work in jeopardy. Something needed to be done to put those two back together or find some equilibrium between them. We had the goods on Chang and in two weeks we were going to infiltrate Erhart.

Later in the evening, I texted Ray and Laura that I would not be home for dinner. By the time I returned to Brooklyn, it was nearly midnight. It was bad protocol to take rooftop parkour routes after dark. Most residents were overly sensitive to thumps overhead while they were sleeping. I took the

Circus Route as quietly as possible until I stood overlooking our home. The moon was full over my shoulder, illuminating the townhouse. There were no lights on. They were asleep.

I took out the camera and zoomed in on their bedroom window. Laura was tucked into bed, her fist balled up under her chin, pushing out those sweet, pouty lips. Ray was not in bed with her. I looked around, then walked six paces left and looked again. It was as I expected, but the sight of it made me sad. How long had he been sleeping on the floor? Had he been doing it all this time, ever since they got to New York? Six months ago I might have felt a little glee. Instead I empathized with him. I'd been through something like this before with Laura. First came the pleading and arguing, followed by the long silences, and finally, with a few words in a short note, the end.

CHAPTER TEWENTY-SIX

"I heard you get up. There's a fresh pot." Laura nodded to the coffee machine. It was eleven-thirty in the morning. I poured myself a cup and sat down at the counter across from her.

"Where's Ray?" I asked, but my question was answered by footsteps coming up from the basement.

"Nice job," he said with a smile as he joined us in the kitchen. Laura grinned.

"We all took turns looking. I just happened to sort the right pile."

"It's more than that," Ray said. "You got one piece and then connected the dots to dozens of other piles."

"I'll send it off to Charles after I get a bite."

"Don't sweat it," Ray said. "I've already sent it. Listen, after you eat, do you want to go over to Central Park for a run?"

"Sure."

"I'm heading over to Erhart. I'm going to try and pick up the bot by sending in another," Laura said. She'd managed to get a spider bot into the ventilation system at Erhart but had lost communication with it as it wound its way through the tower. "I figured out that I can use them as repeaters to carry my signal back to the first." She looked at our faces. "Yeah I know, you guys told me to order more. They're coming."

I was amazed they were both in such high spirits after the fight. Ray stood next to Laura, who put her arm around his waist. It was as if nothing had happened.

Two hours later, Ray and I arrived at Central Park. It was a long way to go for a run, but we had an ulterior motive. George Kennard lived in a 2,700-square-foot luxury condo above Central Park. With all of our work on Hochberg, we'd never had a chance to get over and even look at the neighborhoods of the Upper West Side. A run was a great way to get the feel for the area, though on this day, we ran exclusively in the park.

Eventually we made our way to the 85th Street entrance and started walking down Central Park West toward Kennard's building. As we were walking, Laura called; we sat down on a bench and Ray put her on speaker.

"Hey, I'm in as far as Kennard's secretary. He's headed home early. She just called for his car. If you hurry you can put eyes on him going into his building."

"Nice work," I said.

"You don't know the half of it; navigating these shafts is like the "Portal" game from hell. Speaking of which, I'm going to be several more hours. I've got to navigate a unit into his office and drill through the drywall. Don't wait up. Oh, look, there he is. That should give you about fifteen minutes. Love you," she added and then hung up.

Kennard's building was just another block down. We started walking, eventually taking up seats against the park, across the street from the building.

"I'm still trying to figure out who she was saying 'I love you' to," Ray said, kicking out and crossing his legs.

"She was totally talking to me," I said, mirroring him by kicking out my legs and locking my fingers behind my head. Ray twisted his mouth to the side and rolled his eyes.

"I'd laugh if we weren't going through a patch."

"Oh, I'm sorry," I said with sympathy. "Have you spoken to her about it?" I could tell by his expression, he bought my feigned ignorance.

"Yeah, it didn't help. Did you two go through anything like that? I mean... after...a patch with no sex."

I pulled my legs in, sat up, and looked at him thoughtfully. "Ray, I don't think this is something we should be talking about. You're relationship with Laura is yours, and ours is in the past where it needs to stay. We didn't end well and I don't really want to dredge up bad memories from when things were going downhill."

Ray pulled his legs in and sat up, "Yeah, you're right. I'm sorry; it's not your problem."

"It is my problem if you two not getting along jeopardizes the work. Let me ask you a question. Do you feel Laura is off-task in any way?"

"No, it's the only thing on her mind."

"So, I'm going to give you some general advice. "

"Okay."

"I'm not getting sex either. I don't think it would be wise to risk blowing our cover by dating and I'm certainly not one for an escort. Right now, I'm totally mission-oriented; you need to be too. I know that sucks because when Laura shines her light on someone it feels like you can sing and dance an entire Broadway show. Put your relationship on hold for now—not indefinitely, just until we've wrapped up our current projects. Then the three of us can sit down and we'll convince Laura we need to take a break, a vacation. You guys can go off and work on your relationship. I'll put the kibosh on adding any new companies. "

We sat there, saying nothing. Twenty minutes ticked by.

"I'm going to take that advice. It's not going to be easy," Ray said.

"We can run more," I teased.

"Ha."

"I'll tell you one thing about a mistake I made with Laura. If she needs to be totally mission-oriented, then the best thing you can do is support her completely. Don't just play at her level, exceed her level."

"That's what I've been doing," he said, showing his frustration.

"Yeah, you have, and the three of us have been getting along like family. None of us are having sex, but we have love and trust between us and we're doing something we believe in. Stay focused and don't be selfish." Ray nodded and scanned the road again, looking for anyone that appeared to be pulling up.

The advice I gave Ray was sound and valid in the moment. In the back of my mind, where I stored all of my feelings for Laura, there was a twinge of guilt. I ignored it.

"I don't think Kennard is coming," I said. "Will you stay here and keep an eye on the door? I'll be right back." I ran north and turned west on 86th Street, then went into a specialty book shop called Cultured Oyster Books. The store smelled of old parchment, a divine scent I associated with childhood afternoons spent in our small town library. The shopkeeper eyed me curiously, no doubt because I was dressed in my sweats and running shoes. Most of the volumes of this store were locked in cabinets and carried price tags above $4,000. I found a $100 volume of poetry by Joan Didion, printed in 1987. *Really, a hundred dollars*, I thought as I laid it on the counter. Behind the clerk was wrapping of royal blue, purple, and dark green.

"Do you have a plain wrap and a box? I need to ship it."

"Indeed. It will be extra." I nodded and the clerk trotted off into the back to retrieve them.

After it was wrapped, I borrowed a pen and in my neatest handwriting (making sure the clerk could not see) wrote out the name 'George Kennard,' followed by his address.

With package in hand I left the store, walked two blocks, and approached the doorman of his building.

"I have a package for"—and I stopped to look at the package as if I'd forgotten— "George Kennard," I said, holding the package out for the doorman to take.

The doorman was an inch shorter than I, stout, and wearing the traditional uniform complete with cap and epaulettes. He took off his cap, revealing his baldness, and smiled wide.

"George Kennard? Well I'll be. That's a name I haven't heard in a while. I'm sorry but Mr. Kennard hasn't lived here in a long time. He moved out to Brooklyn."

"Oh, my mistake. Do you know his address?"

He scowled, "Are you new to New York?"

I shot him my best "fuck you" look.

"Well then you should know I can't tell you that. So you've got two choices. You can take the package back or you can leave it with me. I can make some calls and see if I can find him. I'm sure he still has friends in the building. If I can't find him, I'll call you to pick it up."

"Yeah, I don't know what the boss will want me to do. I'll take it back. Thanks for helping," I said in my most disarming voice. A car pulled up behind me. I got out of the doorman's way and headed south. I looked across at Ray and nodded for him to follow. We caught up with one another at the next subway stop and headed down.

"Our intel was old. He doesn't live there anymore."

"Well there's a fucking wasted day."

"Nah," I said, handing him the book. "I got you this gift."

"Is it a book?"

"Yeah, poetry, for your artist soul," I said and got a skeptical look in return. "It cost a hundred dollars."

"It's that good?"

"I don't know, maybe it was only good enough to run a hundred copies and now there are only eighty left."

Ray rolled his eyes and dropped it into the guitar case of a busker before we entered the train. We sat and I pulled up my phone to look for new parkour routes. Two stops later, Ray leaned over my shoulder.

"So, I'm going to need a new hobby. Why don't you teach me?" I nodded my assent and then went back to my phone.

Before we left the island a tall, leggy brunette with blue eyes came aboard and sat across the aisle a few seats down. I went back to my phone barely noticing the flirtations that were flying between them. Next thing I know, we'd stopped at Borough Hall, the woman gets off and Ray goes strolling after. I rushed to catch him, knocking my hand against the door and nearly dropping my phone. By the time I looked around and got my bearings she was already up the stairs, with Ray following casually behind.

I ran through the crowds and caught up with him standing on the edge of Court Street. The woman was getting into the back of a town car. She looked up and met eyes with Ray. She smiled and Ray gave a little wave back.

A few seconds later the town car rolled up and the back window opened.

"You boys want a ride?" she asked, in what I thought was a Russian accent. Ray nodded and I wasn't willing to let him disappear, so we got in the back.

"I'm Ileana. I'm headed to the Heights."

"So are we," Ray exclaimed enthusiastically (we weren't).

"We're not going too far," I interjected. "Just to Hicks."

"Will that be okay?" she asked the driver.

"Of course, ma'am," he replied.

The car eased into traffic and she closed the partition. Ileana proved to be quite talkative. We learned that she was a dual citizen, Hungarian and U.S. She'd come to America to model, had gotten her master's in Art, and now worked at a downtown gallery. From then on she and Ray discussed art with great passion. This saved Ray from telling her more about us than she needed to know.

The drive to Hicks Street was a short one. I opened the car door and heard Ray ask for her number.

"I don't think my husband would like that very much," she said holding up her ring finger.

"I'm so sorry, your eyes, our conversation...I didn't even look," Ray explained.

"I enjoyed our conversation too," she said, and then handed Ray her card, "but only for the art," she added with a thoughtful smile.

Ray stood on the curb and sniffed her business card. At this point, my annoyance with him was transparent.

"I had to try," he said. "You know, just to see if I could."

It had been my plan to double back and board the train, but I spotted a low wall not too far away that gave me an idea.

"You wanted a new hobby; no time like the present. Follow me and do what I do."

We took off, ran about a mile, and then for the next mile I forced him to hop up to every third step we passed and on every low iron fence until someone came along and chased us away. It's not easy to jump onto a three-quarter-inch piece of metal, three-and-half feet off the ground, and stand there. After about thirty minutes of this, Ray was crying that his abdominals hurt too much to go on. We walked for another twenty minutes until we came to the side of a building that had a small protrusion of brick, at the division of the first and second floors.

I explained to Ray how to climb the wall, then did so myself, hanging from the protrusion on just the tips of my fingers.

"So now you do it. Don't try and hang, just touch the top of the brick. We'll work on hanging later."

We took turns running at the wall. Occasionally we'd draw the attention of passersby who would stop and watch for a second, but then quickly get bored with such routine practice. Ray seemed to be making some progress, so I pulled off to let him squeeze in more tries. I noticed a jogger had stopped across the street. He quietly watched, and then seeing that I was looking at him, proceeded to come over and stand beside me.

"This is that thing," he said, snapping his fingers.

"Parkour," I replied.

"Yeah that's it. So how is it done? Can you show me?"

I turned to look at the man closely. He wore shorts and a tight shirt, was in good shape, and in his early fifties. I looked at the sandy blond hair and the piercing blue eyes. He smelled more of lotion than of sweat, and his clothes looked as though they'd never been worn more than once. I nearly fell over; I was standing next to George Kennard.

I smiled and stuck out my hand, "Hi, I'm Jason Kohn and this is Steven Howard," I said, loud enough for Ray to hear. "Like my friend here, I can show you the basics but it's up to you to practice. Also, it helps if you can do this." I started running in place and then did a back flip in front of him. His face lit up like a child's.

"Are you done with your run?" I asked. "We're headed this way." Taking a guess, I pointed west.

"Yeah, I'm George Kennard," he said shaking hands with Ray and me. I gave no sign that I recognized his name, and thankfully, Ray followed my lead. We all started walking together.

"How long have you been doing parkour?" Kennard asked.

"I'm just visiting from out of town," Ray said, "but Jason has been doing it for years."

"I've always thought it was impressive. I keep very fit, but I'm not sure I can do that."

"I need to stop and get some water," Ray said.

"Come this way. I live just around the corner." Kennard ushered us around the block to a beautiful, renovated brownstone. He led us through the gate, up the stairs, and unlocked the door. Inside the elegant foyer hung a giant mirror above the entry table where he threw his key. Kennard quickly tapped out a code on the keypad by the door. I was able to reverse the code in the reflection of the mirror.

We followed him down the hall and into the kitchen, where he handed us water bottles from the fridge. Graciously, he entertained all of our questions about the house.

"I'm from Brooklyn and it was useful to live in the city when I was starting out, but when I was a kid, I used to walk these streets and dream of living here one day. It took three years to renovate this place."

He then took us on a tour, divulging a history of everything from the delicate scroll work surrounding the chandelier hook to the lettering on a basement brick, an indicator that it had come from the Aldridge Brick Company of Dutchess Junction around 1905. The only place we didn't go was the attic.

He was warm and personable; he spoke fondly of his only son, who was now at Harvard Law. Looking over family pictures in the den, we learned his wife was on her way to their second home in the Adirondack Mountains. She sat on the board and worked daily in the New York Public Library. He would be joining her for the weekend, and he shared their very touching love story of twenty-five years. Sweethearts since college, they grew up five miles from each other but didn't meet until Harvard.

Ray and I wisely stuck to our cover stories, the only true part of mine being that I'm a day trader, mostly retired. All in all, we spent two hours chatting him up, or rather, being chatted at; by the end I had a very distinct impression of George. He was a type-A personality, driven and aggressive in business, but when it came to something athletic he could only appreciate vicariously; he was a total fanboy. Given the way he would not stop talking and his hasty invitations to have us back for dinner, go to his gentlemen's club, and tour New York in his company chopper, I got the feeling that he had few real friends.

When his car called to confirm his ETA we left, caught a cab at the corner, and were home fifteen minutes later. Laura had not returned and I could tell this bothered Ray, so I turned the subject back to George.

"I got the code. Why don't we get some sleep and break into the townhouse pre-dawn tomorrow?" I asked, taking a seat in the family room off the kitchen.

"I can't believe he's such a nice guy," Ray said, grabbing a beer and then sitting across from me.

I found Ray's misguided enthusiasm bothersome.

"He had us in his house just like that," Ray continued. "Two nobodies from off the street. He could be living on the Upper East Side and instead he's living in Brooklyn."

"Villains never think they're villains. Remember, this guy isn't only working for a company that has knowingly caused the death of people; he personally made it his mission in life to deny the victims compensation. I have no doubt when he walked out of court it was with a great deal of pride for doing a good job. He is just like every other lawyer who tells themselves that winning is proof of integrity. He did such a good job of screwing people over that the board of directors made him CEO. It doesn't matter how nice he appears. What he deserves is the same slow, agonizing torture and eventual death his company's drugs have inflicted on others. Had I shot him dead today and walked away, we would have been showing him a kindness and mercy he doesn't deserve."

Ray raised his hands, "Whoa, take it easy man. I don't disagree; I'm just trying to process it all."

"That's fine," I said, calming down a bit. "All those years you cried that the government was oppressing the people, all the times you spoke to a crowded room about a loss of freedom, I want you to remember it's men like George Kennard that are the cause. They get away with everything they do for one reason: they have the money to buy our politicians."

As I was talking there came into my mind the idea that we could do something more: that we could take this further than exposing and killing CEOs. I tucked the thought in the back of my mind for another day.

"You're right, "Ray apologized. "To be perfectly honest I didn't see it before; even a year ago I wasn't seeing it. These guys are the people that manipulate the system."

This seemed like a good opportunity to further smash some of Ray's long-held ideas.

"And I should add, they aren't part of the Illuminati, the Trilateral Commission, or Masons. They are not part of any of these secret groups. They don't need to be."

When Laura returned, we brought her up to date and made plans for the morning. Her robots had arrived and she would spend tomorrow getting them into place. One of the robots would infiltrate the server room at Erhart and hack into the company system.

The following morning, we went into Kennard's place dressed as specialty home theatre installers. Once there, we put microphones and cameras throughout the house. There was only one computer, belonging to his wife. We learned from Laura that Kennard didn't use a computer. Anything he couldn't do on his smartphone went through his secretary.

We had gone into the attic as a way of placing bugs into the floor below.

This was where we found his writing room. It contained a collection of fountain pens, inks, and parchment. Throughout his house there had been the occasional famous speech, framed and written in calligraphy. I had dismissed them as authentic but now realized that they were handmade reproductions crafted by Kennard.

It was weird that during the tour of his house he had not chosen to share those details. We did find, written in calligraphy, a list of Kennard's emergency passwords for all the computers he trusted other people to use on his behalf. Among those passwords were the access codes to a bank in Switzerland with forty-five million dollars.

"Since I found this, does that mean I get to drain his bank account? I can't decide if I want to split it up among us or disappear to go backpacking around Europe," Ray joked.

"Now is not the time to tap it; we need to wait until Charles is done."

We had excellent, but not perfect coverage of the inside of Kennard's Brooklyn home. After the Kennards' return, Ray, Laura, and I took a trip to the Adirondacks and infiltrated their second home.

It took six months, three new drug releases, and another wave of lawsuits before we got the goods on Kennard. This time the physical data was the smaller part; the majority of the evidence was video and audio of Kennard incriminating himself. We had him on video ordering negative study results to be kept from the FDA: verifying that he personally knew the drugs were not safe under certain conditions. We had video and audio of him directing lawyers to "punish" families who filed suit against the company and dictating exactly how it should be done, including discussing in detail the profitability to the company while he, literally, rubbed his hands together.

We wrapped up all the evidence and sent it to Charles. Charles was in the middle of conducting the trial on Chang. At the conclusion of that trial he would release the evidence and the video of the proceedings simultaneously.

During the Donaldson trial Charles had put the whole thing online and then sent out press releases. This time he'd stepped it up considerably, turning the conviction into a massive release party. Since the conviction of Donaldson, membership in the Justice Syndicate had risen to over a million people.

Some of the more radical, lay members of the Syndicate called themselves Jurors. When they gathered in the streets or at parties they all wore the same plain white mask which they first numbered one through twelve and then decorated to their own distinctive personal tastes. It was quite a sight to see a crowd of these people walking through the streets with arms locked and their faces in numerical order.

CHAPTER TWENTY-SEVEN

While Charles processed the evidence against Kennard through the Justice Syndicate, the three of us decided to take a break. Though not the vacation I had promised Ray, this was a small recess to enjoy ourselves until we saw the public outcome of the Syndicate's release.

I didn't know–and didn't want to know–the status of Ray and Laura's intimate relationship. What was obvious was that they had embarked on a new level of friendship. They planned to use this time to take horseback-riding lessons. In addition, Laura insisted that we all return to shooting practice with high-powered rifles.

I used my time to walk the streets of Manhattan and ruminate on the idea I'd had while arguing with Ray about people like Kennard. I started going to lectures, sitting in on classes at NYU, and standing on the edges of protests.

While Ray blamed society's problems on elaborate conspiracy theories, in my view, the problem was money in politics. Legislators are more apt to respond to those who fill their campaign chests than they are the citizens who elected them. If the playing field between billion-dollar corporate interests and the voters could be leveled, we'd have a very different country.

Unfortunately, the Supreme Court has ruled that money equals free speech. Their ruling in *Citizens United v. Federal Election Commission* opened the floodgates to corporate money in politics. This paved the way for super political action committees that can spend unprecedented amounts of money to manipulate elections.

The only way to change this ruling would be to pass a constitutional amendment affirming that corporations are not people and do not have a right to free speech. A well-written amendment could put restrictions on all political contributions and lobbying of government officials, and eliminate the ability of public officers to cash in by trading political favors for sweetheart jobs when they left office.

Like all proper zealots, we needed a manifesto. We needed to issue demands. I began researching, writing, and sharpening my message for the moment when I would present it to Ray and Laura.

As Laura spoke, I noticed her lip held a mark where she'd been biting it. "I can't wait much longer. We need to get Ray on board and do this thing.

Donaldson might not even be in Charleston anymore; in all this time, the little worm could have bolted."

"He's still there," I said.

"How do you know? Seriously, how the fuck do you know? Everything we had on him has gone dark! We're not into his computers anymore and there hasn't been an alert on him that isn't really about the Justice Syndicate." She was flushed; her anxiety had come back.

I'd hoped that this little break would be a chance for her to relax. But in reality, I knew better. Laura needed to feel useful all the time. She hadn't been eating much recently.

She'd found me down in the basement, typing at my laptop. I'd been putting the finishing touches on the demands. I closed my laptop and set it aside. I gave her my full attention but said nothing, hoping the silence would calm her down.

"Kyle, how the fuck do you know?" She shouted my name as if I were ignoring her.

"Because I contacted a Realtor the second I got to New York and tried to buy his house. I told her I'd heard the news, was guessing he might be anxious to sell, and that I'd hoped to get his property for a song. He's refused to sell. She goes by once a month and makes an offer. He's holed up and not going anywhere. Besides, his wife is here in New York. She has a boyfriend and is not too worried about anyone finding out."

The tight spring Laura had wound herself into suddenly snapped. She sank down onto the couch. I moved my feet as she crashed down next to me.

"I told you I would do this. I'm not going to let it go. I've got your back."

Laura reached over and squeezed my leg, just above my ankle.

"Thank you." She said it in a weak voice. She heard herself, covered her mouth, and gently started to cry.

I wanted to reach out for her. Kiss the tears off her face and hold her in my arms. It was clear to me–clearer anyway–that ever since Cassandra's death, Laura had been in pain. She'd been in pain and hiding it the best she could. I should have known and done more to comfort her. Instead I'd been preoccupied and let her down again.

"Laura, I want what you want. I'm in this with you completely, until the end."

She looked at me and nodded. "I'm sorry, sometimes I forget the people I love—love me back."

I sat up and grabbed her hand in mine. I intended to pull her toward me when I heard Ray at the top of the landing. He started down the stairs. I let go of Laura's hand, stayed in my corner, and folded my legs under me.

"Hey," Ray said quietly as he came into view. "Is everything okay? What's going on?" He looked at me briefly then knelt down beside Laura and put his hand on her knee.

With a look, Laura urged me to tell him. *Why not*, I thought. *Now is as good as any.* She was prepared to tell him our plan, but I thought I could lessen the brunt.

"Do you remember Cassandra and Lucy?" I asked. "You saw their pictures. Cassandra was the daughter of a coal miner killed by Blake Donaldson. Lucy is her mother."

"Okay, sure. I remember you guys took them to lunch."

"They're dead. Donaldson is to blame."

"Oh geez, I'm sorry," Ray said, rubbing his hand across Laura's thigh.

"As soon as Charles publishes, I'm going back to Charleston to kill Donaldson."

"I'm going. Kyle is helping me," Laura asserted.

Ray stood up and took a step back so as to look at both of us. "Alright, I get that you're upset, but this is still fresh. I don't think we should be so hasty. "

"It's not fresh," Laura replied. Ray cocked his head.

"So how long have you two been keeping this from me?"

"Don't sound so conspiratorial," I interjected. "It's not about you."

"Since before we left home," Laura said, cutting me off in the process. "It's the reason Kyle agreed to help us—why he's doing all this."

A momentary flash of anger stretched across Ray's face and was quickly buried.

"The point is, it's my op. I'm going to do it with or without you. It's why I've been training," she said.

It seemed Laura really wanted to lead this conversation. I stretched out my legs and sat back.

"I don't think you realize what you're getting into," Ray lamented. "He's got to be under constant surveillance since the sentence came out. You'll get picked up."

"It's not hasty, nor is it up for debate. I'm going."

"I understand that you want to do it, but why do you *need* to?" Ray pleaded.

"He needs to pay. They all need to fucking pay!" Laura stood, regaining all the anger she'd shed earlier.

"I agreed to help. No one will blame you if you don't go." Though I said it without emphasis, I knew Ray would take it as a challenge.

Ray pursed his lips and scrunched up his forehead. "I'm not saying..."

"Sit. This is actually much bigger than Donaldson and it's time we talk about it," I said, standing up and motioning for Laura and Ray to take the couch. He paced back and forth, but finally–with some urging from Laura– took a seat next to her. She reached out and put an arm around him, immediately placating his agitation.

"If we continue to act like the secret investigative arm of the Justice Syndicate, we're wasting an opportunity to change the way government functions. When we kill Donaldson, it's going to send a different message. It's going to scare the shit out of guys like Kennard and Chang.

"That alone isn't going to make the corporate world change its behavior. They will fire their CEOs, use their PR firms to whitewash their deeds, and in the end make it that much harder for us to find evidence of their wrongdoing."

"What are you suggesting?" Laura asked.

"That after we kill Donaldson, we issue a public statement and a single demand. This will distinguish us as a separate group from the Justice Syndicate.

"During the height of the conflict between Britain and Ireland in the '70s and '80s the aboveboard political arm fighting the British was called Sinn Fein. The name is Irish for "we ourselves." The terrorist organization was called the IRA, or Irish Republican Army. We are going to follow this model: we'll be the IRA and the Justice Syndicate is going to be Sinn Fein. We're also going to need a name."

Ray was on the edge of his seat. "I can see how this would work. All that typing you've been doing—you have been working on a manifesto?"

"I have been working on a statement and list of demands," I said, grabbing the legal folder from my desk in the corner. Laura was sitting back in deep thought. I handed them each a copy. Laura quickly scanned it, and then nodded her head, dismissing it as if she'd thought of it herself.

"Yes, that's exactly right, excellent work," she said. Ray was still reading and digesting his copy but upon hearing Laura's endorsement stopped short. "Have you come up with a name for our band of thieves and assassins?" she asked.

"I have some ideas. I don't want to sponge off the Justice Syndicate, but at the same time I don't want to go with something colonial like Minutemen. I was thinking about the President's kill list and the use of drones to perform assassinations. I thought naming ourselves after a drone might be a great idea, but a name like the Predators or the Reapers sounds too—predatory. It undermines our political message."

"It undermines our patriotism and our love for this country," Ray exclaimed. "We are patriots, and our name needs to reflect that."

"Alright. I'm open to that, especially since our statement is not one of open rebellion. It's a demand for a single amendment, but it will be viewed as a declaration of war."

We sat in silence for a minute. Ray went back to reading the statement. When he was done he lifted his head. "This is good, Kyle. If I'd written it, I'd have gotten bogged down in the ways the Constitution has been subverted. This is better," he said, holding it up. "It's clear and concise!"

"So you recognize how this would make it possible for real people and not corporations to control their own government?"

"I do," Ray said. "I consider this a last resort before a civil war."

"Well then, you and I have come a long way," and as I said it I could not repress a genuine smile of relief. Maybe we weren't done arguing about politics and conspiracies, but for just once in our lives it felt like Ray and I had finally found some common ground. Then Laura stood up and slapped her hands together.

"I've got the name: Patriots of Last Resort!"

"The PLR. I like it," I said. "What do you think, Ray?"

Ray burst out, "I fucking love it!"

CHAPTER TWENTY-EIGHT

We sent Charles a message demanding he delay the release of the next trial. It was imperative that we execute Hochberg within minutes of the trial release. If we waited–even an hour–his level of protection might become impenetrable.

Determined not to make any mistakes, we cleaned the house completely. If someone broke in while we were gone, or if one of us got caught, there would be no chance it would lead to the Justice Syndicate or our true identities. The one exception to this was Ray, who had a criminal record and was in the system.

We put on clean suits and scrubbed the house of every hair and every fiber, then poured a gallon of bleach down every drain to ensure we wouldn't leave even a trace of DNA. This was overkill. We knew that, but just like we never stopped exercising or eating right, we also never stopped double-checking our precautions. Our final check was to role play from the viewpoint of a federal investigation. We pretended we were the FBI and tried to catch ourselves, each taking turns against the other two until there was no avenue of exploration remaining.

"I can't believe it's been a week and we haven't had five minutes alone together," Laura said to me. "I've been waiting to tell you something,"

We were on the upper level of a parking garage overlooking Brooklyn. We were waiting for Ray, who had just left to pick up food for the trip to Charleston.

"I really love it here," I said, "but only because we can afford it. The income inequality is so staggering. Sometimes it's hard to remember I'm no longer the little kid who felt like he was being branded with a hot iron every time they punched his free lunch card in the school cafeteria. If we can get this amendment through, then politicians will have to actually work for the people who elected them."

Laura put her arm around my waist and pulled mine over her shoulder.

"I'll sacrifice anything if it will give kids a chance I didn't have. I couldn't even get through high school without selling drugs and I couldn't get through college without stealing the diamonds. No one should have to stoop to that."

I took my arm off Laura's shoulder and clasped my hands together.

"When you came to me from law school, I never expected to feel like I needed someone so badly, like I was going to die without them. It's all different now. You're here; you're my friend and not my lover..."

"Stop," Laura said. She slid around in front of me. "I told you. I have something to say. You need to hear me, everything I'm telling you, before you say another word. I stopped having sex with Ray, with anyone, because it was the only solution I could find. Everything we're doing here is more important than me and what I want. I won't sacrifice it just because of what I feel."

"What do you feel?" I asked. She gave my chest a sharp punch.

"I told you to listen." Her voice calmed, "I love you Kyle. I love you more than I ever have before. I can't change that I'm not with you. I won't sacrifice the mission, but if I had to choose–and maybe it's easier to say this because I've chosen not to choose–but I choose you.

"When we first met, I needed something from you. At first it was just plain attraction, but I grew to love you because of your kindness and understanding. I left because I needed you to follow me on my path and you wouldn't go. We both needed to grow, but I never should have demanded that from you. Maybe we could have followed our own paths and stayed together. I don't know... I was foolish.

"What I'm really trying to say is that I know you now. I know you as an adult. I know you better than I ever have. I love you enough to want your happiness. I'm so attracted to you, I have to hide it all the time, but the way I know I truly love you is that I want you for you, more than I want you for myself. Sorry, I'm not saying this right. It's just that, for the first time in my life I want for you to be happy. I don't want to take from you or need from you. Shit, I don't even know if that's healthy, but it feels healthy. Fuck, is this making any sense at all?"

"Completely," I answered. I kissed her, holding our embrace until the minutes drained away and we had to leave. "That's my last indulgence. When you think about that kiss remember I feel the same way about you."

"Man, that smell reminds me of being in prison," Ray said as we past the stench of refineries along I-95. "The Hoobich Refinery was just three miles from the prison and on a bad wind day that smell would get carried in to the air system; there was nowhere you could hide. It was like that for the first two years until the Correctional Union filed suit. No one gave a fuck about the inmates, but because the guards sued, the state had to put in a half-million-dollar filtration system. You could still smell the reek of rotten eggs, but nowhere near as bad as it had been."

I was only half listening. My mind had been stuck on Laura, who was up ahead driving the rental car. We'd stash the van in Pennsylvania and then get another rental car, switching back and forth until we got to Virginia. There we'd purchase a beater to get us to Charleston. Sitting in the middle of the back seat, it was hard to hear him and that gave me an easy excuse to ignore him and be with my own thoughts.

"Hey, there's something I want to tell you," Ray said, trying to get my attention.

I slid to the right so I could better hear him. He was wearing a hat and sunglasses, and underneath he had on a false chin and nose. I wore the same when I drove, as did Laura, driving four car lengths in front of us. The disguises and the pull-down sunscreens on the front windows were to fool the traffic cameras.

"Sorry," I said, "I've been daydreaming. What's on your mind?"

"I wanted to clear the air about why I agreed to do this—to kill Donaldson."

"Sure," I said, though I already had an opinion on the matter.

"I notice you and Laura don't seem to have any reservations about killing again. I do; I met guys in prison who had multiple kills. I worry about becoming like them: cold and dead. Those guys are animals. They'll turn and kill on an imagined slight. You and Laura are so prepared to be assassins, I didn't want to start an argument by telling you I fear for my soul."

"You don't have to do it. I refuse to take responsibility for your soul."

"I know, but I'm in because you guys are in. Don't take that the wrong way. I believe in what we're doing as much as you two, but it's not something I would do alone like Laura. The reason I'm doing it is because we're family now." He paused and, having forgotten he was wearing a false one, tried to scratch his chin.

"Kyle, you and I have been friends for such a long time. We were on the outs, but now it's like we never were. In my mind we've stayed friends since the seventh grade. I've wiped out any memory of bad blood. From here on we are always going to be friends."

"That depends," I said.

"On what?" Ray asked, sounding dejected.

"On whether you keep up with all these sappy speeches," I joked.

"Man, I'm serious."

"I know you are and I appreciate it."

"There's more and it's important. When you came back I thought we were going to have a problem over Laura, that maybe you two couldn't be friends. It's been really cool."

"I think we've all been too focused on the work to have those kinds of problems."

"Laura and I still have our issues, but your advice was solid. I feel closer to her now than ever. It feels like we're friends now in a way we weren't before."

"That's good, Ray. I'm glad. I'm glad we're friends again." I sank back into my seat and closed my eyes.

At the time I meant it. Then slowly, over the rest of the way to Charleston, I kept fighting a growing resentment. Laura loved me. She had chosen me over Ray. I had chosen her over Ray as well. We didn't need him. He was helpful though; an extra pair of hands is always helpful when you have a job to do.

CHAPTER TWENTY-NINE

"We have to find it," Laura said, breathing out her frustration. "I've called half a dozen funeral homes. No one handled the bodies. I did a search for the obituary and came up with nothing. I'm running out of ideas. I don't see any other way but to call the city."

We were standing down by the water at the Haddad River Front Park, looking over at the fall foliage across the Kanawha River. The leaves of orange, yellow, and red shone at once in a single bright mosaic that proclaimed the season still and solemn. Then all at once, a crisp breeze raced along the river in icy wisps, chilling the backs of our necks. Spines straightened, our eyes watched as the shifting tiles of the mosaic now blazed with the motion of fire cast from branches and thrust down: burning embers that rained upon the water and floated away.

Calling the city and asking questions might be problematic in light of the Justice Syndicate's sentence. It might trigger questions in return.

"Let me try something," I said and dialed the city's newspaper. "Hello, I'd like to place an obituary."

"Hold please," came the elderly voice across the line. This was followed by a slightly younger voice.

"Classifieds Department."

"Hi, I'm...excuse me, were you with the paper a year ago?" I asked.

"I've been with the paper for the last twenty-five years. Are you wanting to place a personals ad? You might want to try the city weekly."

"Ah, no, it's just that the last time I was in town I was taking pictures and took some of Cassandra and Lucy Clark. I just found out what happened and..."

"Hold please," she said, cutting me off abruptly. The hold was short and a new, younger voice came on the line.

"Diana Holston, how can I help you?" She sounded preoccupied.

"Well, I was talking to classifieds and she transferred me to you. I'm wondering if there was ever an obituary published for Lucy or Cassandra Clark." On the other end of the line I heard the woman scoot in her chair.

"No, there wasn't any money. Her attorney settled the family's case with the government, left enough for a burial, and kept the rest for fees. Why do you ask?"

"Oh, how sad—last time I was here I took some pictures and accidently caught Cassandra and her mother in the background. I thought the family might want them."

"Their story is the most well-read story I've written in a year. I'd like those pictures. If they're clear and good I can see you get $50 a piece for them."

"I'd rather just give them to the family. If they want to they can sell them to you."

"Oh, they will. Her family is all in Spencer, about an hour drive out of the city. Probably should talk to her aunt, Dorothy Gillespie—if you can catch her sober."

"Is that where they're buried?"

"Yes. Can you save me a trip and send me some thumbnails? I don't think Dorothy has a computer, much less knows how to use one. "

"Thank you. Look, I'll just ask her if it's okay and if she says yes I'll send them to you."

"Alright, thank you," said Holston.

I hung up and turned to Ray and Laura.

"You need to get flowers in town. If we leave in fifteen minutes we can get there just before dusk and hopefully not attract any attention."

The drive on Route 119 meandered through beautiful hills the entire length of its one lane. We drove past clapboard shack after shack, set back off the road, surrounded by trees and pockmarked with rusting cars. It was rural and quaint and we might have punctuated the drive with hillbilly jokes were not our purpose so somber. Every empty space in the car was filled with flowers; the windows were cracked in order to keep us from drowning in the sickly sweet smell. Their bright colors all but shouted at us to maintain a quiet respectfulness for the memories of Lucy and Cassandra.

The town of Spencer was a blink that we only had to half endure: Route 119 entered the town at the middle. We drove to the north end and found the cemetery, also divided in half: split by Hill Street. We parked and started on the north side; it sat on a hill above the south side and held all the old graves—the pillars and the crosses from the '1800s. There were a few new stones, a handful more were just markers. We walked the length of the field twice. When we couldn't find it, I watched Laura sigh and trudge on foot across the road to the south, with Ray following behind her. I brought the car around and turned into the half-circle road that came into the cemetery and exited back out onto Hill Street.

The whole patch wasn't the size of a football field. It was littered with markers but not a single raised stone. I parked, got out, and joined them. We formed a line and made a sweep with our heads bowed low. The same family names repeated over and over. We wondered if this was the pauper's side.

"Why are there no real flowers anywhere?" Laura asked, not hiding her dismay. It was true. There were lots of flowers, some that had withstood many a season, but not a single flower that had lived, grown, and blossomed for those they honored.

Not a hundred paces from the car, five feet from driveway edge, we found their markers. Across Cassandra's stone the wheel of a mower had dragged and smeared fresh-cut grass, leaving a sharp green line. Laura knelt and sobbed, tried to rub it out with her hand and when she couldn't, wet her hand with saliva and tried again. She scraped at it with a fingernail, managing to remove only some of the stain. Ultimately, she gave up and anointed it with her tears.

"Please bring the flowers," she asked, motioning to Ray and me standing alongside her.

I signaled for Ray to wait as I scanned the area. There had been one family at the upper cemetery, but they were out of sight now. Another, an old woman, had been here straightening and arranging the plastic stems in a black cone on the far side, but she'd left as I'd parked. Still, there were occasional cars on the road and when they passed they drove slowly.

"For now, just one bouquet, the smallest one," I said to Ray, who dutifully retrieved it. I tossed him the keys and he went off and brought the car forward, closer to where we were standing. The sun was beginning to disappear. "Another three minutes," I said softly, looking at the clock on my phone.

Laura stood and sang:
I cannot say and I will not say
That she is dead, she is just away.
With a cheery smile and a wave of hand
She has wandered into an unknown land;
And left us dreaming how very fair
Its needs must be, since she lingers there.

And you-oh you, who the wildest yearn
From the old-time step and the glad return-
Think of her faring on, as dear
In the love of there, as the love of here
Think of her still the same way, I say;
She is not dead, she is just away.

"That was lovely," I said, choking back tears of my own. Ray nodded in agreement, and in the thirty seconds that remained we emptied the car of flowers. "Did you write that?" I asked her.

"No," she said, nodding her head, "it's a poem by James Riley."

We got in the car and made the return trip to Charleston without speaking. In case our call to the newspaper resulted in being tracked, I removed the battery, smashed my phone, and dropped it in the first can I found.

CHAPTER THIRTY

I ran down Beauregard Street and stopped to take in the hand-cut stones that formed Saint Paul's Lutheran Church. There are churches everywhere in Charleston, a testament to the wealth they've sapped from this largely poor community. I shook my head and ran on, listening to techno music on my replacement phone.

Before leaving the hotel, I stopped by Laura's room. She had the pictures of Cassandra and Lucy spread out on her bed. I hadn't been aware that she'd printed them. I'd hugged her and she'd whispered in my ear, "I need a day, and then I'll be ready."

I left her and went to Ray's room. I opened his door to find he had transformed himself into a middle-aged man. He'd put on pounds around the middle and lost much of his hair; what remained was gray and scraggly. I was impressed.

"In Hollywood, actors spend four to eight hours in a chair for even a short shoot. I did all this by myself in ninety minutes."

"I lack the words to express my awe at your artistic prowess. It's genius."

"Genius. That's the word, "Ray replied. "I'm going to use this disguise to go to Donaldson's house and get some pictures."

"What's your cover?" I asked him, my fingers running across the colored disks in his makeup case.

"I'm carrying a camera to take pictures of birds. If I get stopped that's all they'll find on the memory. I'm using these binoculars with a hidden camera inside to take pictures of the property."

"Perfect."

From the freeway to the river was barely a mile; I could only zig and zag so much before finding myself back at the water's edge. I stood looking across to where I knew Ray was wandering through the backyards of this town's wealthy, trying to appear guileless and perhaps a little doddering. I had wanted so much to instruct him. *Make sure you know what birds you're looking for and can name the birds you shoot. It wouldn't hurt to practice a few calls, at the least know a whip-poor-will and have a story to cover why you'd be hunting for a common bird.* I didn't say any of those things.

I had prepared myself this way more than a year ago, but never had to call upon the knowledge. I didn't press Ray. He had a bird book, he'd done such a great job with his makeup, and I told myself he was a smart adult who–outside of going to prison that one time–hadn't really screwed up yet.

Still, he was most at risk. A simple arrest, after checking his fingerprints he'd have a whole new set of problems.

I picked up my pace, running along the river this time. Though it nagged at me, I hadn't said anything. I tried to let him do this alone, without my micromanaging. Should I have offered more instruction? Did I not say those things because I was impressed with his makeup, because I didn't want to offend him, or because I secretly wanted him to get picked up? He wouldn't go back to jail, but it would be a good excuse to burn him from the rest of our operations. Laura would be mine.

I imagined what that would be like, for her and me to be a team. It would be a beautiful marriage, the only kind you can have when two people share not just attraction, but a deep abiding set of driven, core values and years of shared experience. At this point in our lives, for either of us to start over would be impossible. Who could understand where we've been? If we ever tried to find outside relationships it would require that our truest selves always be hidden.

Laura had hidden a part of herself from Ray, the part that I knew and understood. It was the part had that brought her back to me. Wasn't she now mine, even though we weren't together? From then on I couldn't see our relationship any other way. I kept these thoughts to myself, but in my heart I saw us together and it clouded my judgment.

CHAPTER THIRTY-ONE

Laura was two paces ahead of me; we were dressed in black. The woods were not thick but we had only night vision to guide our way and a great need to be quiet. She raised her hand and signaled. I stopped and waited while she made a quick 360-degree scan with a thermal image camera.

"He should be two hundred yards ahead," she whispered. "So far he's showing no signature."

I was less worried about Ray camouflaging his heat signature than I was about a security presence lying in wait. Ray had gotten into position this morning in the pre-dawn hours. "Radio on," she said tapping me on the shoulder.

The lights of the house were now in view. We avoided looking directly at them; otherwise they'd flare up our night vision. I split off to the right, moving slowly so as to not crack a twig in the underbrush. Eventually I found my way into the shadow of the house and took my position as backup for Laura.

"I'm killing him," she said yesterday while we plotted over the photos Ray had taken. "It has to be this way."

Ray was wisely silent, but I had promised to do this for her and now she was taking it away.

"No it doesn't. Why do you think so?" I asked sharply.

"Because I know both of you would die to protect me. I'm killing Donaldson. Kyle, you are going to take out Chang. And Ray, it's your job to kill Kennard." Ray started to open his mouth. "I won't debate it," Laura said.

I looked at Ray who shrugged, said nothing, then smiled and winked at Laura with a jerk of his head and a sly smile.

"Fine," I agreed. "But Ray, kill Kennard? He likes the guy."

"Fuck you, Kyle. I don't like the guy; I said he was polite."

"Oh, so you can do it?"

"Yeah, I've done it before," he said. I stared at him, incredulous. "In prison, I killed a guy." Then seeing the shock on our faces added, "I'm just not like you two. I don't need to talk about it." Laura looked even more shocked, perhaps a little betrayed. "This will work out better," Ray said. "After Donaldson is done, I'll take his car to Virginia, ditch it, and take the rental to the airport. I'll fly to Ohio and start setting up for you to come and do Chang. When Chang is done, Kyle can fly ahead and set up for Kennard."

"When? Who?" Laura gently probed. Ray shot a look at her, then nodded for her to drop the subject. She sat staring at him for a moment than added, "The one?" Ray looked deeply annoyed, his face a mixture of fear and anger.

"Yeah. We don't need to talk about it." He was indignant. He stood up from the bed and backed away as she reached out to touch him. That was how I learned Ray was raped in prison.

The issue was settled and now, outside Donaldson's door, Laura had her goggles off and her mask on. We'd chosen to wear the painted masks of the Jurors so that if we were spotted by a hidden camera it would suggest that The Patriots of Last Resort came from the ranks of a much larger random group. Laura wore a number 1, I wore a 6, and somewhere in the dark hiding under a thermal blanket, covered in forest floor, was Ray with a 12 pulled above his head.

"I'm in position," I whispered over my radio.

"You're clear," Ray said. "I have the code. He's drunk, passed out in the living room with the TV on. "

That was welcome news. I'd asked the real estate agent to come by this morning and ordered her to bring Donaldson a bottle. That Ray had the code meant Donaldson had disarmed the system to open the door for her. That he'd gotten drunk and passed out was a bonus. I wondered if, as I expected, the real estate agent was now his only friend. Ray would know how long she stayed and how they seemed to get along, but I wasn't going to break operation protocol to satiate my curiosity.

"9-4-1-7," Ray said.

Laura moved along the edge of the wood between the yard and the forest. Crouched low, she stopped every couple of paces and checked the firmness of the ground, stepping to minimize footprints. There was a double flood light over the back, and once she was under the beam she moved forward to the door. In less than a minute, she'd picked the bottom lock and the deadbolt.

I heard the click of the locks over her radio; they sounded like twigs breaking. Laura's hand was now on the handle of the door.

"Hold," I whispered. "Ray, double check—are we clear?" I could hear Ray's breathing intensify. I was being overly cautious, but the speaker in my ear was throwing off my location hearing. It did sound like a twig break in the front yard.

"You're clear. Laura, go," Ray commanded before I could move to the front and check. Damn it, Ray. I put my hand on my gun. Behind it was my stun gun, and on the other side were two flash grenades. On my forearm was my phone screen; we were in Bluetooth range. The phone produced such a bright light that I hadn't wanted to use it, but now I brought up the feed from the camera scope mounted on Ray's rifle so that I could watch Laura more clearly.

Laura slipped into the house; this triggered a beeping on the security panel by the door and a synthesized voice over the house intercom system: "Back door." Laura punched in the code, then knelt down and pulled her weapon.

"No movement," Ray confirmed.

Laura screwed on her suppressor and crept forward on the wood floor. Donaldson was just around the corner in an overstuffed chair. When she reached the carpet of the family room she stood quietly and made her way around in front of him. She paused. That was a mistake. Masked or not, she was clearly visible through the back window from Ray's position and I had to assume she was also visible from the two windows in the front.

She pulled her gun arm back hard and I was sure she was going to hit Donaldson in order to wake him up. We'd talked about this. I opened my mouth to speak. She thought better of it. She fired, emptying her entire clip: half in the head, half in the heart at close range. With most of his brain now on the back of the chair, she did not have to wait to confirm the kill.

From outside we heard only the faintest *pop*, *pop*, *pop*. Laura changed her clip and boldly strode out of the house. When she got to the threshold of the door, she looked out in the direction of Ray. Her voice was euphoric.

"That fucking bastard is dead. I feel like a god."

She stepped out into the yard, lifted up her mask, and with the back of her gun hand wiped her forehead.

That's when I heard the distinctive sound of a smartphone shutter click. I covered my phone screen and looked around the corner to put my eyes directly on Laura. That's when I heard it again. On the other side of the house, opposite Laura, I saw a small figure, its arm outstretched toward Laura. *Fuck*. Ray must have heard it too.

"I'm on it," he said. It took him a second to refocus his scope.

"Eyes only," I pleaded back. "Stand down. Laura, put your mask down, now!"

"It's a woman," Ray said, "She's alone. I have the shot."

"No Ray, I said stand down!" Finally Laura woke to the danger. She began to pull her mask down but turned toward the woman rather than away. I heard another click, but I was already off and running at the sound. I reached around and pulled out my stun gun. Laura heard the click, turned away, and started to run in my direction before getting a clear look at where she was going. Seeing we were about to collide, I dropped and slid toward her. Laura jumped high, allowing me to pass under her. I fired my gun. The two tiny electrodes propelled forward, extending a trail of wire that lodged into the shadowy woman. Fifty thousand volts coursed through her slender body. She fell to the ground unconscious.

"Nice work," Ray said.

I couldn't have been more pleased with Ray. Through this whole ordeal he never once moved from his perch until we were clear of the scene.

Laura and I pulled the woman into the light and laid her on the ground.

"Who is she?" Laura asked. I scanned through her phone.

"Diana Holston," I said. "She didn't get a single picture, they're all too dark." I pulled the battery and dropped it on the ground then stuck the phone in my pocket. "I can't believe she didn't think she'd get spotted. She's pretty fucking ambitious for a West Virginia reporter."

"I fucked up," Laura said, "What if she saw my face?"

"First—yes, you fucked up royally, but I doubt she saw much of your face, certainly not enough to identify you."

"What are we going to do, kill her?" Laura asked.

"I'll kill someone to save your life, but not for finding us out. Besides, if we killed her we'd have to take her away and make it look like an unrelated accident. If they check her phone records they'll know she pinged on a nearby cell tower. It's unlikely we could pull that off." I found Diana's purse and rifled through, finding her driver's license and Social Security card.

"I have a better idea," I said and tucked them into my pocket next to her phone. I went in to Donaldson, picked up one of Laura's casings off the floor, and used it to scoop up a drop of his blood. I placed the shell in the part of her wallet where the license used to sit and let the blood spill out. I then closed it all back up and put it away in her purse.

"Is she wearing a watch?" I asked Laura, who was bent over the body. "Yeah."

"If she wakes up, choke her out," I said. I dug around in my sleeve pocket until I found the thumb drive containing my copy of the PLR letter and proposed constitutional amendment and put it under Diana's watch band. I held it in place as Laura tightened the band.

"She wanted a story. Let's give her a choice. When she wakes up she'll notice the drive and then have to decide whether to risk losing an exclusive by turning it over to the police or hurry and get it to press. For added security, the next time she goes for her ID she'll know we know exactly who she is; the bullet and blood will send a message."

"I love it," Ray laughed over the radio.

"Ugh, what is that smell?" Laura asked.

I looked around and then called back, "It's Diana; the shock released her bowels."

We took another few minutes to scour the yard and do our best to remove any trace of our presence.

Laura and I backed out the way we came. Ray would leave a few minutes later but head in a different direction. We would not see him again until Ohio.

We changed into clothes we'd stashed earlier on the other side of the woods. I wiped down all the weapons and we placed them and the operation clothing into backpacks. Then we filled the backpacks with rocks. Using alcohol wipes, I cleaned Laura's forehead where she'd smeared blood and gunshot residue.

"I'm sorry," she said, then kissed me. I did not resist her; we kissed in the dark until I felt my heart racing.

"Come on, it's not safe here," I said. There were no cars on the road. We slipped over the train tracks, down onto the road, and then across to the river. I swung around hard, throwing the packs into the center of the current. Even if they were recovered, the water would clean away any missed evidence.

We walked back to the car. Inside we put on wigs and hats and the briefest touch of makeup, then drove off as slowly as would be expected from the old couple we were pretending to be. Later we ditched the car, removed the costumes and makeup, and wandered into our hotel as if we'd been out drinking all night.

We opened the doors between our rooms and waited together two angst-filled hours. Laura and I sat at the table holding hands and looking silently at one another. The sun would be up in twenty minutes. Our eyes had grown bleary by the time Ray signaled that he had gotten away and was far from Charleston. He'd stopped to rest and would start again in the afternoon.

Ray would go east, catch a plane in Virginia, and fly into Ohio. We would drive north and meet him there in a couple of days.

In this moment we were free. I stood and she stood with me. I gently tugged her toward me.

"I...we need to sleep," I said.

"I know. Next to each other," she replied. I agreed. We stripped down to our underwear, crawled into bed, and barely exchanged, 'I love-yous,' before falling to sleep in one another's arms.

It was one o'clock when I woke up. On the table Laura had laid out breakfast. The water was running in the bathroom. Out of bed, I grabbed a quick bite from the table, used the bathroom in my room, and returned to the sheets where we'd slept. The sound of the hair dryer in the background provided a terrific white noise that lulled me back to sleep. It seemed I'd just closed my eyes when I was hit hard round the waist.

"Oh, no you don't, mister," Laura said, straddling me, wearing nothing more than a hotel robe and her heavenly scent. "You're not getting away from me this time." Leaning down and speaking in a malicious whisper, she added, "I fucking killed a man last night, so don't think I won't rape the shit out of you."

Her coarseness shocked me. Was this how it was going to be now—we're just cold-hearted killers who quip about murder in the same way we joke about everything else? The lightheartedness of her intentions were made more clear as she let out a squeal of delight while sliding her pelvis from my abdomen, across my hip bone, and down my thigh.

"Wheeeee! Roller coaster," she exclaimed with childlike giddiness.

I shook off my reservations. It would be wrong to judge her behavior by some arbitrary expectations of propriety. We were soldiers now. We're at war, we kill, and if we're very lucky at the end of the day we have someone we love, who loves us back.

All the ferocity, all the training, and all the discipline it takes to be a good soldier we converted into passion that day. Our lovemaking was a reenactment of our earlier crime.

We silenced each other with our tongues; I pulled my lips across her body, clothing her as if my kisses could hide her from the light of day. My hands moved slowly along her figure, mirroring the slow methodic pace with which we'd approached the house: cracking no twigs, there was no sound but our gentle breathing. She knelt, picked the lock, and opened the door, and this time we strode forth together in a tender entwine. Where before there had been the whisper of radio static now the only communication was the long-awaited words, "I love you," said between us over and over. We crept forward patiently, confident that through our long preparation the mission would be successful. When the moment was right, we stood above our prey and fired. *Pop, pop, pop* and in the aftermath we lay beside each other. We felt like gods.

CHAPTER THIRTY-TWO

Later we rose, we ate, and like good soldiers, we returned and *practiced* late into the next evening. The following morning we woke early, packed, and checked out of the hotel. We drove north on Highway 84 to Cincinnati, stopping for a day.

Around noon, the news broke that Blake Donaldson had been killed. My gamble on Diana Holston had paid out. She not only broke the story, she snuck back into the house to take pictures of Donaldson's body and then cast herself as a star detective.

I'd taken her phone intending to deprive her of a camera, but apparently Ms. Holston had one in her car. She must have woken up, taken the pictures, and then called the police. She'd dumped her paper overnight and traded up. Her story in the *Washington Post* told how she had received a call inquiring about Cassandra and that this led her to drive out to the grave site. She claimed that the flowers around Cassandra's grave stuck in her mind. That night, she couldn't sleep and decided to drive over to Donaldson's house on a hunch. She arrived too late and was surprised by what she called "a gang of twelve," who tased her, but let her live.

"I can't fucking believe that bitch," Laura said, pulling down the newspaper. I looked at her over my tablet. "She didn't publish the demands or the amendment."

"Wait a day." I said, "From the online edition, it looks like they are teasing out the story. Please turn on the TV."

At a huge press conference in D.C., Diana stood in front of the cameras. She told the world that members of the Jury killed Blake Donaldson, all while touting herself as a stoic survivor of a brutal attack. After she stepped aside, they cut to a deputy director of the FBI, who threatened to find us and to take action against the Justice Syndicate.

When the television finally cut to Charles, he was unapologetic. "The Justice Syndicate does not condone the use of violence, but we will not stop the release of the next trial. The action that was taken against Blake Donaldson is the fault of the federal government's failure to prosecute him. Had they done their job he would not be dead; he would be alive and well in a federal prison."

"You know, when we met him he was like a baby-faced twenty-something and now look at him," Laura said in admiration.

"Turn off the TV and come here," Laura clicked it off and joined me on the bed.

Later we went back to the TV and watched the pundits condemn us and the Justice Syndicate for our "crimes." However, online there was a different story. Under the hashtags "#deadDonaldson," "#JusticeSyndicate," and "#Jurors" we were largely proclaimed heroes.

Laura and I ate, showered, and made love again. We slept through the night and in the morning awoke to a new story by Diana Holston.

The headline read: Donaldson Killers Claim "We are the Patriots of Last Resort."

As I was packing up to go, Laura read from the paper.

"They printed the whole list of demands," she said then began to read.

The terrorists who killed coal industrialist Blake Donaldson have threatened to kill again. They have released a set of written demands and proposed an amendment to the United States Constitution which they believe will end corporate influence in U.S. politics. The assassins, after killing Blake Donaldson and attacking this reporter with a stun gun, hid a thumb drive in my purse containing two electronic documents. The first is a set of demands that read as follows:

"We are the Patriots of Last Resort. The time has come to end the influence of commercial money in American Politics. We call upon the citizens of this great nation to rise up and enact the following reforms:

Political donations should be capped and restricted to private individuals. Political advertisements must be paid for exclusively from the lawful campaign funds of a candidate running for office. We call for an end to private lobbying by insisting that all meetings be recorded, broadcast live, and permanently archived for the public. Enact a ban permanently preventing government employees and elected officials from ever acting as lobbyists, or working in an industry that was within their purview while in office.

We will continue to punish those who violate these terms until the United States Constitution has been amended to make these reforms the law of the land.

When the Constitution has been amended we will come forward and plead guilty to our crimes."

192

"It directs readers to the paper's website to read the amendment," Laura said.

"That's good enough for me. At least, it's going to get the ball rolling. What do you think is going through Charles' mind right now?"

Laura thought about it a moment. "Well, knowing how much he respects you he's probably thrilled," she said.

"That's not what I mean. I'm not looking for worship," I said, adding a snort.

"Don't worry about it. This is totally in line with the goals of the Justice Syndicate. Besides, we'll know what he thinks about it soon enough. It's not like he doesn't have reporters from around the world beating down his door every day."

Laura came over and kissed me. The thought crossed my mind that it was never too late for Laura and me to disappear. Once the Justice Syndicate released Chang's name we were going to have to be twice as efficient if we hoped to kill him. There would be no room for mistakes. I pushed back the fear that I might lose Laura to an operational error.

"Let's hope Ray hasn't had any trouble with the drone," I said as we exited the room. Laura walked ahead of me to the elevator. All I really wanted to do was tear off her clothes again. My emotion for her left me terribly compromised. As the elevator doors closed behind us, I stole another kiss.

"Do you feel guilty?" I asked.

"About Ray? I know I should, but I don't, this feels right. I don't want him to be hurt. I still love Ray. We can't tell him," she replied with a reluctant sigh. "I think he'd lose it and we'd blow the whole operation."

The drive to Columbus was only an hour and forty minutes. We reviewed our plans along the way and then sat quietly, not speaking for the last forty minutes. Again, the thought crossed my mind that we didn't need Ray and I wondered if there was a way to get rid of him. I began to feel guilty and wondered if Laura's remorse would set in during the operation.

I looked at her until she turned and smiled at me.

"When we get to Columbus, I—"

"You don't need to tell me, Kyle," Laura said, cutting me off. "We're going to be all business."

"Good," I affirmed.

"Except when we're not," she said without a smile.

CHAPTER THIRTY-THREE

We stopped at a storage unit just outside the city and loaded up the car with our gear. We traded vehicles, switched identification, and retrieved new phones.

"Hi," Laura said sweetly. "We just pulled away from the unit. We're driving to the hotel now. Uh-huh, that doesn't sound good. Did you try the mic on his phone? What about at home? All right, I'll tell him. We're going to check in, get some lunch and I'll bring you some food. Love you, bye."

Hearing her say "love you" to Ray pierced my heart a little. Then I told myself that I should get used to it. If Ray ever found us out, who knows what would happen. The last thing we needed was a shootout over Laura.

"Chang's cell phone is no longer responsive; Ray thinks he's swapped it out," Laura reported. "He said there has been a train of black SUVs in and out of the Hochberg all day and that Mrs. Chang had met with a couple of guys at the house and shown them around. Ray thinks they were security professionals."

"Fuck," I moaned. "Clearly he suspects he's going to be a target. What about his route home?"

"He's still taking the same route home and the cameras in the house are still up. So that's good news."

She was right, it was good news. Our plan was to hit him on the drive home with a sniper shot. When he left the office he always used the same car and driver. We'd run this drill five times on five different days using a laser and every time I'd been able to make the kill. Tomorrow, once he was in his car and on the way home, we'd send a signal to Charles, who would release the trial on Chang. Ten minutes later Chang would be dead.

Separately, Laura and I checked into our rooms. I unpacked, opened my computer, and tied into the server to access our surveillance. Ray had the drone circling Hochberg. Our access into Hochberg's servers was still active and our GPS tracker on Chang's car was functioning.

Mrs. Chang was at home. She was in the master bedroom. Her phone tap was active, and she was talking to René.

"This is his thing," Margaret said, exasperated. "I told him that if he goes into lockdown I'm not staying in this house. I'll drive into the city and get a hotel. What's that place by you, the Becksted? I don't really care. I'll be at your place, not in the hotel."

There was a knock on my door. I left Mrs. Chang laughing on the phone and opened the door for Laura.

"Aren't you supposed to be taking food to Ray?" I asked.

"They're making it," she said, kicking off her shoes. "That gives me at least fifteen minutes."

"You're insatiable," I said. "I thought we weren't going to do this?"

Laura pointed to the background window with the drone footage.

"It's safe," she purred. "We have time, Captain."

"Oh, have I been promoted?"

"If we're going to be soldiers, someone has to be in charge," she said, now standing naked in front of me.

Afterwards I held her in my arms with one eye over her shoulder, watching the computer to see that the drone was still up. I did not want to let her go. We'd just finished and already I was overcome with the desire to nibble every inch of her body.

"Laura," I said tenderly.

She became stern, "That's General to you, Captain."

"General? I thought I was in charge."

"Oh, silly man," she said, standing and getting dressed. "If I wasn't a general I wouldn't have the authority to promote you to captain." Then she came and kissed me sweetly, turned, and without further word walked out the door.

CHAPTER THIRTY-FOUR

The message had come from Charles that he was under heavy surveillance. He was raided by the FBI, but had been ready for them and came out largely unscathed. The feds had not been able to uncover the next target. I was worried that they would prevent Charles from uploading by shutting down the Justice Syndicate website. Charles assured us that it would not matter. The sentence against Chang would be delivered simultaneously on multiple feeds. We put our trust in Charles and began the operation.

The Jack Nicklaus Freeway, Interstate 270, is the belt loop around Columbus, Ohio: three lanes in each direction, separated by a span of grass and plain metal guard rails on either side. During rush hour, barring traffic accidents, the highway is busy; traffic often slows but is seldom bumper-to-bumper.

The Ohio Department of Transportation allowed trees, bushes, and other foliage to grow in the sloped fill dirt surrounding the east-side, south-facing abutment of the Roberts Road overpass. From this vantage point I had excellent coverage and a clear view of northbound traffic. We had devised an excellent perch that allowed my body to lay flat and my weapon to sit comfortably on its bipod.

On the east side of Roberts Road, just past the off-ramp, was the Lion's Den Adult Superstore. In the parking lot Ray waited in the cab of a stolen semi. Twenty yards from me we'd stashed a dirt bike which would act as my getaway vehicle. Laura was stationed six miles away in the parking lot of an abandoned factory complex, flying the drone that was circling over Hochberg.

Lying in this position for so long without moving was by far the hardest thing I had ever attempted to do in my life. When I first learned parkour there were plenty of missed steps and poorly executed falls. I'd had my fair share of scrapes, bumps, and bruises. Once, I even sprained my ankle so badly I couldn't fully put weight on it for two weeks. None of it compared to the tediousness of lying flat at a hide site, wearing a ghillie suit. I'm meant to be in motion.

It was made more aggravating by the fact that Ray loved it. He had been overjoyed to sit outside Donaldson's house, half buried in the ground for an entire day. When I suggested my turn would be unbearable, he bragged and offered to do it for me. Then he smugly teased me for half an hour.

I felt there were a couple of differences in our sniping. Ray had something to do: he got to observe Donaldson and get the alarm code. Over the hours he had a worthwhile task to occupy his mind. My prey was still a twenty-minute drive away. All I had was the endless stream of traffic to keep me focused. I endured the tedium by meditating, and I drowned out the memory of Ray's earlier taunts by smugly recalling that I was fucking his girlfriend.

"He's on the move," Laura said over the speaker in my ear. A minute later she followed with, "He's out of the gate."

"I've requested the verdict, awaiting confirmation," Ray returned, then added, "Does he have a follow?"

"Two men entered one of the SUVs beside his car but they're holding. I'll keep eyes on it as long as I can without losing the target," Laura reported. "Stand by," she said, "target's ETA is nine minutes." A few minutes later she came back, "I've lost the SUV. Maintaining visual on the target."

Through his mic I heard Ray start the semi.

"Still no verdict," Ray said and then joked, "For afterwards, I've purchased us all sex toys and love dolls. Yes, it's been that long."

Neither Laura nor I said a word.

"What?" Ray continued. "I thought we were all a team here? Did you guys slip out for prostitutes or something?"

"I've got confirmation," Laura exclaimed, setting off a little feedback in our ears. "Via Twitter, a sentence of death for Felix Chang," she read.

Ray was now moving. He pulled onto Roberts Road and took the on-ramp. He pulled the truck across a lane and a half of rush-hour traffic, stopped, got out of the cab, and ran off the freeway. A hundred yards, through the brush, was Old Roberts Road. There, Ray took his helmet and jumped on the seat of the waiting motorcycle. He headed south across to Wilson's Road. In a few minutes he would be behind Chang and able to provide backup in case I needed emergency extraction or an alternate shooter. Traffic began to slow.

"He's just passed under I-70," Laura blurted. That put Chang just about two miles away and past the only exit from which he could have hoped to escape.

"I'm in position below Trabue," said Ray. Trabue crossed over the freeway, but there was no exit or entrance onto the interstate. There was no guard rail at this point on the highway below. Ray had taken the southern frontage road, which came to the edge of the wood between the highway and some private residences. There was a footpath through the wood that offered Ray's motorcycle access on to the freeway. It wouldn't be easy, but if Ray had to he could ride alongside Chang and get a good shot at him.

"Trabue in ten seconds, "Laura counted, "nine...eight...seven..."

"I've got eyes on him," Ray shouted, cutting off Laura. "He's through the underpass, center lane."

"There's a Ryder truck," I remarked. Traffic had now slowed to a crawl.

"Hang tight," Ray shot back, "he's moving around it."

"Got it," I said. "I've got the hood. The lanes of traffic were now alternating as cars took turns trying to get around the abandoned semi up ahead. I just needed the Ryder truck to move over or for Chang to move up a single car length. Then I'd have my kill shot. I waited.

Some do-gooder in the far left lane stopped and started waving cars through from the right. The Ryder truck pulled forward, completely obscuring Chang.

"I've lost visual," I said.

"Incident management is four miles out, coming from the north," Laura reported, then added, "I've got two state troopers inbound. One is westbound on I-70. I give him twenty minutes. The second is crossing over on Fishinger. About fifteen, maybe twenty."

"Roger," I said. "This fucking Ryder truck is in my way.

The left-hand traffic started moving again. Chang's car came into view. "I have visual," I said. Chang's driver was clearly in my scope. "Now I have the driver. Chang was on the passenger side. Suddenly Chang's car surged forward, out of my scope. Quickly I refocused, retrained my gun, and had Chang's form drifting through my scope. My finger was in place around the trigger as Chang came into my crosshairs.

"Who the fuck are these guys?" Ray shouted over the radio. "I've got two motorcycles, uniformed, not police northbound, moving fast between cars."

"I see them," Laura barked back. "And a black SUV west bound coming up behind you on Trabue."

It didn't matter: Chang was in my sights, my finger was on the trigger, and I began to pull. Then, Chang's car did the unexpected: it turned sharply to the right and spun 90 degrees. The bumper connected with the guardrail and Chang and the driver ducked below the windows.

"Fuck, fuck, fuck," I screamed. "He's gone. I've lost the shot. It's a fucking wash."

"The SUV's on the north spur of the frontage road," Laura shouted.

The two motorcyclists came into view. They skidded, bringing their bikes to a halt at Chang's car. The two armed men laid the motorcycles on the ground. They opened the back door of the car. One of them covered Chang's body with his own while the other fitted Chang with a heavy protective vest and his own helmet.

"The SUV just hit the logging yard adjacent to the highway," Ray said. There was a loud cracking as the SUV rammed a chain-link fence, taking it down, then ran over some young trees. It pulled right up to the highway. The two armed men ran with Chang, crouched low through traffic, and put him into the SUV. Then they ran back to their motorcycles. The SUV backed up with the same speed at which it had torn onto the scene. Just like that, Chang was gone.

Laura had been giving a play-by-play. The sound of Ray's bike came over the radio, followed by his voice.

"I'm following," Ray said. Four minutes later, "I've got visual. These guys aren't fucking cops."

"Well, when you're worth half a billion dollars," I said, "you can afford paramilitary security firms."

"You've got to get out of there," Laura said. "You've got a ten-minute window."

That was far more time than we'd expected had I killed him. I broke down the gun, stored it in the backpack and took off on the motorcycle.

CHAPTER THIRTY-FIVE

Chang was rushed home where he was met by additional security forces. They shut every blind and closed off every possible hope of assassination. Two hours later, FBI agents began pouring in from the Cincinnati field office. Eight agents stood outside the Chang home, conferring with the head officer of the private security force. From their friendly salutations it appeared the leader of the security force was former FBI. Together they entered the house and approached the living room where Mr. and Mrs. Chang had been quarantined.

"Mr. Chang, this is Special Agent in Charge Topher Correll."

"Thank you Paul," said Agent Correll, and then to Mr. and Mrs. Chang in what seemed his most charming voice, "I have two orders: the first is to make your personal security my top priority, the second is to investigate and apprehend those who are trying to do you harm."

"Thank you," said Mr. Chang gruffly, cutting him off. "As you can see I have my own security services, so I'd like to save the taxpayers as much money as possible. I ask that you please coordinate directly with Mr. Williams," Chang said, pointing to Paul. "I caution you to not get in their way. If another situation erupts, and Paul needs assistance, he will request your backup. This should free up the FBI to immediately zero in and neutralize the threat. Is that agreeable to you, Agent Correll?"

"It's Special Agent, Mr. Chang, and of course my men will coordinate with Mr. Williams and allow them to take the lead. Mr. Williams and I are going to confer about security while we do a quick walkthrough of the house. Afterwards we will withdraw to the street."

Mr. Chang nodded his agreement. Mrs. Chang spoke up unexpectedly.

"Special Agent Correll, I will be moving downtown. I'd like a single agent to accompany me to the hotel."

From the expression on Mr. Chang's face, we could tell her announcement was unexpected.

"Margaret," Mr. Chang intoned. "But why?"

"I'm not a target. I have work to do as well. Two days from now I have to be in Paris... can't afford to get pinned down here."

"Darling, but surely you must take some of Mr. Williams' men?" Chang pleaded.

"My love," she said, with disarming tenderness as she rubbed his shoulder, "I want every one of these men protecting your life. I've already called an international security service." She knelt down next to him. "They'll be here in fourteen hours. You know I have to have a detail that can operate anywhere in Europe." She concluded by kissing him on the cheek.

This was probably the only time anyone had ever seen Chang look defeated. With a nod he acquiesced to his wife. Then he turned to the men in the room.

"Will you please excuse us for a minute?" Williams and Correll left the room, closing the door behind them.   "Marge, don't worry, this will all be over soon," he said to her.

Margaret Chang's next words were quietly spoken, but sharp and biting. "You have embarrassed me, Felix, with this scandal. I have received calls in the last four hours from five of the world's top charities refusing my foundation's donations, and I'm sure that's only because the rest of the world is still sleeping."

"You know this will pass," he said, then added a smug rebuttal. "Nothing this terrorist organization has posted about me can be prosecuted."

"You had better hope not. If you've permanently damaged my reputation," she said, standing and holding up her hand to stop herself from saying more.

Chang stood up and gave her a hug. "Oh my love, I'm so sorry. You know I will fix this. Please, let's stick together. We are stronger as one."

Margaret appeared to be choked up and answered him by shaking her head no.

"I beg of you. Stay with me tonight," Chang said, running his hand through her hair. "At least until your detail arrives."

Again Mrs. Chang shook her head. She pulled away from him, a tear on her cheek.

"I love you, "she said to him, "Oh Felix, please fix this." She walked to the door, put her hand around the handle, and then turned back and added, "I'll be at the Becksted."

Laura grabbed a computer and started scouring the logs.

"She made a reservation online with her phone. I can't believe I missed it," she said, then quickly turned to her own phone and dialed up the Becksted. The phone connected and she walked into the bathroom.

"I can't believe they haven't swept his house and uncovered our bugs," Ray said with great pleasure.

"I'm not complaining," I replied. "They don't suspect. They're worried about a shooter. By now they have to know that truck was part of an attempt."

"She's got the top-floor executive suite. The best I could do was to get a basic room on the top floor," Laura said, returning and gathering her things. "Ray, let's go. If we hurry we can get a camera in her room."

Ray hopped up and performed a quick inventory of the equipment.

"Margaret's in the master bedroom packing," I said.

Ray walked out the door. Laura turned back, gave me a wink, and a smile, and blew me a kiss before following him.

For the next two weeks we were separated. One of us was always at the Becksted, though neither Margaret Chang nor her husband was ever there. She spent her time around the block in the luxury condo of her lover: René Olivier. We'd broken into René's house and set up cameras, and found an open apartment below his from which to monitor them.

Whoever was not watching one of the two camera stations was tasked with following Chang and trying to find a hole in his security. This proved insanely difficult; his defenses were practically impenetrable. However, observing the movements of a world-class security company and a squad of FBI agents was highly educational.

Once Chang realized that the FBI was not using Special Agent Corell to pursue a criminal investigation, he relented and allowed the agents to use part of his home as a command center. This brought all of their planning directly in front of our cameras throughout the entire operation.

The job of following Chang was fraught with difficulty. He traveled in a small caravan of three SUVs. Tailing him on a day-to-day basis meant constantly changing cars, license plates, costumes, and driving styles. Occasionally it required us to suffer through the pulse-raising experience of getting spotted, a fact we were only aware of because of our surveillance at the command center. Had we not such access, one of us would surely have been detained and arrested. Despite the anxiety of it all we got better, much better at tailing, surveillance, and evasion than we ever could have hoped.

The most entertaining assignment was watching René's condo. Their unusual mating choreography was not an anomaly. It was the norm. The three of us were aroused and awed by their daily performances.

Laura drew from her childhood and selected the terminology to describe their intimate moments. We referred to Margaret and Rene' as the dancers; their lovemaking was the dance. Each time they began, whoever was on duty would cry out through the radio, "Curtains up!" Each phase we called a movement. First movement was flirting no touching, second movement touching but no penetration, and the third movement was broken into two phases we called, "third movement build" and "the climax." It was the responsibility of the person on duty to call out each phase to the others, and at the conclusion to stand up and clap.

Two of us were tied to permanent locations, the third was mobile, but as a result of the daily dance we were all constantly aroused. On any day in which either Laura or I were mobile we could do something about it: whoever was roaming could sneak back to the other. We did this far more frequently than we should have.

When one of us was watching the condo, frequently Laura and I joined the dance.

"We had better still fuck like this when we're their age," Laura said, while watching over my shoulder during the middle of our own two-step.

"I promise we will be; so long as we're fucking each other," I quipped back.

"I've decided," she said during the third movement build.

"What?" I asked. But then our breathing increased and she didn't answer.

"I'll never leave you again," she cried during the climax.

Later that evening while I staked out the condo, the three of us began a video conference to brainstorm a new method of dispatching Chang.

"I've got nothing," said Ray. "Short of a bomb, I have no idea how we're going to do it."

"I've got a plan," Laura said in that confident and determined tone that always left me worried about what was coming next.

"Let's hear it," I said.

"We infiltrate Hochberg Chemical. We go in blended into a group from lunch and hide out in the Sales and Marketing building. It's the closest to the President's building, but its security isn't as tight. There's an hourly sweep during the day and random badge checks, but nothing after four when Chang leaves. There are utility closets on every floor, and I can hide in any one of them until it's time to move. After Chang leaves for the evening, security drops to a skeleton crew.

"At five, there is a mass exodus. That's when I'll cross over into the President's building. You two will create a diversion to draw away the security team while I hide in the top-floor utility closet. Once inside, I'll cut through the drywall in the rafters and tunnel across until I'm over the executive washroom.

"The next day, when Chang uses the bathroom, I'll shoot him dead while he's taking a piss," Laura concluded triumphantly.

"No way, that's fucking suicide. How the hell will you get out?" Ray asked, not hiding his contempt for the plan. "Even with a suppressor the sound will likely draw a guard into the bathroom."

"When he comes I'll drop a flash grenade, and then make my way back to the utility closet and onto the roof. I'll rappel down the side of the building where the security guys park their motorcycles. I'll steal a bike, bolt across the campus, and disappear into traffic."

Ray was right. This idea was suicide, though I was never going to say that out loud. As crazy as her plan was, it was still the best plan we had. Perhaps there was a better way to do it.

"Let me play devil's advocate a minute," I said. "What if you get made when you first get onto the campus?"

"I'll be carrying anti-Hochberg leaflets," she said. "I'll pass myself off as a protester. Worst-case scenario, they pick me up on a minor trespassing charge. I'm a former protestor, I know the lingo. Most likely I won't even get charged; they'll just escort me off the property."

The number of protestors surrounding Hochberg Chemical had quadrupled since the Justice Syndicate released the evidence on Chang. Sometimes the protestors were very aggressive; it was not uncommon for Chang's motorcade to get hit by a balloon full of paint.

"That's a big 'if,'" I replied, "And when they search you and discover you're carrying a flash grenade and enough rope to rappel twenty stories?"

"The rope won't be a problem. I'll thread it through loops sewed into ribbons, and turn it into a large circular purse. As for the flash grenade, I'll make my own and carry it in parts. They'd have to be specifically looking for the parts to be able to find it. As for my belay, put a carabiner on it and it's a key chain."

"And let me guess, you'll sew your harness right into your shorts?" I asked.

"No, I'll just wear a uniform rappel belt," she said, and laughed, though her tone had been defensive.

"You'll never get on the campus and into the building," Ray said. "No, I'm not willing to risk you."

Afraid that the idea that she was Ray's to risk might set her off, I quickly interjected, "Hang on, let's all take a deep breath. We're brainstorming; all ideas on the table."

Laura was undeterred.

"I know I can make it onto the campus and into the building."

"Oh, and how do you know that?" Ray snorted, taunting her with a cock of his head.

"Because I've already done it—so fuck you."

"You did what? When?" I asked. The thought of her running such a risk simultaneously left me angry and terrified; that she had accomplished it and gotten back out awed me.

"Two days ago."

"And you didn't tell us?"

"That's so not cool," Ray chastised. "Not cool at all."

"You guys would never have believed it possible if I didn't do it first."

"No, I wouldn't have," Ray shot back, "but that doesn't mean you endanger the entire team by going off and running your own op completely blind. What the fuck has gotten into you?"

"Enough!" I shouted, loud enough to get them to stop bickering. "It's over and done with. We can talk about the risks we should and shouldn't take tomorrow after everyone's had a full night's sleep. We've been working too damn hard. Just drop this until tomorrow."

"Fine, whatever," Ray said, tipping his chair over while standing and crossing his arms. "I need to get out of here and go for a run anyway."

That sounded like a good idea to me. I could have used one myself; nothing clears my head like a brisk run.

"Holy shit," I uttered in surprise loud enough that it drew Laura and Ray back to the conference. "Curtain's up."

"Again?" Laura and Ray said in unison.

"Well at least someone is getting it," Ray said, looking at Laura and then turning away from her.

Watching the two of them I was inspired with a solution to kill Chang. Laura would not have to put herself in danger.

CHAPTER THIRTY-SIX

Felix Chang was a proud man. In the face of the damning evidence presented by the Justice Syndicate, he was unapologetic. The agricultural industry's reliance on modified seed grain and weed-killing chemicals insulated Hochberg Chemical from profit loss by boycotts.

Internally, the board of directors, Chang's own public relations firm, and the chief of police urged him to publicly leave Ohio until the protests thinned out. Chang defiantly refused, writing to them by email, "I will not be bullied."

The marketing department at Hochberg had already placed in the works a plan to change the name of the company with a seventy-five million dollar rebranding campaign. They were just waiting for enough time to pass before rolling it out. By committing to spend this money, by pre-buying ad time on major television networks, and an intense publicity push, they minimized negative media.

Chang's wife was a different story. In private, he pleaded for her to return. At her insistence, he removed himself from their charitable foundation, turning over to Margaret complete control of three quarters of a billion dollars. Afterwards he sat alone in his office, sweat-drenched and shaking, as he stared at a picture of his wife. He then picked up the phone, placed a call, and used his own funds to double the budget of a separate rebranding campaign for the foundation.

Though the foundation's public relations campaign significantly rehabilitated its reputation, Margaret did not return to her husband. Felix Chang would never apologize to anyone for his criminal actions, not even his wife. However, in order to get her back, he came as close as he ever would. Sitting at his home desk, Felix Chang placed twelve very personal calls that, from the sweat on his brow and the look on his face, caused him more pain and humiliation than he had ever before endured.

Individually, and in three different languages, he called the directors of some of the world's top charities. They were all people with whom it was clear he had previously enjoyed a close personal relationship. With the utmost humility he told each of them that Margaret should not be blamed for any of his perceived personal failings, told them of his removal from the foundation, and then sought to elevate them with praise for their admirable contributions to humanity. In some he confided that, "until this whole thing blows over, Margaret and I—are taking a little break."

A week later—after confirmation that his attempts to improve Margaret's and the foundation's reputation had been successful—she still had not returned to him. When she returned his phone calls they were short and strained. In the privacy of his bedroom he paced and tore at his hair. He tried flowers and expensive gifts, but they languished in her hotel room and were often stolen by the maid staff.

At the height of his frustration, a plain manila envelope arrived by mail to Felix Chang's house. The envelope was addressed to Margaret Chang to assure that Felix's security team would scan it for hazards, but not open her private correspondence. The handwritten envelope had René Olivier's name and his condo listed as the return address. The envelope sat undisturbed for one day on Chang's dining room table before it came to his attention.

A little perplexed and hesitant, Felix opened the letter to discover the best of those wonderful photos I'd taken from René's neighbor's balcony across the street. There could be no doubt that it was Margaret and René making love in those pictures. From the close-ups of her face during the climax, there could be no doubt she deeply enjoyed it.

I was not sure what Chang's demeanor would be after he saw the photos. I was a little worried based on his lack of expression that he had, with the flick of an emotional switch, completely written her off. He placed the pictures back in the envelope, folded it up, and stuck it in his breast pocket. I presumed that tomorrow he would show them to René as he was firing him.

He then went down to his security detail, informed them that he would be going to dinner in the city, and called his favorite restaurant asking that his standing table be made ready. Fifteen minutes later at the restaurant Chang ordered a bottle of sake, the bluefin tuna, smoked salmon tartare with warm mayonnaise, and white sturgeon caviar. After his waiter left the table he stood up and walked to the bathroom at the back of the restaurant.

"He's on the move," Laura reported from inside the restaurant. "I'm on him." Seconds later she said, "He's gone out the back."

In the apartment under René's condo, I got ready. We'd reduced our presence to a single laptop, which I now closed and stored in its case.

"He's entered the building," said Laura, the radio crackling in my ear. "You called this perfectly. He's in the elevator." I threw the laptop bag over my shoulder and exited the apartment dressed in black slacks, a pale blue dress shirt, and a reversible jacket. I had a shoulder holster with my secondary weapon, a smoke canister, and a flash grenade. In my hand I carried my weapon with its suppressor already screwed in place. I took the stairs by twos and threes up to René's floor.

I pulled down my mask; tonight I was wearing a number 1. I entered the ninth-floor hallway and approached the elevator.

"Passing the fifth floor...sixth floor...seventh floor," Laura counted off in my ear from the lobby below.

Far down the end of the hall, a door opened and a couple, dressed for the evening, exited their apartment chatting giddily. Without hesitation I pulled the smoke grenade from my belt, simultaneously releasing the pin, and rolled it down the hall toward them. The smoke began to unfurl as the elevator chimed.

The door came open. Chang was standing in the elevator with the open manila envelope in his hand. His face was an explosion of fury. He wore the look of a man about to take his revenge. Then he saw me and was awash with panic. He reached out toward the elevator buttons. I fired three rounds into his heart at close range. There was a scream down at the end of the hall where I'd thrown the smoke. Chang stumbled backward. I turned my head. Through the smoke I could not see the screaming woman. Back to Chang, I fired three more shots into his chest and then four into his head at point blank range.

Chang collapsed to the floor, releasing the envelope as he hit the ground. I reached in, picked up the envelope, and placed a thumb drive in his hand. The drive contained the same files as the one I'd given Holston. It also contained an encrypted message and the requisite public key. They sat outside the file system where only a detailed forensic analysis would find. It would leave no doubt that this assassination was committed by the Patriots of Last Resort. I pulled out the stop on the elevator, causing the bell to ring continuously.

As I stepped from the elevator, the second elevator door opened and Laura waved me inside. I hid my mask in her bag, and then we helped one another with our wigs and makeup: we found pretending to be old people reliably disarming. In this case it proved unnecessary. The police and fire departments responding to calls from the frightened tenants, were still ten minutes away.

Laura and I had no trouble making our getaway, though we stopped briefly before returning to Ray. More than five miles away from the growing chaos at René's building, we removed our costumes. We pulled off the freeway and onto the first darkened stretch of road we found, shamelessly making love on the hood while cars buzzed by on the freeway.

Later that evening we took three separate cars. Ray drove to Cleveland, Laura drove straight to New York to begin the set up for killing Kennard, and I drove to Virginia, where I retrieved our van and headed home.

CHAPTER THIRTY-SEVEN

With Chang dead, René Olivier was appointed CEO of Hochberg Chemical. There was speculation in the press as to why Chang inexplicably eluded his own security detail to attempt to visit René. No one blamed the FBI or the members of High Ridge Security, the company that had been protecting Chang. René took over at Hochberg, High Ridge Security was gobbled up by one of the world's largest private military contractors, which in turn was purchased by Hochberg and renamed Bonus Security International (BSI).

The thumb drive I'd placed on Chang's body left no doubt who was responsible for his death. René and Margaret knew why Chang had come to visit that night. That knowledge led to the discovery of our surveillance at René's condo and at the Chang residence. René used Bonus Security to remove it, as far as we could detect, but did not share that information with Homeland Security.

On the surface it appeared that René made some effort to restore the company and steer it away from its previous bribery scandals. It was really too soon to tell if he would define himself as a different kind of leader. That he surrounded himself with twice the security that Chang employed could have been a reaction to our intrusion into his personal life. It could also have signaled his intent to be twice as aggressive as Chang had been. In any case, should he need reminding, we had enough video of him and Margaret to release a hundred sex tapes.

Chang's death sent a shock wave around the world. CEOs of oil and gas companies, of firearms manufactures, of the behemoth banks all increased their internal security, many of them relying on BSI for their expert security services. Fortunately, George Kennard did not consider himself at risk.

He either saw himself as a small fry, or—I suspected—he simply didn't believe he'd ever done anything serious enough to deserve Chang's fate. When I arrived in New York, I found Laura and Ray in the basement, monitoring the cameras in Kennard's homes.

"Welcome back," Laura said with a smile as I came down the stairs.

"Thank you. What's the 411 on Kennard? Charles is anxious to publish the next trial. He says he's beginning to hear some movement out of the tech industry. There are some proposals to cut off all funds for government lobbying."

Through an ecstatic grin Laura said, "That's unbelievable. We never expected that."

I pointed to the monitors.

"We've been watching them for hours. They've been acting kind of buggy. Sometimes they cut out for five minutes at a time. Ray thinks there's some interference."

Ray nodded in agreement, then stood and patted me on the back.

"I think we'll be ready to go in a couple of days," he said.

"So you have a plan?"

"Yeah. Simple. I use the key we made to his house, walk in, and shoot him dead while his wife is in the Adirondacks. How was the drive? You must be starving."

"It was very long. And yes, I'm starving."

Ray smiled and started toward the stairs. "I made dinner earlier, there's leftovers. I'll just pop up and warm them up for you."

"Thank you," I said with as much gratitude as I could muster. Ray didn't usually make dinner. I assumed he had done so in an attempt to patch things up with Laura. I suddenly felt a twinge of jealousy. What if he had? Laura and Ray had just spent a day and a half together alone. As much as I trusted and loved her, I wasn't fool enough to believe her loyalties weren't divided. She was, after all, cheating on Ray with me.

Laura gave me a hungry look and patted the couch beside her. I took a seat and she leaned over and whispered in my ear.

"God I missed you. Ray's been so horrible I had to give him a hand job just to keep him off of me."

I yanked my head back, shocked. Laura raised an eyebrow and then shook her head.

"You need to learn to trust me again. I told you, I'm yours," she said, and then bizarrely licked the side of my face. "And you belong to me."

Surprisingly, I found this deeply reassuring. I smiled at her, patted her on the leg, and then turned my attention to the monitors. Kennard was in the attic working on his calligraphy, making a very authentic-looking copy of the Bill of Rights.

Ray came downstairs carrying a tray of food. As I ate we went over the details of Ray's plan. We batted it back and forth a little, but in the end I had to admit it was solid. It was simple, clean, and above all, easy.

I eased the car into a residential spot just two blocks from Kennard's house at noon on the day before we planned to execute him. I had a special fondness for this spot, next to an alleyway, which led to an unpublished parkour course I'd discovered by accident. Not everyone liked to share their routes, preferring to master the route well ahead of the competition. Some of the best routes went unpublished for as long as possible.

I particularly loved this course because, like the Circus route, it went across several sets of rooftops. Running across strangers' roofs was wildly fun, but finding courses that did was rarer than one would expect in a city this size.

I took one of two full gas cans out of the trunk and topped off the tank. This zippy little Mini was going to be our emergency getaway car. I put the can back in the trunk, put on my parkour gloves and shot down the alleyway to the drainpipe that led up to the roof. In a few minutes I was passing Kennard's house on the roofs of the townhomes across the street. Given his knowledge of my face and his love of parkour, I considered it fortunate that there was a large tree blocking my view of his house and his view of me.

Running on, I came to a jump that required leaping from the building to a lamppost and sliding to the ground. I jumped without hesitation and found my decisiveness rewarded with a clean catch of the post and a quick but gentle descent to the ground. I shot down another alleyway that turned left and terminated at a busy street. I needed to cross to pick up the route on the other side.

In the road there was a terrible accident: a semi-truck had collided with a black town car. The town car was smashed, flipped on its side, with its passengers displayed in grisly repose. The driver had been ejected halfway through the windshield, and his body had been run over by the rear wheels of the semi as it drove over the hood of the car. As the semi-trailer had continued its travel off the car, it had flipped it as if it were a tiddlywink.

A female passenger sitting in the backseat had been ejected from the rear door, but then crushed underneath it as it hit the ground. She lay face up with her eyes open, blood pooled around the back of her head and from her body at the edge of the car. Her lovely face was pale and unmarred from the accident. Her lips still held freshly painted crimson lipstick.

She was Ileana, the woman with whom Ray had flirted. Beautiful Ileana, who had given us a ride into this neighborhood, ultimately leading to the discovery of Kennard's house.

I turned away from the gruesome scene and walked home with a knot in my stomach. It did not seem feasible to tell Ray, especially not one day before he needed to be clear-headed enough to kill Kennard. The walk home passed slowly; outside I stood and composed myself before entering. I could see no benefit in burdening Laura, either.

Images of Ileana's dead body pulsed in my head. For the first time since we'd begun these operations, I was glad someone else was pulling the trigger and not me.

CHAPTER THIRTY-EIGHT

The following night I waited at the car. Laura was back at the house monitoring the live feeds. Ray, wearing a hoodie, walked steadily toward Kennard's front door. I followed the action on my radio. As I sat in the car the images of Ileana's broken body kept washing through my mind. Ileana and Laura were approximately the same age. The thought that Laura could die as a result of our activities kept pressing into my mind and upsetting my concentration.

Sitting down got to be too much. I got out of the car and walked down the alley, toward the pipe that marked the start of the parkour route. It was dark here, which gave me room to pace. I put on my parkour gloves and when the pacing didn't work, I expended a little excess energy by running up a nearby wall and doing a couple of backflips.

"Fifty feet," Ray said to indicate his distance to Kennard's house.

"Requesting verdict," Laura said, and then spoke again just thirty seconds later. "The verdict is in—you're a go. He's in the master bedroom, packing."

It was highly unlikely we would need a getaway car on this operation, I told myself. I grabbed the drainpipe and climbed to the top of the roof. I took a deep breath in the cool night air.

"Entering," Ray said as he slipped the key into Kennard's front door.

"I've got you on the front foyer camera," Laura replied. From now until Kennard was dead, Ray needed to be silent. Laura provided the play-by-play.

"He's through to the family room. He's entered the rear stairwell." There was no camera covering the stairwell. She would pick him back up on the hallway camera at the top of the stairs. I heard static behind Laura's breathing.

"Fuck! I've lost him. I've lost the cameras," Laura said in a panic.

"You said they've been buggy, let's just play it through," I said calmly. Below me a gate opened into the alleyway. A man stepped out and started walking slowly toward the street.

"You don't understand, I've lost his radio too," Laura intoned.

"It's probably the same interference that's messing with the cameras," I whispered. "Let's give him a few minutes."

The man in the alleyway began to run toward the street—his hands together in a familiar pose. By the car, I heard the screeching of tires and saw the flashes of blue, red, and white light.

"Fuck, I've been made. Laura you know what to do," I said quietly, then turned and ran across the rooftops until I was standing in front of the tree across the street from Kennard's house. I jumped into the tree, loudly cracking some of the branches and smashing my radio in the process. I climbed down the tree and ran across the street, into Kennard's house. Pulling my gun and locking the door behind me, I ran up the stairs and bounded toward the master bedroom. The suppressor at the end of the gun in Kennard's hand told me he'd wrested it away from Ray. I immediately fired two shots, dropping Kennard to the ground. His body fell to the carpet next to Ray's mask and radio, which was lying in pieces.

Ray dropped his hands and picked up his gun. "He surprised me as I came into the room."

"Follow me, I was made."

We ran down the back stairs and into the kitchen. I grabbed Kennard's car keys from off the wall and we headed to the garage. There, we took his Porsche. We pulled out into the back alley and headed out on the side street. We turned onto the cross street and pulled slowly away as several police cars came rushing past. Once we were out of the Heights we ditched the car, split up on foot, and went to our emergency rendezvous point in Prospect Park.

I sprinted through the park and was the first to arrive at our meeting point in the woods near the music pagoda. My great fear was that Laura had been arrested. If that happened, I already knew I wouldn't let her take the fall alone.

By the light of a full moon I stamped around with my foot until I found the canister we'd buried earlier. I opened it up and took out the three cell phones, three passports, and a few thousand of the money we'd stashed there. I left behind the extra firearms and the med kit, and then buried it back in the ground.

It was late, but there were still plenty of people in the park, many of them joggers. When I heard someone coming at a quick pace I crouched low and waited for them to pass. The figure stopped in front of me and gave out a little whistle. I emerged from the thicket and hugged Ray fiercely.

"Fuck man, I'm glad you are okay," I said. "Did you see any sign of Laura?"

"No, not a thing," Ray said, sounding concerned.

Laura had one hour, at which point we would split up again for twenty-four hours and meet at a second rendezvous point. If she failed to show, according to our plans, she had two more chances before we left New York. But those plans had all been made before Laura chose me. I would not leave New York without her.

The hour was up. We heard someone coming down the road. Ray and I retreated into the woods. As the person got closer we could hear the panting of a dog. We laid flat until owner and dog passed. Just as the dog had made it around the bend we heard fierce barking from two dogs and then those dogs shot into the woods headed away from us: their owners cussing at each other while they ran after them. Because of the dogs we gave her an additional ten minutes.

"That's it," said Ray. "She knows better to come here now. If she can, she will be at the next rendezvous."

Resigned to the fact that he was right, I reluctantly nodded my agreement and stood up.

"Alright, I'll see you in twenty-four hours."

"Don't look so sad, Kyle; it's much better that she didn't come."

I shot him a look, but I doubt he could see it in the dark.

"Now she won't see you die," Ray said, pulling his gun and shoving it into my stomach. "You should've stayed in the car. I really wanted to see if she was going to stay by your side while you awaited execution."

"Ray—I'm sorry."

"Fuck you, you're sorry. I'll bet you've been plotting to get Laura from the second she 'bumped' into you. You think stealing my girl was part of some brilliant execution on your part, huh? You can't think it was an accident. She'd been spying on you for weeks to see if you could help us."

"If you're going to kill him, Ray, then you should kill me too." Laura's voice came out of the darkness; from the path in the direction the dogs had begun fighting.

Her voice startled Ray and me.

"Laura!" Ray exclaimed turning his body toward her and simultaneously turning his gun from me. I saw my opportunity and jerked my arm down to grab the slide lock of his weapon and keep him from firing. Just as my hand touched his gun, Laura fired a round, shooting Ray clean through the chest. Ray instinctively fired his weapon. The shot hit the path and ricocheted. I turned my body away, but not Laura. She held her gun steady on Ray and watched him fall to the ground. He lay on the ground, eyes open, with a gurgle of spit rolling back and forth across his lips with each dying breath.

"You betrayed us," she said to him, with more contempt and vitriol in her voice than I've ever heard. She said, "Quickly, take everything off him except his pants and his shirt."

With great urgency I removed his jacket, his shoes, and his holster. I took his wallet and checked his pockets.

"When they find you, all they will know is that you are just another washed up ex-con gone wrong in New York City," she said, and then stuck her fingers on his neck to check his pulse. "Fuck, he's dead. I hope he heard that."

We headed off into the woods, carefully avoiding the park police trying to zero in on the two gunshots that were heard echoing through the park. I slipped Laura her passport and a new cell phone. We split up, agreeing to meet in the morning at an airport motel before purchasing tickets to L.A.

CHAPTER THIRTY-NINE

I watched as Laura disappeared into the night. Then I disposed of Ray's things. I tied them up in his jacket along with a couple of rocks and threw them in the lake. I made my way out of the park and headed toward Queens.

It would have been easy to take a cab or hop on a train to the hotel, but we would have run the risk of being seen, ending up on camera, or engaging in conversation. Walking would take longer, but it meant I could keep my head low and meander away from people.

Laura had spied on me, Ray had said, trying to unnerve me before he killed me. I turned north on Utica. In my mind flashed the images of Ray, illuminated by moonlight. Much of his face had been in shadow, making it hard to read his expressions. How long had he known? He must have caught onto us in Ohio. When his gun was trained on me, did his face reflect the pain of betrayal or the anger of vengeance?

I'd seen both looks many times before when we were boys. Usually when Ray would come running out of the house fresh from a fight with his mother or her latest boyfriend, who sometimes beat him. Back then, our young, unmarred faces showed an innocence we'd never really known.

There was a terrible tightness in my chest, followed by a weakness in all my limbs. I stopped walking, stretched my arm to a nearby wall, and rested my head against the brick. I took a deep breath and then another. Each time I opened my mouth, I felt the desire to moan and then to cry, but it would not come naturally and so I walked on.

Ray had been willing to send me to jail. He'd been ready to kill me. How much had he told the police? Knowing Ray, he hadn't told them anything. I brought up the phone from my pocket and tapped into the security system at our townhome. It had not been entered. I checked the cameras: Laura had done an excellent job of pulling out. She couldn't erase the fact that people had been living there, but she was able to hide our terrorist operation.

The media had already reported Kennard's death. I checked the cameras in his house. The FBI was there. I switched over to the camera in the master bedroom. Leaning over Kennard's body was Special Agent Topher Corell.

Had he been reassigned to the New York office? My guess was that after the death of Chang (or perhaps even Donaldson) he'd been placed in charge of all things having to do with the PLR. It hadn't even been three hours since the murder. If he came from Ohio, he must have done so on a private jet.

From the bottom of my screen I could see that Laura was also accessing the footage. At least that meant she was okay. I logged off and continued walking.

Passing row after row of endless shops, now closed—most covered with rolling metal doors and security gates—made me long for greener pastures. Laura and I were supposed to go to L.A.; from there we would begin investigations into new companies. Perhaps it would be better if we took a break to mourn our loss, go on vacation, and relax a bit.

Lots of times in the past, too many really, I'd indulged in the fantasy that there was no Ray—that I had Laura all to myself. Now that it had happened, I tried to talk myself out of the guilt. Although I had considered the possibility, I would never have tried to send Ray back to jail. Nor would I have killed him just to get to Laura.

I crossed under Atlantic Avenue and started walking next to the twisted metal railing that separated the sidewalk from the Boys and Girls High School to my left. I had a long way to go before I got to Queens.

As far as I could see in the dark, Laura had not hesitated. She had walked up, her steps hidden under the sounds of the barking dogs. She'd heard enough to get angry, to set off her violent indignation. The same motivating force that drove her to break a pitcher's arm in college and to shoot Donaldson had taken hold. In both those cases, when her red hot anger subsided, she had returned to normal. If she'd ever suffered any negative residual effects from those acts of violence, I never saw them.

Surely this was different. She had been a friend and lover to Ray for more than five years. They'd lived together in a shared intimacy. Unlike our relationship, theirs had not been marked by any difficulty—that is, until I came back into their lives. If Laura was able to compartmentalize this death like she had the others, then it couldn't possibly be healthy. Then again, who was I to say what was and wasn't healthy? I told myself, *this time she will be affected.*

As I crossed over Broadway I began to feel the signs of fatigue. It wasn't that late. I had not expended so much energy that I couldn't make this walk. Nevertheless I began to feel like a zombie, like I could fall down anywhere and go to sleep. As I walked my eyes fell on every bench, corner, and alleyway to find a place where I might lie down and catch a nap.

I saw many opportunities to go up instead of down. There were plenty of fire escapes. I could have run up a wall, grabbed one, and easily made it to the roof. The thought of climbing drained me even more. Eventually, I deduced that something was wrong with me. I'd not been shot. I knew that much. That left only one other option—Ray's death was getting to me. This was shock.

I turned left on Knickerbocker, feeling as if I couldn't take another step. I pulled the new passport, phone, and cash out of my pockets and shoved them down the front of my pants. Just another block ahead was a park. I walked in and moved toward the darkest part. Avoiding the playground and basketball areas, I found myself walking up a small grassy hill. I knelt to the ground, extended my hands, and brought my face into contact with the stiff grass.

When I woke my gun, my watch, and the extra phone I'd never given Ray were gone. The ephemeral glow of the predawn bathed the park in blue light. I considered myself lucky to still have my shoes. I got up, peed, and resumed walking.

Twenty minutes later, a steady flow of cars and people filled the street. A block and a half away, I took the train and made my way into Queens.

We were meeting at one of a slew of hotels around LaGuardia. I checked my phone and discovered a concerned message from Laura, sent over an hour ago. I boarded an inbound bus, took a seat at the rear, and texted her back an ETA of fifteen minutes.

"Look at you. What the hell happened?" Laura said, as she ushered me in the door. She was clean, showered, and had already had breakfast. In the corner were two small suitcases: she'd retrieved our emergency clothes.

"I—I think I'm in shock," I said, jarred by the hoarseness of my own voice.

Laura retrieved a bottle of water and forced me to drink while she steadied me with a hand on my shoulder. She gave me a tender, reassuring smile and spoke in a soothing, confident voice.

"Don't worry. I'm right here. Everything is going to be okay." I swallowed and she kissed me fervently on the mouth. "Thank you for coming back to me," she said, and began helping me out of my clothes. She put me in a bath, fed me, and tucked me into bed, crawling in beside me and keeping her body pressed to mine while I slept.

I had bad dreams that left me feverish; often my body felt so heavy I could not move. This went on for days. When, despite not having the strength to do so, I complained that I needed to get up, Laura refused me.

"Stop worrying, just rest. I'll let you know when it's time to get up."

When she did go out, it was never more than thirty minutes. She did not talk about Ray and refused to voice an opinion about what had occurred. She didn't stop me from talking about him, and she listened if I told stories from when we were kids.

"No, it doesn't bother me," she said, "especially because I know it helps you; it's what you need to do." She paused with her mouth open. I waited patiently until she spoke again. "I grieve differently. The Ray I loved was already dead. He died when he admitted picking up the phone to turn you over to the FBI. The person I shot in the park was a stranger who was trying to kill the man I love. When I think about what happened. I didn't kill Ray at all. I fired my gun only to save your life."

I found Laura's attitude healthy and admirable. Knowing she thought that way helped relieve my own grief.

That night we cuddled in bed and for the first time since Ray died, I felt my passion return. Laura felt it too. She continued to nurture this feeling by climbing on top of me and rocking me slowly between her thighs. After we'd expended ourselves, she collapsed and laid her face under my chin. I felt moisture on my neck and wondered if it was her perspiration, joy over my recovery, or the last tears she was going to shed for the memory of Ray.

CHAPTER FORTY

Upon touching down at LAX, we received a message from Charles. We came out to the street to find Katrina Varma waiting for us with a car. She smiled, greeted Laura with sincere warmth, but seemed to shy away from me. In the car she informed us that she had prepared a new safe house for us and had disposed of the old one. She then pitched the plan she and Charles had devised.

They wanted Katrina to be our third team member. She would not do any direct field work, at least not initially. Katrina added the aside, "Not until you think I'm ready."

We told her not to get her hopes up until we'd had a chance to discuss it. It would be a lot easier on Laura and me to have a subordinate, particularly one who didn't have a romantic relationship with either of us.

The Silver Lake home Katrina had chosen was spacious, semi-secluded, and well stocked. It was close to the freeway and provided multiple avenues for escape. Though we were not particularly bothered we found its proximity to Hollywood odd, until we discovered Katrina's penchant for reading celebrity gossip magazines. Also in her favor, Katrina proved to be an amazing cook, a willing housekeeper, and overall a highly efficient assistant.

When Katrina cleared out the old safe house she packed everything in boxes, labeled them in black sharpie, and stored them in a back room. Eventually, Laura and I wandered back there with box cutters and began to unpack.

"Katrina, please give these to Goodwill," Laura said, unceremoniously, of three boxes containing Ray's clothes.

A large stack of cardboard boxes contained various pieces of surveillance equipment. Tucked among them was a wooden box, closed with a latch and fastened with a padlock; along the sides the word Fragile was painted in red, stenciled letters. Katrina had not been able to find a key. Laura grabbed her pick set and in a minute had sprung the lock.

As we pulled back the styrofoam packing, Laura gasped. At first, looking down into the box, I wasn't sure what it was—some bronzed-colored object. I reached in and lifted up the statue. It was the sculpture that had sent Ray to prison. Laura closed the lid to the small crate and I placed the figure on top. We all stepped back to admire it.

Laura gulped. "Last I checked, it sold for 1.5 million."

"He must have purchased it after I gave him the money," I said. "He certainly deserved it."

Laura had not moved; without taking her eyes from the statue she gripped my forearm hard. The words stuck in her throat.

"I was so sad when Nick died."

"You knew him?" I inquired.

"Yes, we were in college together. He graduated my freshmen year." She paused as a thought dawned on her. "You don't know, do you?"

"This was all Ray's thing. It's a beautiful statue, but if Ray hadn't stolen it our lives would be vastly different.

"Kyle, I posed for this statue. I was the model."

Other than the night Ray stole it—when I had a backpack full of stolen diamonds and was preoccupied by a fear of getting caught—I'd never seen the statue. It showed up a couple of times in newspaper clippings, but at that time it was just a bad memory I chose to forget about. Standing here beside her, I looked past the cybernetic elements of the statue. Once I took away the telescopic eye and robotic leg, it was obvious this was Laura.

"Ray said that from the moment he saw me on your arm he fell in love with me. I would get mad at him for telling me how he felt about me when I was with you. I've always wanted my time with you and my time with him to be separate and distinct parts of my memory.

"When he saw the statue in Owens' house, he immediately recognized I was the model. When he was in prison, he told me I was the reason he stole the statue. I was flattered, but I never liked the idea that I played even a tangential a part in his incarceration."

The statue was lit by a beam of sunlight coming through the wood blinds. We stood in silence until the light moved.

A tear ran down Laura's face.

"I need some time," she said. "Please put it back in the crate."

I did not see her for the rest of the day.

In the coming weeks we focused on Katrina. We had her train physically. Laura took over general fitness, I schooled her in combat. She was consistently fearless and never once complained of the cuts and bruises she received. After six months she had made remarkable improvement, and though always very slender, she'd added considerable muscle. I simultaneously began teaching Laura and Katrina free running and parkour. Both women did well, but Katrina excelled. Perhaps because she was younger, she pushed herself harder and took more risks than Laura; though I didn't hold this against Laura, who exceeded Katrina in every other measure.

Laura took the responsibility of drilling Katrina in firearms. The particular focus of Laura's drills was intended to mentally prepare Katrina to take a life. Laura's methods involved a lot of shouting while Katrina shot from various positions nonstop. Often Laura came across as mean, sometimes degrading, during these drills. There simply was no way of knowing how well Katrina was going to function under the stress of a real combat situation. Laura did everything she could think of to simulate that stress beforehand.

My relationship with Laura couldn't have been better. We lavished attention upon the minute details of our relationship and displayed affection in the tiniest of courtesies. In bed, we built upon the stylized romance we'd observed between René and Margaret then fabricated our own creative lovemaking rituals to rival theirs.

We spent so much time together that we both agreed it was a good idea for us to force ourselves to spend some time apart. Laura started making weekend camping trips once a month and I took advantage of our proximity to the ocean and the warm weather to learn to sail. Katrina, who already knew French, Spanish, and Mandarin, began studying German. Being single, Katrina had no hesitation in going out and finding lovers, though she never brought them back to the house or stayed with them very long.

The year went by quickly, and in that time much changed. Charles used his notoriety to push the tech sector to form a consortium. Led by Google and joined by heavyweights such as Apple, Microsoft, and Samsung, they pulled together over twenty-eight thousand tech companies and created a binding contract that none of them would spend money on lobbying the federal government or donate to a single campaign.

Instead, they used their money to expose those who lobbied. Google created Google Government, an application that made it easier than ever to track campaign funds and lobbying activity, and to trace the political activities of every business and political action group on the planet.

They were met with challenges, of course. The federal government sued the consortium, alleging that it was acting in violation of federal antitrust laws. The consortium fought back hard, driving the case to the Supreme Court. The justices quickly overturned a lower court's ruling and paved the way for tens of thousands of new businesses to join the consortium.

The Supreme Court ruling was a major victory for Charles, whose reputation was greatly rehabilitated by the fact that the Justice Syndicate had not published any more trials and there had been no further killings. The

Justice Syndicate was now free, and had the stature to begin lobbying for the constitutional amendment that had been proposed by the PLR. Two bills, variations on the proposed amendment, were introduced to Congress.

With this in mind Laura and I decided to operate without turning over any more data to the Justice Syndicate. We began new investigations into companies with a plan to hold our discoveries in hopes of an amendment getting passed.

We started work on three targets. The first was a California real estate investment bank that knowingly forced families into the street by foreclosing on homes the company claimed to own but didn't actually have the physical deed. The second was a Seattle-based health insurance carrier that bribed officials in the Health and Human Services department to grant them special exemptions—allowing them to put hundreds of thousands of high-risk policies into a separate, bankrupt shell company that the federal government was then forced to bail out. The third was a group of select members of the board of the NRA.

The NRA was a matter of much debate between Laura and me. I argued that we couldn't very well accomplish our goals without guns, and that the NRA made it possible for us to easily get untraceable weapons by protecting our ability to buy them at gun shows and through private buyers. Laura argued that my reasons were exactly why we needed to go after them. We had never had a disagreement of this nature before. We both debated passionately, but never allowed it to come to raised voices or hurt feelings. In the end we agreed to make our cases to Katrina and let her decide.

After a lengthy hearing, with a great deal of trepidation and after many reassurances that her decision would not damage the team, Katrina ruled in favor of Laura. I acquiesced gracefully, then privately teased Laura that with all of her military-style drilling, she'd brainwashed Katrina to do her bidding.

"She'll follow you anywhere," I chided.

"Good, and well she should," Laura replied curtly and without a trace of humor.

At the time of Katrina's decision, I got one concession. I requested that if we ended up carrying out the assassinations, we do so with a bomb and do everything possible not to shoot anyone. I thought it was important to sidestep the gun debate completely and firmly believed that if we were successful with the operation; the death of a dozen board members would adequately terrify the rest.

Laura agreed to my request with her jubilant smile and an affectionate kiss that never failed to make me feel as if I'd won the war for having just lost the battle. Sinking into her tender embrace made it much easier to push away the notion that, on all fronts, I had given her exactly what she'd wanted all along.

We spent the rest of the next year methodically collecting data from our targets. Katrina proved herself invaluable, utilizing her knowledge as a CPA to analyze the California real estate firm. She was able to trace money and interpret complex financial dealings in a way that made my knowledge as a trader seem woefully inadequate. We then let her work in the field during the infiltration of the Seattle health insurance company and on the NRA. In addition to the help she provided on our new operations, she also combed through our old data from Hochberg and Erhart and uncovered dozens of patterns that allowed us to make new market trades and double our wealth.

CHAPTER FOURTY-ONE

It took a tremendous amount of direct pressure by the consortium and the Justice Syndicate to force Congress to take a vote on the amendment. The first bill got stuck in committee and then the representative who sponsored it withdrew the bill. It was generally believed that he did so under pressure from the oil and gas lobby, which subsequently added ten thousand jobs to his state. The second bill came to the house floor but was defeated by a failure of a two-thirds majority to attend the vote.

Feeling that there would not be any more progress in Congress we sent an encoded message to the Justice Syndicate indicating we would begin again. In order to preserve his political effectiveness Charles announced to the world that there would no longer be any trials, but that he would immediately release and publicize any raw data he received from the PLR. This proved to be a much better way to function, as it allowed us to execute our targets without forewarning them.

Our first target was Don Chappell, whose real estate offices were in a downtown L.A. high-rise. His window facing office on the twentieth floor made him an easy target for a quick kill from a hotel room directly across the street. We'd rented the room parallel to his office and cut a hole in the window large enough to accommodate the rifle. We were prepared to kill him the next morning, but then he took an unexpected trip to San Francisco to close a deal with a surprise seller. We decided to take shifts and wait for his return. Katrina took the first shift, I took the second.

Upon arriving that morning, I entered the room to find Katrina naked, fresh out of the shower. We were both embarrassed, though I was first to react: she just stared at me with a single eyebrow raised until I turned around and waiting until she got dressed. Afterward, we made our apologies and she left the room, leaving me behind—intensely aroused by her brown skin and small, round breasts.

After she left, her naked image stayed with me and I found myself fantasizing about what it would be like to make love to her. This made me feel shameful and so I compromised and imagined it a threesome with Laura. Still feeling guilty, and overly stimulated, I called Laura and begged her to come spend the night with me in order to relieve my discomfort.

She showed up dragging her travel case and wearing a very sexy red dress.

By this time, I was in a deeply frustrated state. She refused to give in to my advances until I confessed why I was so aroused.

Laura branded me a "silly man," claiming I was only guilty of being human. This however, did not stop her from exercising power over me the rest of the evening, making me beg and demanding my absolute obedience to her sexual whims. The next morning we made love again. Afterwards we cuddled in bed.

"Kyle, I'm never going to fault you for a fantasy so long as it stays a fantasy."

"Understood," I said, kissing her bosom and feeling ready to have her again on my terms.

"But if something ever happened to me... Katrina. She is definitely a woman I'd approve."

Her comment caused me a twinge of guilt. If anything ever happened to me I could think of no man I would approve of. I really didn't want to think too hard about this; I was now preoccupied with Laura's nipples.

"Cross your hands behind your head," I ordered her. She happily complied and for the next hour we reversed our power exchange.

Later, I showered, packed up my bag, and went out to bring back lunch.

"About time. Where the hell did you go?" Laura asked, indignant at my hour-and-a-half delay.

"I knew you would want your favorite sushi."

She softened and looked surprised. "You didn't have to drive all the way to Cheviot. Thank you my love," she added gratefully. "Will it keep? I've been dying to take a shower." I nodded that it would. "Go ahead and start without me, I'll only be a minute," she said, disappearing into the bathroom.

I began eating and carried my food over to the window to look out at Chappell's office. He was still not there. On my way back to the table I accidentally kicked over Laura's bag; out poured a stack of pictures. They were pictures of her and Ray from the years after he got out of prison. She looked happy in these pictures, much happier than I cared to ever see.

The water shut off in the bathroom and so I hastily replaced the pictures and went to sit at the table.

Watching her while she ate, I contemplated the meaning of the pictures. Was she feeling guilty or missing Ray? What did this mean for our relationship? I remembered the words she said to me in New York, the words she sealed by licking my face. "*You need to learn to really trust me. I told you, I'm yours.*" I didn't lose her to Ray. This was a test of my ability to trust her. In her own time, she would tell me about the pictures or not at all.

So long as our relationship continued the way it had been going, it didn't matter.

I got up from the table, kissed Laura on the top of her head, and walked over to the window. Chappell had still not returned. Laura finished eating, brushed out her hair, and came back into the room.

"The words 'I love you seem' so insufficient for how I feel," I said to her.

She leaned against the dresser, smiling at me with a penetrating stare. She was only wearing her red bra and panties. She walked over to me and guided me to the bed. We removed our clothes and began making love without speaking a word. There was no power exchange this time. This was as sweet and tender as one can possibly physically communicate the phrase *I love you.*

Laura, usually so vocal, was deliberately not speaking—never replying to my repetition of the phrase. The more she resisted the greater was my desire to hear her voice. I listened more intently to the words encoded in the cadence of her breath. Her breathing, at first whispered, became a song of exhalation that collapsed into an unnaturally held rest. Upon the next heave, it escalated again in multi-tone guttural noises that–having passed her lips, broke her resolve. The many sounds escalated and grew into one irrepressible scream.

Her arms closed around me as her body convulsed. Her nails drove deep into my flesh as if clinging to my back was all that held her from a great descent. It was in this moment I whispered in her ear.

"This is how much I love you. Don't ever forget it."

Laura's eyes found mine and filed with tears. She bit her lip and shook her head that she would not. Together we shared a final climax.

That evening Laura lay on her side, staring out the hotel window while I lay cuddled up to her from behind. Many times that evening she had turned and looked at me in amazement: as if she had expected to find one person, but found another, more acceptable person instead. Each time she touched me, as if steadying herself, and said, "I love you." An hour passed. In the dark, she turned to speak again, but over her shoulder a light came on. Chappell had returned.

Without turning on the light we dressed and pulled out the assembled rifle from under the bed. I put on my radio and positioned to take the shot. Laura used the radio to call out to Katrina and put her on alert then left the room, taking everything but the go-bag into which I would collapse the rifle.

I had my shot, but had to wait until Laura cleared the hotel and readied the getaway car. Over the radio I could hear Laura's feet rushing down the stairwell.

Across the street, Chappell was moving around his office with great excitement.

"He must have closed his deal in San Fran because he's practically dancing."

"I'm almost to the car," she replied. "Take the shot."

Chappell was bouncing around, clearing a buildup of paper off his desk. Once he had created a space he set his briefcase on top and opened it. He sat down, reached inside and pulled out a document with both hands, using the tips of his fingers as if he were lifting a fragile thing that might crumble in a breeze. It was at that moment I splattered his head all over the far wall.

Quickly, I disassembled my gun, loaded it into the go bag, and slipped on a mask bearing the number twelve. I bounded from the room and ran smack into a portly couple. The man fell to the ground. The woman, upon seeing my mask, screamed.

"I heard that," Laura said over the radio. I pushed past the woman, exited the stairwell and raced to the ground floor. I stopped at the bottom of the stairs and peered into the hall. Then I ran straight across and through double doors out into a loading area.

"Security guard, unarmed, smoking on the back dock," Laura said, over the rumble of the Ford's powerful engine, "He's a big one."

Had the couple not seen me—I presumed they were calling someone about it—I could have afforded to wait. I pulled my stun gun from the go-bag and bounded through the doors and into a cavernous storage area, then on to the back exit that took me to the dock.

The guard was not much taller than myself, but was twice as thick. He stood up and started moving toward me. I held out the stun gun hoping this would deter him. It did. He stopped moving but raised his radio.

"Dispatch, I have an armed, masked ma..."

Before he could finish his sentence I fired my Taser, dropping him to the ground. I rolled off the dock. Laura screeched to a stop in front of me. A few minutes later we entered the 110 freeway and joined the flow of fast-moving traffic.

"I know this would have gone smoother if we hadn't been fucking on the job," Laura said. "But I wouldn't change it for the world. I love you."

The next morning we learned that Chappell had purchased the soon-to-be tallest building in San Francisco. The owners of the still-under-construction building had run into financial trouble and reluctantly sold their majority stake to him. As a result of his death, the deal fell through. Eventually they found a new investor and when the building was completed a year later they named it the Evergreen Building. They named the tallest part after the man who had only owned it for a single day, and though every tour guide taking people to the observation desk pointed and proclaimed, "That's the Chappell Spire," no one ever walked away remembering the name Don Chappell.

CHAPTER FORTY-TWO

"Guns get a lot of political notoriety; ammunition has gotten off with barely a murmur of controversy," Laura had said eight months ago. A month later, using the skills we'd learned from Ray, Laura altered her appearance. She added twenty years to her age and became Susan Hesse. In this guise we purchased a small ammunitions manufacturing company out of Irvine.

Doubling the amount of ad space in gun magazines led to greater recognition for the company, but only a modest increase in sales. The company did not have a great reputation in the firearms market and compared to other ammunition makers, the product quality was merely average.

The ads, however, did get the notice of our NRA representative who called continuously, offering to provide the full weight of the organization if we'd like to increase our annual contribution to the NRA from twenty-five thousand to fifty thousand.

"Tom, I would love to do that, but we just leased a new 100,000-square-foot factory floor, and were spending over a million and a half on the new build-out," Laura said over the phone to our NRA representative. She clutched the phone with one hand, talking to him while signing a lease on a new factory. "Tom, a year from now we're going to be manufacturing world-class ammunition. What I need from you kind folks down at the NRA are sales. Not a year from now, I need them now. So, tell me what can you do for me?"

"Well if you double your contribution I can help get the word out about your new facility."

"Tom, you sound like a really sweet, young man. Maybe you're not use to dealing with strong women. Money is not the issue. I have no problem writing out a check for a hundred thousand dollars to the NRA if I thought you could do something for me that I could not do for myself." On the other end of the line it sounded like Tom had swallowed something down the wrong pipe.

"With a couple of calls, I could help you get more favorable placement at trade shows around the country," Tom said. Laura sighed with frustration. Tom quickly cut in, "And I'm talking the Shot Show in Vegas too. I realize you pay for the size of your space, but not all similarly priced spaces are the same. We have some sway."

"Tom, listen carefully, I'm taking out my pen," Laura clicked her pen close to the phone to be sure Tom could hear it. "And I'm writing a check to the NRA for a hundred and fifty thousand dollars. I'm putting today's date on the check. That means it's good for ninety days. Now, you've already got twenty-five thousand from us for this year and if you can help me out quickly then I'll send this check in. I imagine, for you personally, it will be a really good year."

"Tell me what I can do for you, Ms. Hess?"

"Why Tom, do you realize we've been talking for ten minutes and that's the first question you've asked me? Tom, I have a warehouse full of half a million dollars of ammunition that isn't moving. I need to get rid of every last piece of it so I can fill it up with bright, shiny, new, high-quality ammunition. Now, maybe you can use your pull to find me a government buyer for this ammunition, maybe a private buyer? I don't care, as long as it's a legal buyer. I'm fifteen minutes from an international port; once it's sold it can go on a boat to anywhere in the world. Do you understand me, Tom?"

"Yes ma'am, completely."

"It's a one-time thing, Tom. A year from now, long after we've opened our new factory, I'm hoping to double my contribution. You'll still be my representative a year from now, won't you?"

Tom laughed. "I think I will."

"Good. Tom, is that something you can help me with?"

"I'll get right on it."

Two days later, the military placed an order for all of our back stock of ammunition. We shipped a full container to a military base in Kuwait even though it was below the quality requirements for government use. On the day the ammunition left the docks, Laura mailed a check to the NRA, tucked into a nice thank-you card for Tom.

A week later, Tom called to thank her for the note (and the check).

"Tom, I'm throwing a party. It's a very small guest list for a big luxury party. My guests will have full accommodations at a five-star hotel, all their transportation will be covered, and well... it's a party so I promise they'll have a good time. My guests each have some special expertise. You see, a bunch of them have worked in key positions in the government. One of them use to work in manufacturing, and some have strong relationships with the very suppliers I use to make my ammunition. I have several other names that have very strong relationships with my key and potential customers. This extravagant party is to celebrate the groundbreaking of my new factory. I've got fifteen shiny gold shovels ready to stir some ceremonial dirt, then afterward I'm going to take about two hours showing them the factory. We'll have lunch and later that evening a very wonderful time. Tom, I just have one problem and I'm wondering if you can help me out."

"I think I can," Tom said with enthusiasm.

"I need a persuasive young man like you—"

"I'm 33," Tom said.

Laura laughed. "A young man like yourself," she continued, "to hand out the invitations and make sure they all show up."

"That doesn't sound too hard."

"Now Tom, that's what I like to hear. If you need to sweeten the pot, let anyone who's reluctant know that there's a ground-floor opportunity to pick up some shares."

"Is there now?" Tom asked. "Please, send me your guest list and be sure to include a few alternates."

Word spread quickly among the NRA board members, who clamored to get a spot at the table. Fifteen turned to twenty, at which point Laura had to turn down further requests.

There was no doubt this was Laura's operation. She had that look in her eye, the one I used to fight against when we were younger. The plan was entirely hers. As soon as the mission was decided, she stole a page from my book. She built a wall replete with maps, photographs, and step-by-step mission plans. I came and stood beside her to look over the plan.

"You have my enthusiastic endorsement," I said humbly, trying to remind myself I was Captain to her General. "It's a solid plan."

"I'm sensing a 'but' in there somewhere," she replied.

"No buts. I'm just worried about you. You seem more stressed than I've ever seen you."

"I'll be fine once the mission starts." I rubbed her shoulders. She relaxed into my arms, her voice drifting. "I'm just afraid of making mistakes."

"Can I ask, why the NRA? We don't have a smoking gun of criminal activity like we did with the others."

Laura seemed incensed by the question. She pulled away from me.

"What's the matter, they haven't killed enough people for you?" she said with more sharpness than she would have liked. She dropped her tone and said, "I know, they aren't like the others, but this is the right direction for the PLR: now we're taking the fight right to lobbyists. The people who buy and sell our government should be scared for their lives."

"There are lots of lobbyists, and you aren't even going after the entire

NRA. These names, the people you want to take out, this is a very specific list."

Laura turned and stared at me.

"Alright, I'm ready," her voice was methodical. "I've never told you where my father made his money. He ran guns. He ran small arms across state lines. He distributed the kinds of guns that wind up on the street in New York or Chicago in the hands of small-time criminals. Eventually, he built up his business and ran guns south across the border into Mexico. He's indirectly responsible for the deaths of thousands of people.

"The names on this list, these are all board members of the NRA who have taken a strong stance on keeping in place the kind of laws that let my father get away with his business. Because of them he could make straw purchases in Virginia and drive guns to New York. He could come out West, buy hundreds of guns at gun shows, and move them right across the border."

"Why have you kept this a secret from me for so long?" I asked. "You trust me, don't you?"

"Oh darling, of course I do," Laura strained. She took a deep breath and in a pained voice said, "I've never told you because I'm ashamed. When I was in high school, before I knew any better, I helped. I went with him when he bought and delivered guns.

"I've seen the faces of the buyers and then saw them again; later, when they'd be arrested for murder..." She added tearfully, "I read the stories and saw in the news the bodies of the people they killed. Young kids who died because of the guns that my father—that I sold them."

There it was the anger and the pain, rising in her. I'd seen it many times, but never with this understanding of where it came from. I could not begin to fathom the burden of guilt she carried within her. I saw her differently, more completely than I had before. I've always told myself that she put the violence behind her when it was done. Now I was uncertain.

"My father thinks he's a fucking hero, carrying out the wishes of the Founding Fathers," Laura continued. "He believes that any gun control at all should be illegal. He takes joy in breaking the law. He believes he's John Hancock, running rum while signing a big declaration of 'fuck you' to the federal government."

I grabbed her hand, turned her back to her operational plans, and embraced her. It was clear to me now. This mission is what she needed. This operation was closure for her father, for Ray, for all of her guilt.

"Direct me," I said. "I'm your soldier. You are my queen. I'll carry out any order you need me to."

The groundbreaking was held on a Saturday. The factory floor was littered with heavy wooden boxes full of production equipment. The boxes were empty. There was a photographer present, painted gold shovels as promised, and a few random people made up of five temporary hires, three caterers, and the shuttle driver who'd brought the guests from the hotel.

Laura read her speech and cut the ribbon at the gate. Then the NRA board members and Laura all picked up a small scoop of earth, held their shovels steady and smiled for the camera. The caterers rushed inside and finished setting up the lunch in the boardroom. The temporary workers climbed into back of a waiting truck and drove away. Laura took the memory card from the photographer while her guests entered the factory. The photographer drove off with cash stuffed in her pocket. Laura sent the shuttle driver away and joined her guests for a tour of the factory floor.

Katrina and I watched through the factory security cameras while hiding in a van a mile and a half away. As Laura presented the tour she worked the room; I was reminded of the day I met her. She charmed each board member until they felt special and valued. She spoke to their strengths and was not afraid to hint at what she needed from them.

"If you follow me to the boardroom," she said. "Lunch is waiting." While walking toward the stairs she enticed them, "I've been saving it as a surprise, but we have some spectacular, 'intimate' entertainment planned for this evening's party. I've assigned a lovely host or hostess to guide each of you through the festivities." That bit of news had them chattering quietly to themselves.

The cameras were clear in the boardroom. Once everyone was seated, comfortably eating, and the CEOs were watching a video, Laura would excuse herself, locking them inside, and run from the building, using her remote detonator to discharge the bomb strapped to the underside of the conference table.

"That food looks expensive. The budget for this operation is off the charts," Katrina said.

It was the first time she'd brought up the subject of money. It struck me rather amusing that she had not said a word when we spent over 4.5 million dollars to buy a faltering ammunition business. Perhaps she saw potential in the company, even though we'd planned to abandon it at the end. For some strange reason, the thought of all the food going to waste raised her accounting hackles.

"If you're hungry, I brought some food," I offered with a whimsical smile. Katrina only looked more agitated. "Is something bothering you?" I asked. Katrina looked at me and then down at her hands.

"If it's between you two it's none of my business, but have I done something wrong?" She sounded tearful.

"Absolutely not," I cut in. "We couldn't be happier with everything you've done." I tried to soothe her but when I put an arm around her shoulder, she winced.

"I haven't caused a problem between you and Laura?" she pleaded.

"No, what would give you that idea?"

"I've just heard her crying," Katrina said softly.

"What? When?" I asked, feeling perplexed and embarrassed to think it might be true.

"At night, she comes down to the main floor and cries in the bathroom. I know she thinks no one can hear her, but I share a vent with that room, and when the air is off, the sound is very clear."

"We never fight," I said defensively.

"I know," Katrina said. "That's why I thought it was about me."

"I'm sure it has nothing to do with you," I said, hoping to reassure her, though I found the idea of Laura's crying to be completely unnerving. The thought that, after all we had been through, there was something I didn't know about my partner, lover, and best friend made me bristle with failure.

Katrina looked at me with a pained expression, put her hand on my arm and said with great gravity, "Kyle is it possible Laura is seeing someone else?"

This, I knew, was wildly off base. If Laura had fallen in love with someone else, the first thing that would have suffered was our love life, as had happened to Ray.

I asked, "Seriously, what would make you think that?"

"All her solo camping trips," Katrina said, raising her voice into a question.

Perplexed, I shrugged my shoulders.

"It's just that was her and Ray's thing," she said. "They went camping constantly all over the country."

At the mention of Ray, and more particularly the thought of Ray and Laura enjoying an activity she and I did not share, turned me off from the conversation. I turned my attention back to the monitors.

The twenty members of the board had just finished serving themselves.

"While you eat, I'd like you to enjoy a short film about my company," Laura said, pushing a button that slowly dropped a projector screen from the ceiling.

"That's the signal. Get ready," I said to Katrina, indicating that she should be prepared to move to the front seat and drive us to Laura for her extraction.

I turned back to the monitor. I was looking over the back of Laura's shoulder. The screen had dropped into place. Several of the members had stopped eating and were looking at it with a befuddled, somewhat concerned look.

"I'm sorry," Laura said loudly enough for everyone to hear.

"Fuck, the stupid projector must not be working," I said, incredulous. "It's a brand-new building."

We fixed our attention to the monitor. Laura turned and moved out of frame.

The conference table at the center of the room rose off the floor. The faces in the room turned upward and for one frame the camera caught their expressions of abject terror. The table cracked in half and the screen filled with the bright blot of overexposure. The camera went dead.

"Laura!" I shouted, but my voice was muted as the sound of the explosion buffeted the van and deafened our ears. I covered the sides of my head and stood. "Drive!" I shouted. "Drive!" Laura needed pick up. She couldn't have had time to get all the way out. Katrina was looking at me with an anguished expression I couldn't comprehend. I got angry that she wasn't moving. I shouted again, "DRIVE!"

Katrina shook her head. *The bomb—it must have damaged the van*, I foolishly thought. I pulled my hand away and moved toward the cargo door. Katrina stepped in front of me. My anger only grew. "Get out of my way!" Katrina put the flat of her hand on my chest. It enraged me. I moved to put my hands on her, to force her out of the way.

Katrina hit me hard in the chest. I growled at her and she punched me again and again: hard, fast, and furious. Despite all of her training and muscle, Katrina was still comparatively small. I grabbed her wrist and tugged her to the side, tossing her against the shelf that held our monitors and equipment. I pulled at the cargo door but it wouldn't open. *Did the blast seal the door?* I wondered. It was locked. I released it and pulled back the handle, sliding the door open with a slam.

Before I could step off, I felt a pull on the strap of my shoulder holster, restraining me. I reached back to release whatever had hooked me and found Katrina's arm. *That fucking bitch, what is her deal?* I thought and then felt a sharp stab in my neck. I hit the crook of her elbow using my full force and broke her hold on me. I stumbled out of the van, began to feel woozy, and fell to my knees.

Katrina, undeterred, jumped out and got in front of me. Again she pushed on my chest as I tried to stand. I rose to my feet, my body in a hunch, and tried to push her away. The world around me became blurry. The ground felt spongy.

"Kyle, she dead, she's dead Kyle," Katrina kept saying as I tumbled backward into the van.

CHAPTER FORTY-THREE

Kyle,

I told myself that I didn't do it, that I wasn't responsible. It worked for a while, but it didn't change the fact that I missed him. It didn't change the fact that I ended his life.

The love I have with you is more perfect than I could have ever imagined possible. It cannot erase the specter that haunts my nights. It seems the closer I become with you, the more I try to seek solace in your arms, the louder and more violent Ray's ghost becomes. I can no longer put it to rest with pills, sex, or violence.

I never told you, but after we broke up I almost didn't make it. I let Ray pick me up and he bought my loyalty by putting me back together. Later, I was in awe of the fact that you didn't need anyone to survive. In that ability, you have a strength I cannot fathom.

It is yours now. Please honor my love for you by continuing what we started.

Laura

I awoke in my bed, feeling the effects of sedation. The clock said it had been a week. There was no one in my room. I rolled on my side and on the night table saw several brown bottles and a syringe. There was a cup with water and a flexible straw. My throat was parched though my lips felt as if they had been freshly coated with balm. I reached for the water but only managed to rap my knuckles on the side of the table.

I let my arm hang over the bed and tried to breathe in deeply, so as to collect my strength. Expanding my lungs fatigued me and I lay there unable to enjoy more than shallow breaths. Small footsteps approached me.

"Shhhh, here you go," Katrina whispered as she guided the straw between my lips.

I slept, and in the early morning hours when the sedation was at its weakest, I rolled over to find Katrina sleeping next to me. There was tape on my thigh holding a catheter in place.

My slightest movements woke Katrina. She rose, fed me small bites, and sedated me again. One afternoon I opened my eyes and looked past my feet to the dresser. An envelope lay against the mirror. My name, in Laura's hand, was penned across the front. I was too weak to get to it. I accepted that she was gone; being gone sounded nice.

More time passed.

I slept and woke, thought more about Laura and wondered what the letter might say. I wanted to die. When Katrina came and knelt beside me, I angrily grabbed at her arm. In her alarm, she hastily grabbed the needle and jabbed me again.

As I sunk back into sleep I whispered to her, "Thank you."

The next time I woke she was there with food. I ate as much as I could bear before sleeping again. Katrina smiled at my progress.

There was a man who came from time to time at the height of my sedation. He and Katrina would stand in the corner and talk about me in whispered voices. I assumed he was a doctor.

On one visit he put his arms around her, but she pushed him away. I assumed he was also one of her lovers.

The urge to move my bowels drove me to the bathroom. This was the first time I stepped out of the bed. In the bathroom I heard conversation below. On the toilet I struggled with the catheter bag.

I exited the bathroom. The voices had moved outside, just beyond the front door. I searched the bedroom for my gun; even the one I'd hidden was gone. From the window, I saw Katrina walking him to his car. In that moment I collected all my strength. I made it through the top floor and down to the second, but I could not find a gun.

I heard the car pull away. I did not have the strength to climb the stairs and rested on the couch.

"You won't find one," Katrina said, closing the front door behind her. She looked at me and something she saw forced her eyebrows into a look of concern. "What have you done?" she asked, as if I were a recalcitrant child. She sat beside me, touched the head of my penis, and then brought up her hand to show me a drop of blood. She shook her head at me and pulled my arm over her shoulder.

"Come on; let's get you back to bed." It was a struggle, but we made it to the top of the stairs. My eyes caught Laura's letter and I started to sob uncontrollably.

"That's good," Katrina said, as she laid me into the bed. "That's really good, Kyle." She ran her hand over my chest and helped me turn on my side. I felt her fingers along the side of my face and repeatedly through my hair. "If you've stopped trying to kill me, I'll reduce your medication."

I did not feel like I wanted to kill her or that I ever had. Thinking on it brought back vague recollections: a tussle followed by a sharp electric pain. I ran my hand over my side and found a tender spot and two small scabs close together.

I'm sorry about that," she said and brushed my cheek. "You didn't give me any choice."

After two days of reduced medication she removed the catheter. Though I was able, aside from going to the bathroom, I chose not to get out of bed. I put Laura's letter in a drawer. I cried some more.

Katrina filled me in on the effects of our work and all the political wrangling. I didn't really listen, except to hear that there was a new attempt at an amendment. I doubted it would go anywhere.

In the night I pulled Katrina's body close to mine. She let me hold her. I cried some more.

"I need you to get better," she said while I ate. "We have a job to complete in Seattle. I can do it alone, but I shouldn't." I was off sedation, but it didn't feel like it.

I slept. I held Katrina more. I cried less. I was numb.

Time passed.

The moon was bright and I could no longer sleep. I'd lost track of the number of full moons. I no longer wanted to stay in bed. I was angry at my body for living when my mind wanted to die. I was angry at my muscles for twitching and wanted to stretch. I held Katrina from behind, too tightly, but she let me. She smelled good. Her skin was soft. Squeezed tightly by my arms, she breathed uncomfortably. I was angry at my erection, but she let me. I was angry at my pumping, but she encouraged me.

We moved. We went to Seattle.

ABOUT THE AUTHOR

Christopher Wilde is an author, poet, and screenwriter. Follow him on
Twitter @ChrisWilde801

www.ingramcontent.com/pod-product-compliance
Lightning Source LLC
Chambersburg PA
CBHW030920120626
46554CB00001B/215